THE LITTLE BOOKSHOP BY THE SEA

ELIZA J SCOTT

Ebook ISBN: 978-1-80508-538-6
Paperback ISBN: 978-1-80508-539-3

Cover design: Rose Cooper
Cover images: Shutterstock

Published by Storm Publishing.
For further information, visit:
www.stormpublishing.co

ALSO BY ELIZA J SCOTT

Welcome to Micklewick Bay Series

Summer Days at Clifftop Cottage

Finding Love in Micklewick Bay

Life on the Moors Series

The Letter – Kitty's Story

The Talisman – Molly's Story

The Secret – Violet's Story

A Christmas Kiss

A Christmas Wedding at the Castle

A Cosy Countryside Christmas

Sunny Skies and Summer Kisses

A Cosy Christmas with the Village Vet

Heartshaped Series

Tell That to My Heart

To my fabulous friends Jessica Redland and Sharon Booth,
thank you for your support and encouragement.
You're awesome! Xxx

ONE

Spring had returned to the pretty Victorian seaside town of Micklewick Bay, a welcome respite after the weeks of lashing rain and gale-force winds that had battered the coastline. Above, the sky was a broad splash of clear blue, the sun a ball of cheerful yellow, its rays glinting off the ripples of the North Sea. A flotilla of little fishing boats bobbed about on the waves while seagulls circled above, hoping for rich pickings, their piercing cries scooped up by the gentle breeze and carried along the bay.

Happiness raced through Florrie Appleton's veins as she made her way to work along the top promenade that Monday morning. The wheels of her vintage bike whirred along the cycle path, skimming over the flagstones, her scarf flying out behind her. She pushed her glasses back up her nose with a gloved finger and sucked in a lungful of the fresh, salty air, a smile spreading across her face as her eyes drank in the familiar sight of the beach that stretched out to the left of her. The tide was rushing towards the bank of shingle that edged the shoreline, culminating in a frothy mass, before scurrying back. The usual handful of die-hard early morning surfers were floating on the breakers by the lanky metal legs of the pier. They were always there, whatever the weather, and from this vantage point, dipping in and out of the waves in their shiny black wetsuits, they could easily pass for a bob of seals.

Florrie pedalled harder, spurred on by a surge of exhilaration, her brunette bob fanning out from beneath her red beret. Up ahead, she saw a man wearing a long grey overcoat and flat cap who'd strayed into the cycle lane. His head was bowed and he was ambling along as if he had all the time in the world.

'S'cuse me!'

She gave a quick jingle of the cycle bell and he jumped out of the way, scowling and almost dropping the mobile phone in his hand.

'Sorry!' she said, pulling an apologetic face as she passed, a ping of recognition firing in her mind. It disappeared before she had a chance to catch hold of it and put a name to the face. She frowned; it would niggle her until she remembered where she knew him from.

Florrie loved days like these, invigorating and brimming with optimism. It was as if the small seaside town was emerging from the long winter months, unfurling, fresh and ready to face the new week ahead. Already, her mind was running through the list of jobs she was keen to tackle when she arrived at The Happy Hartes Bookshop. *And I know exactly where to start*, she thought as the dusty bookshelves piled high with second-hand books in the storeroom pushed for priority. Though she knew her suggestions of what to do with said books would be met with resistance from her boss, Mr Harte, she figured it was always worth a try.

Her nose twitched as the aroma of freshly ground coffee beans pulled her out of her musings. 'Hi, Nadia.' She waved at a well-wrapped up young woman who was busy setting out chairs and tables around the Crows' Nest coffee kiosk. It was situated just next to the steps – all one hundred and ninety-nine of them – that zig-zagged their way up from the bottom promenade; a welcome sight to those who'd braved the climb and finally reached the top, legs aching, gasping for breath and desperate to quench their thirst.

'Morning, Florrie. Lovely day at last!' Nadia smiled, pushing her hair off her face.

'It's gorgeous.' Florrie beamed.

She pushed on, smiling and nodding at the slew of familiar faces she saw every day, walking their dogs or taking an early morning run. She glanced up at the imposing Victorian houses across the road to her right. Five storeys high with tall, looming chimneys and exquisitely carved corbels and lintels, each afforded a much-coveted vista of the spectacular seafront. Despite most having been converted into flats years ago, they still clung onto the haughty air they'd displayed in more affluent times when they were inhabited by the well-heeled members of Micklewick Bay's society. Florrie often wondered what they'd been like in their heyday.

Standing alongside them, occupying occupying an entire block of its own, was the vast Micklewick Majestic Hotel. Not so very long ago it had been the jewel in the crown of Micklewick Bay; a place where anyone who was anyone came to be seen, where music tinkled softly in the background and conversation was murmured in such hushed tones you could hear a pin drop. But in recent years it had fallen on hard times and now looked neglected and forlorn, with boarded-up windows, tiles slipping from its roof, and a battered "For Sale" sign flapping noisily in the breeze. It hadn't taken long for it to become an eye-sore. If the rumours were to be believed, its owner had lost his fortune owing to his gambling addiction and now the sharks were circling, waiting to sink their teeth into their pound of flesh.

As the path swept round, it opened up the view of the bay where the old part – or Old Micklewick as it was known to locals – was nestled down by the beach at the foot of Skitey

Bank. Micklewick Bay had its origins there, in the tiny cluster of whitewashed cottages that teetered on the precipitous cliff side, smoke curling from their chimneys, their once thatched roofs now replaced with cheerful orange pantiles. To Florrie, it looked as if all it would take was a mere nudge to send them sliding right into the sea. A characterful pub called The Jolly Sailors sat amongst the ancient, cobbled rows. It was a favourite Friday night haunt of Florrie and her friends; they'd spent many happy hours there. The little area was steeped in history with stories a-plenty of smugglers and pirates and a tunnel leading from the "Jolly" – as it was affectionately known – right up to the grand house of the legendary Micklewick gentleman, Benjamin Fitzgilbert, who'd led a double life as a member of the landed gentry and a prolific smuggler. It wasn't until Victorian times, when the well-to-do, whose pockets had suddenly become well-lined thanks to the burgeoning success of the industry that clanged away several miles up the coast, had cottoned-on to its charms. Soon, building began in earnest, and the new town sprang up in a matter of months, perched on the opposite side of the bay where it appeared to be looking down its nose at the old part of town.

But the view that made Florrie's soul tingle every morning, no matter what the weather, was that of the mighty Thorncliffe. The towering cliff stood majestically, like a giant sentry guarding the coastline, shoulder-to-shoulder with the cliffs that lined the North Yorkshire Coast. It stirred something deep inside her whenever she set eyes on it. Local historians claimed its name was derived from Thor, god of Thunder, in a nod to its powerful presence, and judging by the booming sound the waves made as they crashed against its feet in stormy weather, Florrie could well believe it.

Sunlight raced over the patchwork fields of Thorncliffe Farm spread out on the cliff top, skimming over the row of white-washed coastguards' cottages and, in the field behind them, the quaint Clifftop Cottage, home of Florrie's friends, Maggie and Bear Marsay. The cottage appeared to squat down into the ground, bracing itself against the wild weather that often hurled itself straight from the sea. The little building looked every bit as achingly cosy from the outside as it was inside.

Florrie took a sharp left, her breath coming out in short bursts as she pedalled along the road that led to the town centre and the shops. 'Hi, Dennis,' she said as she swerved around the postman. He was busy stacking letters in his hands as he stepped out into the road.

'Morning, Florrie, love. Grand day.'

'It certainly is.'

A minute later, she was in Victoria Square, cycling towards The Happy Hartes Bookshop which sat at the top end of a row of shops. It was a double-fronted building with large, bowed windows and worn black and white quarry tiles leading to a half-glazed door. She hopped off her bike, throwing a cursory glance at a tall man with dark hair and a floppy fringe who was loitering by the window. She wheeled her way towards the private door to the right of the shop that gave access to the flat above, her eyes alighting on the peeling, dull-brown paintwork. She sighed, running a finger over the windowsill; it had looked bad last year, but it hadn't fared at all well over the winter. Something needed to be done about it, and soon.

Sensing she was being watched, Florrie glanced across to find the tall man looking over. The warm tone of his skin and the sun-kissed highlights in his hair suggested he'd recently spent time in sunnier climes. Her stomach gave an unexpected flip; he was seriously "hot-to-trot", as Jasmine would say.

'Morning.' The handsome stranger smiled at her. A friendly smile, the sort you'd give to someone you knew, though she was convinced she'd never clapped eyes on him before –there was no way she'd forget someone as out of the way good-looking as him! She quickly rifled through her brain in the hope of jogging her memory, but to no avail.

'Morning.' She returned his smile, scanning his face, feeling somewhat surprised at the thought that there *was* actually something vaguely familiar about him. He looked about her age – thirty-two; was he someone she'd been at school with but hadn't seen for a while? The thought flittered through her mind but was gone before she had chance to dwell on it. *Bugger!*

'Nice day,' he said in a North Yorkshire accent that had had the edges smoothed off. His smile widened, sending a cheeky little tingle running up Florrie's spine.

'It is.' *Oh, my days!* It wasn't just his good looks that had put all her senses of attraction on high alert; there was something else at play here. Such a reaction was completely out of character for her and she was struggling to manage it. *Calm your jets, Florrie!*

'You work here?' he asked, nodding towards the shop.

'Mm-hmm.' She felt suddenly tongue-tied, like a teenager talking to the school heart-throb on whom she had an enormous crush. She hoped it wasn't as obvious to him as it was to her suddenly pounding heart. 'Yes.' *Where on earth is this coming from? Get a grip of yourself, woman! Don't forget about Graham!*

'Right.' He nodded, his sunny beam crinkling the corners of a pair of eyes Florrie would happily melt in. She watched him process her reply, her insides a juddery mess. 'Sorry, I don't mean to pry, it's just... well, I used to visit here as a small boy, that's all. The bookshop has... um... special associations for me.'

'Oh?' was all she could manage to vocalize while her brain took off, scrabbling through her memories, hoping to pin-point him, but without success. She gazed up into his eyes that she noted were a deep shade of navy-blue and framed with ridiculously long, dark lashes, though it didn't escape her notice that dark circles hung beneath them. And he really was incredibly tall – she'd put him at well over six feet – towering over her petite five-feet-two. 'It has special associations for me too, and not just because I work here.'

He nodded again, flashing that smile and wearing an expression that, if she wasn't mistaken, looked as though he knew exactly what she meant. 'You're keen; I see the shop doesn't open till nine-thirty.'

Florrie nodded. 'I always arrive an hour early so I can have breakfast with my boss; it's something I've done since his wife passed away.'

'That's very kind of you.' His smile faltered slightly, and she was sure his eyes seemed to dim.

'Not really, Mr Harte – he's my boss – is good company, and he's been very kind to me over the years; he's actually more like family than my employer.' Their eyes locked and a frisson of attraction suddenly crackled between them, knocking her even more off kilter than she already was. She felt her cheeks burn and hoped he hadn't noticed. Clearing her throat, she asked, 'So what brings you back to Micklewick Bay?'

He pulled his eyes away from hers, casting them down to his feet, scuffing the floor with the toe of his shoe. 'Um...it's been a while since I was here... I just fancied a visit... wondered what the old place looked like.'

'Right.' Florrie was intrigued but something made her reluctant to push further.

They stood in silence for a moment until she spotted the number forty-two bus heaving itself around the corner; she was usually tucking into breakfast with Mr H before that arrived. She glanced at her watch. 'Oops! I'd best dash; Mr H will be wondering where I've got to,' she said, wishing she didn't have to tear herself away.

'Yes, of course.' His eyes met hers again. 'It's been nice to meet you, Florrie. I'll be sure to pop into the shop later when it's open.' He flashed a smile that made her heart skip a beat. 'See you later.'

'See you later.' Florrie watched him as he walked away, his hands stuffed into the pockets of his padded waxed jacket. She had the overwhelming feeling there was more to his visit than he'd let on, especially if the dark circles beneath his eyes and the slightly weary air about him was anything to go by.

She turned, making her way to the flat, stopping dead in her tracks, her brows knitting together. How did he know her name?

TWO

Florrie wheeled her bike into the entrance area of the flat, her stomach all of a dither. *What was that all about?* The sound of paws thundering down the stairs made her look up as she leaned her cycle against the wall. 'Good morning, Gerty. How are you today, eh, girl?' Smiling, Florrie bent to ruffle the glossy ears of the black Labrador who was now nuzzling into her legs with her usual enthusiastic greeting. 'Well, this is a lovely welcome.' She gave Gerty's solid body a resounding pat. 'And how's Mr H this morning? Has he got the kettle on yet? D'you think he's in the right frame of mind to talk about having the outside windows repainted?'

Gerty pressed her paw against Florrie's leg, looking up at her with happy brown eyes, her tail swishing across the floor. 'Come on, let's go and see,' Florrie said, and the Labrador jumped to attention.

Florrie grabbed her backpack from the basket of her bike and followed Gerty up the threadbare runner of the stairs and into the kitchen of the flat. Though it had barely been updated since the nineteen-seventies, the place was spotlessly clean and neat, like every other room up there.

'Morning, Florrie, dear.' Bernard Harte smiled at her as he peered over his half-moon spectacles. He was sitting at the table, his white hair combed back neatly, his navy-blue V-neck pullover stretched taut across his rotund middle. He had a mug of tea in one hand and the local newspaper spread out in front of him. A small pile of newly delivered post was set to the side. As usual, there was a selection of warmed croissants and pains au chocolat arranged on a plate in the centre, and this morning they smelt particularly divine.

'Morning, Mr H.' Florrie gave him a wide smile as she pulled off her beret, her hair instantly floating about as static made mischief with it. Smoothing it down proved futile so she unwound her scarf and slipped off her coat. 'Oh, yum! They look delicious; I'm absolutely famished, the fresh air always gives me a raging appetite, and it was particularly fresh this morning, I can tell you,' she said breezily, doing her best to push the conversation with the handsome stranger out of her mind, promising herself she'd give it some serious thought later.

As he did every work-day morning, Mr Harte prepared breakfast for himself and Florrie using freshly made supplies from Seaside Bakery, the artisan baker's shop two doors down. Tuesday to Saturday, it was chunky doorsteps of toast or thick, oven-bottom muffins with lashings of butter and strawberry jam or tangy marmalade, but on Mondays Mr H always treated them to a selection of croissants and pains-au-chocolat, it was his way of creating a bright start to the week. The bookshop opened at nine-thirty and Florrie had fallen into the habit of arriving an hour early so the pair could enjoy a leisurely breakfast, washed down with copious cups of tea while they discussed their plans for the day, and – whenever Florrie felt brave enough – her ideas for bringing the bookshop a little more up-to-date. Granted, her suggestions were usually turned down, but it didn't stop her from trying.

'I'm pleased to hear you're hungry, you could do with

having a few more pounds on you, you're no bigger than a spar-row. And judging by the roses in your cheeks, I assume you've cycled half-way around the town to get here.' He gave a chuckle that lit up his deep-blue eyes.

Florrie grinned as she went to hang up her coat. Used to the familiar routine, Gerty settled herself by the little pot-bellied stove in the corner, her eyes never leaving the pastries on the table. 'Mr H, you know very well I can't let a day go by without having a fix of the view along the prom. Cycling along there first thing in the morning, while the town's waking up, is no hard-ship; it's more than worth the ten minutes it adds to my journey. I don't think I'll ever tire of looking at Thorncliffe.'

'Ah, yes, I do know what you mean.' He took off his glasses and sighed. 'My Dinah used to speak of it as fondly as you do; she couldn't go a day without getting a glimpse of it either. I used to feel the same, but I can't bring myself to look at it now.'

Florrie's heart squeezed at the sadness in his voice. The eighty-four-year-old had lost his wife two years earlier. She'd suffered a stroke and had become increasingly reliant on a wheelchair the year before she passed away. Every day, Mr H would push her along the top promenade where they'd sit and gaze out at the cliff, sipping coffee from the Crows' Nest, watching the boats and surfers.

Florrie gave a small smile as she made her way over to the table, pulling the hem of her berry-red turtle-neck jumper over her black skinny jeans. She topped-up Mr H's mug of tea before pouring one for herself. 'There's something about that cliff that gets right under your skin. I could honestly never live anywhere else but here.'

'Hmm. I wish young Edward felt that way. I'd love nothing better than if he came to live here. He doesn't seem settled in London.'

'Oh?' She pushed her glasses up her nose. For as far back as she could remember, Mr H had been estranged from his son,

Peter, and daughter-in-law, Suzanne, and as a sad consequence, his thirty-four-year-old grandson, Edward. She didn't know the full ins and outs, but she'd gathered it was something to do with an explosive argument between Mr H and Peter over the bookshop. Though neither Mr nor Mrs H had spoken much about it, she could tell it had caused them enormous pain, especially as it had deprived them of any contact with their only grandchild who'd been a young boy at the time. No one was more surprised than she when six months ago, out of the blue, Mr H had received a letter from Edward who'd tracked him down, stating he was keen to build bridges and get to know his grandfather. Mr H had been in raptures and hadn't wasted a moment in rushing down to London to see his grandson. Since then, he'd paid him several visits, returning each time with a renewed zest for life.

It had warmed Florrie's heart to see her boss looking so happy, though at the back of her mind there was a little niggle that warned her the reunion might possibly be short-lived, especially if Edward's parents had anything to do with it. She'd kept that to herself, hoping upon hope that he wouldn't let his lovely grandad down.

Mr Harte lifted a postcard from the top of the pile of post and waved it at her. 'He sent me this.' He slid his glasses back on.

'Oh?'

'Yes, and judging from the variety of postmarks, it's taken a while to get here. Anyway, the poor boy's been so busy he hasn't had time to call or email. He works too hard; all the hours God sends by the sound of things.'

Florrie pushed down the doubts that were starting to surface before Mr Harte was alerted to them. He'd known her all her life, and having worked for him and Mrs H since she was thirteen years old, he'd developed the ability to read her like the books that lined the shelves of his shop. But it still didn't stop her from worrying that Edward had been having doubts about his newly restored relationship with his grandfather. Mr H would be devastated if he had.

'And reading between the lines...' Mr H paused, scrutinizing the postcard, '...hmm, I think young Edward's a bit lonely. Yes, lonely, that's the feeling I'm getting. Edward is lonely, which is a terrible shame for a wonderful young man like him.'

'Lonely?' She took a sip of tea and peered over her mug at him, her glasses steaming up. She wondered how he'd drawn that conclusion from the smattering of words on the postcard.

'Yes, don't ask me what it is that makes me think that, it's just a feeling I'm getting, call it grandfathers' intuition.' He frowned at the postcard, pursing his lips together. 'Maybe I should invite him to stay here for a while; he could have a little break. What do you think?'

'I think that's a great idea. I'm sure he'd jump at the chance to spend time with you.' She beamed at him, garnering as much enthusiasm as she could to stifle her doubts. The thought of Mr H being disappointed by his grandson made her heart ache.

He chuckled, his rheumy eyes twinkling. 'Well, you seem as excited as I am at the prospect of him coming to Micklewick Bay.'

What? No! 'It's just that I know how much a visit from him would mean to you; you could take a few days off so the pair of you can catch-up; a break would do you good too.' She hoped her explanation would be enough to stop his mind from heading down *that* route; since he'd made contact with Edward, he'd regularly commented on how he thought Florrie and his grandson would "make a lovely couple".

'Yes, that's very true. Come to think of it, a few day trips with young Edward would be rather splendid. And you could show him around the town, couldn't you? Take him under your wing with that rather jolly group of friends of yours?'

Florrie had all on not to choke on her tea. *You've got to be kidding me!* Conscious of Mr H watching her, she steadied herself. 'Erm... well... I suppose so... yes.' She shuffled uncomfortably in her seat.

'Splendid! It'll do him the world of good to get some fresh seaside air in his lungs. He spends far too much time indoors, painting or whatever it is he does now.' Mr Harte sat up straight. 'A couple of weeks here in North Yorkshire would be like a tonic to him.'

And it would be like a tonic to you too, she thought, looking at him fondly, seeing the colour had returned to his cheeks. She felt herself soften. 'If I were you, I'd get onto it straight away, before he makes other plans.'

'Yes, good point.' He paused for a moment, thinking. 'So, can I just double-check, you'd be happy to let young Edward tag along with you and your chums while he's here? I'm sure he'd find the option of being able to spend some time with folk closer to his own age more appealing than being stuck with an old fogey like me for the duration of his stay.'

Florrie groaned inwardly, she felt torn; the prospect of having to entertain Edward Harte with Mr H not-so-subtly playing cupid in the background wasn't remotely appealing. But seeing the hopeful look on her boss's face made it impossible to refuse, so she forced a smile, and, trying to stop reluctance from lacing her voice, said, 'Yes, as long as he can put up with us.' *What have I just agreed to?*

'Excellent!' Mr H's eyes lit up. 'I'm sure he'll be able to. I'll call him just as soon as we've had breakfast. Now, come along, dear, tuck in, I know how you enjoy a pain-au-chocolat. Oh, and it was Jasmine who served me with these; she said to say hello.' He pushed the plate of breakfast pastries towards her.

Florrie mustered-up a smile, though it didn't stop a sense of misgiving setting in.

The usual Friday night get-together at The Jolly Sailors

with Jasmine, Stella, Maggie and Lark wouldn't come around soon enough after this conversation, but the sudden thought of Edward Harte joining them made her heart plummet all the way down to her black ballerina pumps. How was she going to explain that to them, especially since Friday nights were strictly just the five of them? She stifled a sigh; she knew just how much it meant to Mr H. But, either way, it had taken the edge off her appetite.

A whimper came from Gerty's direction, reminding them of her presence. Florrie glanced across to see the Labrador looking at her as if to say, 'Come on! What are you wating for? There's food to be had!' Florrie couldn't help but smile. In typical Labrador fashion, Gerty's appetite clearly remained unaffected by whatever was unfolding around her.

As she reached for a pain-au-chocolat, Florrie sensed the weight of Mr H's gaze on her. She lifted her brown eyes to see him looking at her intently over his glasses. 'Is everything all right, my dear? You seem a bit distracted this morning, it's not like you.'

Florrie's heart lurched, regretting that he'd sensed the change in her demeanour. 'I'm absolutely fine; I'm just making a mental list of the jobs I need to tackle, that's all.'

'Hmm,' he said, taking a sip of his tea, his eyes never leaving her.

'And I read till quite late last night, so I'm a bit tired. Maybe that's what you're picking up on. I'll have to make sure I get an early night tonight.' She laughed, switching her gaze from him. Even to her own ears, Florrie's excuses sounded flimsy.

'And how are things with that young man of yours? You haven't mentioned him much recently. Is everything all right there?'

Oh, here we go. Let the meddling begin! She knew exactly where this line of questioning was heading. Much as she was relieved to get away from the topic of Edward, she'd rather it didn't switch to Graham. Time to change the subject!

'Everything's fine, thanks.' She pulled a corner off her pastry. 'By the way, did you say Miss Davenport would be popping in today?'

'Yes, I rang her on Saturday evening to let her know her book had arrived; she said she'd call in for it sometime this morning.'

Florrie nodded. She had a soft spot for Miss Davenport, an old friend of Mr and Mrs H's, and a regular at the bookshop; she often called in for a chat as much as to buy a book. And though Florrie was aware Miss Davenport kept herself busy with the variety of clubs she was a member of, she rarely mentioned family. Florrie suspected she was lonely. 'Hmm. I was thinking about her the other day; wondering if she's read any of Julie Spelton's novels. They're getting really popular; I think she'd enjoy them. They're the same mix of romance and humour as Tilly Turner's books, which, as we know, are Miss Davenport's favourites. They're set in the Scottish Highlands too, which ticks another of her boxes.'

'Yes, now you mention it, I think you're right. I'll look into ordering a couple.'

Phew! The distraction had worked. Florrie beamed. 'Good.' It gave her a thrill to find new authors for their customers, particularly ones like Miss Davenport. Over the years, Florrie had grown very fond of her, and had got to know her well as they'd chatted over the counter. And she'd become quite adept at seeking out new authors for her to try.

Mr H tapped the postcard against the palm of his hand and pursed his lips. Sensing his mind was moving back towards the matter of her love-life and Edward, Florrie acted quickly. 'It's a shame she never married or had a partner.'

'Who?'

'Miss Davenport. She's such a warm, kind-hearted soul, and

judging by the sort of books she reads, it's obvious she loves the idea of romance. I think it's a terrible shame she's had no one to share her life with.'

'Yes, it is a terrible shame; Jean never seemed to recover from having her heart broken by Johnny Jackson when she was a young woman. Stunned everyone when he dropped her like a hot potato.'

'That's so sad.' Florrie knew Mr H was averse to gossip and whenever their conversations touched on Miss Davenport he never elaborated on the same scant details he always shared, but she couldn't shake the feeling he knew more than he let on. Maybe a little nudge would help reveal more, and this morning felt like the perfect moment to try. 'I wonder what really happened?'

'No one knows the ins and outs, but one minute Johnny and Jean were madly in love and looked destined to head down the aisle together, and the next he was in the arms of Elsie Norwood who was Jean's best friend at the time. He shocked everyone by leaving town and marrying Elsie in something of a whirlwind. Rumour had it a baby followed six months later, but no one knows for sure. Johnny never returned to Micklewick Bay after that. Dinah and I could never see what he saw in Elsie, we always had the impression she was rather conniving.'

'Goodness, I didn't know a baby was involved, no wonder Miss Davenport was so devastated.' It saddened her to think that her friend's heart had been so badly broken she'd felt unable to open it up to love again.

'Yes, well, I've said too much; I'd be grateful if you would keep what I've told you to yourself.' He coughed and mumbled something under his breath.

'Of course. How about another cuppa?' Mr H may have shared more than he intended, but Florrie still had the feeling he was holding something back. And that something had piqued her interest.

'Yes, thank you, my dear.' He watched Florrie as she topped up his cup. 'And did you and your young man go anywhere nice this weekend? Did he take you somewhere wonderful for a slap-up meal, or did he take you dancing?' There was that glint in his eyes again. 'A charming young girl like you should be treated like a princess; I hope he knows how lucky he is to have you on his arm.'

Florrie set the teapot down, averting her eyes from his. 'Graham was away on a business trip at the weekend.'

'I see,' Mr H said slowly, smoothing his hand over his chin. A loaded silence stretched out between them. 'Well, it's a shame young Edward wasn't here; it would've been the perfect opportunity for you both to get acquainted.'

Florrie's stomach lurched at hearing Edward's name again and she felt her face flush. Mr H, the wily old fox, couldn't have been less subtle if he'd tried. But two could play at that game, she thought, as she resolutely pushed Edward from her mind; it was time for a little bit of give and take. If she'd just agreed to take his grandson "under her wing", then surely Mr H couldn't refuse a request to tackle one of the jobs he usually, very deftly, brushed under the carpet as soon as she mentioned them. She seized the moment. 'I meant to mention, when I arrived this morning, I noticed the paintwork outside has suffered quite badly over the winter, and I really think we should get it repainted before it gets any worse; the wood's at risk of rotting if we leave it. I'm more than happy to get some quotes and organise it all for you.' She finished with a hopeful smile, ignoring the reluctant face her boss was pulling.

'Must we? Is it really that bad? I'm sure it was fine the last time I checked out there; and, if I'm being honest, I don't really have the heart for anything like that. Since I lost Dinah there doesn't seem much point any more,' he said, his eyes losing their sparkle.

Which was exactly the problem, and why Florrie was now

feeling terrible for bringing it up. Since Mrs Harte had passed away, the shop had become increasingly neglected, and she couldn't help but think it was why customers were trickling away. Florrie did as much as she was able without causing offence to her boss, but there was so much wonderful potential in the shop and she knew that Mrs Harte would be sad to see how it was fading into a shadow of its former self.

'Well, how about doing it for Edward? For his visit?' Florrie popped a piece of pain-au-chocolat into her mouth and chewed. 'Tell him you're doing it in honour of him coming to see you, then he won't be able to refuse.' A little guilt-trip sent in Edward's direction might just do the trick – just in case there were any doubts about calling to see his grandfather lingering in his mind.

'Oh, I hadn't thought of that. And now you mention it, I wouldn't like him to see the shop looking shabby. Yes, let's do that, let's get the place looking ship-shape again.' Mr H looked suddenly brighter. 'If you're sure you don't mind finding someone to do it, I'll go and see if I can get hold of Edward right now.'

'Brilliant.' She smiled, rubbing her hands together. It gladdened her heart to see Mr H looking so animated. She hoped with all her might his grandson wouldn't disappoint him.

THREE

It was in 1873 that Mr Sidney Harte took possession of the key at number four Victoria Square, and proudly established Harte's Bookshop; the very first in the newly well-to-do Micklewick Bay. Immediately, he'd set about commissioning the fitting of the wooden shelves that still lined the walls of the shop today.

In 1948, Mr and Mrs Billy Harte purchased half of Bunty's Haberdashery, the store directly to the left of the bookshop. The owners, a Mr and Mrs Cotterill, had fallen on hard times, and selling a slice of their building to the Hartes got them out of a hole without them having to give up their business altogether. As soon as the purchase was signed, sealed and delivered, access to the newly acquired portion of property was created via a new doorway at the rear of the bookshop, and a wall separating it from the haberdashery was constructed. The extra room would provide much-needed storage for the thriving book store. Everyone declared themselves happy with the new situation.

Very little had changed since those early days, other than the addition of electricity, the carpeting of the floor, and the expansion of the sales area into the back room where the original Mr Harte had his office and took his tea-breaks – that being relegated to what was once a store cupboard.

The current Mr Harte had taken over the running of the shop with his wife in 1980, heralding another generation of Harte caretakers who would put their own stamp on the business. This they did by adding a couple of rows of free-standing bookshelves along the middle of the shop, a collection of low seating in the children's corner, and branching out into stationery – much to the dismay of Mr Harte's father, who thought such diversification would be the shop's demise. He couldn't have been more wrong, and Harte's Bookshop thrived.

Florrie's first memory of the shop was at Christmastime when she was four-years-old. She could still recall so clearly the feeling of wonder that glowed inside her that frosty December afternoon. Her little mittened fingers were resting on the windowsill, her nose – red from the cold – was pressed to the glass as she gazed up at the window display. A gaggle of snowmen were grinning happily back at her against a backdrop of midnight-blue satin and glittering paper snowflakes suspended on invisible thread that wafted around each time the door was opened. Children's books with brightly coloured covers were set out on the cotton-wool snow and were sprinkled with glitter that twinkled in the light. It was a magical memory that still triggered a rash of happy goosebumps whenever she thought of it.

Once her mum had managed to tear her away from the scene, Florrie was taken inside where it felt as if the warmth of the shop had wrapped its arms around her and enveloped her in a deliciously book-scented hug. It was an aroma she soon came to love and associate with a feeling of happiness. Holding her mother's hand, she walked along gazing up at the books, her eyes wide with wonder. There were shelves and shelves and shelves of them.

They'd queued to see Father Christmas in his snowy grotto

in the children's section of the store, a mix of excitement and fear fizzing in her stomach. Florrie had come away gripping tightly onto the book he'd given her, her eyes shining happily. The first seed of her love for books had been sown and it felt utterly magical. She still had the book today, tucked safely in her box of treasures.

Florrie's mother, Paula, was a voracious reader and took her daughter with her to the bookshop every weekend. Florrie was content to study the shelves of books, running her little fingers along the rainbow of spines while her mother lost herself in the romance section. And, as soon as she was old enough for pocket money, Florrie would spend it there.

The Hartes had grown very fond of their young customer. 'What is it that you like so much about our shop, Florrie?' Mrs Harte had asked one day.

Pausing for a moment, six-year-old Florrie had tapped her chest earnestly and said, 'Because it makes my heart happy.' Mrs Harte had chuckled delightedly, but it had set an idea brewing in her mind. It wasn't long before a newly painted sign sat above the store declaring it to be "The Happy Hartes Book-shop" in cheerful, bold lettering. Florrie's face had lit up when Mrs H told her she was the inspiration behind the change of name.

As she got older, Florrie would ask to stay at the store while her mother finished the rest of her shopping. 'That's fine, Paula, lovey,' Mrs Harte would say. 'We'll keep an eye on her, not that she'll need it; she never strays far from the kiddies' section.'

'Don't rush!' Florrie would say excitedly, making her mother laugh and shake her head. But to Florrie, nothing compared to the joy she got from being surrounded by books or savouring the peaceful atmosphere within the walls of the book-shop. She became such a regular fixture at The Happy Hartes Bookshop, Mr and Mrs H came to regard her as their "unoffi-cial" granddaughter, providing her with biscuits and beakers of juice whenever she called in. Florrie repaid their kindness by tidying the shelves and straightening books.

At the age of thirteen, Florrie thought she would pop with happiness when the Hartes offered her a weekend job. It was just a few hours on a Saturday afternoon, but it meant the world to her. Her hours increased as she got older, and she loved every minute she spent there, never tiring of the thrill of opening newly delivered boxes of books, arranging them in a display, or – best of all – of recommending them to people, which was something she quickly became skilled at.

* * *

When the time came for her to go to university, Florrie had purposely accepted a place at York to study English Literature, it being the city closest to Micklewick Bay. Being an unashamed home-bird, York was far enough away for it still to offer an element of adventure, but not so far away as to risk that stomach-churning feeling of homesickness that hounded her whenever she was away from home for longer than a week. Florrie could trace the torment back to an ill-fated week-long school trip where none of her friends had been happy, their misery spreading like wild-fire around their little group until a cloud of gloom had sat over them, quashing even the slightest glimmer of fun. As far as she could recall, nothing had been able to shift it. To eleven-year-old Florrie, who'd cried herself to sleep every night, it had been the longest week of her life and one she'd consigned to the darkest depths of her memory. But its effects still lingered in her subconscious such that she'd even considered living at home and commuting to university. It was thanks to her parents' gentle encouragement that she'd eventually agreed to stay in student accommodation.

'Just give it a try for the first year, lovey, and if you don't like it, then you can live here and commute for the rest of the time,' her mum had said kindly. 'And, at the end of the day, whenever you feel like popping home, it's really not that far. You can just jump in your little car, and you'll be back in Micklewick Bay, quick as a flash.'

'True.' Florrie had nodded, her mum's words nudging her towards the little en-suite room they'd seen on the student accommodation website. She fancied she could make it quite homely with her own bits and bobs dotted about the place, her favourite books on the shelves.

'We just don't want you to regret not doing it, flower, and it's not even as if you'll be away a full year. I reckon you'll have a whale of a time; York's a wonderful city, nice and compact. And it's got that little second-hand bookshop you love so much,' her dad, Charlie, had said, beaming at her. 'And, if you really wanted to, you could always come home at weekends.'

Which was exactly what Florrie chose to do. It had been the perfect compromise, and it also meant she could keep her job at the bookshop.

By her second and third years at university, Florrie had swapped the halls of residence for shared accommodation with her friends into which she'd settled quite happily – though she still worked at The Happy Hartes Bookshop and came home at weekends.

It was on one such weekend that her world came crashing down.

A few weeks before her final exams, Florrie was poring over her books at the picnic table in the garden, its wide umbrella shielding her from the heat of the sun. Birds were chattering in the trees by the boundary fence, while bumble-bees danced from flower-to-flower, humming away as they busily gathered nectar. She was pulled away from her studying by the sound of her parents' voices wafting through the open window of their bedroom. Their tone jarred in Florrie's ears; it sounded as though they were having a heated discussion, which was something they rarely did. She froze, listening intently, her heart thudding against her chest, but she was only able to snatch the odd word thanks to the occasional car driving by and the intermittent sound of someone nearby struggling to start a lawn-mower.

There was a sudden lull in the noise, allowing her dad's voice to come out loud and clear: 'You've got to tell her, Paula; it's only fair. She's going to find out sooner or later.'

'Shh! Keep your voice down, Charlie, she'll hear you!'

Florrie pressed her hand to her mouth as her heart went into freefall. What was her dad so keen for her to know? Her mind started racing, her thoughts pulling in one direction and settling on her mum. It hadn't escaped Florrie's attention that she hadn't looked well recently. When she'd commented on it, her mother had just waved her concern away, saying she'd been over-doing it and hadn't been getting enough sleep. Her explanation had pacified Florrie. Until now.

Rather annoyingly, the lawnmower struck up next door, drowning out the possibility of hearing anything further. Florrie raced to the house; there was no way she'd be able to read another word of her book or do another stroke of work until her parents had told her exactly what was going on.

At first, Paula tried denying anything was wrong, telling Florrie she'd misheard, brushing her daughter's concern away with a feigned light-heartedness. Seeing Florrie wasn't convinced, she'd given some vague reason that had made such little sense, Florrie couldn't even recall what her mother had actually said. But the anguish on her dad's face spoke volumes, leaving Paula with no choice but to concede defeat and agree, albeit reluctantly, to tell Florrie the reason for their heated words.

It was in the familiarity of the cosy family kitchen – the room Florrie usually associated with happy times and delicious

Sunday dinners – that she learnt her beautiful, fun-loving, kind-hearted mum was seriously ill.

'But what does it mean? You're going to be okay, aren't you? Please tell me you're going to be okay.' Florrie's voice was tight with emotion as tears rolled down her cheeks, her mind in turmoil.

'The team at the hospital are brilliant; your mum's in good hands,' her dad said, squeezing his wife's arm, his eyes wet. He mustered up a watery smile. 'She'll be right as rain before we know it.'

'Of course I will,' Paula said, reaching for Florrie's hand. 'I just wish the timing had been better, that's all. The last thing I want is for it to affect your studies, lovey.'

'You're more important than my studies, Mum.' Florrie threw her arms around her, sobbing into her shoulder. 'I love you, Mum, I just want you be okay.'

'Oh, sweetheart, don't cry. I've got every intention of being okay; I've got too much to do.'

The upshot was that Paula Appleton had found a lump under her arm. That, coupled with a series of high temperatures, unbearable night sweats and sudden weight-loss – which her naturally petite frame could ill-afford – had meant she'd made an appointment to see her GP, albeit after a nagging from Charlie.

Before she knew it, she'd been whipped into hospital for a biopsy, blood tests and a scan, the results pointing undisputedly to Stage 1B Hodgkin Lymphoma.

Paula dealt with the diagnosis stoically, initially wanting to keep her illness to herself, until it became apparent that she'd need chemotherapy followed by little bit of radiotherapy as "extra insurance" – as her consultant had worded it. There was no way she'd be able to keep that a secret.

'The prognosis is good,' she said to Florrie. 'The consultant,

Mr Shevis, says they've caught it in its early stages and they expect me to make a full recovery.'

Florrie nodded, feeling numb as she sat back down, her eyes never leaving her mum. 'That is good.' She could hardly believe she was having this conversation.

'And I intend to get my head shaved before my hair starts falling out.'

The words had sent a chill running up Florrie's spine; her mum had always had thick, glossy hair.

'Then I'm going to treat myself to a couple of fabulous wigs. I've always quite fancied having a luxurious headful of Pre-Raphaelite curls.' She feigned tossing them around, flicking them back with her hand. 'And I might even go for a funky purple crop. Imagine your dad's face when I rock up wearing that!' Mother and daughter fell into a fit of the giggles at the expression on Charlie's face.

That was eleven years ago and Paula had since been given a clean bill of health. But shock at how close she'd come to losing her mum had left an indelible scar on Florrie's soul. It had made her acutely aware of her parents' mortality; made her realise they wouldn't be around forever. To this day, Florrie still felt the constant need to keep an eye on her mum, checking for any telltale signs that things weren't right. It still had the power to keep her awake at night, panic gripping her at the thought of how her mum's life could so very easily have been cut short. She pushed her roots deeper into the ground at Micklewick Bay, vowing she'd never take her family for granted, nor would she ever stray too far from them.

* * *

By the time Mr and Mrs Harte had started to think about retirement they reached out to their estranged son. They'd hoped that the passage of time had softened Peter and that his opinion of the bookshop might have changed such that he'd consider taking the reins. It hadn't been easy to track him down, but a curt, cold response, telling them he and Suzanne had other plans – they were travelling the world in their campervan and couldn't be persuaded otherwise – meant their efforts had been in vain. Peter had even suggested his parents sell the property, which was never an option. Mr and Mrs H had been dreadfully disappointed, especially since their son had ignored any further efforts at reconciliation.

That aside, Florrie found, things usually had a way of working out, and it just so happened that the Harte's planned retirement coincided with her finishing her degree and returning to Micklewick Bay full-time.

'I have a suggestion for you, Florrie, my love.' Mrs Harte smoothed her hand over her grey hair that was kept tidy in its usual bun. The pair were on their break, sharing a pot of tea one Saturday morning.

'Oh, now I'm intrigued.' Florrie sat forward, pushing her glasses up her nose.

'Well, I was wondering what your plans are when you finish university?'

Florrie gave a noisy sigh and flopped back in her seat. 'I haven't got any really. I know I want to move back home – I love it here – but there aren't many local jobs for anyone with an English Lit degree except, perhaps, teaching, but I don't fancy doing that full-time. Dad suggested I advertise offering private tuition to school students, which I quite like the idea of.' *And I want to be close to my mum.*

'Mmm, I think you'd be good at that; you've got the patience for it and a nice way with you,' Mrs H said, nodding.

'Thank you.' Florrie gave a quick smile. 'And, if it's okay with you and Mr H, I'd like to keep my Saturday job; I can't imagine not working here.'

'Oh, of course, lovey. The shop wouldn't be the same

without you. In fact, it leads me very nicely to that suggestion I mentioned,' Mrs H said, her eyes glinting as she rubbed her plump hands together. 'As you know, Mr H and I had plans to retire this year, but with Peter and his wife not being keen to take over, it's forced us to have a re-think. Selling the shop is out of the question — Bernard wouldn't countenance it being owned by anyone who wasn't related to us Hartes, and neither would I for that matter. Anyway, now the time's actually arrived for us to retire and we've had a chance to think about it properly, neither of us is particularly keen on the idea just yet; we're both fit and healthy and have years left in us.' She smiled at Florrie.

Florrie smiled back fondly, Mrs H always took the long way round to ask a question. 'That's true, and neither of you look your age.'

'Ah, bless you, that's very kind, my dear.' She reached across and squeezed Florrie's hand. 'Having said that, we do quite like the idea of having a bit more free time to ourselves. So, what we wondered is, how would you like to work for us full-time? That way, Mr H and I could reduce our hours to part-time. It would solve both our problems. You don't need to give us your answer straight away, take your time to think about it, and you mustn't feel obliged to say yes just to please us – not that we wouldn't love to have you. I know working in a bookshop won't be making the best use of your degree, and the wages wouldn't correspond to your qualifications, I'm afraid, but we'd pay you as much as we could afford.' She took a deep breath, looking at Florrie hopefully.

Florrie didn't need any time to think. 'I'd love to work here full-time! It's a perfect solution. Thank you! The bookshop's my happy place.' The thought of being able to do a job she loved while living close to her parents had filled Florrie's heart with a mix of joy and relief.

'Oh, that's wonderful, lovey.' Mrs H hugged Florrie to her

squashy bosom, almost squeezing the air out of her lungs. 'Now, if you'll excuse me, I must go and tell Bernard; he'll be over the moon.' She released Florrie and scurried off downstairs to the shop.

In the time that had passed since that conversation, Florrie was still just as happy working at The Happy Hartes Bookshop as she was then.

FOUR

Later that morning, Florrie had just finished serving a customer when Mr H ventured into the shop. The frown he was wearing, together with the fact he was rubbing his hand across his chin – a habit he had when something was troubling him – put her senses on high alert, her mind immediately flying to his grandson.

'Everything okay?' she asked.

Mr H watched the door close behind the customer. 'I'm not sure. I've just had a phone conversation with young Edward.'

'Oh?' She nudged her glasses up her nose, a sense of doom descending.

'Mmm. Would you believe, he was actually on his way up here? He was going to surprise me with a visit – such a thoughtful boy – when he received a phone call from one of his neighbours saying Luella, that's his ex-girlfriend, had turned up at his flat. By all accounts, she wasn't very happy when his neighbour told her Edward was having a few days away.'

'So where's Edward now?' She couldn't help wondering why his ex would be annoyed at him having some time away.

'He had to get on the next train back to London to sort

things out. Apparently, she'd called him, ranting and raging, saying she needed to speak to him urgently.' A cloud passed over Mr H's face. 'Between you and me, I do believe he's been having trouble with her for quite some time.'

'Right.' Florrie's mind was processing what she'd just heard. Could it be true? she wondered. Or was it simply an elaborate excuse for not visiting his grandfather? Then again, Mr H's reaction suggested he had prior knowledge of the troublesome relationship Edward had with his ex, so maybe there was a grain or two of truth in it. 'That's unfortunate timing.'

'It is.' Mr H sighed. 'But he was right to go back; by all accounts, she's got a bit of a temper on her if things don't go her way. Puts me in mind of—' He pressed his hand to his mouth as if to stop more words spilling out.

Florrie waited for her boss to continue. Much as she was desperate to know who Ed's ex reminded him of, she knew pushing would make Mr H clam-up even further so she remained silent.

She took a deep breath when it became clear he had no intention of elaborating further. From experience, she knew that Mr H was as tight as a clam where personal matters were concerned – his own and everyone else's – and avoided gossip at all costs. 'It's hurtful to those being gossiped about, and potentially bad for business; I can't be doing with it,' he regularly said. It was no doubt the reason he hadn't mentioned any of this to Florrie before now. And, if it were true, then it must be awful for Edward.

'Well, at least this way, you've still got his visit to look forward to when he gets things sorted out with his ex.'

Mr H's face brightened. 'Yes, you're right, and it's definitely best he gets things smoothed over before he returns.'

'Did he say when that would be?'

'He did; he's going to make sure he's got all the loose-ends tied up with Luella, so he's put his visit back to next week, which should give him plenty of time.' He rubbed his hands together, beaming broadly. 'On that happy note, I think I'll pop the kettle on. Fancy a cuppa, my dear?'

'Sounds good to me.' Florrie did her best to return Mr H's enthusiasm, despite the doubts about his grandson gnawing at her insides; she really hoped he wouldn't let his grandfather down.

FIVE

'So he's really coming to stay with Mr H?' Stella asked, her perfectly microbladed eyebrows raised in disbelief as she flicked her long blonde hair over her shoulder. She was looking casually chic in a crisp, fitted shirt, her long legs clad in designer jeans.

'Mm-hm. According to Mr H he is.' Florrie nodded. 'Hard to believe, after all these years.'

'I reckon he'll back out of it,' said Jasmine. 'How long did you say it's been since his last visit?' Jasmine always put Florrie in mind of a pixie, with her elfin features, green eyes and spiky dyed red hair.

'According to Mr H, he hasn't been here since he was a very young lad,' said Florrie.

'I think he'll come; I can sense it,' said Lark in her familiar, other-worldly tone.

'Well, if Lark can sense it you'd better brace yourself; he's definitely coming,' Maggie said resolutely.

It was Friday evening and the friends were sitting at their favourite table in a cosy nook of The Jolly Sailors pub. Chatter and laughter rubbed shoulders with a lively playlist of folk music in the low-beamed bar. It was filled, as always, with an eclectic mix of clientele; fishermen, business men and women, and students alike all seemed to gravitate towards its welcoming atmosphere. The air was infused with the mouth-watering aroma of the chef's signature dish of fish and chips with lashings of vinegar, something in which Florrie and her friends regularly indulged. Fishing paraphernalia was dotted about the place; an old lobster pot was perched on a shelf complete with fake lobster, while glass fishing floats wrapped in rope netting were suspended here and there from the beams. An old, decommissioned pistol reputed to have belonged to Micklewick Bay's most infamous smuggler, Jacob Crayke, was positioned in a display box at the back of the bar. Lighting was courtesy of strategically placed recommissioned hurricane lamps, while warmth was provided by the fire that crackled merrily in the hearth of the inglenook fireplace. An old ship's bell hung above the broad, dark oak bar. Polished until it gleamed, it was rung every evening to call last orders. At the far end was the wooden figurehead of a sailing ship in the form of a busty, golden-haired mermaid. It had washed up on the beach in front of the pub a century and a half earlier and been nabbed by the then landlord. A well-worn mariner's hat was hanging off one of its nipples, which meant craggy-faced local fisherman, Lobster Harry, was about. The first thing he did when he entered the pub was to hang up his hat before ordering a pint of real ale and seeking out his pals for a catch up or a noisy game of dominoes. He was no stranger to a rowdy sing-along when he was on the other side of a few pints of Old Micklewick Magic, which always made for an entertaining evening.

'And how are things going with you and Graham?' asked Stella in her usual bold fashion – a barrister by profession, she always got straight to the point.

Florrie pulled a face, waggling her hand from side-to-side. She'd met Graham here at the Jolly almost a year ago. The pair had got chatting and he'd asked her out on a date. She was beginning to feel disappointed that things hadn't got much more exciting since that night. 'Um, well...'

'That good, eh?' Maggie chuckled, her chocolate brown eyes and rich, dark curls shining in the soft light betraying her half-Italian heritage.

A frown crumpled Florrie's brow. 'Things are *okay* but it feels as if we're both just plodding along with the relationship, you know? I'm very fond of him, but there's just no spark. And, if I'm honest, there never was.' She glanced up at her friends, regret pooling in her stomach. 'On paper, we should work; we're well-suited, but the reality is, well, everything just feels so... so *polite.*'

'Tell us something we don't know, chick.' Jasmine gave a smile. 'We all think he's a nice enough bloke, really we do, but when you're together you look more like friends.'

'As opposed to hot, passionate lovers.' Stella gave a cheeky wink and grinned broadly before leaning down to tuck a folded beer mat under the leg of the table in a bid to stop it wobbling. 'There we are, good as new,' she said, testing it out.

'Trust you to put it like that, Stells.' Jasmine shot her a knowing look. 'I'm not saying there's anything wrong with being *friends* with Graham, but you need to look like you're connected on a more romantic level. Remember what Maggie and Bear were like when they first got together?'

'Don't remind us,' said Lark, her pale-green eyes wide as she shook her head jokingly.

'Steady on, there, Jazz; we don't need things to get X-rated this early in the evening,' Maggie said, chuckling.

'I think what Jazz is trying to say, is that you and Graham don't look like you're a couple, chick,' said Lark, her blonde mermaid plait snaking over her shoulder. 'I hate to say it, but you're giving out pretty strong vibes that say you *like* each another, but you're not really *into* each other.'

'Is there any wonder he's so emotionally stilted with the

parents he's got? I think his father's face would crack if he ever tried to smile, and as for his mother, she's a right cold fish,' said Stella.

'Never one to mince your words, are you, Stells?' Maggie said.

Florrie sat quiet for a moment, absorbing her friends' words, fiddling with a loose thread at the cuff of her Breton top. She knew they weren't being unkind; they wanted the best for her – she couldn't have managed without them when her mum had been so ill. They'd grown up together, had known each other since primary school, been through thick and thin together. The only exception was Maggie who Florrie had met at university and had shared a house with while she was there. Maggie would regularly pop over and stay at Florrie's parents' with her, and had slotted into the group of friends as if she'd known them forever. It was on such a visit and an evening at The Jolly Sailors that Maggie had met gentle-giant, Bear Marsay. Built like a brick proverbial, he sported unruly dark curls and bushy beard, and was clearly smitten as soon as he'd set eyes on Maggie. He'd lived at Thorncliffe Farm with his parents at the time, and the pair had quickly become inseparable. Just a couple of years after Maggie had finished her degree, they moved into Clifftop Cottage, attached to the farm, and got married the following year.

An image of the handsome stranger Florrie had seen outside the bookshop popped into her mind, making her heart flutter. She'd half-expected him to call into the shop after she'd seen him on Monday morning, and had been disappointed when he hadn't. But it hadn't stopped him from occupying a large chunk of her thoughts since then. 'So, Lark, can I ask, do you think, using that special intuition of yours, Graham and I will stay together? Do you get the feeling we have a long-term future? Or do you think we're just going through the motions and we'd be better off calling it a day?'

'The fact that you even have to ask that, answers your question as far as I'm concerned.' Stella looked serious for a moment.

'Fair point,' Maggie said. She was sitting beside Jasmine, a brightly coloured cardigan thrown over her denim dungarees and a red and white dotty scarf tied around her curls. She looked every inch the creative crafter she was. She was Florrie's closest friend.

Exuding her inimitable calm vibe, Lark inhaled slowly, then released her breath steadily. 'If you want my truthful answer—'

'She does,' said Stella, earning a look from Jasmine. 'Give it to her straight.'

'Stell's right, I do,' said Florrie.

'Well, in truth, I've never been able to see Graham in your long-term future; never had the sense that he's your "happy-ever-after". He's a great bloke, but you're just not a good fit.'

'That's exactly what Stella said to that bloke she was getting intimate with the other night.' Jasmine gave a dirty laugh, causing heads to turn at nearby tables.

'Jasmine!' Florrie couldn't help but giggle along with the others.

Despite the dirty look she shot Jasmine, a smile hovered over Stella's mouth. 'I'm going to treat that comment with the contempt it deserves, Jazz. But that aside, there's no way I'm going to let a bloke complicate my life.'

Maggie's eyes switched from Stella to Florrie. 'What you need, petal, is someone to come along and rock your world.'

'And her bed,' Stella and Jasmine chorused, falling about and snorting with laughter.

'Honestly, what are you two like?' Lark grinned. 'I have to agree though. You need to be with someone who makes you feel it right here – and we don't need any smutty comments from you two, thanks, I'm being serious.' She pressed her hands to her chest, her silver bracelets jangling as she gave Stella and Jasmine a mock-warning look.

Florrie was momentarily distracted by a man wearing a familiar long grey overcoat and flat cap entering the bar on a chilly burst of air, triggering the bolt of recognition from earlier in the week. It had snagged on a vague memory at the back of her mind but, frustratingly, she still hadn't managed to place him. He looked to be in his early fifties, and judging by his weather-beaten complexion, favoured being outdoors. She wondered what could be responsible for the permanently dour expression he wore.

'Graham's a nice enough bloke, but he's just a bit... beige.'

'Beige?' Maggie's words pulled Florrie back to their conversation.

'Yeah, Graham, he's kind of beige,' said Maggie, nodding. 'You're a gorgeous girl, Florrie, as well as being intelligent with a wicked sense of humour. If you want my advice, you shouldn't settle for second best, or plod on with the relationship just for the sake of it. Life's too short.'

'Yeah, you're not wrong there.' Sadness flittered across Jasmine's face.

'Oh, Jazz, I'm sorry; I didn't mean—'

'It's okay; I know you didn't, chick.' Jasmine squeezed Maggie's hand. 'Just forget about it and ignore me. I'm fine. Honest.'

Florrie searched Jasmine's face, her stomach twisting with sympathy for her friend who'd been widowed too soon. Though it had happened five years ago, Jazz regularly said it sometimes felt like only yesterday. Florrie could understand why her emotions were still raw. She caught her friend's eye and smiled, relieved to see Jasmine's expression brighten. She made a mental note to speak to her alone, check she was doing okay. It couldn't be easy juggling two young children and two part-time jobs as well as branching out into baking celebration cakes.

'Maggie's right,' said Lark sagely. Florrie turned to her, the pair locking eyes as Lark gave one of her mysterious looks.

'I've always had the feeling that someone's going to come along and sweep you right off your feet when you least expect it.'

'Really? Tell me more,' said Florrie, smiling, 'especially if your feeling includes the words "tall, dark and handsome".' The handsome stranger's dreamy blue eyes slipped into her thoughts again. She hadn't shared details of her encounter with her friends, knowing they'd tease her relentlessly. And besides, it was hardly likely she'd cross paths with him again.

'All I can sa—'

'Here we go, ladies. Two lots of the Jolly's fish and chips.' Lark's words were cut off by the cockney tones of Mandy, The Jolly Sailors' landlady. 'Tara and Immy are right behind me with the other plates. And watch out, they're hot – the plates, that is, not the ladies.'

'Hey, I'd say we're hot, wouldn't you, Immy?' said Tara, grinning.

'Too right.' Immy wiggled her bottom, making them all giggle.

'Oh, wow! That smells delicious. I'm absolutely starving,' said Maggie.

'Mmm-hmm. It so does,' said Jasmine.

'Right, Tara's got the mushy peas as well, and I'll just go back and get the gravy boat.' Mandy shook her head, laughing. 'I'm still getting my head around the fact you have gravy on your chips up here in Yorkshire.'

'You say it like it's something odd,' said Maggie, smiling up at her.

'It's a delicacy,' said Lark. 'We slather everything in gravy. Well, maybe not cornflakes and stuff like that.'

'Yep, Stella's been known to slather it on her men, isn't that right, Stells?' Jasmine chuckled when Stella flicked a finger at her.

'Just as well I love you, Jazz.' Stella turned her attention to

Mandy. 'And I don't think it's just limited to Yorkshire; I think it's prevalent in other parts of the north too.'

Mandy put her hands on her hips, her face ruddy from the warmth of the kitchen. 'Well, you learn something new every day – and I don't mean what Jasmine said about Stella. Anyway, I'll be back in a flash.'

'Thanks, Mandy.' Florrie smiled after her, catching the eye of the mysterious man in the grey overcoat. There was something about that brooding gaze; if only she could remember where she knew him from.

'Hey, Florrie, you never know, Edward Harte might be a real hottie. You might end up hitting it off with him, if you know what I mean?' Stella gave her a cheeky wink.

'That's hardly helpful, Stells.' Florrie shot her friend a look; it was bad enough Mr H trying to matchmake.

'Just saying, that's all.' Stella pushed a forkful of fish into her mouth and chewed, her eyes twinkling mischievously.

'Stells has a point actually,' said Maggie. 'He could be a real hunk.'

Florrie dipped a chip into her mushy peas. 'Hmm. You seem to be forgetting a fairly major detail: I'm already dating someone and am not in the habit of cheating.' She waved the chip at them to emphasise her point, feeling herself blush as she struggled to push the handsome stranger from her wayward thoughts.

'Yes, but, that aside,' said Stella, swallowing her mouthful, 'he could be good for a quick roll in the hay. That'd perk you up.'

'Stells, you think *all* blokes are good for a roll in the hay,' said Jasmine.

'That's so not true. I work with a few that certainly wouldn't tempt me in that department.' Stella gave a theatrical shudder. 'But you never know, Edward Harte might even be the one to rock our little Florrie's world. Lord knows, she needs it; Graham hardly looks like he's packing dynamite in his UPs, does he? No offence, chick.' Her comments resulted in howls of laughter from the friends.

Florrie was still chuckling, doing her best to ignore Stella's comments about Edward Harte, when her eyes wandered over to the bar, searching for the mystery man in the grey overcoat, but he was nowhere to be seen. She started as she made eye contact with pub regular, Ando Taylor. Though well into his forties, Ando dressed like the teenagers he hung out with at the skateboard park, with his battered leather jacket, skinny jeans and trendy trainers. The look was topped off by his familiar baseball cap, his straggly, bleached hair hanging in rats' tails down his back. Before Florrie knew what was happening, he gave her a self-assured smile. She turned away quickly, her face flushing. He'd recently started to pay her some unwelcome attention and she didn't want to encourage him. He really wasn't her type.

SIX

The weekend passed quietly. It had been Florrie's turn to have Saturday off at the bookshop, and she'd made the most of it by re-arranging the attic room of her little terraced cottage; she'd taken delivery of a new bookcase and had miraculously managed to squeeze it in. She relished weekends like this, enjoying the tranquillity of her home.

She'd fallen in love with the cottage as soon as she'd stepped over the threshold, despite the fact it had been in dire need of a revamp and was absolutely filthy. Even the estate agent had struggled to find much positive to say about it and had at least had the good grace to sound embarrassed when he'd described it as "bijou", but Florrie had seen through the detritus and grime; to her it *was* a jewel, a little diamond in the rough. Being in a less than salubrious part of town – or the "wrong side of the railway", as Graham annoyingly referred to it – and being rundown, meant that she'd been able to snap it up for a bargain using the savings she'd accrued with the help of the private tuition lessons she offered two nights a week. It had a postage-stamp of a garden at the rear and a small flowerbed beneath the window at the front, both of which she tended lovingly. Best of all, it was on the end of a row of six houses, and had views of the sea, albeit from her attic window.

That was six years ago, and in that time she'd totally transformed the property, thanks to help from her dad and his building skills. The shabby uPVC door had been replaced with a sturdy one made of hardwood. She'd painted it a deep ocean blue and fitted it with a brushed chrome handle and matching letter box, setting a pot of sea holly at the side. She'd even given it a name: Samphire Cottage. It still gave her a thrill when she opened the wrought iron gate – painted to match the door – and headed down its short path.

She was curled-up in an armchair in the living room on Sunday afternoon, engrossed in a book, a cup of tea close to hand. Though the room was small, it managed to accommodate a two-seater sofa and two mis-matched chairs covered with patchwork throws without feeling at all cluttered. A small upcycled coffee table sat before them, while a tiny side-table with a single drawer was tucked beneath the window, on which was a cream vintage telephone alongside a notepad and floral pot containing a variety of pens. Either side of the cast iron fireplace was a built-in cupboard with shelves above – more of her father's handiwork. They were painted in denim-blue eggshell to match the skirting boards and window frame, and were perfect for housing her small television, a radio and books. Lots and lots of books. She'd chosen a pale, dusky pink for the walls, and coir carpet for the floor, while a mat in retro swirls of blues, pinks and a pop of yellow sat in front of the fireplace. The heavily lined, floor-length curtains were from Lark's Vintage Bazaar, the shop owned by her friend. Lark had picked them up in France, from a market stall selling vintage items and Florrie had fallen in love with them straightaway. The large Victorian sampler and vintage floral prints that decorated the walls were finds from Lark's too. One of Florrie's favourite ways of passing a lazy afternoon was to read in this room, savouring the sense of calm it bestowed upon her.

The shrill ringing of her landline pierced the silence, making her jump. 'Jeez!' she said, pressing her hand to her chest. Heaving herself up, she made her way to the window and picked up the receiver – being vintage, the phone had no caller ID function. 'Hello.'

'Hi, Flo, it's me. I tried ringing your mobile but it went straight to voicemail.' Graham was the only one who called her Flo. He still hadn't got the message she wasn't keen on it; it reminded her of her Great Aunt Flo, who Florrie remembered as being a bad-tempered, picky old bird. Despite her telling him this numerous times, he still insisted on using it. She'd eventually given up saying anything.

'Hi, Graham, how were things in York?' She glanced up at the clock on the mantlepiece; it was ten-past-five, he'd no doubt just got back from his overnight stay at his parents. 'How are your mum and dad?'

'Er, yeah, good thanks.' He paused for a moment, awkwardness travelling down the phone line. 'I'm still with them actually.'

Her eyebrows drew together. His voice sounded different; she sensed instantly something was amiss. 'Oh, right... er, are you okay? Is everything all right?' She knew his grandmother had been unwell recently and hoped it had nothing to do with her. Her frown deepened; she could hear conversation in the background, his father's deep tones resonating in her ear.

'Erm, yeah, yeah, they're fine. Everything's fine... it's just, well... look, there's no easy way to say this, Flo...'

'Say what?' Florrie asked, keeping her voice calm despite her heart hammering in her chest. But she already knew.

'Look, I'm really sorry – and I feel a real shit doing this over the phone but I didn't want to leave it any longer...'

She swallowed. It was the conversation she'd been bracing herself to instigate with him, though she'd been waiting to do it in person. 'I think I know wha—' But Graham didn't appear to hear her.

'I, er... well, we both know things haven't been great between us recently; you can't tell me you haven't noticed we've been, well... we've been coasting, at least that's what it's felt like to me. Anyway, being here with my family has given me a chance to think, get my head straight. I spoke to them about how I've been feeling, and I've come to the conclusion it would probably be for the best if we called it a day, you know, before we start to irritate one another.'

Florrie stood silent for a moment, gazing out of the window distractedly. An expensive-looking sports car was crawling by. She vaguely registered is as belonging to unsavoury local business man, Dick Swales – or Dodgy Dick as he was known. His wife, Wendy, was sitting in the passenger seat – that huge bouffant of jet-black hair couldn't possibly belong to anyone else – and appeared to be surveying the properties on either side. Annoyance flittered through Florrie's mind, she wondered if they were responsible for the recent notes that had been pushed through the letter boxes of residents in the street, offering to buy their houses, allegedly saving estate agent fees. They'd obviously cottoned-on to the fact that the "poky" houses in a not-so-long-ago undesirable part of town were being snapped-up by young, well-to-do first-time-buyers, and the area was experiencing something of a renaissance. There wouldn't be a better time to buy than now; bargains could still be had. If only the houses were up for sale.

If rumours were to be believed Mr and Mrs Dodgy Dick had amassed a considerable portfolio of properties in the town, including a couple of shops in the square. They'd approached

Mr H with a view to taking The Happy Hartes Bookshop off his hands. He'd sent them away with a flea in their ears, and they hadn't been back since. If they knocked on her door today, they'd get equally short shrift.

'Flo? Flo? Are you still there? Are you okay?' Graham's voice pulled her back to the matter in hand.

'Er, yeah, sorry. I'm still here.'

'So, what... erm... do you think?' His voice tailed off.

Much as she agreed with everything he'd just said, the impact of his words was taking its time to sink in. This was it; this was the end. They'd been together for almost a year, and she wasn't the sort of person who could just switch off her feelings, even if she didn't love him with a burning passion. But one thing was perfectly clear now it had come to the crunch: although she felt sad, she was by no means devastated. Out of the blue, an image of the handsome stranger bloomed in her mind, but before she could dwell on it Graham spoke.

'Are you sure you're okay? I wasn't expecting you to be this shocked, this upset.'

She blinked quickly, scattering her musings. 'Yes, I'm fine. And I'm not shocked, or upset.' How was she feeling? 'It's okay.'

'Oh.' There was an unmistakable tinge of disappointment in his voice. 'You're not upset?'

'Well, of course I feel a *bit* upset – no doubt the same as you – but I totally agree with everything you've just said. In fact I was talking to the girls about it the other night, and—'

'What? You talked about our relationship with your friends?' His tone jumped from disappointed to indignant, taking her by surprise.

'Well, yes, I ju—'

'I'm seriously brassed off about that, Flo. Talking about me behind my back to that group of cackling witches, well, it's plain disloyal. There's no other word for it. I'm disappointed in you. I really am.'

Florrie had never heard him sound so irate, but dissing her friends had niggled her and she felt a twinge of annoyance. 'But it's okay for you to talk about me to your family? And, for your information, my friends are not a group of cackling witches, they're decent women and loyal friends to me. And the fact that you insist on calling me Flo drives me absolutely bloody crazy!' Her anger was building.

Before he had a chance to reply Florrie heard the familiar ring of a woman's laughter in the background. The penny dropped with an almighty clatter. 'Graham, is Bethany with you?'

A beat passed.

'I, er... well, yes... erm, she's here.' His words came out in a splutter.

Another beat passed.

'Are you seeing her?'

'Erm, it's just, well, because I've been spending so much extra time at work, Bethany and I, well, we've become close, especially since we were away for that business meeting last weekend. It's actually made me realise how little you and I have in common; how we've just been rumbling on and I...'

His revelation came as no surprise. When she'd called in at his office a couple of months earlier, Florrie had noticed how Bethany, his PA, had hung onto his every word, gazing at him with puppy-dog eyes and positively sparkling whenever he spoke to her. Graham had lapped it up, showing a more light-hearted version of himself than the one he kept for Florrie. If she was honest with herself, she knew it was inevitable he and Bethany would become an item.

'It's fine, Graham, you don't have to tie yourself up in knots explaining yourself to me. You're right, we've been "rumbling on" as you put it, and breaking-up is the right thing to do – for both of us. I wish you and Bethany all the best, and I genuinely mean that; she's a nice girl. Take care. Bye, Graham.' She rested the handset back on its cradle, hearing the faint strain of Graham's voice calling her name. Outside, Dodgy Dick's car had gone, and Florrie's gaze loitered on a ginger tom cat slinking its way along the garden wall of the house opposite, a mix of emotions swirling around her stomach.

SEVEN

'Oh, Florrie, chick, I'm sorry to hear that. Would you like me to come over?' Florrie could feel Maggie's sympathy floating down the phone line to her.

'No, honestly, I'm fine. I just thought I'd let you know, and I kind of feel a bit mean saying this, but the overriding emotion I have is relief. I know breaking up with someone over the phone isn't the best way of doing it, but in all honesty, I'm glad Graham initiated it; it saved me from having to broach the subject. This was way easier.'

'Still, he could've broken up with you before he hitched up with *her*, and he could've had the decency to tell you face-to-face. And, you don't sound mean at all, Mr Beige has gone way down in my estimation. Way. Down. And as for that Bethany tart! Huh! Rules of the sisterhood clearly state you don't chase after another woman's man,' Maggie said disapprovingly.

Florrie's heart squeezed at her friend's loyalty and she couldn't help but give a small laugh. 'Oh, Maggie, I love you and how supportive you are, but quite honestly, I don't mind. You knew how I was feeling from the conversation we had at the pub the other night; it's actually a huge relief. And

Bethany's a nice girl; I honestly think they're well suited.' She didn't like to add that she'd been cheating on Graham in her mind with some sizzling thoughts involving herself and the handsome stranger.

Maggie snorted. 'Why? Is she beige as well?'

Florrie giggled. 'No, she's really beautiful, and from what I've seen, has quite a playful sense of humour. She probably brings the light-hearted side out of him way better than my nerdy, geeky personality ever did or could.'

'This coming from the woman who ran along the beach stark naked before diving into the waves for a dare. That doesn't sound nerdy or geeky to me.'

Florrie groaned and covered her eyes with her hand, her cheeks burning at the memory. 'Arghh! Nope, you're right, that sounds crazy! And I thought you promised never to mention it again.'

'I had my fingers crossed, so my promise doesn't count. Anyway, you made Ando Taylor and Lobster Harry's day – actually, make that *year* – after seeing you in the buff. I bet they're still drooling about it now.' Maggie gave a throaty giggle.

The flirtatious smile Ando had given her on Friday night barged into her mind. 'Don't! And my behaviour that night is exactly why I'll never take on a dare again.'

'Famous last words, and all that.'

'Trust me, I won't.'

'Fair enough. And have you told your parents about the demise of you and Mr Beige yet?'

Florrie sighed. 'Not yet; I know my mum'll be disappointed, she was very fond of Graham.'

'Ah, but much as she was fond of him, she'll want you to be happy. Mark my words, if I know your mum, she'll take it better than you think.'

'I hope you're right.'

'I am. And I'm just glad you're not sobbing buckets.'

'No chance of that! Actually, I'm more bothered about what Dodgy Dick and Wendy are up to.'

'What d'you mean?'

'I saw them snooping down the road in that fancy car of theirs; it was like they were weighing-up the houses. Made me feel a bit uneasy actually.'

'Hmm. I heard Wendy talking to someone on her phone the other day. She was standing outside the deli, clearly wanting everyone to hear her, saying how they're keen to extend their portfolio.'

'Well, they can keep away from my little house. Ughh! And to cap it all, I've heard back from the decorators with their estimate for painting the bookshop; they're extortionate. If I don't find anyone cheaper, I'm worried Mr H will lose interest in getting it done.'

'Funny you should say that, I was telling Bear about you looking for someone to do the paintwork and he said he'd do it for mate's rates. I meant to mention it the other night but I forgot.'

'Really?' Florrie felt herself perk up.

'Really; he's been thinking about expanding into painting and decorating. Said he could grab some paint charts and crack on with it as soon as you'd decided on a colour.'

This was typical of Bear, he was kind-hearted and generous; he and his wife were well-suited.

'Well, if he's sure, I know I can speak for Mr H – he's fond of Bear – then we'd like to accept his offer. Please tell him we're really grateful, and the sooner he can start, the better.'

'Will do.'

With so much on her mind, Florrie found herself unable to settle back to her book. Before she knew it, she'd slipped her coat on and retrieved her bike from the tiny utility room off the kitchen. She felt a sudden urge to go and see her parents.

* * *

'Charlie, our Florrie's here.' Paula pulled her daughter into a hug, squeezing her tightly as she always did. 'Ooh, it's good to see you, lovey, but by 'eck, you feel absolutely nithered. Come in where it's warm. Have you eaten yet? I was just about to serve up. We're a bit later than usual with our Sunday roast since we've been gutting the garage – honest to goodness, the stuff that was in there, you wouldn't believe. Heaven alone only knows why your dad feels the need to hoard so much rubbish.' She smiled, rolling her eyes good-naturedly. 'He's in the kitchen just now, carving the beef; there's plenty to go round.'

Florrie stepped into the porch as the delicious aroma of roast beef, Yorkshire puddings and her mum's legendary onion gravy wrapped itself around her. She felt a sudden blast of nostalgia for the days she still lived with her parents. Her stomach rumbled loudly. 'Ooh, it smells amazing, Mum. Even if I'd had my tea, I wouldn't be able to turn down one of your yummy roasts.'

Paula beamed at her. 'Good stuff, flower. Right, let me have your coat. I'll hang it above the radiator so it'll be nice and warm for when it's time for you to leave. Just prop your bike up there; mind your dad's wellies, I don't know why he's left them there.'

Florrie did as she was bid, smiling affectionately at her mother who loved nothing better than fussing round her and her dad. At only just scraping five feet, it was regularly commented upon how alike mother and daughter were, both sharing the same petite frame, brown eyes and delicate, heart-shaped face.

Paula made her way down the hall to the kitchen. 'Come on, chick; your dad's got the radio on, I don't think his deaf lugs can have heard me telling him you'd landed.'

Florrie walked into the wall of heat that filled the room, the sight of her father leaning over the joint of beef at the kitchen table triggering a surge of happiness. 'Hi, Dad.' She noticed his salt and pepper waves were in need of a trim.

'Florrie, sweetheart!' His ruddy face broke out into a beaming smile. 'Well, this is a lovely surprise. How're you doing, lass? Please tell me you're stopping for some dinner with us. There's plenty to go round; your mother's done enough mashed potato and Yorkshire puds to feed the whole street.'

Paula smiled at him fondly, rubbing Florrie's arm. 'She is, Charlie; I'm just about to set her a place. Can you pass me another table mat from the drawer?'

'Anything for you, my love.' He set the carving knife down and reached into the draw of the old pine table. 'There you go. Now then, come here, Florrie, and give your old dad a hug.'

That was something Florrie would never be too old for. An only child, Florrie was the apple of her parents' eyes. They were enormously proud of her, especially since she was the first person in the family to go to university.

Much as she adored her little cottage, there was nothing like popping home for a visit, even if her parents didn't live far from her. It was always warm and welcoming, the atmosphere cosy and relaxed. And her mum's Sunday dinners were incomparable.

* * *

'Well, I for one, am not surprised, if you want my honest opinion.' Charlie sat back in his armchair, nursing his mug of tea. 'Not one iota.' They'd reconvened to the living room; Florrie had waited until they'd finished eating to share her news about Graham, not wanting to put a black cloud over the meal.

'I'm not either, lovey,' said Paula.

'Really?' This wasn't the reaction Florrie had expected.

Paula nodded, hugging her mug of tea to her chest. 'He was a nice enough lad, but he wasn't for you.'

'He was all right, but to tell you the truth, I'm pleased you've both called it a day. He was boring.'

'Charlie!'

'Well, he was, and don't pretend you didn't think so too, Paula. He quashed our Florrie's sparkle.'

Florrie looked from her mum to her dad. 'Is that really what you thought?'

'Aye, it is, love,' said her dad.

'Like I said, he was nice enough, but your dad's right. We've been concerned about you for a while.'

Well, this was news to Florrie.

'But now you're free for a nice young man to come along and sweep you off your feet.' Her mum beamed at her. 'And he will when the time's right. Mark my words.'

Florrie gave her mother a look; her words had echoed what Lark had said on Friday. 'I think I'm going to make the most of being single for a while, Mum. The last thing I need at the moment is to replace Graham with someone else.' *Not even handsome strangers.*

EIGHT

Florrie woke to the sound of rain lashing against her bedroom window and the wind howling down the chimney of the cast iron Victorian fireplace. Yawning, she rubbed her eyes and squinted across the room where she could see from the chink in the floral curtains it was only just getting light. It was too early to get up, so she turned over, puffed up her pillow and snuggled deeper under her thick feather duvet; she'd wait until the central heating kicked in, let it take the edge of cold off the house.

But try as she might, she couldn't get back to sleep. Her mind had things it was keen to address and kept shifting between Graham – and her parents' surprising opinion of him – Dodgy Dick, and the potential visit from Edward Harte. *Edward Harte*, she mused; she hoped he wouldn't let his grandfather down. Not wanting to dwell on that particular subject, she flicked on her bedside light and picked up the novel on her bedside table. What better way to fill the time before the alarm clock was due to go off than between the pages of a book? She'd read until late last night, putting her book down reluctantly; she'd been known to keep turning the pages until the early hours, losing track of time, which was fine at weekends, but not great when you had to be up for work the next day.

It felt like she'd been reading for a mere matter of minutes when the alarm went off. She slotted her bookmark between the pages and pushed the duvet back. 'Right, Monday, let's see what you've got in store for us.'

Florrie was thankful that the wind had dropped by the time she left for work. And though it was still raining, it was only light and wouldn't stop her from using her bike. Wrapped up well against the elements, and with her chin tucked into her scarf, she cycled briskly along the top promenade, the wheels of her bike splashing through the puddles. Only the hardiest of dog walkers and joggers were out this morning and she pretty much had the cycle path to herself. Dark, brooding clouds scudded across the sky, and the sea looked black and choppy, with white horses charging towards the shoreline, crashing angrily against Thorncliffe. A fishing boat caught her eye as it chugged away from the cove; it was getting tossed about on the waves as if it was made of flimsy balsa wood. And it never ceased to amaze her that, no matter how horrendous the weather, there was always a pod of fool-hardy surfers braving the icy grip of the water. 'Brrr!' It made her feel cold just thinking about them.

She was glad when she arrived at The Happy Hartes Bookshop, dismounting as she passed Seaside Bakery. Through the window she caught sight of Jasmine who was setting out cakes in one of the counter displays, too busy to spot Florrie walking by.

Florrie had only just got through the door, when Gerty came hurling down the stairs, whining and whimpering and looking agitated. It was a far cry from her usual waggy-tailed greeting. Florrie pulled her gloves off and blew on her fingers that were red with the cold, her eyes landing on the floor where the day's post and newspaper were still sitting. Instinctively, she knew something was wrong. 'What's up, Gerty? Where's your dad?' she asked, pushing her gloves into her pockets.

Gerty whined and charged up the stairs. Florrie scooped up the post and newspaper, following quickly behind, a sense of foreboding urging her on. Goosebumps sprang up over her skin when she saw that Mr H wasn't in his usual seat at the kitchen table, and there was no pot of tea with steam curling from its spout or croissants set out. And judging by the temperature, the pot-bellied stove had yet to be lit. She felt her heart lurch. This had never happened in all the time they'd been taking breakfast together. Myriad thoughts raced through her mind as she glanced around. Had he popped out and lost track of the time? Had he gone to Mrs H's grave; was there a special anniversary she'd forgotten about? Even so, it was very unlike him to leave the flat without taking Gerty with him.

'Mr H? Shall I put the kettle on?' Florrie said, her voice raised – though he would never admit to it, he was slightly hard of hearing.

Just as she set the post and newspaper on the table, Gerty ran back into the kitchen, whining and pacing around her, clearly distressed. Florrie waited a moment, listening out for sounds of movement from elsewhere in the flat, but there was nothing. 'This isn't like your dad, Gerty.' The Labrador nudged her nose against Florrie's hand and whimpered again. Florrie's stomach twisted with anxiety. 'Mr H,' she called once more, her voice tinged with concern. When there was no reply she headed out onto the landing, following Gerty into the living room.

'Mr H?' Florrie ran over to where he was sitting in his armchair, keeping warm in front of the old-fashioned gas fire. His head was tilted forwards and his glasses had slipped down his nose, but his expression was peaceful. Florrie's eyes fell to his lap to see Mrs H's favourite scarf threaded through his fingers. 'Oh, Mr H,' she said in a whisper. The thought of him missing his wife and being lonely tugged at her heart. Gerty pushed her head into his lap and began nudging his hand, whimpering as she did so.

Reluctant as she was to rouse him from such a deep sleep, Florrie went to give his shoulder a gentle shake, but the moment she touched him she knew. Her breath caught in her throat and she snatched her hand away, tears swimming in her eyes. 'Oh, no! Mr H! No!' She ran out of the room, down the stairs and out into the street.

'Florrie! What is it? Are you okay? You look like you've had a shock.' Jasmine's face fell when her friend stumbled into the bakery looking distraught, tears streaming down her cheeks.

'It's Mr H,' Florrie said, sobbing. 'He's... he's...' She couldn't bring herself to utter the words. 'I can't... wake him... he won't wake up!'

'Oh, Florrie, no, you poor thing.' Jasmine exchanged a hurried look with her boss, Sarah, before running around the counter and sweeping Florrie into a hug.

'I'll call for an ambulance then contact the surgery,' said Sarah, her voice calm. 'Bring Florrie through to the back, Jasmine.'

Jasmine nodded and guided Florrie around the counter while Sarah made the calls.

'Here you are, drink this, my love. The ambulance and Dr Giffin are on their way.' Sarah handed Florrie a mug of extra-sweet tea.

'Thanks.' Florrie took it, glad of the warmth on her fingers as she nursed it in her hands. Her teeth were chattering and she was shivering from a combination of cold and shock. 'I don't... I can't... believe it.' She shook her head as fresh tears fell. 'He looked so well when I last saw him on Friday... he didn't say anything about feeling poorly... he seemed upbeat and was looking forward to seeing his grandson.' Her thoughts ran to the said grandson. 'I'll have to contact his family, tell them...' She still couldn't bring herself to say the words.

The bell above the shop door jangled. 'I'll get that, Jazz, you stay here with Florrie,' Sarah said, giving a sympathetic smile.

'Oh, petal, I'm so sorry you had to find him like that.' Jasmine pulled up a chair beside Florrie, pushed a box of paper hankies into her lap and started rubbing her friend's back.

'Just the thought of him being alone, it's...' She shook her head and a plump tear landed in her tea. 'Ughh! I kept telling him to call me if he ever needed some company; I would've been more than happy to sit with him, rather than him being in the flat all alone.'

'He wasn't alone, chick, he had Gerty with him and he adored her; they adored each other.'

'Gerty.' Mention of the Labrador stilled Florrie's tears. 'She'll have to come home with me; she can't stay in the flat by herself. Poor lass, she'll be lost without him. Actually, I'd best get back there, she'll be past herself and I think I left the door to the flat unlocked.' Florrie heaved herself up and put her mug on the worktop. Her legs felt like lead and her eyes felt puffy. She sniffed and wiped her nose with the soggy ball of tissue she'd been clutching.

'It's up to you, but you don't have to if you don't feel up to it. Bear's there; Sarah spotted him going into the newsagents so I sent him a quick text and he headed across to the flat straightaway.'

'Thanks, Jazz, that was kind, but I'd just like to say a quick goodbye to Mr H. I feel bad running out of the flat the way I did, leaving him there like that.' Florrie's throat constricted as she fought back more tears. 'And poor old Gerty, she'll be wondering what's going on.'

'Yeah, I get that, chick,' Jasmine said softly. 'Would you like me to come with you?'

Florrie shook her head and pressed her lips into a weak smile. 'I'll be fine.'

* * *

Rifling through Mr H's personal things had felt wrong on so many levels, but spurred on by necessity, and after a quick search of his desk, Florrie had been relieved to find a battered-looking address book in one of the drawers. Wiping her tears, she'd pushed it into her backpack with the intention of contacting Mr H's son when she got home, her stomach in knots at the prospect of delivering such awful news.

Back at Samphire Cottage, Florrie pulled out a seat at the kitchen table, Mr H's address book in her hand, sadness sitting heavy in her chest. 'Right, let's get this over with, Gerty,' she said with a wavery sigh.

Florrie tried all of the phone numbers that were scribbled next to Peter Harte's name with no success. Eventually, after going through the numerous dog-eared scraps of paper that had been pushed between the pages of the book, she found his email address. *Thank goodness!* She crossed her fingers that it would still be one he used.

In the end, it took hours to draft and redraft the email, with her sobbing buckets over every word – no matter which way you chose to deliver it, it wasn't easy contacting someone you hardly knew to tell them a parent had passed away.

Florrie was thankful when Peter replied quickly, despite his cool, matter-of-fact tone, but was taken aback to learn he expected her to take care of the funeral arrangements together with the wake that followed. He told her he and his wife were currently out of the country so it would be a headache for them to organise. His closing line was to say he and Suzanne would do their best to get to Micklewick Bay for the funeral.

'What?' She frowned, scanning over the email again. It

wasn't quite the response she'd expected. Wondering how a couple as warm-hearted and generous-spirited as Mr and Mrs H had managed to produce such a cold-fish of a son, she sent a quick reply, confirming she'd take care of organising whatever was necessary.

She pressed "send" and sat back in her chair, the sorry situation tugging at her heart. Mr H had been the kindest of men and was worth far more than his son's unfeeling, dismissive response. Florrie drew in a shaky breath. If she was going to be in charge of the funeral arrangements, she was jolly-well determined to give her beloved boss the send-off he deserved.

NINE

The following evening, Florrie was slumped on the kitchen floor next to Gerty's bed, her arms wrapped around her companion's warm body as she sobbed gently into the Labrador's fur, when she was startled by a knock at the door. Gerty looked towards the sound while Florrie groaned inwardly and closed her eyes. She'd ignore it, sit quietly and hope whoever it was would go away. Dealing with the funeral director earlier that day, as kind and sensitive as he'd been, had been emotionally draining. Now she just wanted to be left alone with her grief; she'd be no company for anyone and she had neither the energy nor the inclination to make small-talk. And if it was Dodgy Dick, well, he definitely wasn't worth answering the door for.

A moment later, there was another, more urgent rapping at the door followed by the sound of the letter box flipping open.

'Florrie, it's us, let us in, chick.' Lark's voice floated down the hallway.

Florrie dragged her hands down her face, wiping her tears. Her friends, however, were a different matter, so she pushed herself up and went to answer the door, Gerty deciding to stay put. She opened it to see Lark, Stella, Maggie and Jasmine huddled together on the doorstep, a huge foil-covered dish of something that smelled delicious in Maggie's hands, a bunch of brightly coloured flowers from Daisy Chain Flower Shop in Jasmine's, and a couple of bottles of wine in Stella's. Seeing her friends standing there, affection and concern in their eyes, Florrie felt a rush of relief; they were a welcome sight.

Exhausted from crying, she mustered up a smile as best she could. 'Come in out of the cold,' she said as they all filed past her and headed down to the kitchen.

'Ah, petal, dry your tears, we're here with an unlimited supply of cuddles and one of Maggie's killer chicken casseroles to help chase your sadness away.' Lark swept Florrie into a tight hug, kissing her firmly on the cheek. 'And I brought you this.' She pressed a small silk pouch into Florrie's hand. 'Amethyst, helps with grief; keep it close.'

Florrie's tears reared their head again at her friend's kindness. 'Thanks, Lark,' she said, her voice wavering, her fingers rubbing over the purse and the piece of crystal it contained. Lark swore by crystal healing, and though a little sceptical, Florrie was willing to give anything a try to chase away her feelings of despair.

'Come on.' Lark took her hand and they joined the others in the kitchen, watching as they bustled about, setting the table, warming the oven for the casserole and hunting out wine glasses.

'Ah, Gerty, how're you doing?' Maggie said softly. The Labrador's eyes flicked up, a pitiful expression on her face; she'd barely moved from her bed all day.

'Oh, bless her, she's not herself, is she?' said Stella, bending to stroke her. 'Oh, Gerty, you poor girl.'

Florrie looked on, her chest tight with sorrow. 'No, she's not herself; she's lost and confused. I just keep giving her lots of cuddles, which helps us both actually.'

'Well, let's hope these'll cheer her up,' said Maggie, fishing in her bag for a packet of chew sticks. She opened it and offered one to Gerty who gave a small wag of her tail, taking the treat gently in her mouth. 'I see she hasn't lost her appetite, then.'

Maggie's comment coaxed a smile from Florrie. 'No, that seems unaffected, I'm pleased to say.'

'Typical Labrador,' said Lark, smiling. 'She's in the best place here with you, and she'll be fine once she's over her loss. As will you, petal.' She rubbed Florrie's arm.

'Where do you keep your vases, hon?' asked Jasmine, setting the flowers down on the draining board.

'The cupboard on the wall by the door; there's a couple right at the back; you might need to stand on a chair to get one.' Florrie reached for a tissue from the box on the table and dabbed at her nose.

'Who needs a chair when Amazonian Stella's about?' Jasmine grinned at her. 'Stells, get your lanky legs over here, will you? I need you to reach a vase from this cupboard. It's either that, or I'll have to sit on Lark's shoulders,' she said, making even Florrie chuckle.

'Yikes!' Lark feigned a look of horror.

'Hey, I'm not that heavy!' said Jasmine.

'Just joshing, hon,' said Lark.

'On my way. Can you take over doing this, Mags?' Stella asked.

'Sure can.' Maggie took the proffered bottle of Pinot Grigio. 'And please don't think I'm being antisocial by not having any vino myself, but I should imagine as I'm designated driver, you'd like me to get you all home in one piece.' Maggie caught Florrie's eye and crossed her fingers, a hopeful expression on her face. Florrie smiled, understanding Maggie's subtext. She mirrored the gesture, her heart going out to her friend. She knew Maggie and Bear had been trying for a baby for a while, with no luck as yet, which was beginning to bother her friend, especially since her sister, Sophia, seemed to be popping them out as easily as shelling peas. Florrie hoped Maggie wouldn't be disappointed again.

'There's some apple juice in the fridge, Mags, if that's any good?'

'Perfect, thanks.'

The four-inch heels of Stella's black leather designer boots put her at a statuesque six-foot-two. She reached into the cupboard and retrieved the vase effortlessly. 'There you go, I think this glass one's probably the best for the job.'

'Thanks, Stells. Has anyone ever told you you're handy to have around?' said Jasmine.

'And who would we turn to for disastrous dating stories to have a good old belly-laugh at?' said Maggie, an amused glint in her eye.

Stella groaned. 'Ughh! I know where this is going.'

'Come on, ladies, let's get comfy; Stella can bring Florrie and Mags up-to-speed while the casserole warms through,' said Lark, pulling out a chair and gently guiding Florrie towards it. The others followed suit and soon they were all sipping wine and encouraging Stella to share her latest dating catastrophe.

'Give me a minute, I need a mouthful of this before I start.' Stella flicked her hair over her shoulder before taking a generous glug of wine.

'I'm not surprised,' said Jasmine.

'Ooh, I'm dying to hear it, I haven't had all the gory details yet.' Maggie rubbed her hands together gleefully.

'Okay, here goes. So, as you know there's a new tenant in chambers by the name of Jerome Whitely; he's nice enough and is a few years younger than me, so hasn't had time to develop the ridiculous peacock strut like some of the other blokes in chambers.' As she spoke, Stella glanced around the table, making eye contact with each of them, just as she did when addressing a jury.

'Hey, what's six or seven years between friends?' Jasmine said, chuckling into her wine.

Stella pulled a face at her. 'Anyway, we'd had a couple of drinks together at the pub, all very light-hearted, nothing serious, the conversation mostly revolving around work – which is all barristers can talk about when they get together. Yawn, yawn. So, imagine my surprise when he invites me to his flat for dinner at the weekend.'

'That's the sort of thing that usually has you running for the hills, Stells,' said Lark.

'I know, but I found myself thinking, "What the hell? Why not?" Anyway, I accepted his invitation and didn't really think much more about it.'

Florrie listened, relieved to have her mind focused on something other than her grief.

'So, I rock up at his apartment only to find it's way swankier than I was expecting. Turns out it's his parents' weekend bolthole.' She paused for effect.

Maggie scrunched up her nose. 'His parents' bolthole?'

'Oh, it gets better, Mags,' Jasmine said with a chuckle.

'I'm intrigued,' said Florrie.

'Anyway, Jerome leads me into this huge state-of-the-art kitchen where I'm introduced to his mother – a stunning woman who's dressed up to the nines since she's about to head out for a meal with his father – and, just as she's handing me a glass of wine, the man himself walks in, and I honestly don't know who's more shocked, him or me.'

'What do you mean?' asked Florrie. 'Was he someone you know?'

Jasmine snorted. 'Just a bit.'

'Well, it turns out that Jerome uses his mother's surname to practise at the Bar; he doesn't want to be accused of nepotism; he's keen to be seen getting work on his own merit rather than because of who his father is. I can't knock him for that.'

'So, who's his father then?' asked Maggie.

'Would you believe it if I told you it's Tristan Bosomworth-Smythe QC?'

'Tristan Bosomworth-Smythe... didn't you have a thing... No?' The information slotted together in Florrie's mind, her eyes growing wider by the second.

Stella nodded slowly, pursing her lips in disapproval. 'Yep, I had a brief encounter with him when we were both in that tedious fraud trial over in Manchester.'

'But I thought he was divorced,' said Maggie.

'So did I,' said Stella. 'Turns out the bull-shitting bastard lied. And what makes me feel even worse is his wife seems lovely.'

'Bloody hell, Stella, how awful for you,' said Florrie. 'I know how much you hate that type of thing.'

'I felt terrible. And absolutely bloody furious.'

'Hah! Wait till you hear what she did though.' Jasmine gave a throaty giggle. 'And you weren't to blame, Stells; that cheating weasel's the one in the wrong, not you. It's not as if you can go around demanding to see someone's Decree Absolute before you snog them or jump into bed with them.'

'Thanks, I think, Jazz. All the same, I'm usually pretty good at spotting the married or taken ones, but I messed up big time with Bosomworth-Smythe.'

'It's clearly not the first time he's played away,' said Florrie.

Maggie held up her hands. 'Just hang fire while I check the casserole; I don't want to miss any of this. Two ticks.' She pushed herself up and hurried over to the oven.

'Sounds like the perfect time to top up the wine,' said Jasmine, reaching for the bottle.

Soon the friends were tucking into the casserole. Florrie felt better with every comforting mouthful; she'd barely eaten over the last couple of days and hadn't realised just how hungry she was. 'Mmm. This is delicious, Maggie,' she said as the rich, warm gravy brought her tastebuds back to life. The others nodded their agreement, making various sounds of approval.

'Good; I'm pleased you're enjoying it.' Maggie beamed at her. 'So come on, Stells, tell us how you exacted your revenge on Bosomworth-Whatsisname.'

Stella finished her mouthful and set her knife and fork down, a smile twitching at her lips. 'So, after pretending we barely knew one another – which no one doubted since, as you all know, he's in chambers over in Manchester and his practice is over that way, so it's perfectly plausible that our paths wouldn't have crossed – Bosomworth-Smythe and his wife went out and Jerome and I ate the meal "Mummy" had prepared for us – prawn linguine, in case you were wondering. It was divine and proved to be quite useful actually.'

'Useful?' Florrie's grief-fuddled brain couldn't imagine in what context a prawn linguine could be considered useful.

Stella flashed a mischievous grin. 'On a trip to the loo, I passed a room with its door open which was very obviously Bosomworth-Smythe's bolt-hole study. I couldn't resist taking a peek inside and when I spotted his red brief bag by his desk a rather naughty idea sprang into my mind.'

Florrie and Maggie exchanged bemused glances.

'So, not long after, I made another excuse to go upstairs where I opened the said brief bag, sneaked his wig tin out and tucked a couple of prawns into the horse hair curls of his mangy old wig. Then I hid a couple more in the pouch at the back of his robes.' She gave a satisfied smile.

'Stella!' Maggie pressed her hand to her mouth as she chuckled.

'I can't wait for reports of his fishy body odour to start filtering through,' said Stella, spluttering through her laughter.

'Surely he'll know it's you,' said Florrie.

'Don't care; he deserves it for cheating on his lovely wife and lying to me. He's lucky I didn't do more. If I'd been feeling really nasty, I would've hunted out his underpants draw and tucked a few prawns in amongst them. That would've fettled his wandering ways.'

'Remind me never to get on the wrong side of Stella,' said Lark, tears of mirth running down her cheeks.

'Well, if you ask me, it sounds like there's something fishy going on,' said Jasmine, managing to keep her face straight until she collapsed into a fit of giggles.

Florrie groaned. 'Ughh! Jazz, that's so corny.'

'And how've things been with Jerome since then?' asked Maggie.

'They're fine; he's obviously none the wiser, though I won't be accepting any more invitations to his parents' house for dinner. And neither of us thought it was going to be anything serious anyway.' She gave a shrug. 'It was just a bit of no-strings fun.'

'Even so, you'll have to keep us up-do-date with the prawn situation,' said Jasmine.

'Ah, don't worry, I will; word travels fast at the Bar – the robing room's rife with gossip – and I suspect it won't be long before there's something interesting to report.' The look of glee in Stella's cool-blue eyes made Florrie giggle.

As the evening drew to a close, her grief-stricken heart felt a little lighter. She was thankful her friends had turned up unannounced. If they'd given her advance notice, she would have put them off, saying she wasn't up to it, which of course, was exactly the reason they hadn't. But she'd been glad of their company and it had taken the sharp edges off her sadness just as they'd intended.

TEN

The week and a half following the dreadful Monday morning when Florrie had found Mr H passed in a blur. The days she'd reopened the shop – which Mr H's solicitor had advised she could do – she'd greeted customers on auto-pilot. Before she knew it, the day of his funeral had arrived. As if sensing the sombreness required, the weather was dark and gloomy, with a sea fret hanging over Micklewick Bay like a shroud, curling round the houses and smothering even the tiniest glimmer of joy. Mr H had been a well-loved local figure and the pews at the church were jam-packed. Those not fortunate enough to get a seat had to stand at the back. Even the vestibule was full, with mourners spilling out onto the pavement beyond.

Afterwards, everyone gathered at The Jolly Sailors where Mandy had laid on a generous buffet. A playlist of Mr H's favourite classical music was playing softly in the background, and though the pub was rammed, conversation was taking place in reverential tones as was befitting of such a sombre gathering.

'By, Mandy's done him proud with that spread,' said Florrie's dad, chomping on a sausage roll and nodding towards the table, a pint of beer in his hand.

'Mmm. She has,' said Florrie, massaging her temples, her eyes red and puffy from crying. She felt numb, the memory of finding Mr H in the living room still raw and painful. She had a throbbing headache and, delicious as it looked, she had no appetite for food. She scanned the room wearily. 'Did either of you see anything of Mr H's son or grandson?'

Her mother's brow crumpled as she considered Florrie's question, nibbling on a crayfish salad sandwich as she did so. 'Well, there was that couple in the pews up at the front of the church. I didn't really get a proper look at them since there were so many folk there. Seemed to be keeping themselves to themselves, but I'd put money on them being Pete and Suzanne. They're a smidge older than your dad and me but I can—'

'Aye, I saw them, and from where I was standing, they look a lot bloomin' older,' said her dad, butting in. 'Your mother looks like a young slip of a lass compared to Mr H's daughter-in-law; she's kept herself well, has your mum.' He looked at his wife proudly, raising his pint to her.

Paula gave a discreet giggle. 'You make me sound like a cheese, Charlie, saying I "keep well". Honestly, what are you like?'

Florrie couldn't help but smile, it warmed her heart to know her mum looked good for her age. And Paula deserved it too, with the effort she put in to eating healthily and taking care of her body since her dreadful battle with Lymphoma. Paula had been resolutely determined to do whatever she could to prevent its return.

'Well, it's true, and if you want my opinion, all that travelling to the four corners of the world, doing whatever it is they do, playing at life and getting frazzled to a crisp under a roasting hot sun hasn't done Pete and his wife any favours. She could be a good ten years older than you, love.'

Paula looked at Florrie and rolled her eyes. 'Give over, Charlie, you've just got used to looking at me that's all; you don't notice all my flaws. Actually, that reminds me, I need to book us both an appointment at the opticians.' She turned back to Florrie. 'I saw the same couple talking to old Mr Cuthbert – you know, the solicitor from Cuthbert, Asquith and Co. It was outside the church right after the service, just before they sloped off.'

Florrie nodded, her heart lurching as she was suddenly hit with the implications of such a conversation. She had a horrible feeling they'd be keen to sell the bookshop; their actions had already shown they didn't have a sentimental attachment to it, unlike the generations of Hartes before them. Dodgy Dick's face loomed in her mind; he'd already paid the shop a visit that week, sniffing around and doing a poor job of pretending he was looking for a book while he quizzed her about who the shop had been left to. Infuriating, insensitive man!

'There was a young man with them as well, he was ever so tall with broad shoulders, very good-looking actually. I reckon that was probably Mr H's grandson, Edward,' said Paula.

Florrie tensed at hearing his name. *Edward Harte was here!* She didn't know why, but she'd half-expected him not to show. Since she'd emailed his father, she'd wondered if Edward would get in touch, keen to contribute in some way to his grandfather's funeral, maybe do a reading. But there'd been radio silence from the Harte family.

She liked them even less now.

She snorted, unable to hide her feelings, wrapping her coat more tightly around her. Her mum looked across at her and they exchanged a knowing look.

'Aye, they'll be wanting their pound of flesh now, the three of them,' said her dad. 'And Dodgy Dick'll be hovering, ready with his cash offer of thousands of pounds below what it's worth. But they'll be too eager to get their sticky mitts on the money to let it go and that'll be another property snatched up by that greedy beggar and his flash wife.'

Florrie dragged her hand down her face wearily. She knew her dad was right.

'I wonder where they've got to? The Hartes, I mean. I haven't seen any sign of them here,' said Paula, looking around the bar. 'At the very least, I thought one of them would come over and thank our Florrie for organising everything.'

'Just as well they didn't; a wake isn't exactly the best time to give someone a piece of my mind,' said Florrie. Tiredness was catching up with her, making her uncharacteristically crotchety.

'No, lovey, it isn't,' said her mum, giving her a sympathetic look and rubbing her arm.

In truth, Florrie was amazed any of the Hartes had turned up at all.

Florrie went to bed that night exhausted, her headache reduced to a background niggle thanks to a couple of strong painkillers. As she sank back into her pillows, the bedside light casting a cosy glow around the room, a feeling of relief washed over her. Mr H had been laid to rest; he was at peace and finally reunited with his beloved wife.

She yawned; tired as she was, she'd hoped to read for half an hour, but as soon as she found her page, she felt her eyelids getting heavy. In a matter of moments sleep had claimed her.

ELEVEN

'Tell me again what it says,' said Stella. Florrie could hear her friend moving about her apartment as she spoke.

She glanced down at the letter on the table by the phone, gnawing at her bottom lip. 'It doesn't say anything much really, other than asking me to attend Cuthbert, Asquith's office tomorrow morning at nine-thirty for an appointment with old Mr Cuthbert, and that it's regarding Mr H.' She could hear Stella taking a glass from a cupboard, setting it down on the granite worktop of her kitchen, followed by the unscrewing of a bottle and a glug of what she assumed was wine being poured.

'It'll be to discuss the contents of Mr H's will; he might've made arrangements for you to continue working at the book-shop. Not sure why old Cuthbert couldn't just put it in a letter rather than dragging you in for an appointment though.'

'But what if his son wants to sell it?'

'Hmm.' Stella swallowed her mouthful of wine. 'If that's the case, it could be that Mr H has bequeathed you something. Maybe it's that first edition you like? He definitely thought enough of you to leave you something as valuable as that.'

'Oh, I doubt it, that's been with the shop since forever and besides, I couldn't take it. I think it's probably more like arrangements for Gerty; he used to ask if I'd look after her if anything happened to him.'

Hearing her name, Gerty looked up from her place in front of the fire, giving a half-hearted wag of her tail. Florrie's heart went out to her; the Labrador was still subdued since losing her dad.

'Hmm. I hadn't thought about poor old Gerty.' Florrie heard the euphoric roar of a crowd as a television was switched on in the background at Stella's. 'Jase!' Stella said in a loud whisper. The volume shot down in an instant.

'Oh, Stells, I'm sorry; you've got company.' She winced, regretting disturbing her friend.

'Hey, it's fine. It's only Jason from chambers. We've had a bugger of a day with that awful Roberts case so we thought we'd chill over a couple of glasses of wine and a Chinese takeaway.' The sound of cutlery clattering together and being placed on a hard surface followed. 'But getting back to your matter, honestly, don't worry about it; it's not going to be anything bad. And at least you'll find out where you stand so you'll be able to decide what to do. Text me as soon as you know. And good luck, chick; I'll be thinking of you.'

'Thanks, Stells. And sorry again for disturbing you.' She heard Stella take another sip of wine.

'No probs. See you Friday at the Jolly? And don't say you don't fancy it or we'll come and drag you out. You need cheering up and the ladies and me are on a mission to do just that.'

Florrie felt herself smile. 'Okay, I'll be there.'

She'd forgotten Stella had a casual thing going with Jason. They'd been seeing each other for a couple of months now – non-exclusively, as Stella was always eager to point out, and just the way she liked to conduct her "relationships". It wouldn't be long before he got too keen and Stella would give him the push.

Florrie's approach to relationships was the opposite of Stella's; whereas Florrie enjoyed the companionship they afforded, her friend found it stifling. How Florrie wished she had someone to share that companionship with right now.

Looking back, a proper, *loving* relationship was something Florrie had never really had with Graham. Yes, they'd rubbed along nicely, both being even-tempered and ever-so-slightly reserved, but he'd never been particularly demonstrative or tactile, and they hadn't come anywhere near to thinking about taking their relationship to the next level and moving in together. With the luxury of hindsight, she could see there'd been no burning passion drawing them together; what they'd had was more like a half-hearted fizzle. They'd become a habit. Not that she was laying full responsibility at his door, she'd been equally to blame. And now the dust had settled, she was surprised they'd lasted as long as they had. She could say, hand-on-heart, she didn't have a moment's regret that they'd broken up, though she was rather surprised he hadn't been in touch to express his condolences about Mr H passing away; living in the same town, he'd have heard about it. His lack of contact spoke volumes.

Though Florrie didn't miss being with Graham, what she yearned for at this precise moment was for someone to wrap their arms around her, hold her tight and tell her everything was going to be okay. How she'd love to have someone to curl up with on the sofa and watch old movies together, her head resting on their shoulder. Someone she could open up to about how she was feeling without thinking she was bogging them down, who understood her need to stay close to her mum. She wanted the sort of relationship her parents had; one that was filled with love as well as companionship. One that had, thus far, eluded her.

Her mind segued to her friends. They'd been wonderfully supportive since Mr H had slipped away (she still couldn't bring herself to use the word "died", it sounded too cold. Too harsh.

Too final). They'd taken it in turns to check on her every day, their well-timed words pulling her out of her despair. 'Come on, chick, you need to stay upbeat for Gerty; the poor lass doesn't know what's going on,' Maggie had said kindly. 'If you need a hug, you know where I am, flower,' Jasmine had said when she'd popped into the shop with a sandwich and a cup of tea for Florrie, knowing she wouldn't be thinking about nourishment. Florrie didn't know what she'd do without any of them.

TWELVE

'Right, that's me ready.' With nerves fluttering in her stomach, Florrie finished buttoning up her coat over her smart navy trouser-suit. Even though Cuthbert, Asquith & Co's office was just on the other side of Victoria Square, it was still chilly, with the wind sweeping up the broad road straight from the sea; she didn't want to arrive looking bedraggled. 'Thanks for doing this, Hayley, I really appreciate it. I don't imagine I'll be long.' At least she hoped she wouldn't. The only time she'd ever had an appointment with a solicitor was when she'd bought her cottage, and that had been a happy affair. The young conveyancer who'd acted for her had a bright and bubbly personality, unlike what she'd seen of dour-looking Maurice Cuthbert. 'You be a good girl for Hayley, please, Gerty.' She nodded to where the Labrador was curled up in her usual place on her cushion by the counter. Florrie had thought it best for Gerty to come to the shop just as she had when Mr H was still alive. The poor girl had been distraught with grief, and Florrie wanted to continue with what was left of her routine as much as she was able.

'Hey, it's no problem. I hope everything goes well, and if you need a break afterwards to go for a cup of tea or something,

feel free. We'll be fine holding the fort here, won't we, Gerty?'
Seventeen-year-old Hayley turned to the Labrador and smiled,
flashing her mouthful of braces. Hayley was the bookshop's
Saturday girl and had done extra hours to help out since Mr H
had passed away. She was like a ray of sunshine, with her ready
smile and kind nature. And her lilac-coloured hair and
penchant for fluorescent hoodies helped brighten the place
up too.

'Thanks, Hayley, you're an angel.' Florrie hooked her bag
over her shoulder and checked her watch. It was nine-twenty,
just right for making her way over to the solicitors' without
having to sit around and wait for too long. 'I don't think it'll
come to that, but it's kind of you to offer.'

Lark was dressing the window of her shop when Florrie
went by. Befitting her usual boho style, she was wearing a pair
of cheesecloth dungarees in shades reminiscent of the sea, her
loose, blonde plait hanging over her shoulder. Seeing Florrie,
her face lit up with a smile. She waved and mouthed, 'Good
luck', before blowing a kiss.

'Thank you.' Florrie raised a watery smile and gave a quick
wave back.

Her gaze swept over the black and gold cursive lettering on
the window of Cuthbert, Asquith & Co; it looked every bit as
antiquated as old Mr Cuthbert himself. Taking hold of the brass
door knob, she pushed open the shiny black door and stepped
into the dark, wood-panelled hallway, her stomach doing somer-
saults all the while. Following the sign, she headed to the recep-
tion area where a woman in her forties with short, curly hair
was working at a computer. The décor wouldn't look out of
place in Dickensian times; the place even smelled old-fashioned, she thought, noting the three clients occupying the seats
set against the walls – an elderly couple and a younger man
with his head bowed, his eyes focused intently on the fingers he
was twisting anxiously in his lap.

'Can I help you?' The receptionist gave Florrie a tight smile.

Florrie's stomach swooped and she swallowed nervously. 'Erm, yes, I've got an appointment with Mr Cuthbert at nine-thirty.' She didn't know why she felt so nervous, but the atmosphere of the place definitely wasn't helping.

'And you are?'

'Florrie. Florrie Appleton.' She heard a gasp behind her and the sound of feet shuffling on the bristly carpet.

'If you could just sign-in here, then take a seat in the waiting area.'

'Thank you.'

Florrie set the pen down and turned, her eyes quickly scanning the room for somewhere to sit.

She'd just perched herself on the edge of a seat when a voice caught her attention. 'Hello again.'

Florrie looked up, stunned to find her gaze meeting a familiar pair of navy-blue eyes. 'Oh, it's you... I mean, hello again.' She bit down on her bottom lip, shocked to see the hand-some stranger from outside the bookshop. His leg was bouncing up and down nervously; he looked every bit as anxious as she was.

He gave a weary smile which she returned.

She wondered what had brought him to the solicitors' office when she was sure he'd told her he lived out of town.

An awkward air hung between them but Florrie's mind was too grief-stricken to muster-up any small-talk. Instead, she inhaled deeply and focussed her attention on her hands in her lap.

'I need to thank you for arranging my grandfather's funeral.'

Florrie frowned, her brain attempting to process his words. 'Pardon?'

'My grandad's funeral; nobody could've done a better job. And the reading you gave... it was beautiful; he would've been thrilled.' The handsome stranger pressed his lips together in another sad smile.

Florrie felt sure she must have heard wrong. 'Did you just say...?' No, she'd misunderstood. She looked at him, perplexed.

'Bernard Harte is... *was* my grandfather; my parents and I owe you a huge debt of gratitude for organising such a moving service for him.'

'You're Mr H's grandson? You're Edward Harte?'

'Yes, I'm Ed. It's good to finally meet you properly.' He held out his hand to her.

Florrie took it absently, myriad thoughts hurtling around her mind. 'But... but you were... you were outside the bookshop; you didn't come ba—' She was silenced by the buzzing of the phone on the receptionist's desk. They both glanced over to her, apprehension writ large across their features.

'Miss Appleton, Mr Harte, you can make your way to Mr Cuthbert's office. It's straight up the stairs, take a left on the landing and it's the door at the end.'

'We're both seeing him?' asked Florrie, glancing between the receptionist and Ed, askance.

'Together?' said Ed, sounding equally confused.

'Yes, that's correct,' the receptionist said with a curt nod.

Florrie looked up at Ed who raised his eyebrows and shrugged. 'We'd better head up there and see what he has to say.'

THIRTEEN

'Come in,' said a well-spoken voice, soft and wavery with age. Florrie stepped into the room, her mind racing. Maurice Cuthbert was sitting at a large, leather-covered partner's desk. His half-moon spectacles were perched on the edge of his generous nose, and he was bent over a collection of papers illuminated by a green banker's lamp, the sound of his fountain pen scratching as he wrote. The wall behind him was lined with old law books, some of them worn and battered from decades of use. Though the walls had the same dark wood panelling as the rest of the building, the space was surprisingly light thanks to the large windows which were dressed with net curtains, providing privacy for clients.

'Please sit down.' Mr Cuthbert looked up and smiled, screwing the lid back on his pen and setting it down. 'Thank you both for coming here. I'm sure you must be wondering why I've asked you together, but first of all, I'd just like to say how sorry I am for your loss. Bernard Harte was a dear friend as well as being a popular man and a well-respected member of the local community.' He paused for a moment, as if choosing his words carefully. 'Edward, I know your grandfather didn't see as much of you as he would've wished, but you getting in touch with him again brought him untold happiness; he thought the world of you.'

In her peripheral vision, Florrie saw Ed hang his head.

Mr Cuthbert continued. 'Miss Appleton, I know you weren't related, but we're all aware of just how fondly Mr Harte regarded you; he regularly spoke of you in glowing terms and referred to you as his "honorary granddaughter". In his later years, after he'd lost his wife, I know he was enormously grateful for your company and kindness.'

Florrie felt sorrow swoop down, and before she could stop it a lump formed in her throat. Tears swam in her eyes. She blinked them back quickly. 'I was very fond of him too; he was like a grandfather to me. I still can't believe he's gone.' As she squeezed the words out, a tear spilled onto her cheek. She snatched it away, hoping Ed hadn't noticed.

'Yes, you're not the only one.' Mr Cuthbert gave her a sympathetic smile. 'Can I get you anything, my dear? A cup of tea?'

Florrie shook her head, feeling guilty and embarrassed for taking attention away from Ed; he was Mr H's real grandchild after all, not her. 'No, thank you. I'm fine.'

'Very well.' He picked up the papers on his desk. 'The reason I've asked you both here is regarding Mr Harte's will, which he'd instructed me to prepare for him, with the request that you were together when I shared its contents. I can also advise you that he appointed Cuthbert, Asquith and Co as executors. He was extremely thorough and organised and very clear about his wishes, so it's all very straightforward. And he was meticulous in ensuring there would be no inheritance tax to pay, which was a complicated matter, but, nevertheless, something he managed to achieve – his generous donation to the local animal rescue charity is an example.' Mr Cuthbert paused for a moment, clearing his throat. 'I've already applied for probate in order to set the ball rolling; it should take no longer than three months – though I'm anticipating considerably less. And, as we've already discussed, Miss Appleton, he was very clear about you keeping the shop open until probate was dealt with; I've taken care of everything necessary in order that you can do so.'

Florrie nodded, her stomach churning; this was surreal. She stole a sideways look at Ed, who looked back at her, equally perplexed.

'Shouldn't my parents be here if we're discussing Grandad's will and the future of the bookshop? Surely, they'll be the ones who inherit it?'

'Hmm. It would have been preferable if they'd been here too, but I gather they had more *pressing* matters to deal with.' Mr Cuthbert raised his bushy grey eyebrows, disapproval darkening his eyes. 'And you're quite wrong about the bookshop, young Edward. Mr Harte has left the shop, its contents and the flat above to both you and Miss Appleton here. You each get a fifty percent share.' He seemed to take enormous pleasure in sharing the news.

A stunned silence filled the room.

Florrie swallowed. Her head may be filling with questions, but right now she was rendered speechless. Surely she couldn't have heard right?

'Shit!' Edward sat back in his seat, pushing his fringe out of his eyes. 'I didn't expect that! You mean it doesn't go to my parents?'

'No,' Mr Cuthbert said steadily. 'Bernard was very clear he wanted it to go to you and Miss Appleton. Not to them.'

Thoughts ricocheted around Florrie's mind. This was the last thing she'd expected; he'd never given her the slightest hint. It felt wrong; she'd done nothing to warrant such a bequest. 'What... what about Gerty?' It was the only thing she could think to ask.

'Gerty stays with you. Bernard told me you'd already agreed to that,' he said kindly. 'She knows you well and he knew she'd settle best with you.'

'Yes, of course. I'm happy to have her, poor thing, it's the least I can do.' Her mind was whirling so fast she didn't know how she managed to muster a cohesive reply.

'I'm not sure what my parents are going to say about this,' said Ed. 'They had plans to sell the bookshop and buy a house in Antigua with the proceeds.'

Mr Cuthbert's face tightened. 'Which is exactly why your grandfather didn't want them to have it. I'm afraid your parents are going to have to change their plans; your grandfather left them a sum of money, but I'm not sure it will stretch to that. It's a shame they couldn't be here as I requested, then I could've explained it all to them.' He looked intently at Florrie whose colour had drained from her face, her mind still reeling. 'Are you all right, my dear? Are you sure I can't get you a cup of tea?'

Florrie blinked back at him, not really hearing his words. 'I'm, erm, I'm okay, thank you, Mr Cuthbert. I think I just need some fresh air... it's... I just wasn't expecting this.'

'Yes, of course, I understand. But before you go, here's a copy of Bernard's will.' He handed each of them a large brown envelope before taking off his glasses and setting them down on his desk. 'I know it's a lot for you both to take in, but trust me, Bernard was very clear about his wishes and his reasons for them. However, if you need any further clarification, just call me and I'll be more than happy to discuss things with you further.'

'Thank you,' said Florrie, her mind still playing catch-up.

* * *

On the pavement outside, Florrie looked up at Ed. He had his hands thrust deep into the pockets of his jacket. She noted his warm complexion had taken on a pale hue and he looked troubled. She felt a bolt of sympathy for him. It merged with the guilt that had surfaced at suddenly finding herself part owner of The Happy Hartes Bookshop, something she didn't feel entitled to. Something that, by rights, should be his, or at least, his parents. It made her feel like some kind of money-grabber. She felt a tight squeeze in her chest. 'I honestly didn't know anything about your grandad's plans for the bookshop, Ed. I'm just... just so shocked by it all.'

'Yeah, same here.' He looked every bit as stunned as Florrie felt. 'So, are you heading back to work?'

A gust of chilly wind blew up the square and she pulled up the collar of her coat. 'I'm not sure. I'd planned on going straight back, but my mind's all over the place now; I don't think I'd be able to concentrate on anything.' On top of everything else, she was still struggling to get her head around the fact that he was Mr H's grandson.

He nodded, his blue eyes never leaving hers. 'Fancy grabbing a cup of tea somewhere?'

'Shouldn't you be heading back to your parents?' Her words came out harsher than intended.

His face fell, pain loitering at the back of his eyes. 'They're not here. They got the train to London yesterday after the funeral; they're flying out to the States later today.'

'Oh.' They hadn't even hung around to find out what was happening with Gerty. That said it all. She felt a shard of annoyance pierce her grief. 'I should be getting back to work.'

Ed gave a small laugh. 'So, I can't tempt you to have a cup of tea with me? Doesn't bode well for our future as joint-owners of The Happy Hartes Bookshop, does it?'

His words hit a chord with Florrie, as did the flash of resemblance in his eyes, so like Mr H's. She was knocked off balance for a second. She blinked, trying to assemble her thoughts, but her mind felt like it was trudging through mud. A cup of tea with Ed Harte probably wasn't a bad idea, see if they could make headway with this bizarre situation that had been so unexpectedly thrust upon them. She puffed out her cheeks. 'Okay. I'll just send a quick text to Hayley who's looking after things, make sure she's still okay to keep an eye on Gerty, then we can maybe pop over to the teashop.'

His expression brightened. 'Great,' he said, mustering up a smile.

Lark was still working in the window of her shop, her mouth falling open in surprise as she watched Florrie walk by with Ed. She caught her friend's eye and pulled a face, showing her intrigue at the tall, handsome stranger. Despite her sadness and confusion, Florrie couldn't stop a small smile pulling up the corners of her mouth. She could already imagine the thorough grilling she'd be subjected to later.

FOURTEEN

The pair sat in silence as Florrie poured the tea. Her mind was a swirling mass of emotions and she was struggling to pin even a single thought down, never mind process it. The sound of the coffee machine hissed in the background, competing with the cheerful playlist and burble of chatter from the customers. The aroma of coffee beans mingling with freshly baked scones did nothing to tempt her appetite in the way it usually did.

'Milk?' she asked, with an enquiring lift of her eyebrows.

'Just a little.'

She added a splash to each cup and passed one to Ed.

'Thanks.' She could sense his eyes on her and resisted the urge to look up. Instead she picked up her cup, cradling it in her hands as she gazed out of the window, numbly watching the world go by. The fact that he was the handsome stranger who'd occupied her thoughts an inordinate amount was proving something of a distraction, and somehow at odds with their newfound situation. 'Whereabouts are you staying?' she asked, for want of conversation, eager to ease the awkward air that hung between them.

'A bed-and-breakfast in Old Micklewick; Creelers Cottage,

the landlady's a Mrs Tyreman. I'm booked in till Sunday, but I'm not sure if I'll stay the full stretch.'

'A friend of mine, Lark, lives in Old Micklewick. Seashell Cottage; it's one of the little houses on Smugglers Row.' She didn't know why she felt the need to throw that in but, then again, nothing made sense right now.

'Right.' He nodded. 'The cottages are quaint along there.'

'Mm. She runs Lark's Vintage Bazaar; took it over from her godmother, Elfie. It sells all sorts of vintage stuff as well as clothing; it's a real treasure trove. In fact, you'll have seen her, she was dressing the window when we walked by.' More mindless chatter. Where was it coming from? she wondered.

Ed nodded. 'Oh, right.' His eyes dropped to his teacup and a shadow fell across his face.

The uncomfortable silence had returned and Florrie directed her gaze out of the window once more, getting lost in the fog of her thoughts, grief tugging at her.

'I kind of get the feeling there's something you want to say to me.' Ed cut through the heavy atmosphere, a hint of apprehension in his voice.

Her shoulders heaved with a sigh and she raised her eyes to his.

'I can sense a kind of hostility, and I don't blame you; I can see how things must look.'

After what they'd just heard, she didn't think she had the right to feel hostile, but, nevertheless, she could feel it too, simmering away beneath the surface, but it wasn't necessarily directed at him; more his parents. Nibbling at her bottom lip, she didn't feel it was appropriate for her to say anything today, or at all for that matter. But since Peter Harte's cold response to her email informing him of his father's passing, Florrie's grief had directed her focus to the way he, his wife and, yes, it had to be said, his son had treated Mr and Mrs H over the years. She fully understood that Ed couldn't be apportioned much of the blame; he'd been a young child at the time of the argument, after all. But what had stopped him from getting in touch as he'd got older? That thought had been going round and round in her head, and she was concerned that once she started telling him how badly she felt his grandfather had been treated, she wouldn't be able to stop and it would all come out in an angry rush. Added to that, if he'd bothered to make contact with his grandfather, she probably wouldn't have been thrust into this embarrassing situation with the bookshop, looking like some sort of gold-digger. But, she told herself, now wasn't the time for recriminations.

'I wish you'd say something.' His voice drew her back.

Tread gently. 'It's not hostility... it's just...' *Be careful, he's grieving, like you.* She decided to change tack. 'Your grandad adored you; I don't know if you realise just how much. I'd never seen him as happy as he was the day you got in touch. He spoke of you constantly; he lived for the times he visited you in London. And he was so proud of you, proud of your work as an artist.'

'He was proud of me?' Ed's voice wavered and his eyes shone with tears. 'I don't think I deserve that.'

'He was beyond proud.' Florrie felt a pang of sympathy. 'And when you said you were coming for a visit... well, it put a real spring in his step.' An image of Mr H at the breakfast table, beaming broadly, filled her mind. She sighed sadly.

'I had no idea it meant that much to him.' He looked down into his cup.

'Oh, it did. He was just so thrilled you'd come back into his life.'

Ed shook his head, visibly upset. 'I wasn't sure how he'd react. I half-expected him to scream at me down the phone when I first contacted him, tell me to get lost.'

'Mr H would never do that!'

'I should've got in touch sooner. I should've told you who I was that morning outside the bookshop; come in with you, surprised him.' His voice faltered, tugging at Florrie's heart.

She looked on as a tear dropped from his chin and landed on the table. She stopped herself from vocalising her thoughts: *Yes, you should.* Mr H would have burst with happiness at an impromptu visit from his grandson.

The urge to reach across and squeeze his hand was overwhelming, but before she could act on it, he spoke.

'I'm sorry, I can't do this here. Do you mind if we continue our conversation outside? Maybe go for a walk?' He dragged his hand down his face and looked up at her, his blue eyes made all the more striking by his tears. He looked genuinely distraught; Florrie hadn't expected this and she felt suddenly wrong-footed. Plus, if she wasn't mistaken, he seemed more concerned that his parents hadn't inherited the bookshop, rather than the fact that she'd been given half.

'Yes, of course, that's fine. Come on, let's go for a walk along the prom.'

Once outside he gave her a weak smile. 'Sorry about that. It's just losing Grandad's hit me hard and I'm gutted that I didn't get to see him again before he passed away.'

'There's no need to apologise.' Florrie managed a small smile. 'Losing him has been a huge shock – to lots of people. He seemed so full of life and was so excited about your visit. I even got him to agree to having the windows and doors repainted; you've no idea what a battle I've had trying to get things like that done.' She gave a half-hearted laugh. Bear and his offer to do the job slid into her mind. She'd speak to him about it later, when her head was clear.

FIFTEEN

Florrie fell into step with Ed, the pair of them walking briskly as they headed away from the square. She kept her head down, not wanting to catch the eye of anyone she knew, hoping to avoid the uncomfortable task of making conversation and having to introduce Ed. They made their way in silence down the streets until they turned onto the top promenade, the wind hitting them full-on, taking Florrie's breath away. She pushed her hands deeper into her coat pockets as she followed Ed across the road. He headed over to the railings that ran along the edge, creating a barrier to the steep drop down to the bottom promenade. Once alongside him, she stole a look up to see his face streaked with tears.

'Are you okay?'

He shook his head. 'It's just... I mean, well, I'm struggling to articulate how I feel. I could kick myself for going straight back to London when I got the call about...' He cast her a sideways glance. 'I expect Grandad will have told you what happened; about why I had to get back so quick. My ex... things aren't easy...'

'I understand, you don't have to explain.' She nodded

sympathetically. 'Mr H mentioned it, but he didn't go into detail, he was always discreet.'

He gave a juddery sigh. 'Like I said, I should've seized the moment and gone into the bookshop when I saw you that morning. I know that now. I just didn't want to intrude on your breakfast with him – he'd told me all about that, how much he enjoyed starting the day with you like that; thought I'd pop back at opening time. Surprise him then.'

Florrie resisted the urge to say Mr H wouldn't have minded him joining them for breakfast; he was beating himself up enough without her adding that.

'I only wish I could turn the clock back.'

He wasn't the only one.

Florrie glanced over at the mighty Thorncliffe that Mrs H had loved so much, a blast of sunlight finding a gap in the grey clouds, spreading over the fields that stretched out on its plateau. But it did little to shift the ball of sorrow that sat like a lead weight in her stomach. 'He completely understood why you had to rush back; he just wanted things to be okay for you so you could enjoy your visit here without any distractions. And don't forget, he didn't' know you'd arrived *here*, he just thought you were en route.'

'Yeah, that's true.' Ed sniffed and wiped his eyes with the back of his hand. 'I just wish we'd had more time together; got to know each other properly all over again.' He moved away from the railings and headed towards the sand-covered steps that led down to the bottom promenade. Florrie followed him, wincing as the wind rushed by, blowing drifts of sand along the ground and whipping around their ankles.

'Wow, this place looks different from the photos Grandad showed me.' Ed sounded impressed as he took in the newly painted beach huts in delicious pastel shades of blue, pink, yellow and green that stood alongside the wooden cabins that housed an array of independent shops. When Mr H had visited

Ed, he'd gone armed with a handful of photos he and Mrs H had taken of him on his visits as a young boy. 'Shame the building at the entrance to the pier looks shabby; it's letting the side down a bit.'

'I know, no one can find out who owns it to get it tidied up and let out as a café again; it's been empty for years.'

'What a waste.' He zipped up his jacket as they walked along, seagulls wheeling overhead, their cries buffeted by the wind.

'Mmm. There were rumours that an unsavoury business man – known to everyone locally as Dodgy Dick – was sniffing around, trying to get his sticky paws on it, but that's gone quiet, thank goodness.' Florrie tried to marshal her thoughts, her eyes roving the vast expanse of sea, its tumbling, gunmetal-grey waves topped with frothy white crests.

'Dodgy Dick. Sounds like an undesirable character.'

'He is, and he seems determined to get his claws into the property around here.' An image of the man elbowed its way into Florrie's mind, how he'd turned up at the shop and strutted about, as if weighing it up. The smug expression on his face when he'd offered his insincere condolences had made her blood boil. But other things were taking precedence in her mind right now and she needed to get to the bottom of them. She nibbled on her lip, her tastebuds tingling with the salty tang of sea air. 'Ed, can I ask you something?' She turned her head to him, pushing her hair out of her face, her fingers numb with the cold.

'Er, yeah, course,' he said, a wary note in his voice.

'You can tell me to mind my own business; I'll completely understand, but I've always struggled to imagine what could have happened that was so bad it made your parents sever all contact with Mr and Mrs H?' As soon as the words left her mouth she regretted it. She grimaced. 'Look, I'm sorry, you don't have to answer that. I didn't mean to sound nosy, it's just I can't get my head around it; your grandparents showed me nothing but kindness and I can't imagine them doing anything so bad it would make someone want to have nothing more to do with them, least of all their son.'

Ed released a long breath, his broad shoulders sagging.

'I honestly don't know. I was very young when the falling out happened and don't remember anything about it. My mum's parents died when I was a baby, so I'd grown up without having grandparents in my life. I knew nothing different – probably because they were never spoken of – so it didn't seem odd to me. But as I got older, I became curious about my dad's parents and started asking questions. At first they were met with a stone wall but when I persisted they told me they didn't want to talk about it and eventually became angry, which I came to learn was their default mode when faced with a subject they didn't like. In the end, it was easier to ask nothing and, I'm ashamed to say, I just sort of left it.' Ed came to a stop, focusing his attention on a tiny pebble, rolling it around under his shoe. 'But the more I've thought about it, run my mind over the odd comment my parents have come out with over the years, or the snippets of conversations I've overheard, that made no sense to me at the time, the more I'm certain the fall-out had something to do with the bookshop.'

'Right.' Florrie was all ears.

'I can recall overhearing them talking about a bookshop one day, saying that whoever it was they were referring to were mad to want to hang onto it, especially since the people in question were keen to retire. How they'd told them years before that they should've seen sense and sold it then. I can remember the words "early inheritance" cropping up a few times.' His brows knitted together. 'One thing that stands out loud and clear is they weren't very happy about the situation. Putting the odd pieces of the puzzle together, I've kind of come to the conclusion that the initial falling-out when I was a young boy coincided with my parents being bitten by the travel bug. I suspect they were keen for my grandparents to sell in the hope they'd give some of the proceeds to them to help fund their travels – despite the way they've chosen to live their life, my mum's very money orientated, talks about it all the time, so I'm guessing she was the driving force behind the situation with my dad just following suit, not that I think he needed much encouragement. Then later on, when my grandparents were considering retirement, I guess they'd asked my parents if they'd be interested in taking over the running of the bookshop – with my grandparents still being its owners – which, knowing my mum and dad, would be the very last thing they'd want; the money from the sale – or "early inheritance" – would've been far more appealing.' He gave his head a quick scratch. 'I know it sounds crazy, but, despite them being evasive about it, the more I think about it, the more I'm convinced that's at the core of their estrangement.' He glanced at her. 'It sounds like I'm bad-mouthing my parents, but truly I'm not. I'm just trying to explain an unfortunate situation the best I can.'

'I understand, and it doesn't sound crazy; your grandparents had hinted as much.' And, worryingly, it would seem by her accepting a full-time job from the Hartes, Florrie had scuppered Peter and Suzanne Harte's plans of getting Mr and Mr H to sell-up. If Ed was right about his assumptions, she could only imagine how angry that would have made them; no doubt with her too if they'd got wind of what had changed Mr and Mrs Harte's mind about retiring. Her stomach squeezed at the thought. *Best not dwell on that!* 'So how did you finally manage to get in touch?'

He turned to look at her, those blue eyes triggering a flutter in her stomach. 'About six months ago I found an old snippet from a newspaper on the floor in my parents' house – I think it must've slipped out of a pile of papers my dad had been sifting through earlier. It was an article on a bookshop in Micklewick

Bay, reporting on how it had undergone a name change to The Happy Hartes Bookshop. As you can imagine, seeing the name "Harte" immediately piqued my interest. Why would my parents have that in their possession if they weren't connected in some way?'

'Wow. And did you ask them about it?'

'No way! Their earlier attitude – although it was years before – meant I thought it best not to mention it; I had a funny feeling they wouldn't be too happy and I didn't fancy the screaming and bawling that would ensue, so I kept it to myself. After doing a spot of detective work, I managed to track my grandfather down and got in touch with him. I can honestly say, it was the best thing I've ever done.'

'And didn't Mr H say anything about the fall-out when you were with him?'

Ed shook his head. 'No. When I asked, all he said was that my parents must've had their reasons, that I wasn't to dwell on it, and that, as far as he was concerned, it had all been forgotten in the dust of time.'

'Sounds just like him.' Florrie smiled fondly. Such generosity of spirit was so typical of Mr H.

'I just wish I'd found that article sooner.'

'Like I said before, I think everything happens for a reason. I think it was timed the way it was so your parents couldn't try to wear Mr H down and talk him into selling the bookshop; conversations like that would have caused him stress and he was too old for that.'

Ed nodded in agreement. 'Hmm. I think you're right.' His expression darkened suddenly. 'And, you know, they didn't react how I expected them to when I eventually confessed that I'd made contact with him; maybe they thought it was the perfect opportunity to tackle him about selling up again, especially with their plans for the Antigua house. I'm just glad they didn't get the chance.' His relief was palpable.

Florrie studied him for a moment; his face bore the same kindness as his grandad's, and it gladdened her heart that he didn't appear to be from the same cold-hearted, money orientated mould as his parents. 'Me too. It would seem you contacted him at just the right time. And Mr H honestly didn't care how long it had taken; he was just overjoyed to have you back in his life. Like I keep saying, he talked about you constantly.'

'Funny you should say that, what he mostly talked about to me was you; how wonderful you were, how you were just like a granddaughter to him, how much you've done for the shop, for my grandmother, for him. He adored you; they both did.'

Florrie hung her head as sadness engulfed her. She could feel the warmth of her tears as they trickled down her chilly face. 'I adored them too; they were the grandparents I never had. We shared a love of books; that was our bond.' She fished inside her bag for a tissue; pulling one out, she lifted her glasses and wiped her eyes.

'Which was something I couldn't ever share. Being severely dyslexic meant reading was a chore and something I absolutely dreaded.' He pulled a regretful face.

'Oh.' Her tears stopped and she sniffed. 'I can understand why you felt that way; I used to have a student who was dyslexic and I'm aware of how difficult it can make things.'

'A student?'

'I used to offer private tuition a few hours a week until last year.'

'Ah.' Ed nodded. 'I remember Grandad mentioning it now. And you're right, it can make things difficult. Made me feel like I was an idiot.'

'An *idiot*? Why would you think that?' Florrie was horrified he should think such a thing.

'My father; he doesn't get it, the dyslexia thing. He used to say I was lazy, useless, that I couldn't be bothered to learn. That

I'd make nothing of myself if I didn't buck my ideas up, that I was a disappointment to them.'

'What?' Florrie felt herself bristle. Could his parents get any worse? Ed's father sounded like the mother of one of her ex students who just hadn't been able get her head around how dyslexia impacted on her daughter's learning. Florrie had given her a polite dressing down, which had gone some way towards helping the young girl. But, right now, she felt like giving Ed's pig-headed father a right royal bollocking; the damage such an ignorant opinion could inflict on an impressionable child was inexcusable. 'Being dyslexic certainly doesn't mean you're stupid or lazy; it infuriates me when people say that. There are lots of ways to help, and resources that wouldn't have been available when you were at school. And I find patience goes a long way.'

Ed gave a wry laugh. 'Patience, eh?' He bent to ruffle the ears of a golden retriever who'd run up to them from the thin sliver of beach, ignoring its owner who was calling after it. 'Hello there, fella. Having fun?' he asked. The dog dropped a ball at his feet, its feathery tail sweeping back and forth as it looked up at him expectantly, its nose covered in sand. Ed scooped up the ball threw it onto the beach. 'There, go fetch, lad.' The retriever raced after it in a flash, Ed's gaze following as he brushed sand from his hands. 'Anyway, none of that matters now, and I don't want to mislead you, my parents aren't bad people; they're just a bit wrapped up in their own life and way of thinking. They're a couple of free spirits really who abhor the idea of being hemmed in by conventionality and a nine-to-five lifestyle, they'd never be able to settle here and run the bookshop. To them, the world's a small place that needs to be explored, which was something they were keen to do even more of as soon as I was old enough to do my own thing.'

'It must've been quite an exciting childhood with all that

travelling.' She didn't like to say that sounded like her idea of hell.

'It had its moments, but I mostly found it unsettling. I haven't inherited their globe-trotting sense of adventure; I'd have preferred a more stable base. It's not fun always being the new kid at school, especially when you're dyslexic.' He puffed out his cheeks, releasing a slow breath. 'The mickey-taking makes you toughen up pretty quickly.'

Florrie felt a flood of sympathy for him. 'I can imagine. What is it your parents do? For a living, I mean.'

'Depends on what's available wherever they are. They've got quite a bohemian approach to life. Bar work, helping out on market stalls, my mum's an artist so she sells her paintings, my dad's taught English... anything, really.'

'That's quite a mix of stuff.'

'Tell me about it.'

They stood in silence for several moments, both watching the waves race up to the shoreline, spray flying up into the air. It was such a shame he'd grown up feeling the way he had when there'd been the perfect base he'd so badly craved right here with Mr and Mrs H. They would've welcomed him with open arms and given him the happiest of childhoods. Of that she was certain. Her own parents slipped into her mind; she couldn't imagine them putting their own needs first without regard for anyone else, never mind their child. She felt a sudden rush of love for them.

Ed was the first to break the silence. 'Anyway, it doesn't sound like my grandparents missed out on having a grandchild altogether; they had you to fill the void.'

Florrie frowned. She could be mistaken, but she felt sure she'd detected a smack of bitterness in his voice. It wasn't what she needed right now. She headed towards a wooden bench that faced out to sea. They'd been walking head-long into the bitterly cold wind which was now stinging her cheeks and nipping at her ears. She needed to sit down, needed to absorb Ed's words without the wind whooshing in her ears. 'Ed, by saying they were the grandparents I didn't have, I didn't mean—'

He followed close behind, sitting down heavily beside her. Her stomach started churning as his words played over in her mind. 'I could never have replaced you in their hearts. Ever,' she said earnestly.

'Sorry, that didn't come out the way I intended. My head's scrambled at the moment. I'm just trying to make sense of everything.' He heaved a sigh. 'I really didn't mean it like that.' He turned to look at her, his eyes full of sorrow.

'It's okay. My mind's scrambled too. There's a lot to take in.'

'Least of all the backlash from my parents when they find out about the will.' He grimaced at that.

After what she'd learnt this morning, it was the last thing she wanted to think about. Florrie wasn't one for confrontation, least of all with people who seemed to thrive on it. *Mr H, what have you done?* Her stomach curdled with worry, dreading the onslaught of the Harte's reaction.

A seagull landed on the railings nearby, its shrill cry battling with the sound of the waves crashing against the shore. She focused her gaze on a couple of men fishing from the pier, drawing in a slow breath, the air chilly and damp. 'I can hardly believe I'm asking this, but how do you feel about being joint owner of a bookshop with me?'

'I still haven't got my head around it to be honest. Still hasn't sunk it. But, much as I hate to say it again, thanks to my dyslexia, I'm afraid me and books just don't get along.' He pulled a comical face at her, making her smile.

Florrie was about to speak when the hum of wheels being propelled along the tarmac grabbed their attention. The pair glanced behind them to see Ando Taylor whizzing towards them on his skateboard, his lank blond hair blowing out beneath his baseball cap. He was wearing a baggy leather jacket over a tie-dye hoodie, neon trainers and black skinny jeans with slashes at the knees.

'Hey, Florrie.' He raised his hand and winked at her.

'Hi, Ando,' she said flatly.

Ed's eyebrows flicked up as Ando flashed Florrie a self-assured smile and went to flip his skateboard around with his feet. They watched with morbid fascination as Ando leapt into the air, bringing his knees level with his chest, giving a resounding, 'Whoop!' before dropping back down. He must have misjudged his timing and instead of landing back on the skateboard, he clipped the end with his heel causing him to stumble forward, arms flailing, a look of panic on his face as he was propelled closer to the pavement. Righting himself at the last moment, he sauntered off with his usual swagger, his skateboard tucked under his arm, whistling as if nothing untoward had happened.

Florrie clamped her hand over her mouth. She caught Ed's eye and the pair giggle-snorted. 'I know we shouldn't laugh, but really...'

'Yeah, but it's hard not to.' Ed watched as Ando threw down his skateboard again and zoomed off.

'Part of me can't help but feel sorry for him; he doesn't seem to realise that people laugh at him; think he's a joke.'

'Hasn't anyone ever spoken to him about it? Surely it could be said in a kind way?'

'I think his brother tried but Ando doesn't seem to care.'

'Fair enough... if he's not hurting anyone... What does he do for a living?'

'Not much by all accounts; he just seems happy to bum around town or prop up the bar at the Jolly. Like you say, he's harmless though.'

'And he's got the hots for *you*,' Ed said, grinning and nudging her with his elbow.

'Don't go there!' Florrie felt her face flush and pushed her chin into the collar of her coat to hide her embarrassment.

'Hah!' Ed's grin stretched into a wide smile that triggered an unexpected flutter inside her. 'And I reckon he thinks he's in with a chance.'

'He so is *not!*' She nudged him back, feeling the solid muscles in his arm.

'Well, the message isn't getting through to him for some reason.' He cast her a teasing look.

'It's not for the want of trying.'

'Hmm. Are you sure you're just not keeping him dangling? You know? A bit of the old treat 'em mean to keep 'em keen strategy? Works like a charm I believe.' His eyes twinkled at her, their mutual sadness momentarily forgotten.

SIXTEEN

A text from Hayley enquiring as to the whereabouts of a book for a customer meant Florrie was needed back at work before she and Ed had the chance to continue their conversation.

'Look, I really need to head back, but are you free to meet up? I know it's still sinking in for both of us, but it might be an idea to have a chat about the bookshop before you leave.' She looked at him enquiringly, slipping her phone back into her bag. There was so much to think about, and from their brief conversation, she couldn't work out whether he was happy about being joint owner with her or not. A tiny part of her wouldn't be surprised if he sloped off before they got the chance to discuss anything, which she'd rather didn't happen.

He splayed his palms and smiled. 'I'm free any time; I've got no plans, so whenever suits you is good for me.' He was looking at her so intently with those dreamy eyes, it took her a moment before she was able to reply.

'Um, well, I'm at work for the next couple of days... I don't suppose tonight's any good?' *Grab him before he disappears!* 'You could come round to my house for a bite to eat. My mum dropped off a huge shepherd's pie yesterday; it's massive, could feed a family of six. I've no idea how she thought I was going to eat it all myself.'

Ed's face brightened. 'Well, if you're sure? That sounds great, I love shepherd's pie.'

'Honestly, you'd be helping me out.' She couldn't help but smile at his enthusiasm.

'Great,' he said, smiling back at her. 'What time would you like me to land?'

'How does seven-ish sound?'

'Perfect.'

They walked along, chatting about Ed's parents' travels, until they reached the booking office of the cliff lift, or funicular, to give the piece of Victorian engineering its proper name. Florrie checked the notice board for the running times, but seeing she had half-an-hour to wait before the next journey, she decided to take the steps, reasoning it was better than hanging around in the cold. As she turned to speak to Ed she was distracted by a man wearing a familiar grey coat and flat cap. He nodded and gave her a brief smile. 'Morning,' he said, in a broad North Yorkshire accent.

'Morning,' she replied, sensing Ed's interest in their interaction.

'Who's that?' he asked quietly. 'He seems familiar but I can't place him.'

Florrie frowned, the wind nipping at her cheeks. 'Hmm. Same here, I've seen him a few times recently, but he's not a local.' They both looked on as the stranger made his way along the prom then took the steps down to the beach.

'Right then, I'll see you this evening,' she said, smiling up at him.

'Looking forward to it. I think I'll kill time having a mooch along the beach and exploring Old Micklewick.'

'Have fun, oh, and I can highly recommend a visit to the Fudge House on Mariner Street; the coffee fudge is to die for.'

'Thanks for the tip, I'll be sure to pay it a visit; I've got a sweet tooth which is destined to be my downfall.' He was still smiling at her. 'See you around seven.' Before Florrie knew what was happening, he bent and kissed her cheek, sending a charge of electricity through her. *Woah! Where the heck did that come from?*

With her mind reeling, she watched him walk away, his hands thrust into the pockets of his jacket, the wind blowing his hair this way and that. He took the half-a-dozen steps down to the beach and made his way along the narrow arc of sand with long, determined strides, picking up stones and hurling them into the sea. He turned and smiled at her before giving one last wave, bending to pick up another stone.

Florrie cursed inwardly at being caught gazing after him. She felt her face flame as her hand reached for her cheek and the place he'd delivered the kiss, her mind tumbling about in time with her emotions.

She climbed the steps, lost in thought. If anyone had told her the handsome stranger was, in fact, Ed Harte, she'd have told them they'd lost their marbles. She shook her head in disbelief. What a couple of weeks it had turned out to be.

'Miss Davenport! It's good to see you.' Florrie was busy dusting the shelves when her friend arrived at the bookshop that afternoon. Gerty jumped up from her bed and trotted over, wagging her tail happily.

'Hello there, Gerty. How are you, girl?' Miss Davenport bent and patted the Labrador's head.

Sliding the book she was holding back into its place on the shelf, Florrie rushed over and wrapped her arms around the older woman, noting how pale she was looking. Mr H's loss had hit her badly. 'How are you keeping?'

ELIZA J SCOTT

'I'm bearing up, lovey. How about you?' Miss Davenport took Florrie's hands, her eyes loaded with sadness.

'I'm doing okay, but your hands feel bitterly cold. Come and have a seat. Can I get you a cup of tea?'

'That would be lovely, but only if you've got time.'

'Of course I've got time, and you're a welcome sight today.'

'I'll pop the kettle on,' said Hayley, smiling over at them. 'You stay with Miss Davenport, Florrie.'

'Ah, bless her, she's a lovely girl.' Miss Davenport watched the young girl lope off down the shop in her brightly coloured garb. 'And a welcome blast of colour on these gloomy days.' She looked across at Florrie, tears welling in her pale-blue eyes.

Florrie swallowed and bit back tears of her own. 'She is, I'd be lost without her at the moment.'

Gerty made her way back to her bed and flumped down with a noisy grunt, resting her head on her paws.

'And how's the situation here, with the bookshop? Do you know what's going to happen to it? I hope it's still going to be a bookshop; I don't know what I'd do without it now the library's gone.' Worry hovered in the older woman's eyes.

'Well, it's funny you should say that, and please keep this under your hat for the moment, but earlier today, I had an appointment with Mr Cuthbert over at Cuthbert, Asquith and Co to discuss that very matter. And you might be surprised to hear Edward Harte was there too.' Her heart gave a lilt as she said his name.

'Oh my!' Miss Davenport's eyes widened as Florrie shared the details of her eventful morning. Though she was aware Mr H had spoken frequently to his friend of his reunion with Ed, Florrie was careful not to include any mention of how Ed had tracked his grandfather down; that was for Ed to do if he so wished.

'Well, that's a bit of happy news at this very sad time, lovey.

I always knew Bernard thought the world of you, and leaving half the bookshop to you just proves it.'

'It doesn't feel right though. I feel like I've been given something I shouldn't have.'

'Rubbish! I knew Bernard well and he wasn't one for making rash or silly decisions. He'll have thought long and hard about this, and I can see why he would want you to have the bookshop with young Edward. It makes perfect sense; he couldn't have left it in better hands. Do you think Edward will keep his share and work alongside you?'

Keep his share? Miss Davenport's question stopped Florrie's thoughts in their tracks; she hadn't considered that Ed might not want to keep his share of the bookshop. His words, that he and books didn't get along, suddenly took on a new meaning. 'Erm, I don't know to be honest, we haven't had a chance for it all to sink in yet. He's coming round to my house tonight to have a chat about it; I'll see what he has to say then.' She didn't know how she'd feel if he told her he was going to sell up. An image of Dodgy Dick slithered its way into her mind, triggering a squeeze of anxiety in her chest.

Miss Davenport patted Florrie's hand. 'He'd be mad not to, it's a lovely little business and an injection of new ideas is just what it needs – Bernard used to laugh about how you were always trying to get him to move with the times, and now you can. It's just a terrible shame he's not here to see it.' She smiled fondly at Florrie. 'And I mean no disrespect to him at all, he was a lovely man and he and Dinah were good friends to me over the years, but The Happy Hartes Bookshop is ready for a bit of young blood at its helm; you and, from what I've heard of him, young Edward will be the perfect combination.'

Florrie doubted Ed's parents would agree.

SEVENTEEN

Florrie was smoothing a vintage, embroidered tablecloth over the table in her kitchen when there was a knock at the door. She glanced at the clock on the wall to see it was exactly seven pm. Gerty barked and jumped up from where she'd been curled up in her bed and trotted off down the hallway. Florrie followed behind, stopping briefly at the mirror to check her hair which she quickly tucked behind her ears. Her pulse cranked up a notch and a sensation of something unfamiliar swirled in her stomach. She sucked in a deep breath but there was no stopping the wide smile that spread across her face as she answered the door.

'Hi,' she said, her heart performing a quick leap as she clocked Ed's tall frame filling the doorway. Behind him, the sky was just slipping into dusk, the Victorian-style streetlights flickering to life. A solitary blackbird was trilling away from the hedge in the garden opposite, giving his all to his final song before turning in for the night.

'Hi,' said Ed, a heart-melting smile on his face, though Florrie spotted the dark shadows that sat beneath his eyes, hinting at the sorrow that lurked within.

Gerty lunged at him, her tail wagging with such enthusiasm, her whole body wiggled. After spinning around several times, she took off down the hall before racing back again and repeating the whole performance.

'Meet Gerty,' said Florrie looking on, amused.

'Well, hello there, Gerty,' Ed said, laughing as she nuzzled into his legs.

'I get the impression she's pleased to meet you,' said Florrie. It was the liveliest she'd seen her since Mr H had passed away.

'And I'm very pleased to finally meet her. My grandad spoke of her with great affection.'

'That doesn't surprise me; he doted on her.'

'I can see why, she's a grand lass.'

'She is that.' Florrie smiled, her eyes moving to his hands which were laden. 'Oh, how rude of me, please, come in – if you can get in, that is. Come on, Gerty, calm your jets and let Ed through the door.'

'Thanks.' Ed stepped into the hallway bringing with him a blast of cold, salty air as he wiped his feet on the doormat. 'Mmm. It smells lovely in here; I can't wait to dive into your mum's shepherd's pie.'

'I can vouch for her that it's usually pretty tasty.' She closed the door behind him, shutting out the chilly evening. 'Can I get you a drink? Wine, beer, or tea?'

'I'm happy to have what you're having.' The way he looked at her made butterflies flutter in her stomach. Florrie couldn't remember the last time a man had triggered that kind of reaction – certainly not Graham – and it discomfited her slightly.

'I don't normally drink mid-week, but these are exceptional circumstances so I've got a bottle of wine chilling in the fridge. Pinot Grigio okay?'

'Sounds good. Er, actually, can I give you these?' He handed over a bunch of brightly coloured flowers wrapped in cellophane sporting the Daisy Chain Flower Shop's logo, and a bottle of Chardonnay. 'Oh, and I followed your advice and popped into the fudge shop – which was every bit as good as you said it would be – and I couldn't come away without getting you some of this.' He pulled a brown paper bag from his pocket, releasing a cloud of sugary sweetness as he opened it.

'Ooh, coffee fudge! My favourite.' She beamed up at him, touched by his gesture and the fact that he'd remembered.

'Well, the least I could do is bring something for pudding,' he said, flashing that smile again.

'There was really no need, but I can't think of anything nicer.'

'And don't worry, I haven't forgotten about you, Gerty.' He fished in his pocket and brought out a chewy stick. Gerty sat in front of him, her eyes boring holes into the treat. 'Am I okay to give her this now?' he asked.

'Of course; she'd be gutted if I said no.' They both chuckled at the sight of the Labrador who looked like she was ready to burst with anticipation. He handed the chew to her which she took gently and trotted off to the kitchen.

'Come on through,' said Florrie. Ed followed her down the bright hallway, past the wooden staircase, stopping before a collection of antique Victorian samplers that were grouped together.

'They're from Lark's shop,' she said.

'They look great arranged like that.'

'Thank you, I collect them. I've got a few more dotted around the cottage actually.'

Once Ed had been divested of his jacket the pair made themselves comfortable at the table while the shepherd's pie warmed through. Ed poured the wine and they fell into polite conversation with Florrie asking him about his day and if he'd enjoyed his wander around Old Micklewick. In return, he asked her about her afternoon at the bookshop, and she told him about

Miss Davenport who he recalled his grandfather speaking about.

'She sounds like a sweet lady; I remember Grandad saying she had an air of loneliness about her.'

'Mmm. She's lovely and Mr H was right about her seeming lonely. It's the reason I've always encouraged her to join us for a cup of tea at the bookshop.'

Florrie was pleasantly surprised to find that the two of them chatted over the meal like old friends and, before she knew it, every morsel had been devoured.

'That's got to be the best shepherd's pie I've ever tasted.' Ed sat back in his chair, rubbing his stomach. 'My compliments to your mum, it was delicious.'

'You can't beat a bit of home cooking. I have to say, Mum's shepherd's pie is the best and her roast dinners are to die for.' Florrie sat back too, feeling brighter than she'd felt since Mr H had passed away. She was still savouring the rich red-wine gravy and creamy flavours of mashed potato topped with cheese that lingered in her mouth.

'Well, if what I've just tasted is anything to go by, I can believe that,' Ed said, wearing a contented smile.

'Pure comfort food.'

He nodded. 'And talking of comfort, you've made your cottage very homely, Florrie.' He was looking around the sage-green painted kitchen, her collection of vintage crockery on the upcycled pine dresser. She detected a wistful note in his voice. Probably to do with his unsettled childhood with nowhere to properly call home. She was struck by another pang of sympathy for him.

'Thank you; I was lucky when I bought it; I got it for a song as it needed quite a bit doing to it and the area wasn't what you'd call desirable at the time. Now, almost as soon as the cottages come on the market, they get snapped up.'

'I can imagine.'

'A couple of weeks ago we all had a note pushed through our letter boxes from someone offering to buy our homes for a "competitive" price.'

Ed reached for his glass of wine. 'Don't tell me it was that guy you were telling me about earlier. What's he called? Dodgy Des?'

'Dick,' Florrie said.

'I'm not sure there's any need for that.' Ed's voice had become suddenly serious.

Florrie's face fell. 'Oh... no... I wasn't calling you a di—' She spotted the amusement dancing in his eyes, at odds with his offended expression. 'Ah.' His eyebrows quirked up and he gave a mischievous grin. 'I mean he's called Dodgy *Dick*, not Dodgy *Des*.' She giggled.

'Ah, glad we got that cleared up.' His grin widened.

She continued. 'Anyway, none of us recognised the company name on the note, but I've seen him and his wife cruising up and down these streets over recent weeks, as if they're appraising the houses.'

'Really? Sounds like he operates using intimidation.'

'Oh, that's exactly what he does; he can be quite sinister actually.' A shiver ran up Florrie's spine. 'I'd put money on it being him behind the notes.' She paused for a moment, considering whether to tell Ed about Dodgy Dick's visit to the shop and the interest he'd been showing it. But something made her hold back. 'I threw mine straight on the fire; I love my little home and there's no way I'm going to sell it, least of all to him.'

'I wouldn't want to sell it either, I can't remember being anywhere with such a cosy atmosphere.'

'I think what you're feeling is probably the after-effects of my mum's shepherd's pie,' she said with a self-conscious laugh, her face flushing at the compliment.

'Nope, it's down to you, Florrie. How you've decorated it,

the happy vibes you've imbued into the walls; your "aura" as I reckon your friend, Lark, would call it.'

She swallowed, trying to ignore the sparks that were suddenly flying between them. 'Oh, right. Thank you.'

Ed looked down at Gerty, smoothing his hand over her silky black head. The Labrador's tail swept happily over the floor as she gazed up at him adoringly.

'Well, you've got Gerty's seal of approval.' Unsure of how to deal with the undeniable chemistry that crackled between them, Florrie couldn't think of what else to say.

'Yep, at least I've got that.' He continued to concentrate his attentions on Gerty, who wasn't complaining in the slightest.

'How about we grab a comfy seat in the living room? Unless you've got to head off, that is?' Time to get rid of the awkwardness.

'Sounds good to me; I've got no reason to rush off, there's only my room at the bed-and-breakfast waiting for me.'

'Great! You grab the wine, I'll bring the fudge,' she said, trying not to dwell on the trace of loneliness in his voice.

EIGHTEEN

Florrie had lit the living room fire before Ed arrived. The licking flames had now subsided, leaving a glowing base in the grate, making the room warm and cosy. She flicked the table lamps on then went over to the curved bay window and drew the curtains on the night.

'Take a seat,' she said, gesturing towards the sofa.

Ed flopped down, Gerty settling at his feet. 'What a sweet room,' he said. 'No wonder you don't want to sell to Dodgy Dick; I'd never want to leave if this place was mine.'

Florrie was leaning over her tablet on the shelf by the fireplace, selecting her favourite playlist of gentle classical music. 'I don't want to sell it to anyone, not just the likes of him.' Aware of his eyes on her, she re-fuelled the fire then headed towards the chair to the right of the sofa, the seat furthest away from Ed.

The pair sat in comfortable silence, soothing music spilling gently from the speakers. Ed had slipped his shoes off and was absent-mindedly rubbing Gerty's proffered stomach with his foot. The Labrador groaned in ecstasy and stretched out her legs. Florrie caught Ed's eye and shook her head, rolling her eyes fondly. 'Honestly, what's she like?'

'Gerty, has anyone ever told you you're a right old floozy?' he said, looking down at her, chuckling.

Gerty gazed back adoringly and groaned some more.

'I have to say, Gerty, that's not very becoming behaviour for a lady.' Florrie couldn't help but giggle. 'I've never seen her like this before, she's normally quite reserved, but she's really taken to you. It's actually nice to see her looking so happy; poor girl's been very subdued since your grandad passed away.'

Mention of losing Mr H sucked the happiness right out of the room and a shadow fell across Ed's face. Florrie felt a lump form in her throat, the sudden return of her grief taking her by surprise. The last few hours with Ed had managed to make her forget her sorrow, and it seemed to be the same for him.

Gerty, apparently detecting the change, sat up, pushing her head onto Ed's lap, whimpering until he stroked her. 'It's all right, girl,' he said softly.

Florrie's eyes filled with tears and she blinked them away, hoping Ed hadn't noticed. She took a sip of wine.

'I'm grieving, but I feel I've no right to; I'd spent so little time with him.' His eyes were still on Gerty.

'You've every right to grieve; he was your grandfather and by getting in touch you'd resurrected the special bond you'd had as a little boy.' She could sense the weight of his sorrow.

'Maybe.' He let go a juddery sigh. 'It's bad enough not getting much time with him, but I really wish I'd got the chance to see my grandma before she passed away. My parents have a lot to answer for with their lies and their secrets.'

Florrie couldn't have put it better herself. Their selfish, pig-headed attitude meant they'd deprived three people of building a loving relationship. In her mind it was nothing short of heart-less. 'Listen, Ed, your grandad wouldn't want you to think like that, he really wouldn't. He was always so positive, looked on the bright side of everything. I can't deny it would've been good if you could've seen your grandma, but the situation you found yourselves in meant that wasn't possible. There's no getting away from the fact that the three of you have been caught up in a tragic set of circumstances. The blame lies directly with your parents, not you or Mr and Mrs H.' She looked at him intently, hoping to convey just how much she meant her words.

'I could've pushed them harder.'

'Could you? Really? From what you've told me about your parents, it sounds as though pushing would've made them dig their heels in all the more. You've really got to stop blaming yourself. Though there might be no obvious explanation for them, life sometimes throws things at us like that. But, as I've said before, I always think everything happens for a reason, no matter how we might not like it at the time. So, instead of thinking "if only" or "what if", just focus on the fact that you made contact with your grandad, and as a result you were able to spend some wonderful time together. Think about the *happy* things. Think about how much *happiness* you brought into his life. That's what he'd want you to do.'

Ed lifted his gaze from his glass of wine and breathed out slowly. 'Thank you,' he said, turning his face to her. 'I'm so glad I came here tonight, you've stopped me from hurtling towards a vortex of gloom.'

'No problem.' She pushed her lips into a smile, suddenly feeling the need to lighten the mood and bring back the relaxed atmosphere of earlier. She patted her knees, making Gerty jump. 'How about some of that coffee fudge?'

Ed's face brightened as he shrugged off his cloak of sadness. 'Now you're talking.'

'If it's okay with you, I'll make us a little pot of coffee, as I don't think the fudge will go too well with this wine.'

He gave a hearty laugh which helped chase away the final vestiges of the sombre mood. 'Couldn't agree more. Come on, I'll give you a hand.'

Soon, they were back in the living room, sitting side-by-side on the sofa, a tray of coffee on the little table before them, the fudge set out on a plate with Gerty's eyes glued to it.

'There you go – don't worry, it's decaff; you won't be climbing the walls all night.' Florrie handed him a cup of coffee, its rich aroma rising in the steam. Their fingers brushed as he took the cup from her, sending a fizz of electricity up her arm. 'Oh!'

She sat back, trying to ignore the frisson of whatever it was that was currently dancing between them, hoping Ed hadn't noticed it too. She searched for something to say. 'So, what's it like living in London?' She didn't know why, but she imagined him living alone in some kind of boho flat that was a bit scruffy, artwork dotted around the place.

He cleared his throat. 'Frenetic, vibrant, noisy, very different to here. I've had a flat there for a while now, but I've been staying with my parents in Hawaii for a few weeks; they're renting a place there for six months.'

That explained his sun-kissed skin and the highlights in his hair. 'Hawaii? That must've been nice.'

'It was out of necessity really. I'd split up with my girlfriend, and things had got a bit heated. I thought it best for both of us if I put a bit of distance between us, let the dust settle while she shifted her stuff out of my flat. My parents needed a hand painting their little boat, so...' He shrugged.

'Oh, right.' Mr H's words about Ed's girlfriend having a bit of a temper slipped into her mind, making her wonder if it was why he felt it best to get away.

'Didn't quite go to plan, unfortunately.' He raked his fingers through his hair, mussing it up slightly. 'She was still angry, which is why I had to rush back to London that day I saw you in town. I'd had a call from a neighbour saying someone had broken into my flat and smashed things up. Turns out Luella had heard I was back in the country and had landed at my flat so we could "talk". When she found out I wasn't there she trashed the place.'

'Oh my goodness.' Florrie pressed her hand to her mouth. She was desperate to ask why, but didn't want to appear nosy or prying.

'Yeah, she can be pretty volatile. Accused me of seeing someone else – I wasn't.' He paused for a moment, nibbling at his bottom lip, his expression darkening. 'Things had been gradually getting worse; any little thing could set her off. She'd think nothing of throwing plates of food at the wall if she was annoyed, or start smashing things; I'm amazed I've got any mugs left. And she'd taken to screaming at the top of her voice if I didn't say what she wanted to hear. It was getting pretty unbearable – for me and for the neighbours – but she seemed to love it, got a kick out of it; you could see it in her eyes.'

Florrie listened intently, watching pain flicker across Ed's face as he recounted his story. She couldn't imagine being in a relationship like that; it sounded terrifying.

'In the end, I couldn't stand it anymore and told her I thought it would be best if we broke up.'

'I'm guessing she didn't take it very well,' Florrie said, taking a sip from her mug.

Ed gave a sardonic laugh. 'She couldn't believe it, couldn't see that our relationship was toxic. Said our arguments were indicative of the passion we had for one another, which she thought was a good thing. You can imagine my surprise when she said she'd been waiting for me to propose.'

'Propose?' Florrie almost choked on her coffee.

Ed nodded slowly. 'Yeah, she told me she thought we were good together, that she'd always believed we were in it for the long haul. It wasn't until then that I realised how like my mother she was. And trust me, the last thing I need is to be in a relationship like the one my parents have, with situations exploding out of the blue one minute and everything lovey-dovey the next. I can't keep up with it; I've seen how destructive that can be.'

Florrie recalled the conversation with Mr H when he'd described Luella as volatile; he'd just stopped himself from saying who she reminded him of. Could he have been about to say Ed's mum's name?

'Her departing words to me were that my parents were right, I was useless, disappointing, and wouldn't amount to anything without her behind me.' He heaved a weary sigh. 'Useless and disappointing. Those words have a habit of following me around.'

Florrie's heart squeezed for him. 'Well, for what it's worth, it sounds to me like you've had a lucky escape. Luella obviously can't see how her destructive behaviour impacts on others.' Feeling bold, she continued. 'And I know it might seem out of turn, but I think she might benefit from a bit of anger management counselling.'

'Well, I wouldn't like to be the one to suggest it to her!' Ed gave a wry laugh. 'The thing is, I can see a pattern forming; I seem to be drawn to volatile women like her – or "unhinged" as my mate Dev describes them. I'm not proud to say my dating history is littered with failed relationships with fiery women.'

It crossed Florrie's mind that Ed was possibly drawn to volatile relationships because of what he'd observed of his parents' behaviour when he was growing up. Maybe, on a subconscious level, he'd been conditioned to think it was the norm. 'Have you ever considered trying to break that pattern? Considered dating someone with a more easy-going temperament?' She blushed, hoping he wouldn't think she was hinting at herself.

He took a slug of his coffee. 'I think what I need is a break from dating full-stop. I've had enough of the stress and I've come to the conclusion that I'm better off on my own. That way, I can't be a useless disappointment to anyone but myself.'

Ed's gaze drifted to the fireplace, his fringe flopping over his eyes.

Florrie's heart went out to him. He'd had a tough time of it by all accounts. And his childhood had been the polar opposite of hers. She'd grown up in a settled environment, where she felt loved and secure; hearing Ed's story made her appreciate it all the more.

Keen to lift his mood, Florrie thought quickly. 'So you mentioned you'd been staying in Hawaii for a while, it sounds like a beautiful place. Do you think you'll go back?'

'It is a very beautiful place – great inspiration for painting, which is how I make my living – but I couldn't see myself settling there. Not that my parents would either; they still don't seem able to stay in one place for long.'

Florrie nodded; such an unsettled lifestyle, constantly drifting from country to country, held little appeal for her. She could appreciate why Ed would have craved a more stable base as a child. Something he'd said in the solicitor's office suddenly pinged into her mind. 'I thought they had plans to buy a house in... where was it?' She racked her brains for the location.

'Antigua.'

'Antigua. That's it. So doesn't that mean they're keen to put down roots now?'

'On the contrary. They had plans to rent the house out while they continued with their travels and only stay there when it wasn't being used.' He pushed his fringe back with his fingers. 'From what I can gather, there's a lot to look into before you can buy there, lots of red-tape to work around, so it's still all up in the air. They chop and change their minds quite a lot, so I never take what they say too seriously.'

Not for the first time Florrie felt grateful her parents weren't like Ed's. Paula and Charlie were real home-bodies, just like her.

He gave an embarrassed laugh and turned to her, smiling,

pressing his leg inadvertently against hers, sending a rush of something indefinable through her. 'Listen, sorry about that, I wasn't expecting to share my life story with you; it must be the wine. I hope you can forgive me. I'm not usually such a self-absorbed, boring, old fart.'

'There's really nothing to forgive,' she said, laughing. 'And you're none of those things.' Their conversation was giving her a greater insight into him, and she found herself really rather liking what she saw.

Tucking her feet beneath her, her thoughts segued back to Mr H's will, of how Ed's parents would take the news of its contents. A spike of concern shot through her. 'Have you had chance to speak to your mum and dad yet? About the will I mean.'

He pressed his lips together, his expression darkening. 'No, I haven't been able to get hold of them, which is nothing new.' He gave a humourless laugh.

Florrie nodded, waiting for him to elaborate. When he didn't, she asked, 'So how do you think they'll take it?'

Ed puffed out his cheeks, releasing his breath forcefully. 'Well, there's no denying it's been a massive shock – to me, that is, probably even more so to them when they find out. Like I said, when they heard my grandfather had...' He paused, the thoughts clearly painful. He swallowed. 'When they heard my grandfather had died, they didn't hang around making big plans for what they'd do with the money – travel featured highly. It didn't make easy listening, that's for sure. Their cold-hearted-ness never ceases to amaze me, so I'm expecting the news not to go down too well if I'm honest.' He looked across at her, scrunching up his face. 'I'm afraid you'd better brace yourself.'

Oh no! Florrie felt guilt prickle over her skin. She really didn't deserve Mr H's generosity, but nor did she deserve Ed's parents' wrath. 'It came as a huge shock to me too, so my involvement's bound to be a bigger one for them.' She looked away, a feeling of dread rising inside her as she struggled to make sense of her new-found situation.

Since leaving the solicitor's office that morning, Florrie's mind had whirled with the implications of Mr H's bequest, her mind swinging from declining the share to accepting it gratefully. If she opted to accept it, it would be with the intention of making The Happy Hartes Bookshop the very best version of itself possible. And if she didn't... well, that somehow didn't seem right. She'd aired her concerns with her parents who'd been shocked that she'd even considered not accepting her half.

'But that would be disrespectful, Florrie, lovey,' her mum had said. 'Mr H wanted you to have that fifty percent, and, from the sound of things, he'd gone to a lot of trouble to ensure it went to you and Ed.'

'Your mum's right,' her dad had said. 'Imagine how hurt Mr H would be if he thought you'd gone against his wishes.'

Their words had given her pause for thought and had gone some way to assuaging her doubts – not to mention guilt – but now, sitting here with Ed, as they discussed his parents, her worries had swum to the surface once more.

Miss Davenport's question crept into her mind, adding to her concerns. *"Do you think young Ed will keep his share?"* But much as she was burning to know, Florrie didn't like to ask him directly. Instead she said, 'Have you had a chance to think about what you're going to do?'

'It's all I've thought of actually.'

'Oh?' She held her breath.

NINETEEN

'I've been feeling at a bit of a crossroads actually, especially since I got back in touch with my grandfather.' Ed's gaze settled on the flames dancing in the hearth. 'For a while now, I've been a bit disillusioned with my life. Don't get me wrong, I love painting, but I just... I just need something else too, something more, only I'm not sure what.'

Something more? Again, Florrie waited for him to continue, but she was to be disappointed.

'Anyway, all we seem to have talked about is me.' He set his cup down on the table, making Gerty jump up, and putting an end to that line of conversation. He turned to Florrie, a forced smile on his face. 'What about you? What's been going on in your life. Is there anyone special in it? Are there wedding bells on the horizon?'

'Uh, no. I've recently broken up with someone so there are definitely no wedding bells.' Confusion swamped her at his abrupt change of tack. After all, the reason he was here tonight was to discuss what to do about the bookshop.

'Ah, I'm sorry to hear that. And are you okay about it?' He looked at her, his eyes soft. 'Is your heart still in one piece?'

'I'm absolutely fine; we'd been going through the motions, Graham and me. It was definitely the right thing to do.' She was relieved that mention of her ex's name hadn't elicited even a tiny flicker of regret or sadness.

'Yeah, you know breaking up was the right thing to do when it comes as a relief,' he said, picking up on the subtext of her words.

'You got it in one. And I intend to enjoy some time being single for the foreseeable future.' She felt his gaze on her.

'And how's your mum doing – I hope you don't mind me asking, my grandfather mentioned she'd been poorly a few years ago.'

Florrie smiled, her eyes lighting up. 'She's doing great, thanks. She's stayed cancer free which is a *huge* relief. Still doesn't stop me worrying about her though.' Her expression darkened. 'It rocked us to our core when she was going through it, seeing her losing her hair, her looking so ill. Dad and me felt so helpless.' Her throat tightened and she felt the threat of tears.

Ed nodded. 'I'm not surprised; I can't imagine how awful it must've been for you all.'

'It was.' Florrie nodded. 'It was really awful'.

'From what my grandad said, I gather you're a tight unit the three of you; I get why you'd want to stay close after that.'

'Even the thought of living away from them, after that, makes me feel stressed. It's just not an option I'd consider.'

It was a relief he understood without her having to give an explanation – especially considering his own relationship with his parents. Not everyone did. 'Doesn't matter where you live in the UK, you can always get on a train and be back here in a matter of hours,' Joyce Stubbs, one of the town's busybodies, had said when she'd interrogated Florrie about her reasons for staying in Micklewick Bay. 'Don't you think you're wasting your degree, staying here, just working in a bookshop?' Florrie's blood had boiled, but good manners meant she'd resisted the urge to tell Joyce to bugger off and mind her own business, which was something she'd regretted on numerous occasions.

Florrie stole a glance at Ed. 'Yeah, it's the main reason I've never moved, but it's not the only one. I love it here, I feel it's where I belong. It's a beautiful place to live with so much to offer. I mean, it's got the seaside, the moors are on our doorstep, we've got a great choice of shops, pubs and restaurants, my best friends still live here and it's got a wonderful community spirit, oh, and I love my job too.' She listed the reasons on her fingers.

'You sell it well.' Ed grinned, leaning back and stretching his arm along the back of the sofa. 'You're lucky to have a family and a place to live that makes you feel so happy and content with your life.'

Yes, she thought, she was lucky. 'And do you like Micklewick Bay, Ed?'

'Um. I like its quirkiness, and it's certainly different to London.'

His reply pushed Florrie's thoughts back to the bookshop. They hadn't made much headway in discussing his plans, and truth be told, she was keen to get an idea before he flitted back to London and, very likely, never returned. She didn't want to find out from the solicitors' he'd sold his share under duress from his parents before she'd had chance to act. After all, there was nothing else to keep him here. Her eyes went to the clock on the mantlepiece; the evening was slipping away. She needed to act quickly.

'So, you mentioned the bookshop was all you'd been thinking of...' She left her sentence open, hoping he'd scoop it up and elaborate. Dodgy Dick's face floated into her mind, making her suddenly nervous.

'Yeah, it's still sinking in to be honest. Though I can understand my grandfather's actions.'

'You can?'

Ed nodded. 'It's pretty obvious really. He knew my parents

127

had no interest in it, he knew you loved it, and as far as I was concerned, he'd mentioned that he'd always been keen for me to have a family base which, in his mind, was here. I reckon he thought we were the perfect combination.'

'Oh?' she said, suddenly wrong-footed by the thought Ed had picked up on Mr H's romantic meddling.

He raised his palms and laughed lightly, catching her eye. 'Don't panic, I mean purely professionally; I've no intention of interfering with your newly single status.'

Florrie laughed, hoping her face didn't betray her unexpected twinge of disappointment. 'Phew!'

'He kept telling me you had loads of wonderful ideas and how the place needed a young touch, some fresh input, but how he hadn't had the heart for it since he lost my grandmother. In his mind, by leaving the bookshop to us, I think he felt he was safe-guarding its future.' He rubbed his hand over his chin, looking thoughtful. 'It's a tricky one though.'

Florrie held her breath, hoping with all her heart he'd give serious consideration to his grandfather's wishes. It would certainly get Dodgy Dick and his sleazy dealings out of the picture, which would be a huge relief. But Florrie was beginning to realise that it wasn't the only thing that made the idea so appealing. Ed Harte and his easy manner was really rather nice to be around. Maybe a professional partnership between the two of them could actually work. Her eyes slid back to him, taking in his straight nose and strong jawline peppered with stubble that was glinting in the soft light. He seemed oblivious to just how devastatingly handsome he was. She wished she knew what was going through his mind. Did the idea of settling in Micklewick Bay fill him with dread? Was he thinking of ways to avoid it? Or was he tempted to follow Mr H's wishes?

For several long seconds neither of them spoke, Florrie conscious of her heart hammering fiercely in her chest.

Ed turned away, dragging his hand down his face. 'The

thing is, there's a lot to think about and I don't really know what I want at the moment; I'm not sure if the bookshop and staying in this town is the right path for me long-term.'

Anxiety scurried up her spine. She swallowed nervously. 'Oh, okay.'

'Don't get me wrong, you've made it sound wonderful here, and I can see for myself just how happy you are. But, in all honesty, being surrounded by books kind of fills me with dread. And, on top of that, the hell my parents are going to give me...' He released a forceful sigh. 'It just doesn't bear thinking about. And I don't want to make promises to you I won't be able to keep.'

'I can understand that,' Florrie said, her hand gripping tightly onto her cup, fearing a sale of Ed's share to Dodgy Dick drawing nearer. What on earth could she do if that happened?

'But then again, I don't have to make a decision straight away...'

She felt the squeeze of anticipation in her chest.

'I suppose I could do with staying away from London for a bit longer, put some space between me and Luella, maybe then she'll realise we really are over.' He paused, thoughtful for a moment. 'Hmm. So the burning question is, do you think you can put up with me for a few weeks?' He chuckled, oblivious to confusion rushing around inside her.

She mustered up a smile. 'I think I might be able to,' she said in a voice that was brighter than she was feeling.

'Well, that's settled it then.' He turned to her. 'The thought of not heading straight back to my flat is actually more appealing than I expected.'

Settled? Florrie felt anything but settled. As far as she was concerned, the future of the bookshop was still up in the air. But she gave a small smile and said, 'I reckon that's Micklewick Bay working its magic.'

'I'm not so sure it's Micklewick Bay that's doing it,' he said, the tease of a smile on his lips, his gaze holding hers.

Florrie looked away, feeling suddenly shy, her cheeks colouring. Being around Ed Harte was creating all kinds of confusion.

Sensing a change in the atmosphere, Gerty pushed herself up and rested her head in Ed's lap, her tail wagging against the leg of the table. 'Well, Gerty seems pleased with that decision,' he said, smoothing her ears.

'She does,' said Florrie, forcing a laugh, wishing her head wasn't all over the place.

* * *

The fire in the hearth was reduced to a handful of glowing embers, unlike the one that was burning in Florrie's heart, much to her annoyance. Before she knew it, Ed was checking his watch and declaring that it had gone eleven and was time he left. Despite his indecision over the future of the bookshop, she felt a pang of disappointment that their evening was coming to an end.

'I'll give you a hand to wash-up, then I'll be off,' he said, rolling his sleeves up.

'You don't have to rush off on my account, and forget about the pots, it'll take me seconds to do them.' She reluctantly pushed herself up from her comfy spot.

'Are you sure, about the washing-up I mean? I'm happy to help.'

'I'm positive.'

'Well then, I'd better shoot; it's late and I've already taken up too much of your time.' He went to stand which wasn't easy with Gerty stretched out over his feet. The Labrador looked up sleepily, reluctant to move. 'Come on, girl, if I'm not allowed to help with the washing-up, I need to get back to the bed-and-breakfast before I turn into a pumpkin, or annoy Mrs Tyreman by disturbing her household. Not sure which of those options is worse, actually.' He pulled a face at Florrie, who giggled.

'Disturbing Mrs Tyreman, hands down; I've heard she can be pretty feisty.'

'In that case, Gerty, it's definitely time to get moving.'

Gerty heaved herself up with a groan, allowing Ed to get to his feet. He stretched his arms, revealing a hint of taut, tanned abdomen and a smattering of dark hair where his shirt had come untucked. Florrie stole a surreptitious look which triggered a flutter in her stomach. She quickly averted her eyes, hoping he hadn't noticed before she and Gerty followed him down the hall, watching as he pulled his coat on.

As she went to open the door, he looked down at her, his eyes shining. 'Thank you for the delicious meal, Florrie, and for making me feel so at home here. I've had a lovely time, despite the circumstances. You've helped make me forget how sad I've been feeling about my grandfather.'

'You're welcome, I'm glad you came; it's been good to smile again.' She looked up at him, trying to ignore the butterflies that had been unleashed in her stomach. 'And thanks for the fudge.'

'You're welcome,' he said with a small laugh, his eyes apparently reluctant to leave hers. 'Well, I'd best be off.' He bent and kissed her cheek, the spicy scent of his cologne wafting under her nose and setting the butterflies off in a frenzy. 'See you later.'

'Yeah, see you later.' She watched him step out into the cold night air, her mind in a spin. Her promise to Mr H about taking Ed under her wing suddenly sprang to mind. 'We meet up in the Jolly every Friday at about seven-ish. It's usually just us girls, but you're welcome to join us if you'd like,' she said, the words coming out in a rush.

He stopped at the gate and turned to her. 'Are you sure the

others wouldn't mind? I mean, I wouldn't want my presence to put the dampeners on their evening.'

'You wouldn't, and anyway, they'll look forward to giving you a thorough grilling!' She flashed him an amused grin.

'That doesn't sound scary at all. Did you say one of your friends is a lawyer?'

'That's Stella; she's like a Rottweiler when she gets going.'

'Well, when you put it like that, how could I refuse?' He laughed. 'See you at the Jolly.' He raised his hand in a wave and headed off down the street. As Florrie closed the door, she could still feel the warmth where his kiss had touched her skin, it set her already chaotic emotions swirling. She'd been surprised to find how much she liked Ed; he seemed to have an air of his grandfather's easy-going nature about him, as well as a wicked sense of humour. And it went without saying that he was very attractive too. Thought of his navy blue eyes sent a shimmer through her. 'Be careful,' said a warning voice, reminding her that he probably wouldn't hang around for long – he'd said as much himself. Florrie pushed away the feeling of insecurity it triggered; she didn't want to dwell on it right now. And besides, after Graham, she'd already decided she was taking a break from romance.

TWENTY

Florrie had woken early, memories of her evening with Ed floating into her mind, her heart lifting as she recalled how well they'd got on. She'd been surprised at how much she'd liked him, and it had been a relief to hear he wasn't going to rush off straightaway. Hopefully, they'd have time to come to some form of agreement with the bookshop that would work for both of them.

The glow from behind the curtains told her the sun was shining. She wiggled her toes and stretched her arms above her head before throwing the duvet back. She pushed her glasses on, slipped her dressing gown over her pyjamas and made her way downstairs. In the kitchen, she was greeted by Gerty with a bout of prolific tail wagging. 'Good morning, Gerty, it's good to see you looking happy.' Florrie unlocked the back door and the Labrador charged out, spying a cat at the end of the garden and racing after it, giving a territorial bark as she went.

Florrie made a small pot of tea and sat at the table, nibbling on buttery toast while she made a list of the things she'd like to tackle at the bookshop. Top of the list was the stash of old books

Mr H had in the storeroom; it was a tragedy they'd been kept there, practically hidden away for decades, keeping company with age-old clutter. She could understand his reluctance to part with them; there was something about old books, she had to agree – she had a bookcase rammed with them in the attic, but hers were regularly picked up and enjoyed, their words savoured. Yet Mr H had specifically told her he'd bought his collection with the intention of selling them. What Florrie struggled to understand more than anything, was how he'd never minded them being left in the storeroom, gathering dust and being deprived of bringing pleasure to anyone. And it had never seemed to bother him that the room wasn't being utilised properly, that it was a wasted opportunity. It was a good size, and would probably look even bigger once all the clutter was removed; there'd no doubt be a whole load of Harte history contained within. Sorting through it all certainly wouldn't be an easy task.

Maybe that history had been part of the problem, she mused.

As she sat pondering, Florrie found herself suddenly overwhelmed by a wave of sadness. Her throat constricted and her eyes blurred with tears as her mind filled with the last image she had of Mr H, slumped in his chair. She sniffed and wiped her eyes, releasing a shaky sigh. 'Get a grip, Florrie! Mr H wouldn't want you to be like this,' she said aloud. 'Today's all about being positive and moving on, and that's exactly how I'm going to face it.' She scooped up the teapot, topped up her mug and took a fortifying sip. Gazing out of the window, it occurred to her that Mr H would be very happy to think Ed had been sitting in this room with her last night, of how they'd laughed together and enjoyed each other's company. They'd been a soothing balm to one another's grief for that short time. She felt the warmth of a smile spread across her face. Who'd have thought?

* * *

Since Gerty had moved in with Florrie, cycling to the bookshop was out of the question. Not that Florrie minded, instead the pair enjoyed a brisk walk along the top prom, taking the usual route, passing familiar faces as they went. Gerty was in raptures at the miscellany of scents she encountered on the way, trotting along jauntily. It gladdened Florrie's heart to see it.

That morning, the sky was a deep cornflower blue, the spring sunshine glittering prettily on the undulating sea; it was a far cry from the biting cold of the previous day. The view of her beloved Thorncliffe made her heart sing as it stood before her, drenched in golden sunshine, waves lapping at its feet. Florrie took a breath of sea air, savouring the freshness that filled her lungs. Ahead, she spotted a seagull devouring what looked like the remnants of a portion of fish and chips on the pavement by the fence. It was warning off passers-by with its shrieking cry, flapping its huge white wings. They really were formidable creatures and not to be messed with; she'd heard stories of the seabirds actually attacking people to steal their fish and chips. With their sharp beaks and huge wing-span, it was no wonder folk surrendered their food willingly. Gerty clocked the gull and pulled on the lead, her ears pricked in interest. Florrie wasn't sure if Gerty was keen to reach the food or the bird, but she liked neither option so pulled her back. 'Gerty, stop! No!'

Reluctantly, Gerty did as she was bid and the pair gave the seagull a wide berth as they walked by, a low growl rumbling through the Labrador that made Florrie chuckle; Gerty was the most gentle creature she'd ever encountered. 'There's nothing like a bit of big-talk is there, girl?'

As they strode along, it struck Florrie that she should really mention her intention to start work on the storeroom and its books to Ed. After all, they were equal partners, and she was sure some family stuff would be stored in there. It was only right he had the option to get involved. And it would be nice to have some company while she worked through them. Ed's company, in particular, said a little voice in her head, making her heart give a wayward leap. They'd exchanged mobile phone numbers the previous evening; she'd send him a text when she got to work. Hayley was working at the bookshop today, so she could look after the sales area. Buoyed by the idea, Florrie upped her pace. 'Come on, Gerty, let's make tracks,' she said, clicking her tongue. The Labrador obliged.

Passing the old Micklewick Majestic Hotel, Florrie spotted Dodgy Dick's fancy car parked on the roadside next to it. She'd heard a whisper that he was interested in buying the place and seeing his car there added substance to it. Or rather, if rumours were true, the company he acted as frontman for was interested in buying it. Her mood dipped at the thought; whichever way Dodgy Dick got his hands on the property, it could only mean bad news for the town, and wouldn't take long before it too was under his disreputable cloud. She shuddered at the thought.

The pair ploughed on, quickly reaching Endeavour Road which led directly to the Square. As they approached The Cellar – the town's trendy micro-brewery – Bill, its thirty-year-old joint-owner, stepped out onto the pavement armed with a sweeping brush.

'Morning, Bill,' she said.

'Morning, Florrie.' He had a friendly face, his beard and style declaring to the world that he was a hipster. He was quickly followed by his husband and business partner, Pim.

'Hi there, Florrie,' Pim said in his lilting Dutch accent. 'Looks like it's going to be a beautiful day.' He ran his hand through his Nordic-blonde locks.

'It sure does,' she said, returning their smiles.

As she continued along the road, her attention was drawn to a figure walking along on the other side of the road. It was the man with the grey overcoat and flat cap. He looked at her and nodded, giving a small smile, his coat flapping out behind him. She nodded and smiled back, somewhat shocked at the transformation in his usually sullen features. Her mind whirred as to where she recognised him from. *Ughh!* It would bug her until she remembered.

TWENTY-ONE

Florrie rolled up the sleeves of her cardigan and picked up a duster. The storeroom was dimly lit and got very little natural light thanks to the shutters at the windows being permanently closed. The walls, painted a depressing dark brown, didn't help either and made the place seem gloomy, but she was reluctant to push back the shutters until the room was in a respectable state. She guessed the windows would be thick with ancient dust too, which would drive her mad until she'd cleaned them, but today she just wanted to stick to her plans.

She was eyeing the wall of old books and wondering where to start when the bell above the shop door went, followed by a voice she recognised. Her heart gave an unexpected flip and she headed into the sales area, her face breaking into a smile when she saw Ed. He was bent over, fussing Gerty, who was ecstatic to see him.

'Hi,' she said. 'You came.'

'Hi, I did,' he said, looking up, pushing his fringe back and flashing her a broad smile. She was pleased to see his face seemed less drawn than it had the previous morning; he had a dash of colour in his cheeks and his eyes were brighter, the shadows beneath less intense.

A few beats fell before she realised she must be grinning at him inanely. 'Erm, oh, right, let me introduce you two. Hayley, this is Ed Harte, he's Mr H's grandson. Ed, this is Hayley Medd, she's a student and works here on a Saturday and during her holidays as well as doing the odd day when she's not at college – like today. She's been with us a good few years now and knows the bookshop inside out; we'd be lost without her.'

'Hi,' said Hayley, looking moonstruck at Ed, her face a vivid shade of crimson.

'Hi, Hayley, it's nice to meet you, and it's good to know the bookshop's in such reliable hands.' He seemed oblivious to the effect he was having on the teenager.

'Thank you,' she said, giving an uncharacteristically shy giggle.

'Ed's come to help me sort through the books, but if you need me at all just shout up,' said Florrie, happiness thrumming through her.

'Okay, will do. Good luck.' Hayley beamed at them as they made their way to the storeroom, Gerty following close behind.

Once in the room, Ed took off his jacket and hung it over an old ladder-back chair. 'Wow! It's chock-a-block in here. And that's some hoard of old tomes.' He made his way over to the groaning bookshelves, running his hand across the light stubble of his chin as he went.

Gerty found a comfy spot, circled a couple of times then flopped down, resting her head on her paws and gazing at Ed with adoring eyes.

'I've been itching to tackle them for ages but Mr H wasn't... now seems as good a time as any.' She pulled herself back from the pool of grief that was never far away whenever she thought of Mr H.

Ed smiled and said softly, 'It does. Do you have any idea what my grandfather intended to do with them?' He picked one up and started flicking through it, sending a small cloud of dust into the air.

'He'd originally planned to sell them; he was quite keen on antiquarian and rare books. But I think he grew too fond of them and couldn't bear to part with them.'

'Sounds just like the man I was getting to know.' Ed laughed fondly, putting the book back down. 'So what can I do to help?'

'Well, I think we should start at this end and work through them; maybe make separate piles relating to the categories they belong to. They all need dusting down and cataloguing; I've got a notebook for that here.' She pointed to the table where an A4 pad was open, a pen lying across it. 'Then I'll transfer the details to a spreadsheet, which should make it easier to see what we've got.'

'Sounds like a plan. I'm more than happy to help with the dusting.'

'Then, when we've done that, we need to do a bit of research online to find out if there's still a market for any of them. Over the years, I've lost count of the number of people who've come in asking us if we could source out-of-print books; particularly the ones on vernacular architecture and Yorkshire poetry. I'm not sure about the others though.'

Ed nodded, listening with interest. 'You mean with a view to selling them?'

Florrie looked at him, hoping to gauge his reaction. 'It could be a way for the bookshop to branch out; selling and sourcing rare and antiquarian books.' She gave a small shrug, lifting her eyebrows a little. It felt strange speaking of them in the context of business partners – however long that may be.

He nodded slowly. 'That sounds like a great idea. An extra string to the bow of The Happy Hartes Bookshop has got to be a good thing, right?'

Florrie beamed, relieved he wasn't averse to it. She'd grown accustomed to all of her suggestions relating to the bookshop being shot down in flames, and it felt surprisingly good to finally have a positive reaction. 'Absolutely! I've got loads of other ideas too, but I think I'll save them for another day,' she said, suddenly wary of swamping him with too many plans.

Ed laughed. 'There's no harm in telling me about them as we work through that lot.' He nodded towards the books, picking up a duster.

'Okay, but you might regret saying that.' She feigned a warning look, making him laugh again.

* * *

Florrie and Ed had made great inroads into their task. She found him to be easy company; there was no edge to him and there'd been no awkward silences which was a relief. He'd answered her questions quite happily, asking about her in return, listening attentively. He'd responded to her ideas of setting up a reading club, holding story-telling sessions for school children, poetry readings, and author signing events with great enthusiasm. In turn, Florrie was thrilled with his suggestion of a Happy Hartes Bookshop loyalty card. He'd kept the mood light by telling self-deprecating stories and cracking jokes, mostly at his own expense.

'I can understand why my grandfather lost the joy he once felt for the place when my grandma passed away. But it's time The Happy Hartes Bookshop was brought back to its former glory, just as it deserves.'

'Hear, hear,' said Florrie, raising her duster in the air and waving it about, sending dust motes floating about in the air around her, making her sneeze.

'Bless you,' he said, chuckling. 'And thank you for bringing me up-to-speed with everything; your ideas and enthusiasm for the place are infectious.'

'I'm pleased to hear that.' She felt a swell of happiness and a flicker of something else as her eyes ran over his broad shoulders, the muscles flexing beneath his grey t-shirt. Her gaze settled on his mouth, which was full and turned up at the corners as if in a permanent smile. A wayward thought raced across her mind: *What would those lips feel like on mine?* They'd certainly felt soft and warm when he'd pressed a kiss to her cheek twice the previous day. The memory made her pulse rate take off and she felt the heat of a blush creep up her face. *Calm your jets, you've only known him two minutes!* But through her sorrow, her heart seemed to have other ideas and she'd found him occupying her thoughts an awful lot. There was no denying it, she really quite liked him... well, more than *quite* liked him. If she was honest with herself, she was beginning to like him rather a lot. And maybe, if she was being *completely* honest, this *liking* malarkey had spilled over into the realms of finding him really quite fanciable. She dreaded to think what her friends would have to say when they guessed – which they would – especially Jasmine, who wasn't known for her subtlety.

Finding him attractive and good to be around was proving to be a heady combination but it came to an abrupt halt courtesy of a jabbing reminder of Ed's uncertainty about what to do with the bookshop and staying in Micklewick Bay. *What are you thinking? You're only just out of a relationship and had promised yourself some breathing space. Going all puppy-dog eyes over Ed Harte is a bad idea especially if he's not going to stick around! Oh, but there's something about him that's so... uhh!*

Florrie groaned inwardly; never before had her emotions been in such conflict. It wasn't like her at all; she was usually cautious, measured, took things slowly.

Her thoughts were silenced by the ringing of Ed's mobile phone. She looked up to see him frowning at the screen.

'I should take this,' he said reluctantly.

'Okay; it's probably a good time for a break anyway. I'll go and put the kettle on.' She followed Ed back into the shop, watching as he headed outside; she hoped it wasn't bad news.

TWENTY-TWO

Ed returned, joining Florrie at the counter where she was chatting to Hayley, sipping tea. Florrie did her best to quell her curiosity as to the identity of the caller who'd made him frown. She had a horrible suspicion it had been his parents, but it couldn't have been bad news as he was smiling now. When he didn't enlighten her, she continued telling Hayley about their plans for the bookshop, Ed joining in with great enthusiasm, which came as a relief to Florrie.

Hayley was explaining about her college work when the door went, flooding the shop with the sound of a motorbike roaring by. Florrie glanced across to the customer, taking a few seconds to register that it was the mystery man she still hadn't managed to put a name to. Gerty, who was dozing on her cushion by the counter, briefly opened her eyes, but deeming the man not sufficiently interesting, closed them again.

'Hello there.' Florrie greeted him with a friendly smile.

'Hello.' He pulled off his flat cap. Though he was smiling, his eyes bore the dark, brooding expression that was annoyingly familiar.

'Can I help you?' she asked, taking a sideways look at

Hayley whose mouth had fallen open. The girl had started fidgeting as if she was walking over hot coals. Florrie looked back at the man, her brow furrowing; was his identity the reason Hayley was in such a tizz? With her interest piqued, she hurriedly scrabbled around her mind to put a name to the face, but to no avail.

'No thanks, I've just come in for a browse, if that's all right?' His broad North Yorkshire accent was rich and velvety. He pinned Florrie with his deep, dark gaze, making her feel slightly discombobulated as he headed further into the shop, looking around him all the while.

'Oh, er... yes, of course, that's fine.' Her eyes followed him as the penny dropped with an almighty clank. There was only one person she knew who had a voice like that: nationally renowned Yorkshire poet and author – and infamous hot-head – Jack Play-forth! His profile had recently soared since he took on the role of narrator of a popular North Yorkshire countryside programme, *Breath of Yorkshire*, his voice perfect for the job. His trademark long, dark wavy locks had been cropped short, which was why she'd struggled to recognised him. *Oh, my days! Mr H would never believe this!* She could hardly believe it herself. An author of Jack Playforth's standing, here in The Happy Hartes Bookshop? Was she dreaming? She steadied her jittering stomach and took a deep breath, hoping she'd done so discreetly. 'Just let us know if we can help you with anything.'

'Thank you.' He gave a small smile and headed towards the poetry section where he was soon hidden behind the book-shelves.

Florrie turned to face Hayley who was jumping up and down on the spot, her face matching the colour of her bright pink hoodie. 'Jack Playforth's just walked into the shop!' said Florrie, as if she didn't quite believe her own words.

'I know! Omigod! Omigod! Omigod! He was rumoured to be in the running for poet laureate! Wait till I tell my mum; she absolutely *loves* him! She thinks he's really *hot!*' Hayley covered her mouth, stifling an excited squeal.

'Shh! He'll hear you!' Florrie said in a whisper, though she couldn't help but laugh. 'My mum's a huge fan too; so am I actually.' She glanced across at Ed who was looking bemused at Hayley's sudden giddiness.

'That's Jack Playforth?' he asked in disbelief, pointing his thumb in the poet's direction.

Florrie and Hayley nodded, grinning inanely. 'Yes!' they said in whispered unison.

'The author famous for writing in North Yorkshire dialect?'

'Yes,' Florrie and Hayley chorused softly, their eyes dancing.

'The author who's won all those awards?'

'Yes!' Florrie and Hayley nodded enthusiastically, their smiles widening.

'Are you sure? I mean, he looks so different, and he's a lot shorter than I imagined – as is his hair; he's famous for wearing it long, isn't he?' Ed said quietly, leaning back on his heels in an attempt to steal a better look at their customer. 'Grandad raved about him.'

'His short hair is why I didn't recognise him to start with. And everyone's small compared to you, Ed,' Florrie said, smiling up at him.

He caught her eye and grinned, sending an unexpected thrill through her. 'Hmm. I suppose you have a point, but it's hard to get a good look at him without looking like I'm gawping.' He turned, craning his neck before hurriedly turning back to face them. 'Look sharp, he's on his way back over here.'

Jack Playforth ambled over to the counter, a smile playing over his mouth. 'I don't suppose you have a copy of the new book of poetry by Peter Skelthorpe, do you?'

Florrie composed herself as best she could. 'We do, yes, they're just over here. I can show you—'

'Actually, we've only got one left; they've been selling like hot cakes,' said Hayley. She was still bouncing up and down; anyone would think she had springs fixed to the soles of her shoes.

That Florrie wasn't aware of how many books they'd sold was proof of how tied-up in her grief she'd been. She was usually on top of every sale, particularly newly released, popular publications; it gave her a thrill each time one was sold, taking joy in the pleasure they'd give the reader.

Jack Playforth's smile grew wider. 'Just as well I called in when I did then. If you'd be so good as to point me in the right direction; I couldn't see it when I was looking before.'

'It's fine, I'll get it for you.' Florrie headed towards the poetry section, returning in a matter of moments, handing him the book. 'I hope you don't mind me asking, but you're Jack Playforth, aren't you?' She hoped she didn't sound too starstruck.

'Aye, I am, for my sins,' he said, almost shyly. 'I'm renting a cottage here in Old Micklewick for the next couple of months; hoping to be inspired by the sea and all the tales of smuggling and mermaids as well as the rousing sea shanties.'

'Oh, I'm sure you will be. Micklewick Bay's super-inspiring; loads of people think so. It's crammed with legends and stories and colourful characters from the past, like the infamous smuggler Jacob Crayke. You've *so* come to the right place.' Excitement was making Hayley gabble.

'Well, from what I've seen so far, it's definitely captured my heart,' Jack said, placing his hand on his chest. 'But it's not the only motive I have for visiting here; I have a family connection that I'm keen to explore.'

Florrie was itching to ask more, but not wanting to sound nosy, held back. 'I've think I've seen you about town a couple of times, but didn't recognise you until just now when I heard you speak; you've got such a distinctive voice.' She set the book on the counter in front of Hayley; she thought her assistant might like to serve their auspicious customer.

'It's the hair,' said Hayley, picking up a colourful lock of her own. 'It was as distinctive as your voice, that's why Florrie didn't recognise you until you spoke.'

'Ah, yes.' He reached up and touched his newly cropped dark hair, shot with strands of silver. 'It's afforded me a considerable degree of anonymity since I had it cut,' he said with a chuckle. 'It was time for it to go; can't say I regret it.'

'My grandfather raved about your work,' said Ed. 'We watched you on that countryside programme, *Breath of Yorkshire*, last time he came to stay, you were reading some of your poetry; it was amazing, especially with the moors as a backdrop.'

'Ah, thank you, it's very kind of you to say so. I enjoyed doing it enormously. It was filmed last summer; I was sitting on the moortop in amongst the heather, overlooking Lytell Stangdale on the moors. It was a wonderful experience and I was particularly glad the weather was kind that day; it wouldn't have been much fun if it'd been chucking it down or the place was swathed in a thick fog.'

'Yes, I can imagine.' Ed nodded, his expression animated. He stole a quick look at Florrie before turning back to Jack. 'Okay, I'm going to go out on a limb here so please feel free to tell me if you think I'm being cheeky.' He paused for a moment, all eyes on him. 'I don't suppose you'd consider doing a reading of your work here, would you? I know it's not exactly the moors, but Florrie and I have just taken over the bookshop and are looking at ways to bring it back to life; you doing a reading here would be amazing.' He looked at Jack hopefully.

Florrie's eyes widened and her eyebrows shot up; she hadn't expected Ed to ask anything so bold. And, much as she thought the idea was fabulous, she was searching her mind for something to say to give Jack an escape route without causing offence, or for him to unleash his infamous temper. 'Oh... erm... it's a wo—'

'I'd love to,' said Jack, his dark eyes dancing. 'An intimate reading in this wonderful bookshop is right up my alley.'

Florrie clasped her hands to her face. Had she heard right? 'Are you sure? I mean, wow! That's fantastic.' Her eyes met Ed's, their gaze locking for a moment.

'That's amazing, thank you,' said Ed, who looked as surprised as Florrie. 'Of course, we'd pay you for the trouble.'

'Absolutely.' Florrie hoped his fee wasn't going to be extortionate.

'I wouldn't dream of taking anything. I'm here on holiday, and doing a reading in this place would be a pleasure.'

Now I really need to pinch myself! Her mind was swirling with excitement. Had Jack Playforth really just agreed to do a reading for free here at The Happy Hartes Bookshop? *Oh, my days!* If so, where could they hold it? They were tight on space as it was. Ed's thoughts were clearly on the same track.

'There's a room through there,' Ed said, pointing his thumb in the general direction of the storeroom. 'Florrie and I are in the middle of sorting it out, but if we crack on with it, give it a fresh lick of paint, then we could host it there.' He looked across at her, his eyes smiling.

Florrie bit her lip as she awaited Jack's response. She was hoping he wouldn't ask to go and take a look at it in its current state; it was bound to put him off.

'Well, that sounds spot-on to me. I'm looking forward to it already.' He checked his watch. 'Right then, it's time I was heading off. I've got a date with a plate of fish and chips down at The Jolly Sailors in half-an-hour or so. If you don't mind, I'll settle up for my book, and I'll pop back later so we can make plans for the reading.'

'Of course. And this is on the house.' Florrie took the book Hayley had put into a brown paper bag and handed it to Jack.

'That's really not necessary.' He held his hand up.

'It's the least we can do,' Florrie said, unable to stop herself from smiling. 'Please take it.'

'Well, in that case, thank you very much, I'll enjoy reading it later this evening.' He pushed the book into his pocket and walked to the door. 'Good afternoon, all,' he said in his rich tone.

'Good afternoon,' they said in unison.

They watched him close the door and head down the street. When he was out of sight Hayley released an ear-splitting squeal, making Ed wince. Florrie looked between them in disbelief. 'Did that really just happen?'

'Sorry, I just got mega excited.' Hayley pulled an apologetic face.

'I didn't mean you, petal,' said Florrie, laughing and squeezing the young girl's arm. 'I meant, did Jack Playforth just come into this shop and agree to do a reading, or am I dreaming?'

Ed nodded, grinning. 'He sure did.'

'Ed! Omigod! You played a blinder! That's some big balls you've got asking someone as famous as Jack Playforth to do a reading for us.' Hayley's face was animated, her voice shrill. 'Oh... oops... sorry about the big balls thing; just kind of slipped out.'

Ed's eyebrows shot up and he stifled a laugh. Florrie snorted.

'Arghh! I mean the *words* slipped out, not your, erm, *balls*. And I didn't mean to say they were big,' Hayley said, covering her burning face with her hands.

'Would you like a shovel to help with that hole you're digging yourself into there, Hayley?' Florrie giggled, exchanging an amused look with Ed.

He looked on as the young girl tied herself up in knots, his smile growing wider by the second. 'No problem, Hayley.

Though maybe I should check my flies, just to be on the safe side.' He looked across at Florrie and the pair burst out laughing.

Hayley groaned. 'Why does my mouth have to run away with itself? Please gag me when Jack Playforth next calls in; I'm not safe to be let loose. Who knows what I could end up saying.' She pulled a face, her cheeks still flushed. 'Actually, he was much nicer than I was expecting. I mean, he's supposed to be a bit grouchy and bad-tempered, isn't he? I was half expecting him to lose it when you asked him about the reading, Ed.'

'Yeah, I'd heard he has a bit of a short fuse, but he seemed perfectly amiable to me; he didn't have to agree to do it. In fact, I think he was pleased Ed asked him,' said Florrie.

Ed nodded. 'Yep, he could've told us to bugger off then storm out, if his reputation's anything to go by.'

'If that's what you were thinking when you asked him, I'm definitely right about your balls,' said Hayley, giving him a cheeky grin.

Ed shook his head, smiling.

Florrie felt a wave of happiness wash over her; reluctant as he was to commit to it, Ed clearly cared about the future of the bookshop. His grandparents would have been thrilled to know it. But the prospect of being in partnership with him still meant a shadow of uncertainty loitered at the back of her mind. There was his parents to factor into the equation too, and their desire to get their hands on some cold, hard cash.

Florrie had had a lifetime's worth of anxiety humming away in the background when her mum had been ill. It had never completely gone away, and she didn't need anything else adding to it.

TWENTY-THREE

They were still laughing and chatting when Miss Davenport came into the shop, her usual shopping bag over her arm. Florrie was thrilled to see her, but it didn't escape her attention that her friend was looking tired and drawn. She'd lost weight too and her anorak hung off her. And she couldn't have been keeping her twice-weekly appointment at the hairdressers since her usually well-groomed hair was hanging lank and untended. It wasn't like her at all, Florrie thought. Losing Mr H had obviously hit her hard.

Miss Davenport looked surprised to find the shop in such high spirits so soon after her old friend's passing, and could barely muster a smile when Florrie greeted her. It sent a ripple of guilt through the younger woman; she hoped her friend wouldn't think she was being insensitive.

'Hello there, Miss Davenport, it's good to see you.' Florrie went over to her friend and gave her a gentle hug, the older woman's jutting bones confirmation of just how much weight she'd lost. Gerty jumped up from her slumber and trotted over, wagging her tail.

'Hello, my dear, how are you keeping? Hello, Gerty.' She gave the Labrador a quick pat on the head.

'I'm doing okay, but more to the point, how are you?' She took her friend's hands to find they were bitterly cold, the pink varnish chipped on her usually neatly manicured nails. Florrie's heart ached for her.

Miss Davenport gave a wavery sigh and looked at her with tired eyes. 'I still can't believe Bernard's gone.' She shook her head sadly. 'I keep expecting to see him standing behind the counter whenever I come in, greeting me with his big smile just as he always did. It's heart-breaking he's not here anymore.'

'I know, it still hasn't sunk in with me, but I keep telling myself he's at peace and back with his beloved Dinah. They'll be sitting together up there, sipping tea, gazing out to Thorncliffe and watching the world go by.' She caught Ed's eye, noting he'd exchanged his smiles for a look of concern. 'Miss Davenport, you remember Mr H talking about his grandson, Ed, don't you?'

'Of course, Bernard thought the world of him. Was thrilled they were back in touch.' She mustered up a smile though sadness still hovered in her eyes.

A shadow flickered across Ed's face and he hung his head, a nerve twitching in his cheek.

'Well, he's here, look. This is Ed.' Florrie smiled broadly as she gestured with her hand in Ed's direction, hoping to chase away his feeling of discomfort.

'This is Edward? Bernard's grandson? Never!' Miss Davenport looked confused as she took in the rangy physique of the man before her. A few awkward seconds passed until her face broke out into a wide smile. 'Oh, my goodness! It is Edward! I'd recognise those twinkly eyes anywhere; so like Bernard's, and always full of mischief, which is exactly how you were as a small boy.' She chuckled, patting his cheek just as she did all those years ago.

'Hi, Miss Davenport, it's good to see you,' Ed said, his smile returning, much to Florrie's relief.

'Do you have time for a cuppa, Miss Davenport? We've got some exciting news you might quite like to hear.'

'Now, that sounds intriguing, Florrie, my love. How could I refuse when you put it like that?'

Florrie checked her watch, realising Hayley hadn't had her lunch break. 'Ooh, I'm sorry, Hayley, I hadn't spotted the time.'

'No worries,' she said cheerfully. A couple of minutes later the young girl was heading off to meet her boyfriend, her backpack slung over her shoulder.

Once Ed disappeared into the small kitchen area at the back to make a pot of tea, Miss Davenport asked Florrie how he'd taken finding himself part owner of the bookshop. Florrie quickly brought her up-to-speed, though she thought it best kept to herself that Ed was unlikely to hang around; she knew it would upset her friend if he went against his grandfather's wishes.

'Well, all I can say is it's a relief to hear he hasn't mentioned selling his half, especially with the likes of that dreadful Dick Swales sniffing around; that would never do.'

Florrie's heart dropped at the mention of Dodgy Dick. 'No, he hasn't mentioned anything about that – not that we've had much of a conversation about it, but I think he knows Mr H would hate the idea.' The thought of being in partnership with such a disreputable bully didn't bear thinking about, and, deep down, she knew it was still a possibility if Ed decided to not to keep his share. The thought set anxiety squirming in her stomach, but now wasn't the time to dwell on it; her friend was here and she needed cheering up. Plus, Florrie didn't want to put the dampeners on their thrilling news.

Miss Davenport nodded and patted Florrie's hand. 'Good, good. And I take it he's going to stay in the flat above here?'

'Oh, erm...' The question took Florrie by surprise. 'I'm not sure, we haven't discussed where he's going to stay yet.' How had they forgotten about that? Probably because they were still coming to terms with their new situation. But much as it seemed like a logical solution, rather than Ed having to fork out for a room at the B&B, she wasn't sure how he'd feel about staying in his grandparents' old home.

The arrival of a customer distracted her from having to dwell any further on the matter. For now.

When Ed returned with the tray of tea, Florrie let him tell Miss Davenport their news about Jack Playforth – she thought it only fair since he was the one who'd orchestrated it.

'He's giving a reading? Here? Oh, my, how exciting! That's wonderful news, and bravo, Ed, for being so bold as to ask him,' she said, her eyes wide with wonder.

Florrie was pleased to see her friend looking brighter than when she'd first arrived. 'I know, my heart was in my mouth for a few seconds until he said yes.' She laughed as she poured tea into the mugs. 'But he was lovely about it.'

Miss Davenport's smile grew wider. 'Can I be the first to reserve a seat? Do let me know how much they cost and I'll pay you straight away.'

It was something else Florrie and Ed needed to discuss, her mind suddenly shifting to how much they needed to do in the storeroom to make it ready for Jack Playforth and his audience. They'd need to find somewhere to relocate the books and clutter. Her stomach fluttered with nerves and she did her best to quell them. 'How would you like to help us, Miss Davenport? You could take the tickets from the guests as they arrive, or help serve refreshments.' She handed her some tea, thinking how something to focus on other than her grief would do her friend good.

'Really?' Miss Davenport sat up straighter in her seat as she took the mug. 'Thank you, Florrie, dear. And if that's a serious offer, then I'd be delighted to help out in any way.'

'That's great, we'd love to have you, wouldn't we, Ed?'

'Absolutely; it'd be good to have you involved,' he said.

Florrie looked up to see him smiling across at her, his eyes soft. Her stomach performed a somersault as she felt the warmth of a blush in her cheeks. What thoughts were going on behind those dark-blue eyes? she wondered.

* * *

Miss Davenport stayed for the best part of an hour, with Florrie jumping up to serve the odd straggle of customers, though most of them had just called in to browse. She really hoped their new plans would help increase their sales.

She was checking through the post when Hayley returned, her bubbly personality boosting the atmosphere of the shop as soon as she burst through the door.

'So, I texted my mum about Jack Playforth and she was totally buzzing. She asked if we'd reserve six tickets for her and her mates, if that's okay? She thinks you're going to sell out as soon as you advertise, so she didn't want to lose out. Oh, man, I still can't believe it.' She slipped her backpack off her shoulders, catching her breath.

Ed beamed at Florrie, holding her gaze for a moment.

'Of course we can; it's great that she's so excited. I've already started a book. I'll pop her name in it straightaway,' said Florrie, excitement pulsing through her veins.

'And can I design the poster for it? We need to get loads dotted around town, in pubs and on social media. It's gonna be totally awesome!' said Hayley, her wide smile treating them to a flash of her braces.

A wave of happiness washed through Florrie as she glanced over at Ed. Was this the start of The Happy Hartes Bookshop's renaissance? She hoped with all her heart that it was.

TWENTY-FOUR

Florrie was pushing the key into the lock of her front door when she heard the ping of a text message from the depths of her backpack. Once in the hallway, Gerty trotted off to the kitchen where she drank noisily from her bowl. Florrie retrieved her phone to see a message from Maggie with a slew of heart emojis attached.

> You still okay for the Jolly tonight, missus? Mx

Florrie fired one back as she made her way to the kitchen, adding a flourish of emojis of her own.

> Too right! Looking forward to it. Got loads to tell you! Fx

A reply landed within seconds.

> I'm intrigued! Can't wait to hear it all!! Mx

She hadn't updated her friends of her new-found situation, preferring to tell them when they were all together. In truth, despite several attempts, she hadn't known where to start with a message to them. Talking face-to-face, she figured, would be way easier.

Florrie shrugged off her jacket and hung it up in the utility room where she tipped some food into Gerty's bowl. 'There you go, girl, enjoy your tea.'

With Gerty fed and watered, Florrie headed upstairs for a quick shower; after spending the day dusting and sorting through the old books she felt decidedly grubby. Friday nights always involved a quick turn-around, not that she minded, she looked forward to the catch-up with her friends, and tonight had the extra appeal of Ed being there. She peeled off her clothes and stepped into the shower, feeling a buzz of excitement. She hadn't felt this way in a long time.

Florrie had put a little extra thought into what she was wearing instead of grabbing the nearest thing in her wardrobe as she usually did on a Friday evening, telling herself it had absolutely nothing to do with the possibility of Ed joining them. Tonight, she'd opted for her new teal cotton sweater with three-quarter sleeves, knowing it went well with her navy ankle-grazers (on anyone else they would be just below the knee) and deep-red cotton scarf which she looped around her neck.

She was tying the laces of her plimsolls when another text came through. She scooped up her phone to see this time the message was from Jasmine.

> Hi chick, running late – babysitter probs! Best if you make your own way to the Jolly. I'll join you as soon as I can xx

Jasmine's house was en-route to the pub and Florrie usually

stopped off for her friend so they could make their way down to the pub together.

'Poor Jazz,' Florrie said aloud. Jasmine's life was regularly a juggling act, which she always somehow managed. And though she often looked tired, she was always upbeat. Woe betide anyone who felt sorry for her.

Florrie sent a quick reply.

> I don't mind waiting with you. Fx

She was pulling on her navy twill jacket when Jasmine replied.

> Could be a while. Best if I see you there xx

She pinged one back.

> Okay, if you're sure. There'll be a large glass of wine waiting for you!! Fx

Florrie smiled as she sent the message, knowing it would lift her friend's spirits.

> Now you're talking!!! xx

Florrie clipped the lead onto Gerty's collar, the Labrador dancing excitedly from paw-to-paw. 'Looking forward to a night at the Jolly, are you, Gerty?' A second later, Florrie found herself being dragged down the hallway to the front door, the leather of the lead digging into her hand. 'Woah, bide you passion, lass!' She chuckled; it was good to see Gerty looking more like her old self. The extra exercise seemed to have helped boost the Labrador's mood; she loved going for a walk, and so did Florrie, for that matter.

Outside was still bright and mild, though there was a subtle nip in the air, which was to be expected at the end of April. Gerty took a left at the gate, following their usual route, trotting along jauntily, her tail swaying. It gladdened Florrie's heart to see it. 'How about a walk along the beach on Sunday, Gerty? It's supposed to be a lovely, sunny day.'

Gerty looked back at her, her tongue lolling from the side of her mouth, her eyes shining happily as she plodded on.

Reaching the top prom, Florrie drew in an invigorating lungful of air. Yes, there was still an undercurrent of sadness running through her, an ache in her heart that took the edge off the brighter moments and prodded at her when she had a minute to herself. She missed Mr H terribly. But Jack Playforth had been in The Happy Hartes Bookshop, for goodness' sake! It had lifted her spirits inexorably, that and thinking how over-joyed it would have made Mr H. *And then there's Ed,* said a little voice. Her heart gave a happy lilt.

As she watched Gerty sashay her way along the pavement, stopping occasionally to investigate an intriguing smell, Florrie found herself feeling very glad of Ed's unexpected arrival into her life. Though he'd only been in the town for a few days, it felt like he'd been here for years. Something stirred inside her as she strode along. If anyone had told her a month ago she'd feel like this she'd have thought they were on the wrong side of a pint of Old Micklewick Magic – The Cellar's award-winning beer had a reputation for being like rocket fuel.

She caught sight of Thorncliffe, imposing as ever, and wondered if Ed had sensed the vibes that passed between them the previous evening. Her mind flashed back to the way those dark blue eyes had looked at her; she was pretty certain he had.

In the next moment, the wary side of her nature made itself known, reminding her that it was still early days, that neither of them had had the chance to think their new-found situation through properly. She shook her head. 'Best get that out of your mind, Florrie,' she said under her breath. She needed to stop herself going down that route. She wasn't strong enough to suffer any more hurt; her heart was still aching from the loss of Mr H.

Before long, they'd reached Old Micklewick, seagulls screeching overhead. They walked by the fishing boats moored up on the jetty, Gerty stopping to give the ramshackle stack of lobster pots a quick sniff. The smell of seaweed hung heavy in the air, mingling with the occasional waft of fish and chips. Florrie upped her speed, her plimsolls brushing over the sand that had blown onto the cobbles from the beach. She caught sight of a couple of glossy black heads bobbing about in the water and smiled; from here it was easy to mistake seals for black Labradors. They were a regular feature in Old Micklewick, as was the pod of dolphins. Seeing either of them never lost its lustre.

'Right, Gerty, I'm relying on you to be on your best behaviour in here, okay?' Florrie's cheeks were flushed, her eyes shining from the walk as she pushed open door of The Jolly Sailors. The delicious aroma of home cooking rushed at them. Gerty lifted her nose into the air, sniffing appreciatively. At quarter-past-seven the place was already heaving with folk crowding round the bar and filling the tables, their conversation drowning out the background music. Friday night was always a popular one at the Jolly.

Florrie stepped into the bar, scanning the room. She didn't need to see Lobster Harry's hat on the figurehead's bosom to know he was present; his throaty laugh gave him away. Ed evidently wasn't here; he was so tall, she'd be able to spot him towering above everyone else. Florrie ignored the pang of disappointment that resounded in her chest and made her way over to the friends' usual Friday night table in the cosy nook of the bar. Maggie was sitting alone, staring into space, her dark curls scooped up and tied with a vivid tangerine scarf, its colour a contrast to her blue woolly sweater. Her cheerful apparel belied the serious expression on her face.

Maggie swapped her frown for a smile as soon as she saw Florrie. 'Hiya, hon, it's good to see you.'

'Hi, Mags, s'good to see you too,' she said before going on to explain why Jasmine wasn't with her.

'Oh, poor Jazz, it sometimes seems like such a struggle for her.'

'I know, but at least she doesn't have to cancel tonight.' Florrie hooked the handle end of Gerty's lead under a leg of the table then took off her jacket. She gave her cold hands a brisk rub together. 'Can I get you another drink?'

'I'm fine with this, thanks.' Maggie held up her glass of wine.

It took a moment for Florrie to click. *She's back on alcohol.* 'Oh, Maggie, I'm sorry, chick.'

Maggie wrinkled her nose and shrugged her shoulders. 'False alarm. Another one. But hey-ho, that's how it goes.' Her smile couldn't muster the strength to reach her eyes.

Florrie reached over and squeezed her friend's hand. 'It'll happen when you're least expecting it, I know it will.'

Maggie nodded, attempting to push her smile up. 'Here's hoping.'

'Hiya, ladies, I can't tell you how bloody glad I am it's Friday night.' Stella joined them, dumping her designer handbag down onto a seat, her crisp perfume wafting in the air around them. Wearing a pair of slim-fitting black jeans and a black fitted jacket in soft leather over a black and white striped boat-neck t-shirt, she could pull off casual chic like nobody else Florrie knew.

'Hi, Stells.' Maggie beamed up at their friend, her sadness shooed away for the moment.

'Hi, Stella,' said Florrie just as Lark swept in, her wavy

blonde hair cascading all around her loose-fitting ethnic tunic top in shades of pink and purple. 'And hi, Lark.'

'Hello, everyone, ooh, I'm looking forward to this.' Lark glanced around, her familiar aroma of essential oils mingling with Stella's perfume. 'No Jasmine?'

'She's running late – babysitter problems. Hopefully she won't be long,' said Florrie. 'In the meantime, can I get anyone a drink?'

'It's all dealt with,' said Stella, making herself comfy on the settle and slipping her jacket off. 'I've ordered a bottle of Pinot, should be here in a sec.'

'Someone's keen,' said Lark, smiling.

Stella sighed. 'There's no wonder with the week I've had. Anyway, park your pants and tell us all about your week, missus,' she said, looking at Florrie. 'I thought you were going to let me know how you got on with old Cuthbert. I'm guessing it wasn't anything bad he wanted to speak to you about.'

Florrie pulled an apologetic face; her head had been so full of Ed and the bookshop, she'd forgotten she had been supposed to text Stella. 'Sorry, Stells, my mind's been in a bit of a whirl; I thought it'd be easier to tell you when we were all together.'

'Now then, ladies,' said Immy in a familiar Yorkshire greeting. She was carrying a bottle of wine in an ice-bucket, a clutch of glasses slotted between her fingers.

'Here, let me help. Looks like a recipe for disaster there,' said Stella, jumping up and sliding the glasses out of Immy's fingers one-by-one.

'Thanks, Stella, I was wondering how I was going to put them all down without creating havoc.' Immy beamed at her. 'Right, I'd better head back to the bar, we've got a bit of a rush on. Have a good night, lasses.'

Stella had just finished pouring the wine when Jasmine rushed in, red faced and out of breath. 'Bloody hell, I'm so unfit,' she said, gasping. 'Have I missed much?' She flopped down beside Stella, leaning back in the settle and puffing out her cheeks, a sheen of sweat glistening on her brow.

'Nope, it's perfect timing, chick,' said Maggie while Stella filled the empty glass. 'Don't tell me you've run down?'

Jasmine nodded. 'Pretty much. I had no idea it was so difficult to run downhill; I've lost count of the times I nearly went A-over-T.' She eased off her denim jacket. 'Ooh, that's better, I'm in a lather.'

'You should come running with me, you'd get used to it in no time,' said Stella. She ran along the beach several times a week.

'Tempting,' said Jasmine, reaching for her wine, her friends chuckling at the sarcastic note in her voice. 'Not!' She raised her glass in their direction. 'Cheers, by the way, lasses.'

'Cheers. Sorry to hear about the babysitter, Jazz,' said Maggie.

Jasmine rolled her eyes and pushed her fingers into her spiky red hair. 'I just wish things could be easy for a change. It'd be so good to have a day off all the stress and juggling I have to do to keep everything running smoothly.'

'Couldn't Bart's parents help with babysitting?' asked Lark.

Jasmine's face dropped and she snorted. 'I've given up asking them to help with anything. They disapprove of me going out, they think I should be in widow's weeds forever more. I dread to think how they'd react if I ever met anyone – not that that's on the cards anytime soon.'

'You'd think they'd be keen to spend time with their grandchildren.' Florrie couldn't get her head around how cold Jasmine's in-laws had been since Bart had died, practically turning their backs on Jasmine and the children.

'I know.' Jasmine shook her head wearily. 'Anyway, it wasn't all bad news; when the babysitter *eventually* arrived, she came with an order for a birthday cake. Apparently, her mum had seen one I'd done for a friend and liked it, so thought she'd ask me to make one for her other daughter's twenty-first. She wants a butterfly theme which I'm really excited about. My head was brimming with ideas when I was on my way down here.'

'Ah, that's fab news, Jazz. And it doesn't surprise me, your cakes are amazing,' said Maggie.

'Thanks, Mags.' Jasmine beamed at her.

'That reminds me, I was going to ask you to do one for my mum,' said Stella. 'It's her fiftieth next month and I was wondering if you could do her one of your fabulous chocolate cakes. I'll leave the decoration up to you; you know what sort of thing she likes.'

'That's awesome, thanks, Stells. I'd love to.' Jasmine's eyes shone happily.

'You should seriously think about turning your cake-making into a business,' said Maggie.

'Ooh, I wish. I'd quite happily spend my day making cakes instead of serving in the bakery and cleaning other people's houses. Anyway, enough about me, how's everyone else doing?'

'Yes, come on then, Florrie, it's time you filled us in on your week.' Stella pinned her with one of her formidable stares. 'How did you get on at the solicitors'?'

'Yes, and who was that rather attractive man I saw you with?' asked Lark. 'He was ever so tall with lovely broad shoulders. Could he be the tall, dark and handsome stranger of your dreams, I wonder?'

Florrie felt all eyes on her. She glanced around at their eager faces and pushed her glasses up her nose. 'Well, you won't believe this but...'

She went on to give a brief outline of what had happened, her friends listening quietly all but for the occasional gasp of surprise and a 'Holy shit!' from Stella.

'Bloody hell! All that happened over the last few days?' Jasmine sat back when Florrie had finished. 'And I thought my life was crazy.'

'So, out of the blue, you're part-owner of a bookshop with a man you know very little about,' said Maggie, eyeing her friend with concern.

'That's pretty much the top and bottom of it.' Florrie hadn't shared the unexpected feelings that made her heart race whenever she thought of Ed. Her head was still whirling with it all. She also hadn't shared Ed's hesitance about committing to the bookshop; she didn't want them wound up about it, especially when there was the chance he'd be joining them any minute. Stella, in particular, would give him a roasting, of that there was no doubt. She had a reputation for taking no prisoners and Florrie felt it wouldn't be appropriate tonight.

Stella sat back, her glass in her hand. 'Well, it explains why Cuthbert wanted to see you personally.'

Florrie nodded. 'Seems so. Though I must admit, I do feel a bit guilty about it, especially when I've done nothing to deserve it and I'm not even a blood relative. I feel like it shouldn't really have come to me; I don't think his son'll be very happy about it at all.' She glanced around at her friends, wondering if they shared her thoughts.

'Listen to me, Florrie,' said Stella, her smile switching to a stern stare, making Florrie feel a little nervous, 'you know full-well Mr and Mrs H thought the world of you; why else would they have referred to you as their "honorary granddaughter"? And let me tell you this, Mr H didn't go to the trouble of including you in his will for you to just give away what he very much wanted you to have. He had his reasons for not bequeathing the bookshop to his son and everyone needs to respect that. You included.' Stella's tone meant Florrie didn't dare argue.

'Stella's right, chick,' said Jasmine. 'When Mr H used to come into the bakery, all he ever talked about was how wonderful you were, singing your praises to the high heavens, saying that you were like a granddaughter to him, and how thrilled he was you loved the bookshop as much as he did.'

Jasmine's words prodded at Florrie's raw emotions and she felt the threat of tears. She hurriedly blinked them back. 'I'm sorry, I don't mean to sound ungrateful, it's just it's come as such as shock, my mind's all over the place with it.'

Lark touched Florrie's arm and gave a gentle smile. 'No need to apologise, flower, we know you're not ungrateful. But Mr H was clearly in no doubt that his son and daughter-in-law would sell the place as soon as they could – more than likely to Dodgy Dick – which must've genuinely worried him. Sharing it between you and Ed gave him comfort in the knowledge that he was safe-guarding its future,' she said in her soothing tone.

'And I agree with all of that,' said Maggie. 'Anyway, you've had a tough couple of weeks, you need to stop beating yourself up. It's Friday night, so push your sorrows out of your mind for a few hours and focus on something positive. Like Jack Playforth, for example. How blimmin' exciting it is to think we'll be able to hear him do a live reading?'

Florrie mustered up a smile. 'You're right, Mags. And I still can't believe it about Jack Playforth.'

'Mmm. I love his voice, I could listen to him all day,' said Jasmine dreamily.

'Me too,' said Stella. Her eyes shifting to the bar, her eyebrows suddenly arched in interest. Florrie knew that expression, her friend had spotted something, or rather, *someone,* she liked the look of. 'Excuse me, ladies, my libido's jumped to attention; I just need to savour a hot man moment.'

'Stells, your libido's always jumping to attention,' said Jasmine dryly while the others followed Stella's gaze.

'Hot man moment?' Florrie's heart leapt when her eyes settled on Ed, realising a moment later he was Stella's "hot man". He looked over, his face breaking into a wide smile as he raised his hand in a wave.

'And he's heading this way,' said Stella. 'Oh, thank you, God.' She pressed her hands together in a prayer as she grinned at the others. 'I've got a feeling tonight's going to be rather fabulous.'

'Stells, close your mouth and put your tongue away, you're practically drooling, woman,' said Jasmine, chuckling. 'It's likely to have him running for the hills.'

Lark sat up straight. 'Oh, wow! Florrie, it's that guy I saw y—'

'Hi,' said Ed, reaching the table before Lark could finish. Resting his hand on Florrie's shoulder, he glanced around at them, beaming, sending her insides into raptures. 'Can I get you all a drink?'

Gerty jumped to her feet, pressing her paw against Ed's leg, her tail thudding against the leg of the table. He bent to ruffle her ears. 'Hello there, Gerty, it's good to see you here.'

All but Florrie looked on in astonishment. Feeling suddenly giddy, she struggled to stifle the giggle rising inside her. 'Ladies, this is Ed Harte, Mr H's grandson,' she said. 'Ed, meet Stella, Lark, Jasmine and Maggie.'

'Good to meet you, ladies, Florrie's told me lots about you.' His smile deepened, creasing the corners of his eyes in a heart-fluttering way.

Florrie felt a kick to her shin under the table. 'Ouch!' She looked across to see Stella eyeballing her.

'Remind me to have a word with you later, madam,' Stella said in a hissed whisper, before turning back to Ed and flashing a smile at him, her eyes roving over him appreciatively.

Florrie batted Stella's reprimand away. 'I told Ed he could join us tonight; he's staying at Creelers Cottage here in Old Micklewick till Sunday.' Her eyes swept round her friends, checking their reaction and hoping the dim lighting would hide the blushes that had turned her face crimson.

'Mrs Tyreman!' Jasmine pulled a horrified face. 'I don't

envy you, Ed, she can be a right sour-faced old witch. You're definitely better off here with us.'

'Jazz's right, she's got a reputation for being a bit of a dragon,' said Maggie. 'Have you eaten yet? We're having fish and chips but haven't had chance to order; you're very welcome to tuck in with us.'

'The Jolly's fish and chips are way the best in town. Florrie can shuffle up and you can sit next to her; there's plenty of room.' Lark switched her gaze from Ed to Florrie. It didn't escape Florrie's attention that she was wearing one of her mysterious smiles. She felt her blushes deepen as a huge wave of relief simultaneously washed over her, thankful that her friends were so welcoming. Even so, they were going to have some fun with this...

'In that case, how can I refuse? But first you really must let me get you all a drink. Is that Pinot Grigio I can see in the ice bucket?'

'It is,' said Stella, her eyes still lingering on him.

'Right, one bottle of Pinot Grigio coming up,' he said and loped off in the direction of the bar, Gerty tugging at her lead to follow him.

All eyes turned to Florrie. 'Right then, miss, you've got some serious explaining to do,' said Stella.

'What do you mean?' asked Florrie, knowing exactly what she meant.

'He's absolutely *phwoar!*' said Jasmine, her eyes following Ed as he walked across the room. 'I love a tall man, and as for those broad shoulders... don't get me started.'

'He is very attractive.' Maggie's eyes headed in the same direction as Jasmine's.

'Which is something you neglected to tell us,' Stella said pointedly.

'Really? I hadn't noticed.' Florrie hoped she'd added a convincing note of nonchalance to her voice.

Stella snorted. 'Hadn't noticed, my arse! The whole *pub's* noticed. I wouldn't kick him out of bed, that's for sure.'

'Stells, you wouldn't kick any bloke out of bed,' said Jasmine, giggling.

Stella shot her a look before tipping her head in the direction of Ando Taylor and Lobster Harry who were standing near the bar chatting. Harry threw his head back, letting rip with a throaty cackle. 'I think you'll find I would,' she said, making the friends chuckle.

'That reminds me, is there any news on Prawngate?' asked Florrie.

'Ooh, yes, I'd forgotten about that,' said Lark.

'Me too. Have any fishy rumours filtered through about Bosomworth-Whatsisname?' Maggie asked.

Stella shook her head. 'Rather disappointingly, I've heard nothing, but it's early days and I'm very patient.' A mischievous grin crept over her face.

'And how about you and Jason?' Florrie was keen to keep the spotlight off herself and Ed.

Stella gave a theatrical roll of her eyes and set her glass down on the table. 'Uhh! Don't! I'm going to have to call time on our little arrangement, he's starting to get a bit too clingy for my liking. The other night when he came round he told me he'd like us to take things a bit more seriously; "become an item" was how he put it.' She curled her top lip in disgust. 'Can you believe that? I mean, I'd made it perfectly clear right at the start that I wasn't interested in a serious relationship and never would be.' She stabbed the table with a varnished fingernail.

'Ey up, that sounds like the death knell to me as far as that little dalliance is concerned,' said Jasmine.

'You'd better believe it. But worst of all, he's taken to sending me the most god-awful dick-pics, it's as if he's trying to tempt me to change my mind. I mean, someone should tell him small ain't beautiful in that department. I'd show you if I didn't think it'd put you off your fish and chips.'

Heads turned at the raucous laughter coming from the friends' table. Maggie wiped tears of mirth from her eyes. 'Please don't, Stells.'

'Fear not, I'm only joking, I deleted them straight away. There's no way I'm having pictures of his inadequate body parts on my phone.' Stella gave a mock shudder.

'I can't remember the last time I saw one, inadequate or otherwise.' Jasmine pulled a rueful face. 'I think I've forgotten what they look like – not that I'm asking to see Jason's,' she said, in a splutter of giggles.

'Well, I'd quite like to see Ed's,' said Stella, waggling her eyebrows. 'But I've got a funny feeling his affections are directed elsewhere.' She fixed her eyes on Florrie.

'I think you could be right, Stells,' said Lark, who was wedged between Stella and Jasmine. She gave Florrie another mysterious smile.

'Behave, you two!' Florrie folded her arms defensively across her chest and looked down at Gerty who was still gazing adoringly in Ed's direction.

'I most certainly will not,' said Stella. 'I'm thoroughly looking forward to interrogating him when he gets his hot little butt over here.'

Florrie felt her heart sink, her eyes darting over to the bar to see Ed heading back, a bottle of wine in one hand and a pint of beer in the other. 'Listen, go easy on him, you lot. There's no time to go into detail now, but there's lots more to tell and not everything is as it seems.' Keen to explain herself before Ed got to the table, her words came out in a rush.

'It very rarely is, chick, which is something I've come to learn in my time as a criminal lawyer,' said Stella.

Florrie was grateful to hear her say that. 'So no aggressive questioning, Stells, okay?' Her heart was thudding against her chest as she sensed him getting closer.

'Okay, I'll tread gently.' Stella held her gaze for a moment, unnerving Florrie slightly. 'Just for you.'

'Here we are, ladies,' said Ed, smiling.

TWENTY-FIVE

Florrie inched closer to Maggie who'd shuffled along the settle, creating a space for Ed; she wasn't sure how he was going to cram himself into it without doing himself a mischief. He set the wine and his glass of beer down on the table and removed his jacket, bunching it up and placing it on the floor next to Gerty, before squeezing in next to Florrie, his body pressing against hers and making her heart gallop. She avoided making eye contact with Lark, Stella and Jasmine; she knew only too well what they'd be thinking, and it would be written right across their faces.

Stella didn't waste a moment. 'So, Harte, how does it feel to be in business with our Florrie here?'

Florrie froze, wondering if he'd detected the undercurrent of warning in her friend's tone. If anything was likely to send him running for the hills it would be that.

'Er, yeah, I think it's come as a bit of a shock to both of us,' he said, smiling cautiously before looking down at Gerty who'd pushed her head onto his lap. He smoothed his hand over her head. 'Did Florrie tell you about Jack Playforth?'

Florrie sensed he was keen to move the conversation on and for that she was thankful.

Maggie nodded. 'She did. I gather that was all your doing.'

'For which we're eternally grateful. I could listen to Jack Playforth's voice till the cows come home,' said Jasmine, pulling a swooning face and making them all laugh.

'And how have you been occupying your time until now?' asked Stella, cool as a cucumber. Florrie was astonished at how her friend had put her obvious attraction to him to one side while she continued with her subtle cross-examination. Well, it was subtle for Stella. Florrie had once observed from the public gallery of the courtroom where Stella was cross-examining a defendant. The man had ended up crumbling to the floor, crying like a baby, his barrister wincing as Stella delivered verbal blow after verbal blow. She'd seen a very different side to her friend that day.

'I'm an artist,' Ed said, his smile never failing. 'It's how I've been making my living.'

'And do you make a good living?'

'Yes, I've been happy enough with it.' A hint of amusement glinted in his eyes.

'And how would you describe your style of art?' Stella asked.

'Well, I mostly paint landscapes but I was do—'

'And how will you be able to focus on that with your responsibilities at the bookshop?'

Florrie's stomach clenched. *Give it a rest, Stella!* She was trying to think of something to distract her when Jasmine came to the rescue.

'Flippin' heck, Stells, give the lad a break, would you?' Jasmine rolled her eyes. 'Sorry about our friend, she falls into barrister mode a bit too easily sometimes.' She flashed Stella a warning look.

'Yeah, ease up, Stells, it's Friday night. Put your wig and

robes to one side and chill, girl.' Maggie softened her advice with a smile.

'It's honestly fine; I can understand why Stella wants to know about my plans.' Ed looked around at the friends. 'The truth of the matter is that it's still sinking in. I'm not really certain what I'm going to do, but after discussing things with Florrie, I'm going to stay in Micklewick Bay for a while. I've extended my stay at Creelers Cottage for another week, so I can help get the storeroom cleaned up in readiness for Jack Playforth's reading.'

Florrie made a mental note, reminding herself to have a conversation with him about his grandparents' flat, rather than forking out for bed and breakfast. She figured that was best done when they were on their own; she didn't want her friends chipping in with their "helpful" comments; knowing them, they'd have him moving in with her before either of them could argue about it. Plus, the last thing she wanted, after their conversation last night, was for him to feel railroaded into anything. If he'd rather stay at Creelers Cottage, then that was fine with her.

Ed turned to Florrie, his deep-blue eyes looking down at her. 'That's if Florrie can put up with me,' he said with a laugh.

She gulped. 'That's great, yep, of course, we've got loads to do.' She could feel the weight of her friends' gazes on her, hoping her answer bore a ring of indifference to chase them off the scent.

Lark clapped her hands together, smiling. 'That's wonderful! It looks like you two are on a mission, and I have such a good feeling about it.' She caught Florrie's warning look. 'The bookshop, I mean. It's great that you're going to breathe new life into it, it'll be good for the town.'

TWENTY-SIX

'That was delicious,' said Ed, putting his knife and fork together on his plate. He sat back, stretching his arm out along the settle behind Florrie, disturbing a waft of his cologne, sending a zing of electricity through her. 'I can honestly say that's the best fish and chips I've ever had.'

Jasmine leaned across Lark to get to Stella. 'Bet it's not all he'll be saying that about before too long,' she said under her breath, flicking her eyebrows in Florrie's direction. The pair giggled conspiratorially, much to Florrie's consternation.

She flashed them a warning scowl, hoping Ed hadn't heard. Having him in such close proximity, feeling the warmth of his body, the solid muscles in his thigh, was having a serious effect on her emotions. Her libido, which had been very definitely lack-lustre while she was with Graham and had practically limped along, had surged back to life with a vengeance. Now desire was pulsing through her veins, sending wicked thoughts into her mind. *Woah, calm your jets, woman! Where's this come from?*

She reached for her almost empty wine glass and took a sip, hoping it would take her mind off Ed.

She felt her gaze being drawn to a familiar figure walking over to a table by the window, his hand in the small of the back of a woman he was guiding to a seat. Graham and Bethany. Her shoulders slumped. As if sensing her watching him, he turned and caught her eye. The smug smile he gave came as a surprise, but it fell as soon as his eyes moved along, resting on Ed sitting snuggly beside Florrie and smiling down at her.

Florrie gave a small wave and Graham tipped her a nod, whispering something in Bethany's ear. Bethany snatched a glance over her shoulder, her face burning. She muttered something to him, shaking her head before turning away.

'What the bloody hell is Mr Beige doing here?' Maggie spotted him, her top lip curling. 'I thought he didn't like the Jolly on a Friday night; thought it was "too loud" for him.'

'Graham's here?' Stella looked as shocked as Maggie.

'Yes, but don't turn round!' Florrie said hurriedly, before leaning into Ed who was looking on, puzzled. 'It's my ex and his new girlfriend; they're the ones who've just sat down at the table over there.'

'Oh, right.' He nodded, stealing a look at them.

'He knows full well we come here every Friday; how pathetic of him to bring his new bit of stuff. It's as if he's trying to flaunt her under Florrie's nose. Prat!' said Stella.

'Honestly, it's fine, I'm not bothered.' Florrie raised her palms. 'We parted on good terms, it was all very amicable.' *Well, almost.*

'Eeuw! And why does he think he needs to slobber all over her? Jeez, that's so *gross*. I think I'm going to see my fish and chips again.' Maggie pulled a horrified face as she watched Graham clamp Bethany's face between his hands and kiss her passionately.

'He's what?' said Jasmine, her eyes wide.

'Please, just ignore it,' said Florrie, morbid fascination rendering her unable to do just that. She was surprised at such an overt public display of affection from Graham; he used to tell her how much he abhorred such behaviour, but this little performance was something else. And she couldn't help but feel sorry for Bethany who, judging by how her eyes were bulging, was wholly embarrassed by his actions.

'Oi, you two, get a room,' Lobster Harry called across the bar. 'You're putting me off this jar of winkles, and that takes some bloody doing, I can tell you.' Laughter ran around the room followed by the odd jeer from some of his fishermen friends.

'Woah! Give 'er one!' Ando Taylor had been propping up the bar since late afternoon and was looking the worse for wear. He lurched forward, leering at the pair before being pulled back by Lobster Harry.

The taunts appeared to do the trick and Graham released Bethany from his grasp. The poor girl looked mortified, hanging her head and wiping her mouth with the back of her hand, muttering something under her breath.

'Oh, my God, how cringeworthy was that?' Jasmine turned to Graham and shot him one of her infamous death stares, mouthing, 'Arse,' before she turned back.

Florrie felt Ed wrap his arm around her, pulling her closer to him. 'He's doing it because he knows he's lost someone special.'

Silence hung over the table as Florrie's friends stared at Ed as if telepathically willing him to elaborate. Florrie looked up to see Jasmine and Stella's eyebrows nestling somewhere in their hairline, while Lark was wearing her calm expression that meant lots was bubbling away behind those gentle eyes of hers.

'Explain yourself, Harte,' said Stella. 'Let's hear your theory on why Mr Beige is behaving like a knob.'

'It's because he regrets losing Florrie. He's clearly had time to think since they broke up, and now realises exactly what he's lost,' Ed said. 'He's trying to make her jealous; hoping she'll want him back.'

Florrie felt all eyes on her as a blush rose up her neck, scorching her cheeks and even making her ears burn. She gave an embarrassed laugh. 'I don't know about that; he seems very into Bethany – as we've just witnessed.'

'I wouldn't be so sure.' Ed squeezed Florrie's shoulder as her friends looked on with growing interest. 'Even I have to admit us men behave in the oddest of ways at times, particularly when it comes to women we're attracted to. Though, it's fair to say most blokes are programmed to act like that when we're testosterone-fuelled teenagers and not when we're adults – I'll bet you can probably recall some of the lads at school teasing you, pulling your hair, leaving frogs on your seat, that kind of thing.'

'Steven Wilson. Remember him, Stella?' Jasmine nodded towards her. 'He tortured you for ages.'

'Ughh! How could I forget? He used to think it was hilarious to shove the stinky, filthy socks he'd worn to do cross-country into my PE bag, making my kit smell *absolutely gross*.' She pulled a face at the memory.

'Then we found out he fancied you,' said Florrie, giggling. 'I reckon he was trying to wipe his pheromones all over your gym stuff, marking you as his property.'

'Yeah, because behaving like a skunk's a real turn-on,' Stella said. 'Anyway, I'd really rather not think about that when I'm trying to enjoy myself.'

'I don't think he ever realised he was wasting his time, did he?' Florrie laughed as much at the face Stella was pulling as Steven Wilson's behaviour.

'Let's hope he isn't still using those wooing techniques; it'll have been bad enough him doing it when he was fifteen, but a bloke in his thirties...?' said Maggie, her shoulders shaking with mirth.

'See, your example has proved my theory right; the reason lads behave that way is because we like you, and are under the misconception that sort of thing makes us irresistible to all women,' Ed said.

'Seriously?' said Jasmine with a look of disbelief.

'Thankfully, for the survival of the species, we tend to grow out of it.' His eyes wandered to Graham. 'Well, most of us do.'

'Judging by his behaviour, that memo hasn't got to Graham yet.' Maggie gave a disapproving snort.

'Cheating, two-timing arse,' Jasmine said with a snarl. 'He's got a nerve treating our Florrie that way.'

The corner of Stella's mouth quirked in amusement and she gave a barely visible tip of her head in Florrie's direction before directing her gaze at Ed. 'Well, thank you for enlightening us, Harte. But just make sure you don't mess our friend about or you'll find yourself with a pair of seriously broken balls.'

Florrie tensed, scrunching her eyes up. Did Stella really just say that? *Ground, please open up and devour me whole!*

'I wouldn't dream of it. Florrie's worth way more than that,' he said, his voice gentle as he gave her arm another squeeze.

Oh, my days! What does he mean by that? Florrie felt a nudge from Maggie and four sets of eyes boring into her. Yet again, she found herself blushing a ridiculous shade of beetroot red. She shuffled awkwardly in her seat, not knowing where to look. Rather opportunely, the sound of a fiddle struck up over by the bar, sending a wave of relief washing over her. Its jaunty tune was soon accompanied by the sweet notes of a tin whistle and the gentle beat of a bodhran. There was a "whoop" from the group next to them and people started tapping their feet and drumming their fingers on the tables. Such impromptu music was a regular occurrence at the Jolly, particularly at weekends. But Florrie's mind was busy and it pushed the melody into the background while Ed's words took centre stage. *"Florrie's worth way more than that."*

Holy guacamole, if her mind was swirling before, it had been whipped into one heck of a whirlwind now.

TWENTY-SEVEN

'Can I just sneak out, please? I think Gerty could do with popping outside for a minute,' Florrie said, leaning in closer to Ed to make herself heard above the music.

'Course, no problem. Actually, I wouldn't mind a breath of fresh air, I'll come out with you.' He manoeuvred himself out of the gap between the settle and the table, then pulled his jacket on before freeing Gerty's lead. The Labrador seemed thrilled at the prospect of going for a walk with her new friend.

'Just taking Gerty out for a wee,' Florrie said to the others.

'Ah, is that what we're calling it these days?' said Jasmine, shooting her a cheeky grin.

'Have fun.' Stella winked at her. 'Don't do anything I wouldn't do.'

'Er, is there anything you wouldn't do, Stells?' said Maggie.

Florrie shook her head in despair and followed Ed across the bar, feeling the weight of Graham's gaze on her back.

She was easing her way through the mass of bodies when Ando Taylor loomed up in front of her, swaying precariously. He was looking at her through bleary eyes and a cloud of breath that was so boozy it could strip paint. She'd noticed he'd been getting progressively more lairy as the night went on and had hoped to avoid him on her way out.

'All right, Florrie, babes. Having a good time?' he said, his words slipping and slurring while his right eye appeared to be focused on the tip of his nose. Up close, Florrie noticed he looked older than his years, with deep wrinkles carved into his weather-ravaged skin.

'Er, yes thanks.' She tried to push past him, holding her breath, but he blocked her way.

'Just want you to know, if you need anyone to walk you home, I'm your man.' He released a beer-fuelled belch and smiled.

I'm not so sure about that! She gave a tight smile, still trying not to breathe in. 'I'm fine, thanks.' She doubted very much if he could walk five feet in front of him, never mind all the way up Skitey Bank and through the streets and snickelways to her cottage.

He went to grab her hand. 'How about that Stella friend of yours? She's a right fit bird. Does she need walking home? Or how about Jasmine? I fancy me a bit of feisty wench; a bit of a challenge, like.'

Not hard to guess why you're single, "fit bird" and "feisty wench" indeed! 'Why don't you go and ask them?' She wriggled free of his grip and hurried to the door. Oh to be a fly on the wall if he dared do that!

Outside, darkness had descended, and the Jolly's lights cast a warm glow over the beer garden, spilling over the stone wall to the beach. The smell of woodsmoke swirled downwards from the pub's chimney, lingering on the damp air. The temperature had dropped and there was a chill in the light breeze. Florrie shivered, regretting not grabbing her jacket. She scanned around for Ed, the only sound the lapping of the waves on the shoreline and the muted music coming from the bar. She spotted him by the wall, a tall shadow, looking out into the darkness that was punctuated by a handful of tiny lights from boats far out to sea. Gerty was sniffing the ground by him.

'Hi,' Florrie said when she reached him.

'Hi.' Ed looked down at her and smiled.

'Sorry about Stella.' She scraped a straggle of hair off her face, looking up at him.

He laughed. 'It's fine, no need to apologise; you did warn me after all. And she's only looking out for you; she's a good friend. They all are.'

They started walking slowly along the cobbles, Gerty plodding along in front. 'I know, but I just wish she'd do it in a less forthright way.'

Ed laughed, pausing before he spoke. 'So that was your ex – Graham, did you say his name was?'

Florrie nodded. 'Mm-hm, that was Graham. Though I can promise you, he never behaved like that when we were together; I'd have run a mile if he had.'

'I can well believe that,' Ed said with a chuckle. 'His display was definitely for your benefit. I think he's still in love with you. He hasn't taken his eyes off you since he arrived.'

'Honestly, you've got it wrong. Our relationship had fizzled out by the time we split up, as had any love we had; we were more like friends. He said as much himself.'

Ed nodded, a few moments of quiet passing between them. 'Can I tell you a secret?'

Florrie's heart began to race, where was this going? Was he going to tell her he was still in love with his ex? That he'd changed his mind about extending his stay in Micklewick Bay? She pushed down the ball of nerves that were creeping up inside her. 'Of course.'

'It's a bit embarrassing so I want you to promise not to laugh.'

'I'm sure it's not that bad, but okay, I promise.'

'Well, I've never felt... I mean, I can feel myself fall—'

He was prevented from saying anything further by Ando Taylor who'd left the pub in a hurry. Spotting Florrie, he lunged towards her, crashing into Ed where he proceeded to vomit all over his feet.

'Arghh!' Florrie jumped back as Gerty barked.

'What the fu—' Ed stood rooted to the spot.

'Sorry, mate,' Ando said, gasping as he wiped his mouth with the back of his hand. 'Shit, I needed that.'

'Not so sure I did,' said Ed as he and Florrie looked down at his shoes in disbelief. Gerty growled as Ando staggered past her, heading away from the pub.

'Ed, are you okay?' *And the Stupid Question of the Year Award goes to Florrie Appleton!* Florrie winced as she took in his brown brogues and the bottom of his jeans that were now plastered with the contents of Ando's stomach.

'I can't believe that just happened.' Ed's eyes were glued to the mess. 'I'm going to have to call it a night; there's no way I can go back into the pub like this. Lord knows how I'm going to get past Mrs Tyreman.'

'You could come back to my house, I don't mind; I could put them in the washing machine for you.' She was struggling not to retch at the smell.

Gerty looked on, confused.

Ed shook his head, wrinkling his nose. 'It's okay, I couldn't expect you to do that. I'll rinse my shoes in the sea, then wade in as far as the mess goes and hope it gets the bulk of it off my jeans.' He shook first one leg, then the other. 'Ughh! Feels disgusting.'

'I can imagine.'

'And you can tell that Stella she's a stuck up, snooty cow!' Florrie and Ed turned towards the slurring voice to see Ando walking backwards, pointing theatrically in the direction of the pub. 'And she's got a right filthy mouth on her, and so has that Jasmine as well. Bad tempered cow, she—' Before they had chance to warn him, he fell backwards onto a bench, his feet flying up in the air.

Ed and Florrie looked at one another and burst out laughing, watching as Ando picked himself up and stumbled off into the darkness.

'Well, this isn't quite how I expected the night to end.' Ed's eyes twinkled. 'But, excluding Ando Taylor's intervention, I've had a great time. Your friends are warm and funny and welcoming – and, yes, before you ask, I've included Stella in that.'

Florrie smiled. 'I'm glad you had a good time with us, and Stella hasn't scared you off.'

'No, that was down to a certain drunken skateboarder,' he said regretfully.

'Hmm. He's going to have a sore head tomorrow.'

'Might make him think twice about getting hammered and doing this sort of thing.' Ed lifted his foot off the floor and Gerty sniffed it tentatively before snorting and backing away, making Florrie and Ed chuckle. 'Right, I'd better go and get cleaned up, but I'll pop by the shop tomorrow and give you a hand with the books.' He handed her Gerty's lead.

'That would be great. Though I'm not sure how much we'll get done; Saturday's our busiest day in the shop.'

'Every little helps.' He smiled, bending down and kissing her cheek. 'Thanks again for a great night. See you tomorrow.'

Florrie felt her heart swoop in her chest as his lips brushed her skin. 'See you tomorrow,' she replied. Her whole body was tingling; she could barely string the words together. How was it her heart was ruling her head over someone she'd only known five minutes? Someone who wasn't going to stick around for long. She needed to give herself a serious talking to.

'Bye, Gerty.' He bent and rubbed between the Labrador's ears before smiling and heading onto the beach, pulling a torch from his jacket pocket. Florrie's eyes followed him as she heaved a sigh.

TWENTY-EIGHT

'What's happened?' Florrie frowned. She'd re-joined her friends to see Immy wiping a beer towel over their table in vigorous swirls. Her eyes alighted on the vacuum cleaner and a tub of what appeared to broken glass standing alongside it, suddenly aware the folk music had stopped and people were regarding them with interest.

'Ando-bloody-Taylor, that's what,' said Jasmine, her face pinched in the way it did when she was annoyed.

'I'm nearly done, hon, then you can sit back down,' said Immy, giving the table one last going over. 'And it should be safe for Gerty's paws; I've given everywhere a thorough vacuuming.'

'Thanks for sorting it out so quickly, Immy,' said Maggie.

'Yes, thank you, Immy, you're a star,' said Lark.

'So what's Ando Taylor been doing?' asked Florrie when Immy had left, slipping in beside Maggie, feeling a hint of dampness seeping into her trousers.

'Behaving like a dick, that's what,' said Jasmine.

'My jeans are soaking thanks to him, and I stink of wine.' Stella wiped her hands over her thighs. 'Would you believe he came over here, or rather, he *staggered* over here, and proceeded to tell me he was going to take me home and show me a good time?'

Florrie heard Maggie stifle a giggle beside her. 'Sorry I'm laughing, but your face was a picture, Stells.'

Florrie bit down on a grin; she could imagine Stella's expression. If Jasmine was famous for her death stares, then Stella was famous for her icy glares that could wither a man to dust.

'Not as much of a picture as his when Stella told him to eff-off,' said Lark.

'Then he turned his attention to me, and announced he was going warm me up in bed which, apparently, only *he* knew how to do.' Jasmine still looked put out. 'And then he ended up sprawling over the table, sending glasses and everything flying; there was wine every-bloody-where.'

'Which is what you caught the tail-end of,' said Lark, turning to Florrie, her pale-blonde brows drawing together. 'Where's Ed?'

'He had to go back to the bed-and-breakfast, which I'll explain about after I've fessed up.' She scrunched her face up.

'Fessed up about what?' asked Stella.

'Ah, well, I think I might be partly responsible for the unwanted attention you got from Ando,' said Florrie, nibbling on her bottom lip before explaining.

'There's only one person responsible for his prattish behaviour, and that's him,' said Jasmine.

'Agreed,' said Maggie.

'It seems Ando's got a lot of people to apologise to tomorrow.' Florrie went on to share what had happened, her friends listening, uttering sounds of disgust and disbelief.

'Poor Ed; sounds like we got off lightly, girls. I'd rather have wine chucked over me than puke, any day.' Maggie patted her soggy jumper.

Someone threw a log on the fire, sending sparks shooting up the chimney and a sweet blast of woodsmoke into the room. A moment later, the fiddle struck up again just as Tara arrived at the table with a fresh bottle of wine and five glasses. 'Here you go, ladies, let's hope you get to drink this one.'

Stella filled the glasses and passed them round.

'Cheers to Friday nights, lasses,' said Jasmine.

'Cheers!' they said in unison. Florrie's mind reached back, wondering what secret Ed had been about to share with her before Ando bulldozed into their moment. She glanced up, aware of Graham's eyes on her once more. His mouth was set in a grim line, his fingers drumming slowly on the table. Beside him, Bethany's eyes were downcast as she worried a fingernail, her body ever-so-slightly turned away from him.

'So, Florrie,' Stella paused, taking a sip of her wine, a mischievous glimmer in her eyes as she peered over her glass, 'what's going on between you and Harte? And don't deny it, we all felt the sexual chemistry sizzling between you.'

Jasmine sat back, an amused smile dancing on her lips. 'We sure did; it was so hot I thought the table was going to catch fire.'

'That's a fine line in corny you've got going on there, Jazz.' Lark feigned an "I'm impressed" expression.

'I do my best.' Jasmine chuckled.

Florrie took a sideways look at Maggie to see her friend grinning at her; it was clear that denying her feelings to her oldest friends would be futile. She took a glug of wine, giving a quick sweep of the room to make sure no one was listening. She spoke softly. 'I think I like him; I mean *really* like him. And I know it's ridiculously sudden, and out of the blue, and I've only known him a few days.' She held up her palms and stole a glance up at the four smiling faces. 'Don't worry, it sounds as bonkers to me as it does to you. And I know I shouldn't be feeling this way when I'm still grieving for Mr H, but blimey, the way I feel when I'm around Ed. I get butter-flies doing crazy things in my stomach and my knees turn to jelly like the worst possible teenage cliché, but I've honestly never felt anything like this before. There's no rational explanation for it.' Her eyes were shining, her cheeks flushed. The wine she'd consumed over the course of the evening had quashed her usually reserved nature, allowing her bolder side to venture out. It was the first time she'd properly acknowledged her feelings for Ed, the first time she'd actually put them into words. It thrilled and scared her in equal measure. She looked up to see her friends beaming at her, affection glowing in their eyes.

'Ahh, Florrie, that's lovely, chick.' Maggie pulled her into a hug and kissed her noisily on the cheek.

'And it's pretty obvious to us he feels the same way about you,' said Jasmine. 'I wish someone would look at me the way he was looking at you tonight – before he was puked on, that is.' They all laughed at that, but Florrie's heart squeezed for her friend who'd been on her own too long.

Across the table, Lark was wearing one of her mysterious expressions. 'There's a totally rational explanation for it, it's called fate, and it's best not to argue with her, Florrie. She has a plan for us all and I always find it's best to go with the flow; there's no point fighting the inevitable, is there? And since he arrived your aura's been way brighter.'

'Wise words, petal.' Jasmine gave Lark a friendly nudge with her elbow. 'If that's what Lark thinks, it must be right. You should listen to her, Florrie.'

'When have you ever known Lark to be wrong?' asked Maggie.

Florrie met her friend's eyes, despite her smile, there was a seriousness in them. 'Erm, that would be never.' She could feel her heart thudding in her chest. 'But here's the thing, he's already told me he doesn't think the bookshop and Micklewick Bay are for him; there's a pretty good chance he won't hang around. He's only extended his stay for a short while, and there's a strong chance he won't come back. And then there's the fact that the furthest thing from my mind is getting involved in another relationship; I'm just not ready.'

'You reckon?' said Jasmine, unconvinced.

'Doesn't mean you should rule out a bit of no-strings fun.' Stella gave her a pointed look. 'It'd do you the world of good after putting up with Mr Beige over there.'

Florrie rolled her eyes, a hint of a smile tugging at her mouth.

'Like I said, trust in fate, flower.'

Lark's words sent a cocktail of emotions rushing through her, ranging from excitement to trepidation and everything in between. Could she do that? *Should* she do that? With so many thoughts ricocheting around her head, Florrie didn't know what to think.

It seemed so unfair that the person who'd stirred such deep feelings inside her was the last person she should allow herself to fall for. It shocked her even to think he'd had this effect on her in such a short space of time; she'd never experienced the like of it before. But to open her heart, even the slightest crack, would be exposing it to the risk of being hurt. And Florrie wasn't sure it was one she was prepared to take. To her mind, there were too many obstacles in their way. The fact that he'd already aired his doubts about the bookshop and making Micklewick Bay his home were two glaringly obvious ones that were potentially insurmountable. Added to that, she'd already told herself to pull up the drawbridge as far as matters of the heart were concerned; there was no room in her life for a man for the foreseeable future. Taking all of this into account, Florrie couldn't deny she'd be mad to let herself fall in love with Ed Harte. But a little voice at the back of her mind told her it was probably already too late.

* * *

As the friends were making their way across the bar and heading for the door, Florrie heard a familiar voice behind her. She turned to see Graham. He was wearing a sanctimonious expression, his mouth pinched tighter than a cat's bottom. She had a struggle on not to laugh. He stepped towards her and she instinctively stepped back.

'You seem to have moved on quickly,' he said in a disapproving tone.

'What do you mean?' She paused buttoning up her coat.

He gave a mocking snigger. 'Well, how about the fact we've only just broken up and you're gadding about with another man.'

'I haven't been *gadding about* with anyone!'

Graham snorted and Florrie felt her hackles rise. 'And the way he's been looking at you and pawing you all night, makes me wonder just how long it's been going on. They're hardly the actions of someone you've just met.'

'You all right, Florrie?' asked Stella, heading back over to her.

'Fine thanks, Stells. Won't be a minute.'

'Okay, see you outside.' Stella flicked her long hair out of her jacket and made for the door, flashing Graham an icy glare.

Florrie shifted her eyes back to Graham. She didn't feel the need to explain Ed's identity, nor her feelings for him; it was none of her ex's business. 'Listen, Graham, I'm not with anyone. I don't want to be with anyone; I'm quite enjoying being on my own actually. And let's not forget, you were seeing Bethany before we broke up.'

'That's not strictly true, I... we...'

'I think we both know it is true, so if you don't mind, my friends are waiting for me outside; it's cold.' She turned to leave, catching Bethany watching them.

'Wait!' Graham grabbed her arm. 'Look, I'll be perfectly straight, Flo, I'm not so sure we made the right decision, you and me. Don't you think we were a bit hasty calling time on our relationship? After all, we were good together; never argued.' He shrugged and gave her, if she wasn't mistaken, a flirtatious smile, making her recoil inwardly. 'I seriously think we should consider giving it another go.'

Flo! Arghh! Did he never learn? Florrie's eyes locked on his, annoyance curdling in her gut. Had he always been so condescending? Yes, she thought, he bloody-well had been, but she'd just chosen to turn a blind eye to it. She took a fortifying breath. 'That's just the thing, see, Graham, we never argued because there was no passion, no fireworks, no oomph. Not even a little spark.' She glanced over at Bethany who was still watching them, feeling a flicker of pity for her. 'And what about Bethany in all of this? You seemed pretty keen on her when you first arrived here tonight; looked like you were trying to eat her face off.' She knew he'd hate that expression.

He flinched.

'No, Graham, I'm not interested in us getting back together, and do you know what really sealed our fate?'

'What?'

She stepped aside to allow a couple of customers pass, waiting a moment until they were out of earshot. 'Knowing Mr H had... passed away,' Florrie still couldn't bring herself to use the word "died", '...you didn't even pick up the phone. You knew he was like a grandfather to me, that his loss would hit me hard.'

'You have your family and friends; I knew you'd be okay. And you seem all right to me; laughing and joking with *that group* all night.'

Florrie felt her grief swim to the surface, tears prickling her eyes. 'It's called trying to switch off; move forward. I was devastated. I still am. I was the one who found him. How awful do you think that was?'

Before he had a chance to answer, Bethany appeared beside

them, pushing her arms into her coat, a tight expression on her pretty face. 'I'm going home, Graham.'

'Wait, Beth! I'm just coming!' The pleading look in his eyes sickened Florrie.

'No thanks, I'd rather be on my own.' She turned to face Florrie, resting a hand on her arm. 'I was really sorry to hear about Mr H, he was a lovely man and I know you thought a lot about him.' She gave a small smile. 'Bye, Florrie.'

'Bye, Bethany, and thank you.' She watched her hurry out of the pub, Graham in hot pursuit, calling after her.

Florrie heaved a sigh. What a night it had turned out to be.

TWENTY-NINE

Florrie was half-tuned into a conversation Hayley was having with a customer who was quizzing her about the rumour Jack Playforth was in town and booked to give a reading at the bookshop. She was checking through the post at the back of the shop, sorting the bumf from what was important, her mind drifting off to the events of the previous evening. Already that morning there had been several enquiries about the poet. Much as this had thrilled Florrie, it had sent nerves scurrying around her stomach, reminding her of just how much needed to be done to make the place ready for the event. Nate, who had a shop selling upcycled furniture along Endeavour Road – and a huge soft spot for Lark – had just taken delivery of forty wooden chairs which Florrie had asked him to reserve for the bookshop; they'd be perfect for the event and one less thing to worry about.

The kettle had just boiled and Florrie was throwing teabags into the pot when the bell above the shop door jangled and she heard Ed's voice. From his tone he was greeting Gerty.

Her heart flipped as she walked towards him, his eyes meeting hers. 'Anyone would think you knew I was making tea.' Florrie beamed up at him and his face broke into a wide smile. He bent to fuss Gerty some more, making her tail bash against the counter.

'I like to think it's a skill I've honed to perfection over the years.' He stood up, brushing his fringe back off his face.

'How did you manage last night, after Ando...?' she asked, grimacing at the memory.

'Ooh, yes, Florrie told me about that; talk about gross.' Hayley pulled a face, making Ed guffaw with laughter.

'I managed to get cleaned up a bit before I got back to the bed-and-breakfast, though I did get a suspicious look from Mrs Tyreman. But I'm afraid my shoes'll need an airing for a couple of days before I can wear them again.'

'Eeuw!' Hayley's face crumpled some more.

'Thank goodness you had something to change into,' said Florrie. 'And, like I said last night, you're welcome to use my washing machine for your jeans and anything else you need washing.' She resisted mentioning the dormant washing machine at his grandfather's flat for fear he'd think she was pushing him to stay there. And, in truth, the thought felt odd to her.

'Thanks, I might take you up on that offer.'

Florrie was suddenly aware of Hayley listening with interest. It triggered a little twinge of awkwardness. 'Right, Hayley, I hope you don't mind, but we're going to crack straight on with the storeroom. I'm starting to feel a bit panicky about how much work there actually is through there.'

'Go for it!' The young girl beamed.

Ed nodded, rubbing his hands together. 'Yep, let's get started.'

'Great, I'll go finish making tea and I'll meet you in there.' Florrie's heart lilted at his smile.

* * *

'Ooh, I wonder what's in here?' Florrie lifted a handful of books down from the shelf to find an old wooden box stuffed at the back. Roughly the size of an A4 notebook and no more than three inches deep, it had tiny brass hinges and a dull brass clasp. Wedged between the wall and the bookshelf, it was almost as if it had been deliberately hidden away.

She blew years'-worth of dust off its surface before giving it a quick wipe over with her cloth. She gave it a gentle shake as she headed over to the desk; the resultant rustle inside suggested its contents were paper. Ed joined her and she handed it to him. 'There you go. I think it's only right that you should open it just in case it contains personal Harte family details.'

'Oh, right...' He seemed surprised at her suggestion. 'I really don't mind you opening it; I'm sure my grandparents had nothing to hide. I can't see them harbouring any dreadful secrets somehow, can you?' He smiled down at her, his eyes warm.

'Hmm. Still, something makes me feel you should be the first to open it.' She pressed it into his hands.

'Okay, if you insist.'

Florrie watched as he set the box on the desk, carefully lifting its lid which opened stiffly. She peered over his arm to see a clutch of letters inside, yellow with age and bound together by a pale blue ribbon. The uppermost envelope bore neat, even handwriting and a stamp Florrie didn't recognise. Beneath them, she could make out a stash of loose papers.

Excitement rippled through her as Ed lifted the letters out, handing them to her. 'Can you untie these? I'm hopeless with this sort of thing and don't want to cause any unnecessary damage.'

'Oh, yes, of course.' She took them from him, and lay them

down on the desk, very gently loosening the knot. She noted the envelope on top bore a Harrogate postmark and was addressed "Care of Mr and Mrs Harte". 'There, done.' She stood back and Ed picked up the first letter, easing the paper ever-so-gently out of its envelope. Florrie moved closer, momentarily distracted by the rhythm of his breathing. That, together with the clean, crisp aroma she'd come to associate with him, set her pulse racing. She made a concerted effort to steady herself, focussing on the cursive handwriting on the page in his hand. From the folds and creases, it had obviously been read a great many times.

'What does it say?' she asked.

Ed frowned. 'I think it might be a love letter.'

A love letter addressed to Mr and Mrs H? She glanced up at him, noticing how red his face had become. In a flash, his words came back to her, "being severely dyslexic meant reading was a chore". She could've kicked herself for putting him in this position. 'Ooh, a love letter. How romantic. May I?' She held out her hand and he placed the piece of paper in it.

'It seems to be an update, or a catch-up if you like, on the welfare of a child called Tommy,' she said. 'And it's signed L and C; how odd they didn't use their full names.' Florrie looked across at him, frowning. 'I don't suppose Tommy or "L" and "C" ring any bells, do they?'

Ed scratched his head. 'Not even remotely. There was this in the envelope too; I wonder if this is Tommy?' He handed her a black and white photograph of a little boy aged, she guessed, around four-years-old. The child was beaming as he played with a ball in a garden. From the style of the youngster's clothing and the way his hair was cut, Florrie thought it was probably taken in the sixties or early seventies; she'd seen photos of her dad as a young boy looking similar.

'Yes, I reckon you're right,' she said. 'And you really have no idea who it could be?'

'Nope, none. I've never heard of anyone with links to our

family called Tommy – not that I heard many names mentioned over the years – but you know how secretive people can be when it comes to family matters – especially mine.'

Florrie rubbed her hand across her chin. 'How about relatives over Harrogate way?'

'None that I can recall.'

They went through more of the letters, with Florrie reading aloud. Each one had the same theme, saying how quickly the child was growing, sharing details of how he was doing at school, the academic prizes he'd won. There was even one telling of how he'd broken his arm falling from a tree. The last, sent on the fifth of August nineteen-seventy-two, contained a colour photograph of the little boy on his seventh birthday. He was stretched out in a hammock in a sunny garden, his hair an unruly shock of curls, a book in his hand and a look of concentration etched on his face. Florrie guessed he'd been unaware he was being photographed, he looked so engrossed in his reading.

'This is a real mystery to me,' Ed said, scrutinizing the last photo more closely. 'But I have to admit, there's something vaguely familiar about Tommy in this one.'

'Really?' Florrie took another look at it. 'I know what you mean, but I'm not sure if it's because we're so desperate to see something familiar, we're trying to convince ourselves of something that isn't there.'

'Yeah, you could be right.' He placed the photograph back on the desk.

The documents beneath the letter didn't make much sense until the final one which had a more formal appearance. It was drafted on thick, cream paper, the sort of which was used for legal documents. It had been typed, the wording formal and legal-sounding.

'Oh, my God!' Florrie clapped her hand to her mouth, her eyes growing wider as she read down the page, finally alighting on a name she knew so well; the signature she'd seen so many times. Her eyes darted over to Ed, her heart racing.

'What's the matter? Is it bad?'

Florrie took a moment to reply, wanting to be sure she'd read things right. She held her breath, marshalling her thoughts. 'Ed, you're not going to believe this.'

THIRTY

'Shit!' Ed said when Florrie finished reading the document aloud.

'Couldn't have put it better myself.' This was hard to take in.

'But why would my grandparents be involved in something like this?' he asked, his brow furrowed. 'And why would the letters be sent here, to the bookshop? It doesn't make sense.'

Florrie nibbled on her bottom lip, attempting to fathom out the logic behind it all. 'Well – and this is just conjecture – it looks to me as if the person who wrote the letters maybe didn't know the address to send them to, so forwarded them to your grandparents in the hope they'd eventually get to the right place.'

'Sounds plausible.' Ed rubbed his chin, staring at the pile of letters on the desk. 'And do you think my grandparents passed them on? I mean, I can't understand why they're still here.'

'Mr and Mrs H were good people, I can't imagine them hiding anyone's mail for a minute; that really wasn't their style. And judging by how crumpled the letters are, it kind of gives the impression they've been read many times over.' Florrie had noted several spots on the letters where the words had run, as if a tear had fallen onto the page. It had touched her heart.

Ed nodded slowly. 'Good point.'

'Actually, I think we should get these put back in the box in case Hayley comes through, not that I don't trust her or anything, it's just with them containing such sensitive information, I'd feel more comfortable if they were out of sight.'

'Of course, I agree. Why don't I pop them up on that high shelf over there for now? If I push the box right to the back, no one will be able to see it.'

Florrie's eyes followed to where he was pointing. 'Good idea. We can move it upstairs with everything else later.' She handed the letters to him, puffing out her cheeks and blowing out her breath. 'Talk about a Pandora's box.'

'Yeah, but I'd like to think they'd bring happiness rather than a load of trouble.'

'Me too.' But Florrie wasn't so sure.

Once they were safely out of sight, Ed flopped down onto a chair. 'So, what do you think we should do about them?' Gerty immediately jumped up from where she'd been dozing and ran over to him, resting her head on his lap and nudging his hand. 'Hello, Gerty-Girl.' He smoothed his hand over her head.

Florrie sat down on the seat beside him, her mind spinning with it all. 'I honestly don't know, but I think we need to give it some serious thought before we do anything at all, just in case the person in question isn't aware of their existence. Imagine the hurt that would cause.' It crossed her mind they might be better off doing nothing than run the risk of causing any further heartbreak.

Ed winced. 'Doesn't bear thinking about.'

The sound of the bell jingling several times in quick succession drew her out of her thoughts. She pushed herself up. 'I'd better go and see if Hayley needs a hand, sounds like there's a bit of a rush on all of a sudden.'

'Sure. Shall I stick the kettle on? Don't know about you, but I could do with a cup of tea.'

'Good idea. Maybe slosh some whisky in mine,' she said, giving a small laugh as she headed towards the door.

'I'll make it a double.' He grinned.

Pushing their recent discovery to the back of her mind, Florrie was pleasantly surprised to see Maggie standing at the counter, a familiar pop of colour in her sunshine yellow jacket, a bright green scarf tied around her head, keeping her curls off her face. 'Hi, Mags, what brings you here this morning?' She beamed at her friend.

'Hi, Florrie, Bear asked me to check if next Thursday suits to start painting the windows and since I was in town, I thought I might as well pop in and do it in person. He says we're forecast a dry week weatherwise, so it'd be perfect timing.'

Bear's request was a welcome reminder; up to that moment, Florrie had put all thoughts of the windows out of her mind. She recalled with a jolt the sign-writer had been booked for the following Tuesday. She'd arranged it when Mr H was still here. It seemed a life-time ago now. 'Sounds good to me.' She looked across at Ed, who'd now joined them. He took a moment to register she was awaiting his input.

'Oh, yeah, sounds good to me too. I like the idea of getting the outside looking smart before Jack Playforth's reading; we want to create the right impression, even if most of the audience will be locals and know what the bookshop's like. Actually, I'm heading over to Prince's DIY shop this afternoon to pick up some paint for the storeroom, why don't I get the paint for the woodwork then?'

'Save yourself the trip, Ed. Bear's got an account with them; he can get it. We're keen to support local businesses as much as possible so he buys all his stuff there and they give him a special rate. Text me the colour and brand and I'll pass it on to him,' said Maggie.

'That's really kind, thanks, Mags, I'll do it right away,' said Florrie. 'We're hoping to make a start this weekend; it'll give us an extra day with us being closed for Bank Holiday Monday.'

'Couldn't be better timed actually, we'll be moving the clutter and books up to the flat by the end of tomorrow, then we can pull the carpet up and have a good clean round in readiness for painting,' said Ed.

'Wowzers! You two are on a mission.' Maggie looked impressed. 'Give me a ring when you're ready to move the carpet, Bear and me can give you a hand. We can drop the paint off then, and he can chuck the carpet in the back of his van and take it to the recycling centre.'

Florrie hadn't even got as far as thinking about what they'd do with the old carpet. 'You're a star, thanks, Maggie.' She squeezed the top of her friend's arm.

They were distracted by the shrill ringing of Ed's mobile. He reached for his back pocket, pulling his phone out, his expression darkening as he looked at the screen. 'I'd better take this,' he said, fixing his smile back in place. 'Nice to see you again, Maggie.'

'You too, Ed.' She and Florrie watched as he headed for the door.

Florrie brushed away her concerns about the identity of Ed's caller, though she felt sure it was the same one who'd made his smile drop the previous day. 'Have you got time for a cuppa?' she asked her friend.

Maggie shook her head, her curls bouncing. 'Sadly, no. I need to head back to finish the teddy-bear I've been making for Samantha Carter; she's coming to collect it on Tuesday morning.' Maggie made soft toys out of vintage fabrics and recycled jumpers, with a preference for cashmere, for which she was building a good reputation.

'No worries.' Florrie smiled, detecting the subtle change in her friend's demeanour. The prospect of welcoming a heavily pregnant Samantha to her home wouldn't be easy for her.

'I'd offer to help out too, but my mum found a glass of smoothie that had gone mouldy in my bedroom and made me promise to tidy it tomorrow – or "muck it out" as she put it,' said Hayley.

'Nice.' Florrie caught Maggie's eye and the pair exchanged a knowing smile.

'Don't worry, chick, we've all been there. I can remember my mum threatening to put all the stuff from my bedroom floor into binbags and take them to the tip.' Maggie chuckled at the memory, hitching her bag higher on her shoulder. 'And on that note, I'd best be off. Don't forget to text me the paint details.'

'I won't. Bye, Mags.'

'Yep, see you tomorrow.' She turned to Hayley. 'And good luck with your bedroom,' she said with a wink.

'Thanks.' Hayley flashed her a wide smile.

'Why don't you take your break now, Hayley?' Florrie asked when the door closed behind Maggie. From the window, she could see Ed, he'd crossed to the opposite side of the road and was pacing back and forth.

'Sure.' Hayley followed Florrie's gaze. 'He's really nice, isn't he?'

'Who?'

'Ed.' She beamed a smile. 'Mr H would be buzzing to think he'd come to work here, following in his footsteps.'

The thought of Mr H "buzzing", as the young girl put it, made Florrie chuckle. 'Yes, Hayley, I think he probably would.' She didn't like to say it was very likely Ed wouldn't be here for long.

THIRTY-ONE

The afternoon flew by with Florrie and Ed completing the dusting and cataloguing of the old books. He hadn't mentioned his phone call, and Florrie hadn't thought it right to ask about it, despite the times she'd caught him wearing a frown, his mind obviously elsewhere. Her thoughts veered from it being his parents, railing about the bookshop, to his ex, Luella. She tortured herself, her stomach churning, thinking of them talking about getting back together, of Ed returning to London.

'That's the last of them,' he said, wiping his brow with the back of his hand, leaving a grubby smear. He checked his watch. 'It's only four o'clock; how about I start taking some of them up to the flat?'

His question caught Florrie off-guard, triggering a wave of anxiety. She hadn't been in the flat since the day Mr H had died. An image of him sitting in his chair flashed through her mind and she felt the sudden threat of tears. She steadied herself; she'd have to face it at some point. After all, they'd discussed storing the books and clutter in the spare bedroom while they painted the storeroom, so she'd known they'd be venturing up there soon, but she'd told herself she'd have time to prepare herself. Which, at this very moment, she hadn't.

'Oh, erm, yes, okay.' She hoped her voice sounded less wobbly to Ed's ears than it did to hers.

He turned from the books to her, his eyebrows knitting together. 'Are you okay?'

She nodded, sorrow clogging her throat. 'Yes,' she said in a barely discernible whisper. She clenched her jaw, hoping to regain a modicum of control over her emotions.

In an instant, Ed was striding over to her. Towering above her tiny frame, he enveloped her in his arms, smoothing her hair with his hand. 'Oh, Florrie, I didn't mean to upset you. I should've realised it would bring back horrible memories of that day. We can do it another time, or find somewhere else in the shop, maybe.'

Gerty, suddenly aware of Florrie's distress, jumped up and ran over to her, pressing her head against her leg.

'It's all right, Gerty.' Ed smiled down at the Labrador.

With her head resting against the warmth of his chest, hearing the strong beat of his heart, Florrie was unable to stop her tears from flowing. 'I'm sorry, I shouldn't be the one who's crying; he was your grandfather. I don't mean to be a wuss,' she said, her words punctuated by sobs.

'Hey, there's no need to apologise. You loved him just as much as if he was your grandfather; it's obvious in the way you talk about him, and I know how much he adored you.' He hugged her closer to him. 'And you were the one who found him. I can't imagine what that must've been like.'

Hearing the emotion in Ed's voice, Florrie reluctantly pulled her head away from his chest to look up at him. He gave her a small smile, his eyes wet with tears. 'Are *you* okay?' she asked, seeing her sorrow mirrored in his face.

'I'm fine.' He sniffed, his hands warm on her back. 'It's early days; the loss is still raw.'

She nodded. 'It is. It just creeps up on you sometimes, doesn't it?'

She felt his chest rise as he drew in a deep breath. 'It does.' He paused for a moment, searching her face. 'But being here with you, somehow makes everythi—'

'Florrie, there's someone here... Oh!'

They turned to see Hayley standing in the doorway, her mouth hanging open, her eyes shining. 'Sorry, I didn't mean to interrupt you.'

Ed released Florrie from his embrace. She pushed her fingers under her glasses and swiped her tears away, feeling suddenly chilly and adrift without his arms around her. 'It's okay, you didn't. I just got a bit upset about Mr H; Ed was comforting me.' What had he been about to say? she wondered, inwardly cursing Hayley's timing.

Ed cleared his throat and took a step backwards. 'We were talking about taking the books and stuff up to the flat and it just got a bit... you know?' He shrugged by way of explanation.

'Oh, right.' Hayley's face dropped; she understood. 'I'm really sorry to interrupt, it's just Mr Pugh's asking when we can expect delivery of the book he ordered. He thought it would be in today, but I can't find it in the usual places.'

'I'll come and have a word. I don't think it was due today, but my mind's been all over the place, so I could be wrong.' She looked up at Ed. 'I'll just be a minute.'

By the time Florrie had spoken to Mr Pugh and helped Hayley with a brace of other customers, she was feeling much brighter when she re-joined Ed in the storeroom. She'd given herself a talking to and decided the sooner they got the books moved, the better. Tackling some of it today would mean she wouldn't have to spend a sleepless night fretting about it.

'You sure you're up to it?' Ed asked when she told him.

'Positive. Come on, let's make a start.' She pulled a key out of her pocket and went to unlock the door at the very back of the shop where another set of stairs led to the flat above, her heart thumping as she did so.

She stood back, letting Ed go first, doing her best to ignore the feeling of dread that was pooling in her stomach. Gerty watched them, surprising Florrie by not following. Evidently, even poor old Gerty didn't relish a reminder of that awful Monday morning.

Upstairs, Florrie was gripped by how empty and hollow the place felt, not to mention cold. She used to love bounding up the stairs of a morning, the sight of Mr H sitting at the kitchen table, his eyes shining happily when she walked through the door, the delicious aroma of toast mingling with woodsmoke from the pot-bellied stove. How she used to relish their chats over breakfast, him reading her snippets from the newspaper, the pair of them having a good old chuckle over them. She recalled him hooting with laughter over a headline one particular morning, his glasses slipping down his nose with mirth, tears running down his ruddy cheeks. 'Oh, Florrie, my dear, listen to this one: "Man Shoved in Manure!" Can you believe that's the main news in and around Micklewick Bay? What a little backwater it is we live in. "Man shoved in manure" indeed.' He hadn't been able to speak for laughing for a good five minutes afterwards and nor had Florrie, so infectious was his laugh. She smiled fondly at the memory.

She hurried past the living room, grateful that the door had been pulled shut, and joined Ed in the spare bedroom. He was glancing around it, hands on hips. It was a bright room, painted a mood-lifting shade of light-blue, with a large window that overlooked the square. It was furnished with a nineteen-forties bedroom suite. A cumbersome, dark wood wardrobe took up a huge amount of wall space at one end, a double bed with a patchwork quilt in shades of blue thrown over it sat opposite, while a three-mirrored dressing table was set to the left of the window, and a chest of drawers to the right of the door.

Ed looked across at her. 'You okay now?'

'Fine, thanks.' She smiled up at him.

It was the first time Florrie had been in this room and she looked around, assessing the best place for the books; she was determined not to let her mind venture over to sadder subjects, much as it was doing its best to pull her thoughts that way. 'What do you think if we move that chest of drawers to the other side of the room? It should make it easy for us to line the books up against the wall.'

'Makes sense.'

She nodded, turning her attention to the window once more, watching a young mum battling to fasten a toddler into a pushchair across the road, the child wriggling, arms flailing until, finally, the woman was successful and strode off looking harassed. 'Have you given any thought to where you're going to stay while you're here?' She'd been reluctant to ask, but here, in the flat, she found the words slipping out.

Ed scratched his head. 'Erm, I'd actually wondered about staying here. How would you feel about that?'

She tilted her face to him. 'It would make sense, as long as you wouldn't mind... well, you know...'

He nodded. 'Yeah, I'd thought about that, but I'm fine with it. There's a nice atmosphere up here. Admittedly it's cold without the heating being on, but it feels welcoming and homely.'

He was right, the kindness and loving personalities of Mr and Mrs H were still very much present up here. 'I agree, and once you get the heating back on and the little stove lit, it won't take long before it's cosy again.'

'True.'

'Your grandad's keys are still on the hook at the top of the stairs; I meant to tell you before.'

'Thanks, Florrie, remind me to grab them when we're finished for the day.' He gave a small smile and put his arm around her, giving her a squeeze, the simple gesture chasing away the sadness that lurked in her chest, replacing it with a pulse of happiness.

* * *

Before Florrie had time to think about it, it was five o'clock and Hayley had locked the shop door and turned the sign to closed.

Florrie smiled, handing her young employee an envelope containing her week's wages as she did every Saturday. 'There you go, Hayley, we've included a little bonus.' Mr and Mrs H used to do the same for Florrie from time to time, and she still remembered the boost their token of appreciation had given her.

'Thanks, but there's really no need.' Hayley looked surprised.

'Of course there is, we wouldn't have got as much done without you.' She didn't want to run the risk of Hayley feeling taken for granted; she was an asset to the bookshop and well-liked by their customers. Florrie was very fond of her too. 'And while I remember, when things get sorted, would you prefer us to transfer your wages into your bank account, or are you happy getting them in cash?' Mr H had been old school as far as wages were concerned and preferred to deal with physical money.

'Erm.' Hayley pressed her lips together as she thought. 'I think I'd prefer them to go into my bank account, save me having to pay them in myself, or spend them before they even get there,' she said with a hoot of laughter. 'Plus, I mostly use my debit card, so it makes sense.'

'Okay, I'll get your bank details off you as soon as Mr Cuthbert gives us the go ahead. In the meantime, have a great night tonight.'

'Thanks, will do. You too,' she said with a mischievous glint in her eye. 'Say goodbye to Ed for me.'

Hayley had just left when Ed came back into the bookshop. 'There, that's the last of them; the books and stuff are all up in the flat now.' His face was flushed from his many journeys up and down the stairs, his floppy fringe dishevelled. Florrie felt her stomach loop-the-loop as she was taken by the sudden urge to run her fingers through it.

'Wow, that's great, you've done loads.'

Ed grinned. 'And so have you. Don't suppose I could tempt you to join me for dinner tonight, could I? Only, I've booked a table at Oscar's Bistro – they rather luckily had a last-minute cancellation. There's no pressure, I'll totally understand if you don't fancy it. I just think we've earnt ourselves a treat.'

Florrie felt a thrill run through her at the thought of spending another evening in Ed's company, not that she wanted him to know that. 'Oh, I'd love to! I can't remember the last time I had a meal there,' she said, failing to rein in her enthusiasm as much as she would have liked.

'Great.' He beamed at her. 'How about I pick you up around quarter-to-seven? I booked the table for quarter-past, so that should give us the chance to have a leisurely walk into town from your place.'

'You don't have to come out of your way to pick me up, I'm happy to meet you there.'

'I insist. I mean, I'd like to, if that's okay with you?' His eyes searched hers.

Inside, her stomach was fizzing. Looking up at Ed now, there wasn't the slightest trace of the obnoxious person she'd expected him to be. Instead, looking back at her was a kind-hearted, considerate man with the softest dark-blue eyes, who was doing funny things with her heart. Her smile widened. 'It's okay with me.' He gave her a heart-melting smile and she felt colour rise in her cheeks. Again. Watch yourself, said a little voice, you're going to get your fingers burnt. But it was getting more difficult to take heed of its warnings.

THIRTY-TWO

Florrie had raced home, puffing and panting, Gerty enjoying the pace as the pair trotted along the top prom.

She was still in her dressing-gown, straightening her hair when her mum arrived just before six-thirty, knocking before opening the front door with her key. 'S'just me, Florrie, sweetheart.' Paula's voice drifted upstairs. Florrie heard Gertie race down the hallway, followed by her mum's friendly tones as she greeted her.

'Hi, Mum, I'll be down in two ticks. Make yourself comfy.'

'Thanks, lovey.' The sound of her mum heading down to the kitchen followed, chatting to Gerty as she went.

Not really one for make-up, Florrie, gave her dark lashes a quick sweep of mascara, completing her eyes with a flick of eyeliner, finishing with a light dusting of blusher over her cheeks.

She slipped her dress off its hanger, the silk cool and smooth beneath her fingers. It had a Mandarin-style collar and fabric-covered buttons that ran down to the small of her back. She'd had it a while now, but it was a firm favourite and always felt good to wear. Florrie loved the contrast of the exotic-coloured flowers against the shiny black background. She teamed it with black leggings and a pair of black Mary-Janes with a three-inch-heel, giving it a less formal appearance, which would suit the bistro perfectly.

Before heading downstairs, she fixed a slide with a silk red rose to the side of her hair just above her ear, then added a slick of claret lipstick to her lips. She checked the time on her watch before taking one last look in the mirror. Her pulse-rate quickened; Ed would be here any minute.

'Thanks for this, Mum.' Florrie walked into the kitchen where Paula was sitting at the table, flicking through a magazine.

Paula looked up. 'You're very welco... oh, lovey, you look absolutely beautiful!' She stood up and walked over to her daughter, pulling her into a hug.

'Thanks, Mum. It's the dress.'

Paula stood back, her hands on Florrie's shoulders, appraising her. 'Granted the dress is very pretty, but you yourself look stunning, my love.' She smiled and hugged her daughter again just as there was a knock at the door.

Florrie jumped, her stomach jittery with excitement as Gerty charged down the hall. 'That'll be Ed.'

At the door, Florrie grabbed hold of Gerty's collar in an attempt to pull her back but to no avail. 'Gerty, how do you expect me to open the door with you there?' She managed to open it a crack and in a split second, Gerty had pushed her nose into it, forcing it open and hurling herself at Ed.

'What a welcome, Gerty-Girl.' He laughed, bending to greet the Labrador. He looked up at Florrie, his mouth falling open. 'Oh, wow! I mean, erm, oh, erm, Florrie, you look beautiful.'

A rush of happiness made her cheeks burn. 'Thank you. You don't scrub up too badly yourself.' She noted his smart blue chinos and jacket the colour of wet sand, beneath which she could see a dark shirt scattered with what appeared to be tiny white birds. She stepped back, opening the door wider. 'Come in while I grab my coat. You can say hi to my mum; she's here to keep Gerty company while I'm out.' She stopped herself from adding that Gerty hadn't lived with her long enough for her to have felt comfortable leaving the Labrador on her own. She'd just lost one owner and Florrie didn't want to make her feel she'd lost someone else.

'Mum, this is Ed.'

'It's good to meet you, Ed. Our Florrie's told us lots about you,' Paula said, grinning broadly.

Mum!

'Good to meet you too, Mrs Appleton. And should I be worried about what Florrie's been saying?' He flashed Florrie a quick grin.

'Paula, please.' She waved a hand at him, dismissing the formal address. 'And Florrie's only said good things.' Her expression changed. 'I'm so sorry about your grandad, he was a lovely man.'

'Thank you.' Ed's smile fell. 'You're right, he was a lovely man.'

'And how does it feel to be in Micklewick Bay? I hope our Florrie's looking after you.' Paula smiled, clearly sensing the dip in his mood, keen to lift it back up.

'It feels really good, despite the circumstances that brought me here, but Florrie's very kindly taken me under her wing, which has made things a lot easier.'

Florrie felt her blushes deepen, aware of her mother's eyes flicking over to her but she resisted making eye contact. 'Well, that's good to hear. Anyway, don't let me keep you young folk. You've got a lovely evening for a walk to Oscar's.'

* * *

'What a great place.' Hanging his jacket on a wooden coat stand, Ed glanced around at the cosy décor of the bistro, with its typically French style. Large arch-shaped mirrors draped with fairy lights were set above wainscotting painted a subtle shade of pale sage-green eggshell to match the walls. Underfoot, the floorboards had been sanded and varnished a rich amber, while a variety of pendant lights with vintage-style bulbs were suspended from the beamed ceiling. At the far-end of the room was a wall that had been stripped back to its imperial-size bricks. It was lined with shelves that were dotted with memorabilia and vintage crystal decanters filled with yet more fairy lights. The mismatched wooden tables of varying shapes and sizes were each sporting an old wine bottle re-purposed as candlesticks, coated in multiple layers of wax from previous evenings of burning. The air was infused with the delicious aroma of freshly cooked seafood while a playlist of French songs could just be heard above the hum of conversation.

Oscar's Bistro couldn't have been more welcoming if it tried. Already most of the tables were occupied, a blend of couples on romantic dates and groups of friends, enjoying an evening catch-up, occasional peals of laughter coming from their direction.

'It's lovely; it's been redecorated since I was last here.' Florrie went to hang up her coat, but Ed lifted it from her hands and hung it over his. 'Thanks. It's nice and warm too.' Which was something she was glad of as it had turned surprisingly chilly outside.

They made their way over to their table, the sound of their shoes clipping over the floorboards. Ed pulled out one of the chairs for Florrie – the bistro-style so iconic with its cane seat and bentwood beech back.

'Thank you.' Smiling happily, her eyes met his.

'Pleasure.' He gave a quick grin.

'Hi there, guys, I'm Nikki and I'm your waitress for the

evening.' A young girl dressed in black trousers and a white blouse was smiling down at them, her long chestnut hair scraped back into a neat ponytail. Florrie recognised her as one of Hayley's college friends. 'Here's a couple of menus for you, the specials are on the blackboard over there – I can highly recommend the moules with crème fraiche and tarragon starter, and the monkfish with beurre blanc and sea herbs is to die for.'

'Thanks, Nikki, that sounds delicious.' Florrie smiled at her as she took the proffered menu.

'Mmm. It really does,' said Ed.

'Now, can I get you some drinks sorted or do you need a minute?' Nikki pressed her hands together, poised for their order.

'How does a bottle of Pinot Grigio sound?' asked Ed, peering round his menu at Florrie.

'It sounds great, as long as you're all right with it.'

He nodded, flashing his familiar easy-going smile. 'It's great with me.'

'One bottle of Pinot coming up,' said Nikki, before disappearing with a swish behind the bar.

* * *

'They were delicious.' Florrie rinsed her fingers in the bowl of lemon infused water before dabbing them dry with a paper napkin. She and Ed had shared a large pan of the moules Nikki had recommended, dipping wedges of butter-smothered baguette into the flavoursome sauce.

'Man, they were seriously good.' Ed finished drying his hands and sat back in his chair, a relaxed smile on his face as he looked over at her. 'I've really enjoyed spending time with you, Florrie. I know I've only been here a few days, but we seem to have crammed so much into that time; I feel like I've known you for ages.'

Florrie laughed. 'I know exactly what you mean; I've enjoyed spending time with you too.' She felt the warmth of a blush on her cheeks; she hadn't blushed so much since she was a teenager!

He picked up his glass, swirling the wine around. 'You've made me feel very welcome here... so at home. It's been a while since I've felt this way, and I really appreciate it.' The flickering candlelight danced in his eyes as he gazed across the table at her.

A memory of something Mr H had said slipped into her mind, "*I think young Edward's a bit lonely.*" Seems he could have been right. 'You don't have to thank me; it's been nice having you around.' The wine may have been making her open up, but she meant every word.

'It's such a shame I didn't get the chance to visit when I was younger, I think we would've....' His voice tailed off as he held her gaze with those dreamy blue eyes again, making her heart leap about in her chest.

A couple of beats passed.

'Mmm. It is a shame.' *What had he been about to say?*

'Maybe if I'd met you then I wouldn't have ... but then again...'

She wished he'd finish what he was trying to say!

'We could've been teenage sweethearts.' His eyes sparkled, making her pulse take off.

It would be so easy to let her emotions run away with themselves. *Be careful!* said a warning voice. She swallowed, feeling suddenly vulnerable 'I'm not sure you realise just how excruciatingly shy I was as a teenager.' She laughed, making light of it as a vision of her seventeen-year-old self popped into her mind. 'My head was way too full of books; there was definitely no room in it for boys.'

'And I dare say I was one of those horrific teenage boys we were talking about the other night. I'd probably have thought a way to impress you would've been to put a slug in your drink or to ping your bra strap,' he said chuckling, the frisson between them dissipating much to Florrie's relief as she reminded herself to keep her emotions in check.

'I'd have been mortified!' She giggled.

The pair of them were still laughing when Nikki brought their main courses over.

* * *

All too soon they were the last in the bistro, their bill arriving on a small plate accompanied by two handmade chocolate mints. Ed insisted on settling up and once done, he helped Florrie on with her coat. She slipped her arms in, aware of the subtle scent of his cologne, the nearness of him, his breath caressing her ear. It sent a shiver of delight through her.

Outside, the air was cool and damp with the hint of a sea fret. Florrie pulled up the collar of her coat and Ed took her arm, slipping it through his as they sauntered their way through the labyrinth of streets and snickelways to her little cottage.

'Have you had any thoughts on what to do about the box of letters?' he asked. They'd agreed not to discuss them at the bistro, not wanting to risk being overheard, but they'd frequently dipped in and out of Florrie's thoughts throughout the day.

'I've thought about them loads, but I still don't know what we should do. Sometimes I think we should just bite the bullet and hand them over to the rightful owner in the hope they'd bring them some joy. Then I wonder if it would be best if we did nothing and just kept them hidden away like they have been for however many years. That way, we'd avoid the risk of resurrecting any unnecessary hurt; I'd never forgive myself if I was responsible for causing anyone pain. For all we know, it could open up a horrible can of worms.'

Seeing a man walking a dog heading towards them, they paused their conversation.

'Evening,' the man said, nodding, the claws of his wire-haired terrier clicking on the pavement. As he drew closer, Florrie could see it was her dad's friend, Allan, from the allotment, beads of mizzle glistening on the shoulders of his jacket. His dog, Scamp, glanced up at them, briefly stopping to cock his leg against a lamppost.

'Evening.' Ed nodded back.

'Evening, Allan,' said Florrie.

They waited to be sure he was out of earshot. 'I know where you're coming from. It's not an easy decision to make,' said Ed.

'And, thankfully, it's one we don't have to make right away. But for now, I think it'd be best if we put it upstairs in the flat, out of the way with all the other stuff.'

'Good plan.'

Florrie felt herself dipping into sadness and was keen to lift the mood. 'On a brighter note, thank you for taking me to Oscar's, the food was wonderful.' She stole a look up at him, his profile handsome in the warm glow of the Victorian streetlight as they ambled along, her arm in his, feeling so right.

'I honestly can't remember eating as well as I have over the last few days.' Ed patted his stomach. 'What with your mum's shepherd's pie, the Jolly's fish and chips and now that amazing meal at Oscar's. I think I'm going to have to start joining the foolhardy folk who jog along the prom every day if I stay here much longer.'

If he stays here much longer? Florrie chose not to dwell on the implication for fear it would take the edge off their lovely evening.

'Well, I'm glad I have a brisk walk to and from work,' said Florrie, opening the gate to Samphire Cottage, pleased to see her mum had put the outside light on for them so she wouldn't have to fumble for the lock.

'Florrie.' She was poised to slot the key into the door when Ed spoke.

'Yes.' She turned to see him standing close, his eyes soft. A thrill rippled through her as he took her hand, smoothing her fingers with his. She looked down at them, seeing his artist's hands; large yet at the same time gentle-looking, sporting callouses from years' of holding pencils and paintbrushes, ink ingrained into his nails.

'Thank you for coming out with me tonight.'

'Thank you for inviting me.' She looked up to see his eyes had become dark pools. She felt her knees weaken. *Uh-oh! I'm in trouble.*

Just as he cupped his free hand against her cheek, the door opened. In a flash, Ed stepped back, his hands falling to his sides.

'Oh, it's you two,' said her mum, pressing a hand to her chest as Gerty flew out, fussing around them, warmth from the hallway spilling out onto the doorstep. 'We thought we heard something, didn't we, Gerty?'

'Hi, Mum,' Florrie said with feigned breeziness. 'We've just got here.'

'Well, you'd best get yourselves inside, it's raw out there, you must be absolutely nithered.'

Before Ed had chance to argue, she gently pulled him in and guided him down the hallway and into the living room where the fire was glowing in the hearth. 'You're right, Paula, it's nippy out there now,' he said.

'Yes, I can feel the cold air coming off you. Brrr! Get your-selves warmed up.' She rubbed her hands up and down her arms, watching Gerty fuss around Ed who was bent ruffling her ears. 'Someone's got a fan.' She gave Florrie a knowing look. Florrie averted her eyes.

'She's a good lass, aren't you, Gerty-Girl?' Ed said. He stood upright, brushing his fringe out of his eyes, Gerty still fussing around his feet.

'Right then,' said Paula, glancing between him and Florrie. 'I'd best be off; I gather you two have a busy day ahead of you tomorrow so you won't be wanting to get to bed too late.'

Florrie felt her cheeks flame hotter than ever. She hoped her mother wasn't implying they were going to sleep together and, worse, she didn't want *Ed* to think her mother was implying it. *Jeez, Mother!* She groaned inwardly.

'How are you getting home, Paula?' Ed asked. 'I'd be happy to walk with you.'

'Thank you, lovey, that's very kind of you, but I came in my car.' She shrugged her coat on. 'Oh, and your dad reminded me to let you know I'm doing a roast dinner tomorrow, about six-thirty-ish, you're both very welcome to join us. There's always plenty to go round, and there's sticky ginger pudding with custard for afters.'

'Sticky ginger pudding.' Ed's eyes lit up as he looked across at Florrie hopefully.

'Sounds good to me, how about you, Ed?' she said. 'I reckon we'll be starving after tackling the storeroom.' Florrie suspected he hadn't had the pleasure of many sit down family dinners when he was growing up.

'Florrie's told me all about your roast dinners, so I'd love to. Thank you, Paula.' He looked inordinately thrilled at the prospect.

'Great stuff.' Paula, picked up her handbag, scanning the room. 'Right then, I think I've got everything. Good luck with the storeroom, don't forget to shout up if you need a hand. Lovely to see you, Ed.' She patted his arm.

'Bye, Mrs, I mean, Paula, it's good to see you too.'

Florrie followed her mum to the front door. 'Bye, Mum, thanks for Gerty-sitting.'

'My pleasure, lovey, she's been as good as gold.' Paula

leaned in to kiss her daughter on the cheek. 'By, isn't Ed ever so tall and handsome?' she said, her voice a whisper. 'Wait till I tell your dad.'

'Bye, Mum, see you tomorrow.' Florrie gave an amused smile, shaking her head as Paula raised her eyebrows at her.

Florrie waved, watching her mum drive away before closing the door. She took a moment to gather herself before going back to the living room, wondering what would have happened if her mum hadn't flung the door open when she did. She was pretty certain Ed had been going to kiss her. She sighed. Is that what she wanted? Yes! In that moment, feeling his lips on hers was what she wanted more than anything. In fact she'd been thinking about it all night. But now? Now the passion of the moment had dissipated and cooled, floating away on the chilly night air, Florrie felt something pull her back. For one thing, she was fresh out of a relationship and had been looking forward to having some time on her own after the plodding tedium of Graham. And for another, she was grieving for the grandfather of the man who was just about to kiss her. How insensitive was that to Mr H's memory? She shouldn't even be thinking about getting involved with anyone. A little niggle ran up her spine. But the thing that was never far from her mind was the fact that Ed very likely wouldn't be hanging around for more than a few weeks. And, much as it pained her every time she thought about it, she had to acknowledge she didn't want to risk investing her feelings in him.

'You okay?' Ed's head appeared round the door, puncturing her bubble of thought.

'Fine, thanks. Just tired; it's been a busy day.' Florrie found herself yawning as she finished her sentence, hoping she was sending out vibes that said she was reluctant to pick up where they'd left off on the doorstep.

He strode over to her, resting his hands on her shoulders. 'You're right, and it's set to be even busier tomorrow. I'd best head off and let you get some sleep.' He bent and brushed a kiss against her cheek, sending a wayward thrill pulsing through her, contradicting every bit of advice she'd given herself about safeguarding her feelings. 'See you in the morning.' He bent and gave Gerty a quick scratch between her ears. 'See you tomorrow, girl.'

Gerty responded with a swish of her tail.

'Bye, Ed, and thanks again for a lovely evening.' Florrie smiled up at him, seeing kindness in his eyes. A spike of guilt tempered by regret added to the mix of emotions swirling around inside her. How she wished things could be simpler, wished Ed wanted to stay in Micklewick Bay, be part of the bookshop. Be with her.

THIRTY-THREE

Ed was already at the shop when Florrie arrived with Gerty just after nine the following morning and, judging from the amount of clutter he'd moved, he must have been there for a good few hours.

'Wow! The room looks so different, and so much bigger with all that stuff gone,' she said as Gerty bounded over to Ed, greeting him as if it had been an eternity since she'd last set eyes on him.

He finished fussing the Labrador and gave Florrie a lopsided grin, pushing his fingers through his hair, his eyes roving over her appreciatively. 'Morning. Great outfit. You look like a land-girl from the forties.'

Florrie giggled shyly, looking down at herself; she'd come prepared for dusty work. 'It's just my scruffy decorating gear.' Beneath her black, boyfriend cardigan she was sporting an old black t-shirt and a pair of roomy cotton dungarees, the cream fabric spattered in a rainbow of colours from previous painting jobs. She'd tucked her hair away under a red vintage head-square she'd picked up at Lark's shop, tying it at the front with a sturdy knot.

'It's cute,' he said, holding her gaze for moment, making her stomach loop-the-loop.

She felt her face tingle as a blush rose in her cheeks. *What's going on with me, for goodness' sake? Get a grip of yourself, woman!* 'Right, what can I do to help?' She plonked her hands on her hips, attempting to look as if she meant business and wasn't the silly blushing schoolgirl she felt she must appear to be.

'Right then, if we get the rest of the stuff upstairs, then we can give the bookshelves a clean before moving them into the shop area while we lift the carpet; I've got a feeling that's going to be a messy job and the sooner we get it done the better.'

'Yes, captain.' Florrie grinned as she saluted him, his eyes twinkling with amusement. 'Lead the way.'

Over the next few hours they worked solidly, both eager to get as much done as possible. The only thing they couldn't do was move the bookcases which, they discovered, were fixed to the wall and wouldn't budge. Florrie was secretly relieved since they looked heavy and cumbersome. Next, they'd gone around the edges of the carpet, setting it free from the vicious shark-like teeth of the gripper. That done, they'd carefully rolled it, thankful to find there was no underlay to contend with. Finally, they tackled the sanding of the deep skirting boards, then the door and the window frame. It was dusty, dirty work.

Ed brushed the dirt off his hands, assessing the lengthy roll of carpet. 'That's going to be too heavy for just the two of us to lift, Florrie.' He nodded towards it. 'I don't want to risk you hurting your back trying to, especially since we need to get it through the bookshop and out into the back yard, which is going to be awkward.'

Florrie wiped her brow with the back of her hand, her face glowing from the exertion; she couldn't argue with that, the carpet was a dead-weight. 'I'll give Maggie a ring so she and Bear can give us a hand; the sooner we get it shifted, the better.'

'While you're doing that I'll go get the vacuum; I've got a feeling there are some rather fine floorboards underneath all this muck.'

Florrie hoped Ed was right; she'd envisaged leaving the floorboards uncovered, with maybe a few large vintage rugs scattered about.

Before they knew it, there was a rapping at the bookshop door.

'That was quick,' said Florrie, hurrying to let Maggie and Bear in.

With their friends' help, they had the carpet shifted in no time.

'Right then.' Bear clapped his huge hands together. 'We'd best get off since my van's blocking the alleyway and I don't want to get anyone's back up.'

'Yep, we've still got a fair bit to get done today,' said Florrie. 'Thanks for all your help, and for dropping the paint off.'

'No probs,' said Bear.

Once Maggie and Bear had left, Florrie and Ed resumed tackling the storeroom.

'I'll get this place vacuumed; I'm itching to see what state the floorboards are in,' said Ed.

'Me too.'

Vacuuming the storeroom took longer than expected, and it was a while before Ed could set to sanding the floorboards with the machine he'd hired from Prince's DIY shop. Gerty was unimpressed by the noise, so Florrie took her for a walk along the top prom. She spotted Jack Playforth cutting a solitary figure as he ambled along on the bottom prom by the pier. She still had to pinch herself when she remembered he'd offered to do a reading for them. She strode on, wondering if he'd had any luck with tracing his family.

By the time the pair had returned, Ed had finished the sanding and was in the middle of giving the floor another vacuuming. 'I know I might sound bonkers, but I'm going to give the walls a quick going over to get rid of the excess dust. Should make it easier to give them a quick wipe over.'

'Okay.' It seemed like a sensible suggestion.

Over the next few hours their hard work had been punctuated by a generous smattering of lighter moments. Florrie had howled with laughter as she'd watched Ed and Gerty race around the storeroom with the vacuum cleaner, Ed "whooping" and shouting, 'Come on, Gerty-Girl, let's do this!' The Labrador had bounded around, a hand-brush clamped firmly between her teeth, loving every minute. In the end, Florrie couldn't tell who was chasing who.

On one occasion, Ed had chased her around the room, the angular carcass of a huge, long-since-dead spider dangling between his fingers. 'Arghh!' She'd squealed and leapt over the bowl of sudsy water, her heart pounding loudly in her chest, Ed in hot pursuit.

'Mwahaha! It's coming to get you!' he'd said in a horror-movie-esque voice. It was soon followed by a loud, 'Warghh!' as he missed his footing, clipping the rim of the bowl, sending soapsuds everywhere. Gerty had joined in the fun, leaping about, charging after Ed, her tail swishing through the foam and flicking it around the room. In her bid to get away from the spider, Florrie slipped in a puddle, falling flat on her backside. Despite the resounding thud it hadn't hurt, and she'd stretched out on the floor, roaring with laughter, her hands clutching her stomach. 'Oh, that was so funny!'

'You okay?' Ed had asked, gasping for breath, grinning broadly, offering a hand to help her up.

'Yep, I'm fine thanks; no damage done.' She'd grinned back, letting him pull her to her feet. She'd dusted herself down, breathing heavily, her cheeks and sides aching from laughing so hard. It had been an age since she'd last had such a good belly-laugh.

'You've got a smudge of dust on your nose,' he said, reaching across and wiping it away gently with his thumb, his touch sending her heart racing. 'Looks cute, but I don't think you'd want to leave here still wearing it,' he said, his voice soft.

'Oh... yeah... thanks.' Their eyes locked for a moment before she turned away to hide her blushes, wishing she could keep her feelings under control.

Their moment over, they set to, wiping the floor dry with a pile of old cloths while Gerty curled up in the doorway, drifting in and out of slumber.

Once finished, Ed threw his arm around Florrie's shoulders, the pair of them ruddy-cheeked and glowing from their efforts as they admired the Victorian pine floorboards in all their glory. 'They look fantastic,' he said, a satisfied smile spreading across his face. 'We make a great team.'

'They do; it's such a shame they've been hidden away under that bloomin' awful carpet for however many decades.' *And I think we make a brilliant team, but it scares me a little bit. Scrap that! It scares me a hell of a lot!*

'It is, but now they're free to be admired. Once we've painted the woodwork and walls, I'll set about varnishing them. But first, I think we've earnt us a large cup of tea.' He squeezed her closer and glanced down at her, making her stomach flutter.

'Come on, Gerty, you've been a good lass, I think you deserve a dog treat or two.' Ed patted his leg, breaking the spell. Gerty didn't need telling twice, she leapt to her feet and trotted after him.

Florrie surveyed the room, her mind wandering to how much she'd enjoyed being in Ed's company today, indeed every day since his arrival in the town. He was so easy to be around, it was as if she'd known him for years. His presence had the knack of making everywhere seem a little brighter. She felt a flash of guilt, wincing as she recalled her coolness with him when they'd got back from the bistro the previous evening, quickly justifying her actions with the reminder that she'd only known him a handful of days and he wasn't likely to hang around for long. She sighed deeply. If only circumstances were different. She had the feeling he felt the same too.

THIRTY-FOUR

'S'just us.' Florrie stepped over the threshold of her parents' house, walking into a wall of warmth and the delicious aroma of Sunday roast. She bent to free Gerty from her lead, watching as the Labrador bounded towards the kitchen.

Paula popped her head around the kitchen door, her cheeks flushed, Gerty fussing around her feet. 'Hello, lovey, hello, Ed. Come on through. Your dad's here too.'

'Hi, Mum, it smells so good. We're starving.'

'Hi, Paula, Florrie's right, it smells amazing.'

Florrie hung up her coat, taking Ed's from him and hanging it on the peg beside hers before they joined her parents in the kitchen.

'Dad, this is Ed,' Florrie said.

'Now then, lad, it's good to meet you.' Charlie, his cheeks every bit as rosy as his wife's, stopped stirring the gravy and made his way over to Ed, his hand outstretched, a welcoming smile on his face. 'Paula and me are thrilled you could join us for dinner.' He pumped Ed's hand enthusiastically, patting him soundly on the shoulder with his other hand.

'It's good to meet you too, Mr Appleton. And thank you for the invitation.'

'Charlie, please. And you're very welcome, son, there's always plenty to go round, and my good-lady wife's Yorkshire puddings are legendary as you're just about to find out.'

'Get away with you, Charlie.' Despite her protestation, Paula sparkled at her husband's praise. 'Anyroad, come and make yourselves comfy, dinner won't be for another five or so minutes. You can start telling us all about your day.' Paula busied herself mashing a mound of steaming potatoes in a bowl, adding a generous blob of butter as she listened.

With the meal over and done with, Florrie and Ed joined her parents for coffee in the living room. Paula and Charlie sat side-by-side on the sofa as they usually did, while Florrie and Ed took the armchairs that flanked it. Gerty went straight for the rug in front of the fire, curling up with a contended groan, her stomach full of leftover beef. Florrie's parents had always been sociable, welcoming folk, and she'd noted Ed had appeared relaxed, tucking into his roast dinner with great gusto. The conversation had flowed freely, regularly punctuated by bursts of laughter. Once again, Florrie found her feelings for him growing.

'Our Florrie tells us you're staying in town till you decide what to do,' Charlie said, nursing his mug on his stomach. 'Seems the sensible thing to do if you ask me.'

'Mmm.' Ed nodded, swallowing his mouthful of coffee. 'I am, for now, till the bookshop situation sinks in and I work out what to do for the best.'

Florrie felt herself tense at the prospect, fearful Dodgy Dick might eventually feature in those plans.

'Aye well, all-in-all, it sounds like it's been quite a week for the pair of you, what with finding out you're suddenly joint owners of the bookshop, not to mention Jack Playforth paying you a visit and agreeing to do a reading. Bloomin' 'eck, makes you wonder what's going to happen next.' Charlie gave a hearty chuckle. 'Your mother and me were just saying the other week Micklewick's such a quiet little town, where not much out of the ordinary happens. Seems we spoke too soon.'

'Seems we did,' Paula said.

The four sat chatting for the next half-hour, Ed totally at ease with Florrie's parents. It was a far cry from Graham's visits. He used to sit on the edge of his seat, his body language saying he'd rather not be there. It wasn't until now that Florrie realised how obvious that must have been to her parents. She felt a sudden twinge of guilt coupled with annoyance at her ex.

THIRTY-FIVE

They'd just turned onto Florrie's street, stomachs full of Sunday dinner, chatting away about their plans for the layout of the storeroom, when Ed's phone started ringing from the back pocket of his jeans. He groaned, unlinking his arm from hers and coming to a halt. 'Much as I'm tempted to ignore that, I'd better get it.'

Florrie's heart sank; she hoped it wasn't the person who had the power to make Ed's smile vanish whenever he saw their name on the screen – at least, she assumed it was the same person and there wasn't a string of them. She stole a glance at him to see his smile had dropped. She groaned inwardly. *Uh-oh, here we go.*

'Ughh!' He rolled his eyes and ran his hand over the back of his neck, the call ending before he answered it. 'Sorry, but I really should call them back.'

'Okay.' She did her best to push down her disappointment, hoping he couldn't detect it in her voice.

They resumed walking, he clearly didn't intend to return the call in her presence. She couldn't shake the feeling that something was amiss. Her mind started racing. Was it his ex? His parents? He hadn't mentioned them in relation to Mr H's will over the last couple of days which had struck her as odd, but she hadn't liked to ask for fear of sounding nosy, telling herself he'd share anything of concern. But now she wasn't so sure.

They stopped at her gate and she forced a cheerful smile. 'Right then...' Awkwardness rushed in, filling the space between them.

'Right then,' he said, echoing her words, pushing his mouth into a smile. 'I really enjoyed meeting your parents; they're great folk, explains why you're so awesome.' His smile broadened and Florrie felt another dreaded blush turn her cheeks crimson.

'I'm pleased you like them – not so sure about the me being awesome part though.' She gave an embarrassed laugh.

'I am. Sure, that is.' His eyes twinkled at her. 'So... thanks for another amazing day, it's been great but, much as I hate to, I'd better make tracks. I'm sure you're sick of the sight of me by now, and I'd hate for you to start dreading the very mention of my name. And, unfortunately, I've got a suspicion this call could be lengthy.' He waggled his phone at her. If she wasn't mistaken, the twinkle in his eyes had been replaced by one of regret.

'It's been fun. Busy, but fun.'

'It has.' He looked down at her, a conflicted expression on his face. 'See you tomorrow?'

'Yep, I'll be there bright and early, wielding my paintbrush like I mean business.' She mimed waving a paintbrush in the air, making him chuckle.

'Thanks again for a wonderful day.' He bent and pressed a kiss to her cheek, lingering for a moment.

She felt a charge of electricity so strong it rendered her

speechless for several seconds. Surely he must have felt it too. 'Oh, erm, yes, it's been a fab day, thanks,' she said when she finally found her tongue. She shyly raised her eyes to his and was met with inky-dark pools, setting her heart racing. *He did feel it!*

Ed blinked quickly and swallowed, turning his attention to Gerty. 'Okay, then, erm, see you tomorrow, Gerty-Girl.' He smoothed the Labrador's ears before flashing one last smile. 'Bye, Florrie.'

'Bye, Ed.' She watched as he headed off down the road, giving a flick of his floppy fringe, his hands thrust into his jacket pockets. Despite her misgivings about her attachment to him, she hadn't been ready to end the day with him just yet.

Once inside the warmth of the cottage, Florrie hung up her coat and flopped down at the kitchen table. Her mind was whirling. 'Phwah!' The last few weeks had been intense, with a whole gamut of emotions bombarding her body, ranging from gut-wrenching grief to finding herself falling hard for Ed, and doing everything in her power to reason against it. It wasn't easy. 'Jeez!' she said, rubbing her face briskly. She didn't know if she was coming or going.

She couldn't shake the feeling there was something bothering him, something he wasn't telling her that had been brewing gradually. And she had a horrible feeling she was going to find out about it soon. It was a shame he'd had to go back to the bed-and-breakfast, confusing even, especially when they'd had such a great day together. It felt like it had been cut prematurely short. But she was too tired to dwell on that right now, all that scrubbing and lugging things about was catching up with her. A twinge in her shoulder made her wince, she reached up and rubbed it with her fingertips, the muscle knotting in response. *Ouch!* She'd know about it tomorrow. What she really needed right now was a long soak in a hot bubble bath, a cup of tea and to lose herself in a good book.

'Oh for the simple life of a Labrador,' she said to Gerty, sighing as she got to her feet. Gerty looked up from her bed and wagged her tail. 'Actually, your life hasn't been very simple recently, has it, girl? Forget I said that.'

THIRTY-SIX

By the time Ed arrived on Monday morning, Florrie had finished painting the long wall opposite the door and was about to tackle the one at the front.

'Sorry I'm late, I lost track of time.' His face was flushed and he was out of breath, the scent of the sea breeze lingering on his clothes. Gerty raced over to him, her tail wagging faster than ever, her whole body wiggling. 'Hi there, Gerty-Girl, it's good to see you too.'

Florrie set her paintbrush down on the lid of the tin. 'No worries, Gerty and I got here really early.'

'So I see; you've made amazing progress.' He stood upright, taking in the freshly painted wall, beaming at her. 'It looks good; so much brighter already.'

Florrie smiled despite the unsettled feeling that was making her stomach churn. She'd woken up a couple of times in the middle of the night, worrying about the phone calls, and they'd never been far from her mind while she'd been busy painting. 'Mmm. It does. We're lucky we've got the Bank Holiday today,' she said, struggling to keep her anxiety out of her voice.

'We are.' He looked at her, searching her face, his smile dropping. 'Is everything okay?'

'Yep, I'm just a bit achy after yesterday, all that lifting and floor scrubbing.' She rolled her shoulders as if to demonstrate, her muscles objecting as she did so.

He tugged at his ear, nodding as he shifted his gaze to the floor. 'That's understandable, you worked your butt off yesterday.' An uncomfortable silence circled the room. 'Hey, tell you what, why don't you have a break while I take over? You said you've been here ages.' He shrugged off his coat, plastering an over-bright smile on his face.

'Yeah, I think I'll take you up on that. Gerty could do with a walk actually.' She drew in a deep breath, forcing a smile that struggled to reach her eyes.

'You sure you're okay?' he asked, frowning. 'You know, if you're in too much discomfort, you don't have to do any more. I'm happy to finish the rest.'

'I'll be fine, I could just do with some fresh air.' She forced another smile.

'Course.' He nodded, swallowing, his eyes betraying his confusion at her coolness.

Her need for fresh air was partly true, but the main reason Florrie was so eager to get outside was to process what she'd just learnt that morning. Until she'd done that, she couldn't look at Ed. She knew she should mention it to him, but she didn't want to speak in haste. She needed to clear her head, work through some recently imparted information that was making her brain ache – her heart too if she was honest.

Florrie had been in the middle of painting when her phone had pinged with a text. She'd climbed down the creaky set of ladders, wiped her hands on an old rag and picked her way carefully over the dust sheets covering the floor. She'd been expecting to see a message from Ed and was surprised to see

Maggie's name. She read it, frowning at the contents before reading it again. 'What?'

> Hi Florrie, hope the painting's going well. I'm sure it's nothing, but I thought I should let you know Bear and I saw Ed talking to Dodgy Dick earlier. Looked pretty serious from where we were standing. Just wanted to make you aware. Forewarned and all that, chick. If you need anything, just holler x

Florrie's pulse had raced. Maggie wouldn't have contacted her if she'd thought it was nothing. Hurriedly, she'd dialled her friend's number; she needed to know more.

The call to Maggie revealed that Jasmine had seen the pair in conversation on Saturday. Apparently, she'd mentioned it in passing when Maggie had popped into the bakery that day. 'We just assumed Dodgy Dick was trying to ingratiate himself with Ed, you know, kind of be the first to find out if he was thinking about selling his share of the bookshop. We'd had a laugh about what his reaction would be when he found out there was no chance, especially with Ed looking like he was sweet on you.'

Maggie went on to say she'd thought nothing more about it until she and Bear had spotted them walking along the bottom prom that morning, apparently deep in conversation, ending it with a handshake and Dodgy Dick looking pleased with himself. 'Sorry, chick, I thought long and hard about whether I should say anything, but me and Bear just got a sense something wasn't right and figured if we were in your position, we'd want to know.'

And she was right, Florrie did want to know. This, together with the phone calls that had the power to subdue Ed's mood, had set anxiety squirming in her stomach. She wondered why Ed hadn't mentioned bumping into Dodgy Dick even in passing, especially after their conversation about him. She chewed on the inside of her cheek, a sense of foreboding inching up her spine. Not three weeks ago her life had been running smoothly, with no horrible surprises to contend with. But since then, she'd had pretty much everything thrown at her. Her existence felt as if it had been turned upside down and given a thorough shaking, and she didn't like it. Not one little bit.

Florrie made her way along the prom with long, purposeful strides, Gerty trotting along jauntily, keeping up with her new owner's brisk pace and oblivious to the turmoil she was wading through. As she walked, Florrie mulled over everything she'd learnt that morning, trying to tally it with the phone calls that appeared to bug Ed. The more she thought about it the more she felt sure they were linked. *It's just too much of a coincidence.*

A straggle of hair had escaped her headscarf, blowing across her face. She scraped it away with her fingers, savouring the cool, head-clearing breeze and the glow of the sun's rays as they bounced off the smooth sandstone walls of the tall Victorian houses. She snatched a glimpse of the choppy sea; it was a dense pewter, dappled with white breakers and peppered with the usual cluster of foolhardy surfers.

She pushed on, her thoughts set against the familiar sounds of the seaside; judging by the level of shrieking, the seagulls were out in force today. She felt her heart rate increase with her exertion and sucked in a lungful of cool sea air, releasing it slowly until her lungs were empty, repeating the action several times over. It did little to calm her jittering stomach.

It was all so confusing. Florrie was certain Ed could feel the strengthening connection between them just as she could. After all, he'd insinuated that he liked her on several occasions. And if the way he looked at her was anything to go by, then there wasn't a shadow of a doubt. Which made it all the more confusing if he was considering selling his half of the bookshop to Dodgy Dick, suggesting he wasn't keen to stay in Micklewick Bay and a relationship with her was the last thing on his mind.

She rubbed her brow with her fingertips. Was he heading back to London? Getting back with his ex? So many dratted questions. But maybe she'd got it all wrong about him selling up. Maybe he'd been discussing something else with Dodgy Dick. That was highly unlikely she thought, dismissing the idea straightaway. 'Ughh!' It was all so bloody confusing. Her stomach churned. It felt like she was teetering on a ledge, and if she wasn't careful she could very easily find herself falling for someone who had no intention of sticking around.

THIRTY-SEVEN

'Florrie! Florrie! Wait up.'

With her face glowing pink from her walk, Florrie ceased rummaging for the shop key in the pocket of her dungarees and turned to see Graham hurrying towards her.

'Graham, what are you doing here?' Confused, her eyes alighted on the huge bouquet of flowers in his hand; he must be on his way to see Bethany.

'Didn't you hear me? I've been calling after you for ages.' He was out of breath, flustered, his usually immaculate hair dishevelled. His mouth lifted in an uncertain smile.

'No, sorry I didn't. Why? Is something the matter?'

He stepped back, his expression morphing to one of disapproval as Gerty stretched out her neck and gave him a quick sniff. The Labrador grunted and sat down on the pavement, her back to him, evidently unimpressed. Florrie pressed her lips together; she had all on not to laugh.

'I need to talk to you,' he said, trying to get his breath back. 'I called at your house first, but you weren't there. Then I went to your parents and they told me you'd be here decorating or something, which judging by your clothes, they were right.' He was looking her up and down in a condescending manner which made her bristle. 'Then I saw you heading this way as I was just about to turn onto Endeavour Road, so I pulled up quickly, abandoning my car in a totally unsuitable place.'

For the first time, she saw him for the prissy, fussy man he was. 'I'm not sure we have much to talk about, Graham. From what I witnessed on Friday night, it's poor Bethany you should be talking to, she seemed quite upset when she left the pub.'

His eyes flickered, taken aback by Florrie's response. 'Bethany's fine; we're... erm... we're not together anymore.'

'Oh, right.' Despite what she'd witnessed on Friday night, Florrie was still surprised to hear this.

He cleared his throat. 'It's just, seeing you at the pub made me realise I still have feelings for you. Strong feelings, Florrie. I think we gave up on us too soon. We'd started taking each other for granted, got too comfortable, stopped making an effort. We became a habit, if you like,' he said, his chest heaving as he ran out of breath.

Florrie wished he'd stop talking, but evidently he had more to say.

'Flo, what I'm trying to say is, I still love you. I've never stopped, and I didn't realise until I saw you the other night, sitting next to—'

She closed her eyes, taking a deep breath. 'Graham, please stop.'

'What?' He stepped closer and she raised her hand, resting it on his chest which only seemed to encourage him. Before she knew what was happening, he'd reached his free hand around the back of her head and pressed his lips against hers, the flowers crushed between them. She froze, her eyes wide as her brain struggled to process what was happening.

She was too stunned to notice a dark shadow pause behind the glass of the shop door, then quickly move away.

Florrie pushed Graham away, wiping his wet kiss from her

mouth. 'What the hell are you doing? In case you forgot, Graham, we're over! Don't ever do that to me again!' She left him spluttering on the doorstep while she rushed into the shop, locking the door firmly behind her, anger bubbling its way through her body. 'Could this day get any flaming worse?' she said, muttering the words under her breath.

Gerty padded off in search of her water bowl while Florrie stepped into the storeroom, still shaken. Ed had made good progress while she'd been out. 'Hi, looks great.' Rattled as she was, she still managed to muster up a smile.

'Yep, got lots done.' His chilly tone took her by surprise though she did her best not to show it.

What right does he have to be arsey with me after what he's been up to?

'Cuppa?'

'I'm fine, thanks. I'd just rather crack on and get this done and get back to the bed-and-breakfast, grab an early night.'

'Okay,' she said coolly, noting his reluctance to make eye contact with her, wondering what had soured his mood. Her mind ran straight to what Maggie had told her about Dodgy Dick. He must've decided there was no need to be friendly if he wasn't going to stick around. Her stomach clenched.

* * *

By the time the painting was finished, the awkward atmosphere between the pair had mushroomed into a thick, miserable fug. Anxiety had squirmed in Florrie's chest for the whole afternoon. She felt exhausted by it. For the first time, she couldn't wait to leave the place.

'I'll just go and wash these,' Ed said flatly, gathering the paintbrushes together, still reluctant to look her in the eye. 'The dust-sheets might as well stay down until the second coat's done.'

'Fine.' Her emotions surged and she felt her eyes swim with tears. She blinked them away quickly, busying herself with folding the rags, wondering what the hell had happened between them. She glanced down at her paint-spattered hands; much as she wanted to wash them before she left, she wasn't keen to join Ed in the tiny kitchen area, reluctant to be in such close proximity to him while this new hostility directed their interactions. She heaved a sigh as she heard him make his way back to the storeroom.

'Right, I'm heading off now.' His eyes flicked briefly in her direction, his face solemn.

'Okay,' she said, her voice as flat as his. Part of her was desperate to ask him what was going on but a stubborn part of her made her hold back. If he intended to sell his share to Dodgy Dick, there was no way she was going to grovel to him, beg him not to, much as she desperately didn't want him to. And if he wanted to leave Micklewick Bay he might as well get gone as soon as possible.

He bent to pat Gerty who was looking up at him intently; she seemed to sense something was amiss. 'See you, Gerty-Girl.' Florrie noted he managed a smile for the Labrador at least. That done, he grabbed his jacket and left the bookshop, Florrie and Gerty staring after him.

'What's his problem, Gerty?' Florrie asked.

THIRTY-EIGHT

By the time Florrie reached Samphire Cottage she was starving, the brisk walk home in the sea air kick-starting her appetite. It was only then she realised she hadn't eaten since breakfast. Thanks to their weird, barely speaking day, she'd abandoned her plans to suggest they grab a takeaway sandwich and a coffee for lunch from the café down on the bottom prom and enjoy them sitting on a bench, looking out to sea. Her mind had been in such a turmoil she hadn't felt hungry.

She slipped out of her decorating clothes and into a pair of comfy old leggings and a loose checked shirt. Turning the radio on, she peered into the fridge and found a tub of homemade tomato soup, tipped it into a pan and set it on the hob. She sliced a couple of wodges of wholemeal bread from Seaside Bakery and slathered them with creamy butter. The wholesome aroma of the soup quickly started to permeate the kitchen, making her stomach growl. Just as soon as it was ready, Florrie set the bowl down at the table and placed the paperback she was currently reading in front of it, and tucked into both.

The soup was delicious and soothing, but Florrie was struggling to concentrate on her book. Instead, her mind was running riot, searching for reasons that would explain the sudden change in Ed's behaviour. She felt stupid for letting herself fall for him. Even worse, she regretted sharing her feelings with her friends on Friday night, blaming the wine for loosening her tongue. Would they think she was stupid too? Lord, she hoped not. It was totally out of character for her; she was normally reserved and took a while to warm to people properly. Why hadn't she bloody-well been like that with Ed? She sank back in her chair, closing her eyes in the hope of erasing the image of him, with his floppy hair, easy-going smile and dreamy eyes, getting cross with herself when it didn't work.

Mr H's intentions had come from the kindest of places, but why did he have to go and bequeath half of the bookshop to her? She'd have been happy just to choose a small memento of him and Mrs H. That would have been more than enough. But though Mr H meant well, it looked as though he was going to be responsible for putting her in a position that was up there with her worst nightmares. It was bad enough that her heart was bruised but if her fears became a reality, then she'd be business partners with the unscrupulous Dodgy Dick. She emitted a loud groan and Gerty look at her quizzically.

She'd almost finished her soup when her mobile phone started buzzing like an angry wasp. Her heart leapt. Ed? She jumped up and retrieved it from the dresser to see it was Maggie's number.

'Hi, Mags.' She tried to inject a breezy note into her voice.

'Hiya, chick. I'm just checking you're okay. I sent you a couple of texts and got a bit worried when I heard nothing back; it's not like you.'

'Sorry, hon, I hadn't spotted them.'

'What's up? And don't say nothing, I can tell by your voice something's the matter. Is it anything to do with Dodgy Dick?'

Florrie released a weary sigh and flopped heavily into her seat. 'I'm not sure, I didn't get chance to say anything to Ed.' She went on to share the events of the day with her friend. Maggie listened quietly, the occasional sound of her sipping from a cup of tea.

'Well, there's no excuse for him to behave like a prat. And as for Mr Beige, what the hell's he playing at? Who'd have thought he'd turn out to be such a knob?'

Florrie couldn't help but laugh at Maggie's turn of phrase. It felt good to share her feelings with her closest friend.

'If you ask me, it sounds like you need a relaxing soak in the bath followed by a good kip, then you'll be ready to face tomorrow all refreshed. And, if you want my advice, I reckon you need to ask Ed about Dodgy Dick. Maybe try doing it subtly rather than just blurting it out. But, quite honestly, flower, if he's doing things behind your back like this, you're better off without him.'

'But I won't be better off being joint owner with Dodgy Dick. That's way, way worse.' Florrie felt the soup churning in her stomach.

'Don't forget there's always the option to sell your share,' Maggie said softly. 'I know it wouldn't be what Mr H wanted, but neither would he have wanted his grandson to put you in this position, nor for his beloved bookshop to fall into the hands of Dodgy Dick. I'd go as far to say he'd be furious.' She tutted and huffed. 'And you really wouldn't want to be tarred with the same brush as that slime-ball. Trust me there's no room in this town for "Dodgy Florrie", and besides, it just doesn't have the right ring to it.' She gave a throaty giggle.

Despite her concerns, Florrie found herself laughing too. 'You're right, I don't fancy being "Dodgy Florrie". And I do need to find out what's going on with Ed. I'll speak to him when he comes to the shop tomorrow.'

'Good.' Maggie sounded genuinely pleased to hear that. 'And how's the decorating going?'

'It's going really well. We've painted all the walls and the woodwork – the skirting boards took ages; they're so deep. We just need to give everywhere another coat, then we're done. Thanks for your help with the carpet, by the way.'

'Hey, no probs, Bear and me were happy to assist. Actually, that sounds like him pulling up in the yard; he'll be ready for his dinner. And I've still got that cashmere teddy bear to give one last check over for Samantha Carter before I hand it over in morning.'

Florrie's heart squeezed for her friend, knowing she'd be feeling apprehensive about tomorrow. 'Okay, chick, good to talk to you, thanks for listening to me being a whinge-bag.'

'It's what friends are for, and you weren't whinging, you've had a crap couple of weeks, you're entitled to spout off.'

'Thanks, Mags.'

* * *

Throughout the course of the evening, Florrie had found herself having to resist the urge to call Ed, so keen was she to talk things over with him, to clear the air. She couldn't deny she'd been cool with him that morning, but to her mind she had good reason. In retrospect, maybe that had been childish of her, but she was utterly confused by his behaviour; it made her feel uneasy, unable to settle.

She had her mobile phone in her hand, poised to dial his number when a text came through, the surprise causing her to drop it with a clatter on the kitchen table. 'Bugger!' She quickly snatched it up to see a text from Stella asking how the decorating had gone. Florrie had a funny feeling Maggie had been in touch with her.

She fired a text back, saying it had gone well, but found herself sharing her concerns over Dodgy Dick and what Maggie had said.

Mere seconds after she'd pressed send, her phone started

ringing. Florrie wasn't surprised to see it was Stella. 'Florrie, listen to me. There's no way you want to get mixed up with that slimy bastard! I know everyone laughs at him as if he's some kind of comedy bad guy, which he might have been ten years ago, but the company Dodgy Dick's acting as frontman for is made up of dangerous people, and you need to keep as far away from him as possible. I can't go into details, you've just got to trust me on this.'

Stella's words triggered a spike of panic in Florrie. 'Oh my God, Stella, you're scaring me. I don't want to be mixed up with him and his company, but I might not have a choice.' She felt goosebumps prickle all over her skin.

'What the bloody hell is Harte playing at? Do you know for certain he's wanting to sell his share of the bookshop?' Stella's voice was steel-strong, so different from the usual tone she used with her friends.

'I don't know... I mean, I don't know what he's playing at, and I don't know if I'm right about him selling his share, it's just with Maggie and Jasmine seeing him with Dodgy Dick, and him saying his parents will be brassed off that they weren't left the bookshop. He's been getting a few calls that seem to make him unhappy and I'm sure it's them. I don't know if I'm putting two and two together and getting a hell of a load of Lord knows what.'

There was a pause down the line, Florrie could almost hear the pistons firing in Stella's mind. 'Right, we need to find out as soon as possible, and if the flaky little shit wants to sell his shares, I'll buy them off him.'

'Stella, I can't ask you to do that!'

'You wouldn't be asking me; I've got some money I want to re-invest and property's the best place for it. I think my mum would be interested too. If not, I'd have to get some sort of mortgage or loan on the balance, but that's not a problem.'

'Oh, right.' Florrie's mind was busy playing catch-up.

'Find out what you can from Harte tomorrow. If he's serious about selling, we need to act quickly. Let me know what he's up to as soon as possible. Okay?'

'Okay.' Stella's tone made Florrie stand to attention.

'Good. Speak to you tomorrow. And, Florrie...'

'Yes.'

'Try not to worry, we'll get this sorted for you; everything will turn out right. We'll make sure of it.' Stella's voice had softened. 'And if Harte's planning on heading back to London, he's not worth shedding a tear over. Got it?'

'Thanks, Stells.' Florrie's throat constricted at hearing the reassuring tone in her friend's voice.

'No probs, chick.'

Florrie sat back, certain of two things. The first was that she had best friends a girl could ask for. The second being it was definitely better to have Stella on your side. Stella Hutton as an enemy? That didn't bear thinking about.

THIRTY-NINE

Florrie hadn't had a minute to catch her breath from the moment she arrived at the bookshop. Despite using the eco-friendly variety, the smell of paint still lingered in the air, masking the familiar, comforting aroma of books. She hoped it wouldn't hang around too long. Since Hayley was at college, she'd had to deal with the barrage of customers and phone calls herself. Rumours of Jack Playforth's reading had created a surge of interest, with most enquiries being in relation to that. But her mind had struggled to focus on anything.

Events of the previous day meant she'd slept fitfully, waking almost every hour despite being exhausted from her long weekend of painting and decorating, Ed never far from her thoughts. Even though she'd had a lie-in, she was still feeling stressed and bleary-eyed this morning, and she really wasn't looking forward to picking up her paintbrush and continuing where she'd left off once the shop was closed for the evening. With a weary sigh she made a mental note to have another chat with Nate about the chairs too. The sooner they could set a date for the poetry reading, the better, she thought, willing her usual enthusiasm to return.

It wasn't until almost ten-thirty that things had finally quietened down, giving her the opportunity to tackle that morning's post. Since Mr H had passed away, Florrie had asked the postman to deliver to the shop rather than the flat – the fewer times she had to venture up there, the better. She was flicking through the mail when her eyes landed on a postcard bearing a picture of Micklewick Bay. She noted there was no stamp or postmark. It must have been hand delivered, she mused. Puzzled, she quickly scanned the scrawled note:

> *Dearest Florrie,*
> *I'm so sorry to tell you like this – I've never*
> *been any good with words – but I've made*
> *the difficult decision to leave Micklewick*
> *Bay. Much as I think you're awesome, my*
> *head's all over the place. Thought it best*
> *to let you know sooner rather than later.*
> *The "useless disappointment" strikes again!*
> *I hope you can find it in your heart to forgive me.*
> *My love always,*
> *Ed x*

Florrie clamped her hand over her mouth, tears blurring her vision as her chest tightened in anguish. She tried to read the words again, a fat tear landing on the postcard. 'Oh, Ed, what have you done?'

She rushed over to the shop door, locking it. There was no way she was fit to serve anyone at the moment. Just as she was turning the sign to closed, Miss Davenport arrived on the doorstep, her face clouding with concern as she took in Florrie's tearful expression.

'Florrie, are you okay?' she asked, her voice muted through the glass.

Florrie shook her head, unlocking the door and letting Miss

Davenport in, quickly locking it again and heading towards the back of the shop. The older woman followed close behind.

'Florrie, my love, whatever's the matter?'

'Oh, Miss Davenport, it's Ed, he's gone,' she said through a sob.

Miss Davenport's face fell. 'Gone?'

Florrie nodded, her face crumpling. Before she knew it, she found herself enveloped in a soft, warm hug. She let the tears fall.

'There, there, lovey, you let it all out,' Miss Davenport said, smoothing Florrie's hair.

Eventually, Florrie released herself, taking her glasses off and wiping her swollen eyes with the back of her hands. 'Thank you,' she said when Miss Davenport handed her a tissue, mopping up her tears and blowing her nose. She looked at her friend to see a pair of concerned eyes looking back at her. Even in her state of distress, Florrie could see Miss Davenport still carried an air of sorrow around her. She felt a rush of concern; once she'd processed this postcard situation, she'd make sure to check her friend was doing all right.

'I don't mean to pry, but I'm happy to listen if you'd like to talk.' Her friend smiled kindly, her sad eyes making Florrie's heart go out to her.

Florrie nodded, dabbing at her runny nose as she was guided to the couple of chairs in the corner of the tiny room. Miss Davenport sat her down and set about making a pot of tea as Florrie, fiddling with her fingers, recounted what had happened over the last few days, her doubts over Dodgy Dick, Stella's offer, and the postcard from Ed. She didn't include the fact that she'd found herself falling for him and that her heart was aching knowing he could walk away from her so easily.

Gerty sat down beside her, nudging her hands with her head until Florrie gave her a pat.

'I don't know why he let me know like this, rather than call me, or text; we could've discussed it.'

'I expected better from young Edward; his grandfather would be devastated if he knew,' Miss Davenport said, tutting and shaking her head as she handed Florrie a mug of tea. 'There you go, lovey, get that down you.'

'Thank you.' Florrie nursed the mug in her lap, the occasional sob jarring in her chest. 'I just feel a bit punch-drunk with it all. So much has happened over the last couple of weeks, everything's feeling a bit muddled.'

Miss Davenport nodded. 'There's no wonder, it'll feel like you've been on a rollercoaster. It's not at all what Bernard would've wanted for you, nor what he would've wanted for Edward, for that matter.'

Florrie took a juddery breath. 'I wish I'd known what his plans were before he had chance to put them in his will, then I could've stopped him and wouldn't be in this situation. Wouldn't have got to know Ed.' Her voice tailed off.

'You care for him, don't you, lovey?' Miss Davenport said softly, leaning across and placing her hand over Florrie's.

Florrie hung her head, tears rolling down her cheeks. There was no point denying it. 'Yes.' She nodded then sniffed. 'Thought he liked me too. Ughh! What a fool I've been.'

'You're anything but a fool. We've all been there at some time in our life.' Miss Davenport squeezed Florrie's fingers. 'And where did you say he was now?'

Florrie shrugged. At this moment in time Timbuktu wouldn't be far enough away for her liking. 'I don't know, in his postcard he just said he was leaving.' She pushed up the sleeve of her cardigan to check her watch. 'I guess he'll be at the station, waiting for the train to York so he can get a connecting one to London.'

'Don't you think it might be worth trying to speak to him about selling his share before he leaves, if that's what he's intending to do?' Miss Davenport dipped her chin, searching out Florrie's eyes.

Florrie gazed back. 'You mean...?'

Miss Davenport smiled, nodding. 'Yes. Now's your chance. I'll stay here with Gerty. The last thing you need is him signing something or agreeing to something with Dodgy Dick before you've had the chance to tell him about Stella's offer.'

Florrie felt a small wave of hope washing over her. She pushed herself up. 'You're right, Miss Davenport. If you're sure you don't mind holding the fort...'

'I don't. Now go on, get a wriggle on, you've only got five minutes before the York train leaves.'

With her heart banging hard against her chest, Florrie flew out of the shop and raced down to the station, dodging in and out of shoppers as she went. She burst into the ticket office to find only a young woman with a toddler at the counter. The woman looked round startled, the cashier flashing her a frown. 'Sorry, just looking for someone.' Florrie gave an apologetic smile before turning on her heel and running out onto platform one, almost colliding with a businessman pulling his suitcase along. 'Oops! Sorry!' She pelted through the subway, the sound of her shoes hitting the pavement echoing around her. Out on platform two her senses were alerted to a cacophony of pigeons cooing from the ornate steel rafters above, the low hum of a train engine and the distinctive whiff of diesel fumes. Her chest heaved as she gasped for breath, scanning the handful of people waiting for trains. Her heart sank; there was no sign of Ed.

A quick look at the train idling in the station told her it was destined for York. Quickening her pace she ran alongside it, searching the carriages through the windows. At the far end she saw the guard alight, checking up and down the platform. Panic filled her as the sound of his whistle rang around the station, shrill and harsh. 'Please wait!' But he didn't appear to hear her and, with a toot of its horn, the train nosed its way slowly out of the station. Florrie raced along beside it, desperately glancing into the carriages, trying to keep up with the train's increasing speed. Finally, she had to admit defeat as she watched it snake its way along the line until it was eventually out of sight.

She leant forward, her hands on her knees, gasping for breath, her heart feeling like it would burst. 'No!' She closed her eyes, tears squeezing between her dark lashes.

It was too late. Ed had gone.

FORTY

Florrie trudged her way slowly back to the bookshop, a feeling of despondency swamping her body, dragging her shoulders down. If only she'd been five minutes earlier she might have had the chance to stop Ed, or at least speak to him. If only she hadn't had that lie-in she'd have got to work earlier, seen his postcard and had time to think about what to do before she got swept up by customers and phone calls. Why was it everything she did at the moment felt like she was wading through treacle? Her life was never usually this difficult. It was calm and ordered and peaceful. Or it had been until a few weeks ago.

Back at the bookshop, Miss Davenport greeted her with eager eyes. 'How did it go? Did you find him?'

Florrie shook her head. 'The train pulled out before I had the chance to check all the carriages. Maybe I should've called or texted him, but then again, he'd probably have ignored my messages.' Her head was thumping, and she felt suddenly weary from crying, weary from the decorating, weary from chasing after the train. Weary from everything.

'Maybe young Edward just needs some time to think. He's had a lot to deal with too,' said Miss Davenport, giving Florrie a sympathetic smile. 'It can't have been easy for him to lose his grandad after just getting in contact with him, then find out he was part-owner of this place, whether he wanted it or not.'

What he'd shared about how being surrounded by books filled him with dread crept into in her mind. That should have been enough for her to realise being part-owner of a bookshop was never going to work for him.

'I suspect you're right. He's had a lot to contend with recently. I know losing his grandad hit him hard, and he's just come out of a difficult relationship, which will have been a stressful mix. But I just wish he'd been upfront with me from the start, told me it was definitely a no-go for him.' Feeling her headache intensify, Florrie gently massaged her temples. 'We could've talked about our other options; maybe he'd have considered being a sleeping partner, then he wouldn't need to be hands-on with the bookshop, wouldn't even need to live here. That way, he would've still respected Mr H's wishes, which was something Ed said he was keen to do.' As she spoke, a nagging doubt crept in as she recalled the phone calls that used to leave Ed looking hassled. 'Having said that, I can't shake the feeling his parents might have contributed to his decision.'

'Oh?'

'Hmm. Something he said makes me suspect they might've been pushing him to sell and give the proceeds to them. I'm actually surprised they haven't contacted me, expecting me to transfer my share into their name so they could sell up.' Florrie didn't like to share the finer details of her conversation with Ed when he'd told her his parents had talked about selling the bookshop when they'd heard Mr H had died. A cold shiver crept over her body. It must have taken the wind right out of their sails when old Mr Cuthbert told them the shop hadn't been bequeathed to them.

'They wouldn't dare!' Miss Davenport pushed her shoulders back, pulling Florrie out of her musings with a start.

'There's no way Mr Cuthbert would countenance that! In fact, why don't you go and have a word with him about the situation with Ed?' She seemed suddenly brighter.

'Mr Cuthbert?'

'Yes, I don't know why I didn't think of that before. He'll put you straight about everything. Maybe you can mention Stella buying Ed's share, if it comes to it, that is.'

'I suppose it wouldn't hurt.'

'You should ring the office now. You need to get an appointment as soon as possible.' Florrie had never known Miss Davenport be so forceful.

'You think so?'

'I most certainly do. Come on, there's no time like the present.' She chivvied Florrie along, tapping her on the arm.

'I suppose Stella did say she wanted me to act quickly.'

Miss Davenport waited while Florrie rang the solicitors' office. The receptionist advised that Mr Cuthbert was with a client but assured her he'd call back as soon as he was able. Florrie felt a pang of disappointment; she'd rather have got things sorted out as soon as possible than hover over the phone until it rang.

'I'm sure he'll call back as soon as he's free.' Miss Davenport gave a reassuring smile.

Florrie regarded her friend. 'So how have you been since I last saw you?' Though she didn't need to hear Miss Davenport's reply to know that the fingers of grief still had a tight grip on her.

'Oh, you know, lovey, taking each day as it comes. I still can't believe Bernard's gone.' She shook her head, tears suddenly glistening in her eyes. 'It's hard to think I won't ever see him again here in the shop, but the thought of you and young Edward running it together had given me a little nugget of hope for brighter days ahead, and I know it will have done the same for Bernard.'

Florrie reached forward and wrapped her fingers around Miss Davenport's hand, regretting burdening her friend with her worries. 'Well, there'll still be something to look forward to if Stella buys him out, and there's no reason the plans I had with Ed can't still go ahead. Stella's very driven in everything she does.'

'True. I hadn't thought of that.' A smile brightened Miss Davenport's face.

'And don't forget about Jack Playforth and the reading; I'm going to need your help with that more than ever, if you're still okay to be involved?'

'Of course. But what a shame Edward won't be here for it, it being his idea and all.'

Florrie was about to reply when the phone rang, making her friend almost jump out of her skin. 'Oh, my goodness! That frightened the life out of me!'

'It's Cuthbert, Asquith's number,' said Florrie, taking the call. Miss Davenport crossed her fingers and went to leave, giving Florrie some privacy. Florrie shook her head and gestured for her to stay put. 'It's fine,' she said, mouthing the words.

Ten minutes later Florrie set the phone down on the worktop and turned to Miss Davenport who was sitting on the edge of her seat, looking up at her eagerly.

'So is everything going to be okay?'

'I'm not sure. Mr Cuthbert's going to have a word with Ed, see if he can find out what's going on, see if he'd be willing to sell to Stella.' Though her heart was still thumping, the solicitor's words had offered some reassurance.

Miss Davenport fell back into her chair, pressing her hand to her chest. 'Let's hope he can talk some sense into him.'

'Yes, let's hope so.'

It transpired that Mr Cuthbert hadn't heard anything from Ed and had sounded most disappointed to think he'd sell his share of the bookshop. 'Tsk. If it's true, Bernard would be enormously saddened to hear it,' he'd said, disapproval heavy in his voice. 'But do try not to get yourself in a pickle, my dear; we don't know for definite that's what young Edward's planning to do.'

Florrie released an impatient sigh, running her fingers through her hair. 'Well, we can't do anything at the moment, so we'll just have to sit tight until Mr Cuthbert manages to get hold of Ed. In the meantime, I just hope Dodgy Dick doesn't come swanning in here as if he already owns the place.' As soon as she'd vocalised that thought another one jumped into her mind. 'Actually, I promised I'd keep Stella up-to-speed with everything; I'd best let her know. S'cuse me while I just send her a quick text, Miss Davenport. She'll probably be in court, but at least she'll see it as soon as she's done.'

'Of course, lovey.'

With the text sent, Florrie turned her attention back to Miss Davenport, saddened to see the older woman still looking pale and wan. She felt suddenly guilty that she'd put her own concerns before her friend's. She mustered up a smile. 'You didn't get finished telling me how you'd been keeping.'

Miss Davenport sighed. 'Oh, you know, I'm plodding on, but I can't seem to shift this sadness that's following me around. And for the first time in a long time, I'm struggling to concentrate on reading. I know it sounds silly, but my days just feel hollow and empty; I haven't had the heart to go to any of my clubs recently.'

'It doesn't sound silly at all. Losing Mr H has knocked the stuffing out of you; you're grieving.'

Miss Davenport nodded forlornly.

'And I know it might not seem like it right now, but getting out to those clubs will help take your mind off things. I know this place is helping me, especially with all the decorating we've been doing; I haven't had time to dwell too much. And of course, my friends have helped too.' *And spending time with Ed.* But Florrie didn't want to linger on him. 'It's when I have time on my own to brood that I feel Mr H's loss the most.'

'I know, and I'd like to go to my meetings; I know they'd do me good, but that busybody Joyce Stubbs goes to them too and she's always meddling in other people's business, pretending to be nice but being horrible behind everyone's back, spreading spiteful rumours. I simply couldn't face her at the moment, I know she'd be trying to prise information out of me about Bernard and his will as soon as I got there. I'm worried I'd say something I might regret.'

'Oh, I wouldn't worry about that one, everyone knows what she's like.' Florrie decided not to mention that Joyce Stubbs had already been in the shop in case it stopped Miss Davenport coming in. She'd turned up a couple of days after Mr H had died, her dark, beady eyes staring out of a mean, pinched face as she'd asked Florrie about the future of the bookshop, wanting to know details of who had found Mr H. Her unfeeling, forthright manner had set Florrie's hackles up, and she'd replied, firmly but politely, that it was something she'd rather not talk about. Joyce had set her mouth into a thin, hard line as she paid for the pen she'd purportedly come in for. She'd swivelled on her heel and left the shop leaving a cloud of disapproval in her wake.

'Don't hurry back,' Florrie had said once the door had clicked shut, anger burning in her stomach.

'Sour old bag,' Hayley had said with a snarl. 'You can tell she's toxic just by looking at her face.' Florrie hadn't been able to argue with that.

It saddened her to think that her friend was confining herself to her empty house because of some spiteful woman who nobody took any notice of, but she could understand it all the same. 'Well, if that's how you're feeling, how do you fancy giving me a hand with some other things? I know you're keen to help out on the night of Jack Playforth's reading, but there's lots of other stuff to do.'

Miss Davenport's eyes brightened. 'Very much, but what do you mean?'

'Now Ed's gone, I could do with some help in organising the reading club. I'm keen to get it started as soon as possible; there's no point hanging around, waiting to see what he's going to do.' She watched her friend's reaction closely, not wanting her to feel she was being pushed into anything. 'Actually, come and see what we've done with the storeroom, I think you'll be pleasantly surprised.'

Florrie made her way through the shop followed by Gerty and Miss Davenport. Her heart lifting a little when she saw the room. It looked even brighter and fresher now the paint had dried.

'It still needs another coat of paint, as does the woodwork, but I'm really pleased with the results.' *And so would Ed be if he'd stuck around.* 'You're actually the first to see it.'

'Well, I'm honoured.' Miss Davenport stepped into the room, her eyes shining as she gazed around it. 'Oh, this is lovely. Such a shame it's been hidden away for all these years. And is this where you plan to host the reading club?'

'It is.' Florrie nodded, pleased to see her friend looking brighter. 'Actually, are you free this evening?'

'I am, why?'

'How do you fancy coming to my house for tea? I'll grab a quiche from the bakery, rustle-up a quick salad. We can eat while we chat about the reading club; I'd appreciate your input.'

'You would?'

Florrie smiled. 'I would.'

'But aren't you busy with your painting once the shop's shut?'

'To be honest, after what's happened in the last twenty-four hours, I don't think I could face tackling it this evening. Another day won't hurt, and besides, it'd be nice to have a catch-up with you. It feels like we haven't had a good old natter for ages.'

'Well, if you're sure?'

'I'm positive. Say six-thirty?'

'Ooh, lovely, I'm looking forward to it already.' The sallow tinge to Miss Davenport's cheeks had been replaced by a rosy glow.

'Same here.' The idea had perked Florrie up too. 'Well, I suppose I'd better get the shop back open for business before folk start wondering what else has happened.'

Florrie was making her way to the front of the shop when there was a knock at the door. Through the glass, she could see Jack Playforth cupping his hands around his eyes, peering in.

'Coming.' Florrie hurried to the door, unlocking it and flicking the sign over so it said "Open", Gerty peering around her. 'Sorry about that, Jack, please, come in.'

He smiled hesitantly, sliding his flat cap off his head and stuffing it in his pocket. 'You sure? I'm not intruding am I?' He bent to pat Gerty's head. 'Good lass.'

'No, not at all, I just had a bit of personal stuff to deal with.' She guessed her eyes must still betray that she'd been crying.

'Okay, as long as you're sure.' He gave a wider smile, nodding to Miss Davenport. 'Hello there.'

'Oh, excuse my manners,' said Florrie. 'Jack, this is my friend Jean Davenport, Miss Davenport, this is Jack Playforth.'

'Pleased to meet you.' Jack smiled, giving a quick nod.

The older woman was suddenly all of a flutter. 'Oh, my goodness, Jack Playforth! I'm pleased to meet you too. I was thrilled when Florrie told me you'd agreed to do a reading here. I'm a huge fan of your work, I could read it for hours.'

'Thank you, that's very kind,' he said almost bashfully. 'It's the reason I'm here actually, the reading that is. Just thought I'd pop in and see how things were coming along with the room, maybe see if we could decide on a date.' He raised his nose in the air, sniffing. 'Seems you've been busy; is that paint I can smell?'

'It is.' Florrie nodded. 'Come this way, you can see our progress for yourself.'

Florrie showed Jack the room, explaining what was left to do. 'The plan was to have you sitting here at this end, with the audience over here.' She walked across the room, her shoes resounding on the floorboards as she went, stopping at a central spot at the back, facing the window. 'Nate, who's a friend of a friend, has sourced us some wooden chairs for the audience. Actually, I'm really pleased you've popped in, 'cos he's found a vintage leather wingback chair too and I wondered if it would be any good for you to sit in while you do your reading?' As soon as she'd set eyes on the slightly battered ox-blood leather seat, it had kick-started an idea of having the storeroom dressed in a Victorian library theme. She'd visualised it as cosy and intimate, Jack's voice filling the room. She and Ed had found plenty of suitable props when they'd been sorting through the piles of stuff. But she wanted to run it by the poet before she got carried away.

Jack beamed as he glanced around, deep creases forming at the corners of his eyes. 'What a lovely space this is, and I love the idea of the wingback chair; it sounds a good deal more comfortable than sitting on a mound of prickly heather and having stray spikes of gorse digging into my backside, or having to worry about ticks sneaking up my trouser legs.' His eyes twinkled as the two women laughed.

Florrie clasped her hands together. 'I can promise you, there'll be no thorns or ticks here. And I'll text Nate straight away and let him know to keep the chair for us.'

'Thank you,' said Jack.

Looking at him today, his expression friendly and relaxed, Florrie found it hard to it match this man to the one in the rumours reporting of his explosive temper; she couldn't imagine him getting cross at all.

The bell above the shop door rang and the three returned to the shopfloor with Gerty in tow. 'Have you made much progress tracing your family tree, Jack?' Florrie asked as they walked towards the counter, her eyes finding the customer who was heading over to the romance section.

'Not as much as I'd have liked, I'm afraid, writing seems to have got in the way of that. This place is that inspiring, words just keep flooding into my head.' He chuckled. 'I can't write 'em down fast enough.'

Florrie turned to face Miss Davenport. 'Jack's not just here to write, he's got a family connection this way and he's hoping to trace some relatives.'

'Really? What a lovely thought, Jack Playforth having family that hails from Micklewick Bay.'

'Actually, you'd do well to talk to Miss Davenport, Jack, she's a mine of information as far as local history and families are concerned. In fact, you're very welcome to join us for tea tonight.' Florrie didn't know where such boldness had come from. Had she really asked Jack Playforth to her simple little home?

'Ooh, it would be lovely if you could,' said Miss Davenport, her eyes shining.

'I'd be delighted; glad of the company actually,' he said, looking equally thrilled. 'Just let me know the time and the place, and I'll be there.'

'That's brilliant!' Florrie reached for the notebook on the counter and scribbled down her address and the time. 'It's nothing fancy – my cottage and my cooking – but you'll be very welcome.' She handed him the piece of paper, catching Miss Davenport's eye, the pair of them exchanging wide smiles. It was good to see her friend looking happy again.

FORTY-ONE

The afternoon had flown by, for which Florrie was thankful since it meant she hadn't had too much time to dwell on Ed. He hadn't been in touch, and she'd resisted the temptation to contact him. And, whenever she felt him popping into her mind, pulling her mood down, making her head swim with confusion, she pushed him away, focussing instead on her evening with Miss Davenport and Jack Playforth. She wouldn't have time to dither about when it came to closing time; the downstairs of her home could benefit from a quick whizz over with the vacuum before her guests arrived.

At lunchtime, she popped into the bakery to grab a quiche, a loaf of crusty bread and a cake for pudding that evening. 'How's things going?' Jasmine asked, popping the cake into a box. The wiggle of her eyebrows suggested she was referring to Ed.

'Erm, okay.' Florrie hadn't had the chance to tell her friends he'd upped and gone and was reluctant to say too much in front of the other customers, one of whom was Joyce Stubbs whose ears had pricked up.

Jasmine nodded, pulling a face to show she understood the

subtext of Florrie's words. 'Fab. There you go, chick, give me a call when you've got a minute, I know you're rushed off your feet at the moment, what with everything that's going on.' She winked, handing over the carrier bag. Florrie couldn't help but smile, she knew her friend had said that for Joyce's benefit.

* * *

Florrie was arranging the flowers she'd bought earlier at lunch time when there was a knock at her door. She set the vase on the windowsill and followed Gerty down the hall.

'Come in, Miss Davenport.' Florrie greeted her friend with a smile, standing back to let her in. She was pleased to see her looking more like her old self, with her hair set in gentle waves, a swipe of pearly-pink lipstick and a flush of colour in her cheeks. The older woman shrugged off her coat revealing a twinset in cornflower blue that flattered her complexion. 'You look lovely,' Florrie said, giving her a quick hug. 'Here, let me hang up your coat.'

'These are for you, lovey.' Miss Davenport handed Florrie a box of chocolates.

'Oh, there really was no need, but thank you.' Florrie kissed her cheek, it was cool and soft and smelt of powder. She was glad to have her evening occupied rather than being alone and free for her mind to fill with thoughts of Ed and Mr H.

Once in the kitchen Florrie looked intently at Miss Davenport, drawing her teeth nervously across her bottom lip before she spoke. 'Before Jack gets here, I'd be really grateful if you wouldn't mention the situation with Ed. It's just, I don't want him to get the impression we're unprofessional, or don't appreciate what he's offered to do for us. If he asks where Ed is, I'm just going to say he had to pop down to London on business.' She searched the older woman's face, hoping to read her reaction.

'Of course, lovey. I can understand why you'd want to do that.' She patted Florrie's arm reassuringly. 'Speaking of young Edward, I don't suppose you've heard anything from him, have you?'

'No.' Florrie shook her head, a feeling of heaviness settling in her heart, pushing aside the flutter of nerves that had been brewing at the prospect of having one of Yorkshire's most revered poets here in her tiny little cottage.

'Well, just put him out of your mind for tonight and let's hope he comes to his senses soon and gets his backside back up here where he belongs.'

Florrie was saved from saying she hoped he'd stay put in London and that she'd be happy if she never saw him again when there was another knock at the door. Her heart leapt and she grabbed hold of Miss Davenport's hand. 'This is so surreal,' she said in a whisper, the pair grinning broadly.

'I know!' Miss Davenport squeezed Florrie's hand. 'Let's have ourselves a wonderful evening, my love.'

* * *

Set to a mellow playlist of Florrie's favourite classical music, the three chatted away like they'd known each other forever. There was no hint of any diva behaviour from Jack, instead he cracked endless self-deprecating jokes, and shared stories of the times he'd recited his poetry in pubs and how he'd had rotten tomatoes thrown at him. 'Aye, it took me a right long time before I'd honed my craft and for folk to stop thinking I was bletherin' on about a load of old codswallop. Seemed to happen overnight. One minute no one would give me the time of day, and the next I was getting booked to do appearances on the telly. It was crazy.' He'd scratched his head as if he still couldn't quite believe his success.

Florrie and Miss Davenport had listened, enthralled.

'And I always said I'd never forget my humble beginnings, nor the kindness of the folk who gave me a leg up, nor the times when I was penniless and living off the bones of my arse.'

'Is that why you agreed to do the reading for us?' Florrie asked, her cheeks pink with the warmth of the kitchen. She was surprised to be feeling so relaxed after the morning's events.

'Aye, it is, lass. Your friend, Ed, reminded me a bit of myself, taking the risk to ask something you think there's not a hope in hell's chance of happening. The feeling when it does is fantastic.'

Florrie smiled, her stomach leaping at the mention of Ed's name. Her eyes shot across to Miss Davenport who gave the tiniest lift of her eyebrows.

'Well, I for one, am grateful you said yes; I'm so looking forward to hearing you read. Have you decided on a piece yet?' Miss Davenport asked, her face animated. 'Having said that, I could listen to you read from the back of a tin of meatballs and think it was wonderful, you have such a magical tone to your voice.'

'Thank you, that's very kind. I'll be sure to bring a shopping basket filled with tinned stuff to the reading; might go down better than my poetry.' He chuckled. 'Actually, now you mention it, I quite like idea of reading the list of contents from a tin of meatballs aloud. Can you imagine the look on everyone's face if I did that?' He gave a mischievous grin before adopting a serious expression, holding an imaginary tin aloft in his hand. He cleared his throat, his sure, rich Yorkshire accent filling the room as he enunciated each word slowly. 'Minced beef. Herbs. Tomatoes. Sage. Onion. Gravy.' He took a dramatic pause, glancing around the room, shaking his head sagely. 'Never, never forget t'gravy. It's *all* about t'gravy.' He took a deep breath, his nostrils flaring. 'Heat thoroughly before serving. Once opened, keep in t'fridge and get 'em down yer within three days.' As soon as he'd finished, the three of them roared with laughter.

'That was brilliant,' said Florrie, taking off her glasses and wiping tears of mirth from her cheeks.

Miss Davenport clapped her hands together, merriment dancing in her eyes. 'Ooh, that was just wonderful. I haven't laughed so much in a long time.'

'Happy to oblige,' said Jack, his eyes crinkling as he smiled.

* * *

Conversation flowed all evening, punctuated by much laughter, the three clean forgetting that Jack was here to pick Miss Davenport's brains about local families. Soon she was declaring it was time she headed home.

'Would you allow me to see you to your house, Jean? It's a dark night for a genteel lady like yourself to be walking home alone,' said Jack.

'Oh, how very gentlemanly, but I wouldn't want to put you to any trouble.'

Florrie almost jumped in; she needed to take Gerty for her last walk so could kill two birds with one stone and combine it with seeing her friend home, but the glow of happiness on Miss Davenport's face made her hold back.

'It'd be no trouble to me at all, it's a lovely evening out there.'

'Well, thank you, that's very kind, though I don't live too far away.'

It was fair to say, Jack Playforth had been a real tonic for both of them. Florrie had barely given Ed a thought all evening.

FORTY-TWO

Later that night, Florrie lay in bed unable to sleep. Her life felt like a spinning coin, whirling out of control, not knowing which way up it was going to land. Today had been an unlikely mix of dizzying highs – Jack Playforth had actually visited her house which was up there as a real "pinch-me-it-can't-be-true" high – and utterly depressing lows – Ed leaving without even speaking to her had taken the wind out of her sails much more than she'd anticipated.

She made the decision to push him very firmly to the furthest point of her mind. It was time to forget about him.

Rousing from sleep the following morning, Florrie's mind was filled with Ed – her resolution had been short-lived. She stirred, the movement making her feather duvet rustle. A lazy smile played over her mouth as his handsome face looked down at her, his fringe flopping forward sexily, his familiar easy grin making his deep-blue eyes dance. They were walking leisurely along the quaint cobbled streets of Old Micklewick, the warmth

276

of the sun caressing her back, his arm flung around her shoulders, the sweet smell of confectionary drifting on the breeze as they passed the Fudge House. He dropped a kiss to her cheek, pulling her closer. She sighed happily. Oh, what bliss! He started to say something to her, she could see his lips moving, but the ear-splitting cries of a herring gull overhead drowned out his words. 'What did you say? I can't hear you?' she asked, straining to hear him. 'Tell me again...'

She blinked her sleep-heavy eyes, as slumber slowly released her. She lay still for a moment, allowing her mind to focus and realisation creep in. Her heart came crashing down. She'd been dreaming. She wasn't with Ed, and the god-awful racket was coming from a seagull that had perched itself on the chimney pot of her cottage. An image of Ed's postcard loomed in her mind, elbowing any lingering dregs of happiness out of the way, allowing sadness to sneak in and take its place. He'd gone. He'd left Micklewick Bay without a backwards glance, taking her hopes and dreams with him.

With a groan, Florrie pulled the duvet over her head. She couldn't bear to think about it.

Over a quick breakfast of toast washed down with a mug of tea, Florrie gave herself a stern talking to, reminding herself she wasn't going to waste another second mooning over Ed Harte. They were business partners – for now at least – he'd have to make contact sometime, whether it be with her directly or through the solicitors, she didn't care how. There were still things that needed sorting out, but if he didn't want to be involved in the running of the bookshop then so much the better; she was happy to manage it on her own. She'd ask Mr Cuthbert to draw up some kind of working agreement for them, keep everything right and watertight. If he was happy to sell his share to Stella, even better. If he insisted on selling to Dodgy Dick, then ... ughh! She didn't want to dwell on that this early in the morning. Her life had been fine before Ed had burst into it, disrupting it with his easy, amiable way, and it would jolly-well be fine now he'd gone. She was going to carry on as if she'd never met him.

Florrie drained her tea, casting her eyes over to her mobile phone which was charging. She unplugged it, checking the slew of messages she'd missed from the previous evening. There was one from her mum asking her to call back, a breezy one from Jasmine checking-in with her, and a text from Stella asking for an update on the situation with Ed "Heartless" – as she referred to him. Florrie chuckled at that. There was nothing from the man himself, but she hadn't been expecting to hear from him.

She replied quickly to the messages, telling her mum she'd ring when she had a quiet moment.

'Onwards and upwards,' she said when she was done. Gerty looked up at her quizzically. 'Time to face the day, Gerty. Come on, let's get this show on the road.' Florrie hoped she sounded more convincing than she felt.

* * *

It was almost half-past eleven when her mum landed, all smiles and rosy cheeks, kick-starting a surge of happiness in Florrie's chest. It had been a long, drawn-out morning, and her mind had kept wandering back to Ed and Mr H.

'Hi, Mum, it's lovely to see you.'

'Hello, lovey, it's good to see you too.' Paula pulled her into a hug that smelt of fresh sea air and her familiar light floral perfume, delivering a kiss to her cheek. That done, she took a step back, her hands resting on Florrie's shoulders, her forehead crumpling with a frown. 'Is everything all right? You seem to have lost a bit of sparkle since we saw you on Sunday,' she said softly, quickly glancing around for customers.

'It's okay, there's no one else here.' Florrie felt herself flop, the scaffolding of the talking to she'd given herself the previous evening bending and buckling on seeing her mum.

'No Ed?' Paula searched her daughter's face, mother's intuition kicking in.

Florrie shook her head forlornly.

'Oh, sweetheart, what's happened?' She squeezed Florrie's shoulders.

'I'd rather not go into detail right now, but he's gone, Mum. Decided he doesn't want to be part of the bookshop after all.' She swallowed, hearing her voice waver.

Paula's mouth fell open. 'But what about the plans you both had? He was so full of enthusiasm for the bookshop, it can't just have vanished overnight.'

'Apparently it can.' Florrie shrugged, sadness creating a lump in her throat. She rolled her eyes and shook her head angrily, annoyed at herself for getting upset. 'Looks like he wants out.' She held her hand up, clenching her jaw in a bid to keep her voice steady. 'Please, Mum, don't be nice, don't give me any sympathy; I don't want to break down and risk a customer coming in and seeing me looking like a wreck.'

Paula nodded, her face etched with concern. 'I understand, lovey, and much as I want to squeeze you real tight, I'll hold back.' She paused, and Florrie knew she'd be searching for the right thing to say. 'Well... what can your dad and me do to help?'

Florrie took a deep breath. 'It's been deathly quiet in here this morning, I'm tempted to close the shop at midday, just for half an hour. Gerty needs a walk and I could do with some fresh air. If you join us, I can bring you up-to-speed then, if you've got time that is?' She hoped her mum would say yes; she was keen to hear her take on the situation.

'Of course I've got time, my love. I just need to nip to the bank and pay this money in for your dad, then I need to call in at the newsagents. By the time I've got done it'll be getting on for lunchtime. Does that sound okay?'

'Sounds good.' She felt a wave of relief wash over her. Her mum always made things feel better.

Florrie had slipped her coat on and had fastened Gerty's lead to her collar by the time Paula returned. The Labrador was whimpering with excitement, looking up at Florrie, eagerly awaiting the signal that they were about to set off.

'I'll just go and pop these in the fridge for you, lovey. It's a ham salad sandwich and a cream scone from the bakery. You can have them with a cup of tea when you get back.' Paula bustled her way to the small kitchen. 'Oh, and Jasmine says hello, by the way. Lovely girl, that.'

'Thanks, Mum.' She gave a smile. 'Yeah, Jazz is great.'

Florrie locked the door, pocketing the key as she slipped into step with her mum. The light, cool breeze felt refreshing on her skin. She waited until they were well away from the main streets of shops before sharing what had happened since Sunday.

'Well, I'm stunned. Your dad and me certainly didn't get that impression of Ed when he was at our house. Quite the contrary in fact, we both thought he was very genuine. Your dad was quite taken with him actually, warmed to him more than he ever did to Graham. Me too. But I suppose grief can make folk act in funny ways.'

'I'm not sure grief had much to do with it, but at least it isn't only me who was fooled by him,' said Florrie, her eyes fixed to the pavement.

Paula took a couple of moments before she spoke. 'Hmm. From what I saw of him, I don't think he was trying to fool anyone, Florrie, love. And, much as I don't like how he's upset you and am disappointed that he chose to use a postcard to tell you he was leaving rather than speaking to you face-to-face, after listening to what you've said, it sounds like he's very possibly being brow-beaten by his parents. It can't be easy for him.'

Florrie turned her gaze to her mum, it was so like her to play devil's advocate. It was the reason Florrie valued her mother's opinion, knowing she'd evaluate a situation by taking all sides into account. 'But would that make him take off the way he did? Without explaining the dilemma he was in? Not giving us a chance to talk it through? Surely he'd know I'd understand.'

'Put yourself in his shoes. What would you do if your dad and me were wittering on at you to do something over and over again, nag, nag, nagging away? You can't tell me our wishes wouldn't weigh heavily on your conscience over and above anyone else's, even if you might not agree with them. And don't forget what he said about how books make him feel uncomfortable. Top if off with the messy break-up with his ex; there's no wonder he needs some space.' She turned to Florrie, seeking her eyes. 'I actually feel sorry for the lad.'

Florrie watched Gerty sashaying along on the end of the lead, her tail held aloft, with not a care in the world. Her mum's words were running through her mind, recalling the numerous calls Ed had taken that had left him subdued. She could see her point, but it still didn't justify him leaving the way he had. 'I completely understand that it must be horrendous if his parents are pressurising him on top of losing his grandfather and all the other things that were stressing him out. But he's a grown man, not a little boy, and he could've spoken to me about it; it's not as if I'm a monster. And he could've stood up to his parents and told them he wasn't going to sell, if that wasn't what he wanted.' She paused for a moment, taking a deep breath. 'I actually think his parents pressurising him has given him the perfect excuse.'

Paula thought for a moment. 'I very much doubt Ed thinks you're a monster, I think he probably found it too painful to tell you in person. Nor do I think he's using his parents as an excuse. If you want the truth, lovey, I think he was probably a bit scared of his feelings.'

Before Paula could elaborate, the whirring of skateboard wheels behind them caught their attention. Florrie didn't need to look to know who it was. 'Don't say anything else till this person's well out of earshot, Mum,' she said in a whisper as Ando Taylor whooshed by.

'Hey, Florrie,' he said, spinning his board round and giving a casual wave before leaping off the kerb.

'Hi,' she said, watching him disappear down the road.

'Anyway, what I was about to say was I think young Ed could be feeling a bit overwhelmed by his feelings,' Paula said.

'What do you mean?'

'Well, as you know your dad and me don't like to stick our noses into your business, but we could see the way the lad was looking at you on Sunday. It's written all over his face; he's smitten.'

Florrie went to object but Paula cut her short. 'Hear me out, flower. What I'm trying to say is that your dad and me thought the pair of you just seemed to slot together quite naturally; you're well-suited. And before you say it, we weren't trying to match-make, we just know what we saw. You seemed happier and more relaxed in his presence than you were in all the time you were with Graham.'

Florrie felt her cheeks burn; there was no point denying her feelings to her mum; she'd see through that straight away.

Paula rested her hand on Florrie's arm. 'I'm just sorry things have turned out the way they have and that you're upset. But, as we both always say, things have a happy knack of working them-selves out. And I've a feeling that'll be the case for you.'

Florrie resisted the temptation to say she didn't want things to "work themselves out". What she wanted was her old, peaceful life back. The one where she'd woken up on a morning and pretty much knew what the day had in store for her. Was that the reason she'd stayed in her uneventful relationship with Graham for so long? Very probably. Though, his recent behaviour had confirmed breaking-up had been very much the right thing to do.

Since the day she'd learnt of her mum's illness, and fear had dominated her waking hours, only releasing its grip when Paula had been given the all-clear, Florrie had come to savour her life being on an even keel. Change and upheaval equated to stress and sorrow to her. It was like throwing a large pebble into a lake; that simple "sploosh" creating far-reaching ripples and the potential for unwelcome consequences. Mr H passing away was a perfect example, poor old soul. If it wasn't for that, she'd never have found herself spending so much time in Ed's company, and she wouldn't have found herself falling for him despite her struggles not to.

And she'd never have had this dreadful ache in her heart.

FORTY-THREE

Back at the bookshop, Paula presented her daughter with a sandwich surrounded by a sprinkling of cheese and onion crisps, and a steaming mug of tea to wash it down, telling her she'd keep an eye on the shop while Florrie ate her lunch in peace.

'Thanks, Mum, you're a star.'

'You're welcome, lovely. Oh, and before I forget, I've spoken to your dad; him and me are coming here after work to help you finish painting the storeroom.'

'But—'

Paula held her hand up. 'No arguments, the three of us will get it done in no time. Many hands, as they say'.

Florrie couldn't argue with that. 'Thanks, Mum.' She breathed a sigh of relief. It would be one less thing to worry about.

Florrie sat quiet, mulling over the conversation she'd had with her mum, absent-mindedly flicking through a magazine Paula had set out for her. If Ed did return as Paula had gone on to say he would, there was no way Florrie could welcome him back as if nothing had happened. She would tolerate being his business partner because it was Mr H's wishes, but that was all she was prepared to be. Nothing more. She wasn't going to risk opening her heart to anyone for a good long while, least of all flaky Ed. Her affections were staying under lock and key for the foreseeable future; she didn't need the hassle.

As she chewed on her mouthful, half-heartedly reading an article on seaside gardens, Florrie's nose twitched, suddenly aware of the heady scent of incense while her ears detected a light, jingle-jangle sound.

'Penny for them,' said a familiar, softly spoken voice.

Florrie looked up to see Lark smiling down at her, the light glowing behind her golden-blonde hair, affording her an angelic appearance.

'Lark, it's good to see you.' Florrie got to her feet and went over to hug her friend, immediately enveloped in a waft of fragrance. 'What brings you over here?' she asked, standing back.

'I couldn't shake the sense you were unhappy, and I just had to come and see you,' she said, appraising Florrie as she fiddled with a bead at the end of one of the fine plaits woven into her locks. 'Are you keeping the amethyst close? You know you can even tuck it in your bra, let it work its magic from there; you won't even notice it.'

'Not so sure my bra's big enough,' Florrie said with a chuckle, patting her trouser pocket 'It's in here.'

'Good.' Lark slipped her patchwork slouch bag off her shoulder and reached inside it, her bracelets sliding melodically up and down her arms. 'I've brought you this, it's a mixture of soothing essential oils to add to your bath or use in a diffuser. It'll have you floating on cloud nine in no time.' She handed Florrie a blue glass bottle she recognised as being from Lark's shop. Her friend was as passionate about the powers of aromatherapy as she was vintage items.

Thank you.' Florrie unscrewed the lid and wafted the bottle under her nose. 'Mmm. Smells heavenly.'

Lark's smile lit up her eyes. 'And this came in the other day; I thought of you as soon as I saw it.' She pulled out a small, flat parcel wrapped in sky-blue tissue paper, tied with a pale pink ribbon. 'It's been laundered, and has the most amazing vibe I've ever picked up in an item; it's so soothing.'

Florrie took the gift, opening it carefully and lifting out a square of silk printed with vivid red poppies with deep green foliage on a creamy-white background. She gasped. 'Oh, Lark, it's beautiful. Are you sure?'

'Of course I'm sure.' Lark beamed. 'It couldn't possibly go to anyone else. And with your love of bold colours, I thought it would go with most of your wardrobe.'

'It so will.' Florrie folded the scarf in half, point-to-point, and tied it around her neck, the delicate fabric feeling luxurious against her skin. She stood on her tip-toes and peered into the small mirror that hung above the kettle, thrilled with what she saw. 'I love it, thank you,' she said, her heart feeling lighter as she delivered another kiss to her friend's soft cheek.

Lark dropped onto the seat next to where Florrie had been sitting. 'So, can you enlighten me as to why I'm picking up such sad vibes from across the road?'

Florrie sighed, feeling her mood slump. 'Cuppa?'

'Sounds serious.'

Florrie nodded. 'It's been interesting.'

'In that case, I'll have a camomile tea, if you've got one.'

Lark listened quietly, sipping her herbal infusion, as Florrie recounted what had happened with Ed, her pale-green eyes growing wide at the mention of Dodgy Dick, nodding slowly when she heard Paula's take on the situation. When she'd finished, Florrie wasn't surprised to hear Lark's opinion echoed that of her mother's.

'It'll all come right, chick, I can sense it. And you won't have too long to wait,' she said in her other-worldly tone.

'Pfft! The only things I'm bothered about coming right are business related; I'm okay to carry on with the plans for the bookshop as long as I'm in partnership with him, or preferably Stella. Definitely *not* Dodgy Dick. And as far as my feelings for Ed are concerned, that's it. I'm not interested; they're over before they got started, thank bloody goodness.' She glanced at Lark who was peering over her mug, a knowing glint in her eyes. 'And you can stop looking at me like that,' said Florrie, unable to keep the giggle out of her voice.

FORTY-FOUR

Florrie was arranging a collection of local history books on a table display when Jack Playforth came into the shop, his face wreathed in smiles.

'Now then, Florrie, lass,' he said, pulling his flat cap off and stuffing it into his pocket as he usually did.

'Jack! Lovely to see you.' It had struck Florrie the previous evening how his smile totally transformed his face from its dour resting expression, like the sun bursting out from behind black thunder clouds.

'I thought I'd better drop by seeing we forgot to set a date for the reading last night. I was enjoying myself that much, it clean slipped my mind,' he said, giving a throaty laugh.

'Me too, the night seemed to go in a flash, didn't it?' She set down the book she was holding and headed to the counter.

'Aye, it did that. I had a marvellous time.'

'Oh, me too.' Florrie reached under the counter for the diary.

'To be honest, I've been that consumed with writing, I haven't had much time to do much else, so it was a welcome change.'

Florrie beamed. 'That's good to hear; I'm pleased Micklewick Bay has been such a source of inspiration to you.'

'Aye, it has that, it's quite a place, got right under my skin, it has. So much so, I'm going to find it hard to leave.'

'Sounds as though the town's made quite an impression on you,' said Florrie, hoping there'd be no mention of Ed. 'So, is there a date that works better for you? And is an evening okay?'

'Evening's spot on. How about next Wednesday?'

Florrie flicked to the page. 'Next Wednesday's perfect. What kind of time do you think?' From the list of people who'd reserved tickets before a date was even set, she knew there'd be no need to advertise.

'Seven? Will that give you enough time to get organised after the bookshop closes?'

'Plenty,' she said, a ripple of excitement rushing through her as she found a pen and wrote the event in her neatest hand, underlining it for good measure. She still couldn't quite believe this was happening.

FORTY-FIVE

Between the three of them, Florrie and her parents finished painting the room quickly. 'I'll come back tomorrow after closing time, and get that floor varnished,' her dad said. Florrie was thankful of his offer since it freed up her time for the next thing on her Happy Hartes Bookshop to-do list, which was to set up social media accounts and look into organising a website; something Mr and Mrs H had dug their heels in about no matter how many times she'd tried to convince them it was a good thing. To them the internet, and all it stood for, caused nothing but trouble and they'd refused outright to have anything to do with it. Yet, she somehow got the feeling they'd be looking down at her approvingly.

There was still no word from Ed, nor Mr Cuthbert, but she was determined to plough on with her plans with or without Ed's input. But it still didn't stop the whole situation with him from feeling like a ticking time-bomb.

* * *

Thursday arrived on a blast of late-spring exuberance as Florrie and Gerty made their way along the prom that morning. Above, the turquoise-blue sky was punctuated by little puffs of cloud that drifted idly by, while the sea was millpond calm, the sun's golden rays pouring over it. The silently majestic Thorncliffe seemed to stand extra bold and proud in the sunshine, exuding power and beauty all at once. The view scooped up Florrie's spirits, lifting them high, chasing her worries away. She drew in a deep breath of salty air; summer wasn't far away.

Bear arrived bright and early, the clatter of his metal ladders outside alerting her to his presence. He set-to straight away, prepping the exterior woodwork, sanding and undercoating. Florrie couldn't wait to see the finished result – when the new sign had been painted, it would offer another photo opportunity for the website.

She'd spent the morning taking photos around the shop, artfully arranging books and snapping away, building a collection in readiness for uploading as soon as the bookshop's social media pages were ready. It had given her a thrill of excitement with the added bonus of steering her thoughts well clear of Ed.

She was taking Bear a cup of tea and plate of biscuits when she spotted Nate leaving Lark's shop, whistling as he set off down the street. 'One tick, Bear, I just need to grab Nate,' she said, before rushing across the pavement. She waited for a van to pass before cupping her hands around her mouth. 'Nate!' The man in question turned to look at her and she beckoned him over, not wanting to leave the shop unattended. 'Have you got a minute?'

'Aye, course,' he said, nodding and smiling. Crossing the road, he loped towards her. 'Now then, Florrie, what can I do for you?' He was almost as tall as Ed, with kind brown eyes and an easy manner.

'I just wanted to ask about the chairs for the storeroom.' She squinted up at him, shielding her eyes with her hand.

'Ah, good, I've been meaning to have a word with you about them.' He nodded, resting his hands on his hips. 'I've cleaned them all up for you, sanded them down and varnished them.'

'That's brilliant,' she said, thrilled to hear of his progress. 'I can't wait to see them.'

'Any idea when I can drop them off?'

She leaned towards him, lowering her voice. 'I'm guessing Lark's told you about our special guest and the reading he's agreed to do for us?'

'Aye, she has.' His eyes lit up at the mention of Lark's name, as they always did.

'Well, I've just booked Jack for next Wednesday, so if we could maybe have the chairs before Monday, would that be okay?' She scrunched up her nose, suddenly realising how many chairs there were. 'I'm happy to give you a hand loading up the van.'

'Thanks for the offer, but Lark's volunteered her services.' A wide smile dimpled his boyish face. At twenty-five, he was seven years younger than her friend.

'Okay.' Much as she was keen to help, there was no way Florrie wanted to play gooseberry with those two and intrude on Nate's time with Lark. 'But just shout up if things change, okay?'

'Aye, will do.' He nodded. 'Right, I'd best be off then. See you later, Florrie.'

'Bye, Nate, and thanks.' She watched him saunter down the street, whistling away. It was a shame Lark was still keeping him at arm's length; his easy-going nature complemented her friend's perfectly.

* * *

The afternoon brought a visit from Miss Davenport. Florrie was pleased to see she was smiling. The roses that had been in her cheeks on Tuesday were still there and her eyes were shining.

'Morning, Miss Davenport, it's a lovely day out there.' Florrie beamed at her.

'Morning, lovey. It's beautiful; feels almost like summer. I'm beginning to regret wearing this cardigan, I'm that warm.'

Florrie took in her friend's rose-pink cardigan and matching skirt teamed with a crisp white blouse with lace collar. She'd swapped her drab look for joyous, summery colours and they suited her.

'Well, you look like a breath of fresh air to me. And I'm so pleased you've called in, I've got news about Jack's reading.' Florrie felt a thrill swirl in her stomach.

'Ooh, tell me all about it.'

Florrie filled her in with the details, the older woman clapping her hands happily.

'Ooh, how exciting! Mr H would be over the moon with all you're doing. And Bear's making a grand job of the paintwork, it looks lovely and fresh. It's such a shame young... I mean, erm, I don't suppose you've heard anything from young Edward, have you?' She arranged her features into an apologetic expression.

Florrie shook her head, a noisy sigh escaping her lips before she had the chance to stop it; she didn't want Miss Davenport to think her question had niggled her. 'Nope. Not a dicky-bird,' she said, adding a smile. 'But that's absolutely fine with me, means I can do things exactly how I want them.'

The older woman nodded, her face serious for a moment. 'Well, I still think it's a shame, and I have to admit to being a bit disappointed in him, letting you down so. Bernard would be devastated. But it's Edward's loss.'

'Exactly!' Florrie said decisively, reinforcing her words with a wide smile. 'And I have too much to do. The last thing I want is to waste my time thinking about him.'

They both knew that was a big, fat fib.

FORTY-SIX

'Jeez, thank goodness it's Friday, feels like I haven't seen you lot for ages.' Jasmine flopped heavily onto the settle beside Stella, joining the rest of the group in The Jolly Sailors. The pub was busier than ever thanks to the beautiful sunny day bringing folks down to the beach so they could start the weekend early over fish and chips and a pint. 'And please excuse my hair, I was running late and haven't had time to wash it. It's still sticky from me icing the cake for Melanie Day's mother-in-law; it's Janice's fiftieth. Male stripper theme, would you believe?' She touched the top of her hair with the palm of her hand. 'Ughh!'

'Tasteful,' said Maggie dryly, arching an eyebrow.

'What? My hair or the cake?'

'The *cake*, you nutter! I was being sarky.' Maggie chuckled. 'And your hair looks fine to me.'

'Can I ask what on earth possessed Melanie to order that theme for her mother-in-law's cake?' Lark's face was a picture of horrified confusion.

'You clearly haven't met Janice,' Stella said with a laugh. 'She's got a riotous sense of humour, and Melanie says she's really let her hair down since her divorce came through. Apparently, she could teach us all a thing or two, if you know what I mean.' She gave an exaggerated wink.

'Well, that's saying something coming from you, Stells,' said Jasmine, nudging her friend with her elbow.

'Haha. Not at all predictable, Jazz.' Stella nudged her back, smiling.

'Does Melanie's husband know about the cake?' asked Lark. 'I mean, do you think he'll be okay about his mum being given one like *that*?'

'No idea, and it's not my problem; I just follow the brief. First time I've made one with male-strippers, mind you; I had to buy the mould specially.'

'What? You mean you can actually buy moulds of male strippers?' asked Lark in disbelief which made Jasmine giggle and Florrie snort into her wine glass.

'Not exactly male-strippers, but naked men,' said Jasmine.

'Butt-naked?' Stella waggled her eyebrows and howls of laughter followed. 'Sounds good; remind me to put in an order, Jazz.'

'I said *"but"* with one "t", Stells, before you get yourself all carried away. Though, I suppose they're kind of, well, yes, "butt-naked" but without the *"parts"*, if you see what I mean. Put it this way, there's nothing small to get stuck in the moulds.' Jasmine gave a cheeky laugh, wiggling her little finger to demonstrate. More sniggering ensued. 'And anyway, I've covered their modesty with gold sugar-paste thongs; it's all very tasteful. I just hope Janice handles it carefully.' Jasmine spoke as if was just an every-day kind of problem which added to her friends' amusement.

'There are so many things wrong with what you've just said, Jazz, I don't know where to start thinking about it,' said Lark as Lobster Harry's familiar gravelly laugh rang around the pub, perfectly on cue.

'Seems Lobster Harry agrees,' said Maggie, chortling.

'And can I ask why your hair would be sticky from icing a cake?' Stella stuck her finger in amongst Jasmine's red spikes, her nose wrinkling. 'Hmm, you're right, it is sticky.'

'Don't go prodding her like she's some sort of exhibit,' said Maggie as she poured Jasmine a glass of Pinot Grigio. 'There you go, hon, sounds like you've earnt this.'

'Thanks, Mags.' Jasmine took a welcome slug of wine. 'It's icing sugar dust; it floats around in the air when I'm using it. Gets everywhere, my hair included.'

'Right,' said Stella, bemused.

'Well, at least the babysitter turned up this week,' said Maggie.

'Yep, being late was all down to me this time.' She directed her gaze at Florrie. 'Sorry I wasn't ready when you called, chick.'

'Hey, no worries, I'm just glad you're here now.' Florrie had sauntered down to the pub with Gerty at a leisurely pace and had herself arrived only ten minutes earlier.

'So, how's things with you?' Jasmine asked, looking at Florrie. 'From the snippets I've gathered from this lot, it sounds like you've been having more drama in your week than I usually have in mine.'

Florrie rolled her eyes as memories of the last seven days piled into her mind. 'It's settled down a bit now, but it started off crazy.' Since she hadn't had time to go into the finer details with her friends during the week, she started from the beginning, filling them in on the events with Ed, her concerns over his parents and the potential involvement with Dodgy Dick.

'Wowzers,' said Jasmine. 'I might just work a couple of doors away, but I had no idea all that was going on.'

'It's not all bad, though, the storeroom's finished and looks fantastic, as does the shop front thanks to Bear's painting skills,' said Florrie. She was determined to put a positive spin on things.

'Yeah, it looks fab,' said Jasmine, agreeing wholeheartedly. 'So have you really heard nothing from Ed since he left?'

Florrie shook her head, her eyes dropping to the table. 'Nope, not a word.' She felt her emotions rising to the surface and pushed them back before they could convert to tears. Fixing a smile to her face, she looked up. 'Which is fine.'

From the faces looking back at her, she was clearly fooling no one.

'Well, I for one am stunned.' Jasmine glanced around at the others. 'I mean, we could all see how he felt about you; it was so obvious.'

'I don't think Florrie's seen the last of him,' said Lark.

'Huh! As far as I'm concerned, if that's the way Heartless is going to behave, Florrie's better off without him,' Stella said firmly. 'I'm just sorry I gave him an easy time of it last week. Weasel.'

Florrie groaned inwardly; after the week she'd had, she wanted to let her hair down with her friends, not dwell on him tonight. *Time for a change of topic*. 'Listen, I'm absolutely fine about Ed. Truly I am. Hopefully, he'll want to be a sleeping partner or be willing to sell his share of the bookshop to Stells, which is my preferred option as I won't have to think about him or see him ever again. Anyway, I haven't told you about Graham, have I?' She glanced around the pub, relieved to see there was no sign of the man in question, nor Bethany, before turning back to see four sets of eyes on her.

'No, but judging by the look on your face, it's something juicy and interesting,' said Jasmine, turning to the others. 'Not that I ever imagined putting Mr Beige and the word "interesting" in the same sentence.'

'Nor "juicy" for that matter,' said Stella, smirking.

'Don't be unkind, you two,' Lark remonstrated gently.

'Come on, spill,' said Stella, ignoring Lark.

Florrie obliged, watching their expressions morph from

confusion to disbelief as she told them of her last encounter with her ex-boyfriend.

'The bloody nerve of the man after his pathetic PDA in here with Bethany last Friday.' Stella's eyes looked ready to pop out of her head.

'I hope you told him to stick his flowers up his ar—'

Jasmine's words were cut off by Immy who placed a bottle of Pinot Grigio on the table. 'Now then, ladies, this is courtesy of Ando Taylor by way of an apology after his little debacle last week.' She lowered her voice, leaning in. 'Between you and me, I think he's a bit too embarrassed to bring it over himself.'

'Ah, that's kind of him,' said Lark.

'Wow! Wonders will never cease,' said Jasmine. 'And bugger "kind", Lark, he gave us all a right soaking last week. What with the glasses he sent flying, it was nearly a full bottle's worth that got wasted.'

'Hmm. Let's hope he doesn't make such a spectacle of himself this week,' said Maggie.

'I reckon he can't be all bad. I mean, we've got to give him some credit for puking up all over Harte's shoes,' said Stella, smirking.

Florrie looked across at the bar to see Ando peering around Lobster Harry, as if hoping to catch a glimpse of their reaction. She smiled and mouthed a thank you. He returned her smile and nodded before disappearing behind the fisherman. Maybe he wasn't so bad after all.

By quarter-past ten, it was just Florrie and Maggie sitting at the table, enjoying the warmth thrown out by the glowing embers of the fire. Gerty was curled up by the hearth, her ears twitching in her sleep. The bar was still busy, resonating with lively chatter and banter set against the lilting tunes of the folk music playlist. The others had cried off early. Stella declaring she had a heavy case to prepare for over the weekend and needed a clear head for it. Jasmine had to get back for the babysitter whose mum had told her she didn't want her back too late, and Lark was heading off bright and early in the morning; she was going on a sourcing trip with her mum and needed an early night. 'Lark's up with the larks,' Jasmine had said, smiling at her own joke while the others groaned.

Florrie's face was flushed thanks to a mixture of the heat from the fire and the effects of the wine. Maggie had moved so she was sitting opposite her, leaning back in her seat, looking relaxed. 'So, chick, tell me honestly how you're feeling about Ed.' She smiled kindly. 'I know you're not feeling as couldn't-care-less as you're making out.'

Florrie felt her cheeks burn brighter. Maggie knew her well; there was no way she'd be fobbed off.

Before she had chance to answer, her friend spoke again. 'Shall I tell you what I think?'

Florrie nodded. 'Okay.' It would be interesting to hear how things looked from Maggie's point of view, and besides, she valued her friend's opinion, knowing it would come from a kind place.

Maggie's eyes fell to the wine she was swirling in her glass, firelight glinting off the golden liquid. 'Well,' she said, choosing her words carefully, 'I think you like Ed way more than you're willing to admit – I know you told us you had the hots for him last week, but I think your feelings run deeper than you let on and I think him leaving so abruptly has really hurt you. I reckon you secretly hoped he'd stay on here; that a relationship would blossom between the pair of you – which I've no doubt it would.' Her expression soft, she glanced across at Florrie. 'Does that sound about right?'

Florrie's gaze remained fixed to her fingers as she continued to fiddle with her nails. She knew it would be useless to deny it.

She sighed and nodded, a rogue tear springing from her eye and rolling down her cheek. It was the first time she'd admitted it to herself, never mind anyone else. 'Sounds about right, Mags.'

'Oh, chick.' Maggie reached across the table and rubbed a comforting hand up and down Florrie's arm. 'What a bloody rotten time you're having of it. What I'd give to have a magic wand so I could put everything right for you.'

Florrie gave a watery smile. 'I wish you did too.' *And I wish I had one for you, then I'd magic up a smiling, chubby-cheeked baby kicking in the crib that's sitting empty in your home.* 'To be honest, I wish I'd never set eyes on him.' She rested her elbows on the table and covered her face with her hands. 'Uhh! I feel stupid for getting it so bloody wrong.'

'You didn't get it wrong, Florrie, and you're certainly not stupid. Ed genuinely likes you, *more* than likes you; we all saw that last Friday, and we can't all be wrong, can we?'

Florrie shrugged and sat back, removing her glasses, enjoying a moment of myopic haze. 'I suppose not, but it doesn't make any difference; he's not here anymore, whether he likes me or not.' She took a mouthful of wine, sluicing away the emotions that were pushing their way back up, feeling the weight of Maggie's scrutiny as she did so.

'Listen, flower, you're still feeling raw from losing Mr H, so that's why your tears aren't far from the surface – Lover Boy can't take all the credit for that. And feeling sad, grieving, is perfectly natural. Just make sure you don't bottle up those emotions, that'd be the worst thing you could do. Trust me, I'm an expert on it.'

Florrie slid her glasses back on, guilt perching on her shoulder. In comparison to Maggie's troubles, hers paled into insignificance. She'd lost count of the times she'd been witness to her friend's heartache as she and Bear desperately hoped to start their family; Maggie's excitement bubbling away as her hopes were raised every month, only to be followed by crushing disappointment. It had gone on for years, yet somehow Maggie never lost her optimism. Florrie's heart squeezed for her friend.

The brass bell at the bar clanged loudly and Mandy shouted for last orders. The two friends looked over, watching the ensuing clamour and calls for refills.

'One more for the road?' asked Maggie, her smile returning.

'Why not?' Florrie beamed back.

FORTY-SEVEN

'Go fetch, Gerty!' Florrie lobbed a fluorescent yellow tennis ball along the beach. It bounced and rolled, skimming the edges of the tide. The Labrador didn't waste a second and tore after it, grabbing it in her jaws and rolling over, kicking her legs about giddily, sand and seawater flying everywhere. Florrie couldn't help but laugh at her exuberance.

The pair had taken a detour on their way to the bookshop that morning, skipping the walk along the prom in favour of a leg-stretch along the beach, taking advantage of it being quiet. Even on glorious sunny days like today, eight-thirty on a Sunday morning was way too early for day trippers to have descended on the town, mapping out their stake in the sand and parking their brightly coloured deckchairs and wind-breaks. The early hour had tempted out only a small handful of dog-walkers and runners and, for once, there wasn't a surfer in sight. The tide was inching out, leaving a broad ribbon of dark, wet sand, while gentle, frothy waves lapped at the line of fine shingle strewn with seaweed.

The beach had been a wonderful playground when Florrie was growing up. She had a whole slew of happy memories filled with balmy summer days and whippy ice creams with their rainbow-coloured sprinkles. Smiling, she recalled the feeling of utter abandon as she'd raced over the warm sand to the sea, the slapping sound of her bare feet as she bore down on the tide, shrieking as the waves splashed up her legs, the water agonisingly cold, triggering a rash of goosebumps all over her skin. 'It's the North Sea, and you'll come to learn, the North Sea's never warm, sweet-pea,' her mum had said, throwing a warm towel around her daughter who was almost blue with cold, and whose teeth were chattering ten-to-the-dozen. Florrie had lost count of the sandcastles she'd built with her dad, decorating them with shells, seagull feathers and toy windmills whose plastic sails made a flapping sound as they whizzed around in the breeze. Their efforts had been elaborate affairs complete with moats, ramparts, and even drawbridges made of driftwood.

Florrie looked towards Thorncliffe, pushing her hair off her face as she soaked up the view. Just beneath the great cliff sat a cluster of rocks, huddled together, still glossy and wet from high tide – a favourite perch of kittiwakes, herring gulls and cormorants. The spaces between the jutting nubs of stone were dotted with rockpools, an exciting place to explore when Florrie was a child. Armed with a bucket and spade, her wellies sloshing with seawater, she'd squat beside her dad, peering into the water, fascinated as he'd pointed out a whole variety of sea creatures that made the pools their home, from limpets to hermit crabs, vibrant sea anemones, starfish and the tiniest of prawns. He always used to joke that come home-time, her wellies contained as much seawater as the rockpools themselves. He'd tip them out while her mum dried her feet with a rough towel, dusting the sand from between her toes. And, oh, that blissful feeling as her mum rolled a pair of dry socks over her still-damp feet, red with cold, thankful of the sudden warmth. With Florrie snuggled up in a blanket, they'd traipse back over the beach, staggering over the pebbles till they reached the steps of the bottom prom. Florrie's bucket would always be laden with shells, sea-glass and the dark-grey fossilised oyster shells her dad used to call, rather scarily, "Devil's Toenails".

The happiest of times.

'Good girl.' Florrie scooped up the sandy ball Gerty had dropped at her feet. The Labrador danced backwards, looking up at her eagerly, ears cocked, primed to retrieve it at a moment's notice. 'Fetch!' Florrie pushed all of her strength into throwing the ball, watching Gerty race after it, but instead of bringing the ball back, the dog bounded on, continuing until she reached a figure in the distance, jumping about him rapturously.

'Gerty! Come back! Gerty! Here!' Her cries ignored, Florrie shielded her eyes with her hand. It was difficult to make out the identity of the stranger in the bright sunshine, but she sincerely hoped Gerty wasn't making a nuisance of herself; though, in fairness, from years of spending time in the shop, Gerty had learnt to distinguish the dog lovers from the folk who weren't so keen, dispensing her affection accordingly. 'Gerty!' She squinted as the figure bent to make a fuss of the Labrador. 'Oh, bugger.' Realisation dawned and Florrie's heart plummeted to her plimsolls. It wasn't a stranger Gerty was pleased to see. It was Ed Harte. Florrie had all on not to turn around and walk the other way.

Get a grip, Florrie, you can do this. Don't let flaky Ed Harte get to you, he's the one who should turn the other way, not you. She took a deep breath, pushed her shoulders back and strode towards him. Her heart might be hammering in her chest but she was determined he wasn't going to see her looking flummoxed.

'Ed, what are you doing here?' She treated him to a cool smile, ensuring it didn't reach her eyes, and ignored the wayward flutter in her heart as her feelings for him sprang to life.

'Florrie, it's good to see you.' He pushed his fringe back off his face. Though his smile was uncertain, his eyes declared he was pleased to see her.

'I thought you were in London.' She kept her tone neutral; she wasn't going to give an inch.

He had the good grace to look embarrassed. 'Erm, yeah, I was, though not at my flat; I've been staying with Dev.'

She nodded, her face set firm. 'So what brought you back?' As if she needed to ask; he was no doubt hoping to sort out his share of assets from the bookshop for the sale to Dodgy Dick to proceed. She seethed at the thought. 'I rather got the impression you'd gone for good.'

' Yeah, sorry about that,' he said quietly. He swallowed, focusing his gaze on Thorncliffe. 'Everything got a bit much. I was feeling overwhelmed, and my head was all over the place with so much happening in such a short space of time. The thought of being tied to the bookshop and tied to Micklewick Bay suddenly felt like a massive weight on my shoulders; it felt stifling. I panicked.' He rubbed his hand over his face. 'It felt like my whole family were telling me what to do: my grandfather's will basically giving me no choice but to move here and run the bookshop, my parents telling me in no uncertain terms that I had to sell my share and give them the proceeds. Then there was Luella, pushing me to go back to London and give our relationship another go. It was too much; I couldn't breathe. I needed to get away, needed to recalibrate, needed to clear my mind.' He looked at her, a shadow of pain fleeting across his face.

'So how long are you here for?' As if she needed to ask.

'That depends.' He looked at her uncertainly from beneath his fringe.

'On what?'

'On you.'

'*Me?*' She frowned. 'But you've just told me the bookshop and being in Micklewick Bay feels like a massive weight on your shoulders. I don't see how I can change that. And I mean... as far as the bookshop's concerned, I was under the impression you were selling your half to Dodgy Dick, especially since you didn't reply to Mr Cuthbert's messages about Stella being willing to buy it.'

'Dodgy Dick?' He looked mortified. 'I'd never sell to *him*! My grandfather would turn in his grave if I did that. I'm not going to deny selling my half hasn't crossed my mind, but it was never my plan to sell it to the likes of that weasel. I'm sorry that my actions made you think otherwise; I can see I should've checked my emails. Stella would've been my first choice though, but it must've been worrying for you thinking I was in negotiations with that creep.'

'You could say.' Feeling tiny fissures appear in her resolve to be cool towards him, she desperately hoped he was telling the truth about Dodgy Dick.

Ed's eyes searched her face. He went to say something but thought better of it. Instead, he scratched his cheek before bending to pick up the ball Gerty had dropped at his feet. 'Go fetch, Gerty-Girl,' he said, throwing the ball hard then dusting the sand off his hands. He turned to Florrie. 'I really am sorry I bolted.' He paused a moment, as if looking for the right words. Florrie jumped into the space.

'I can see you had your reasons,' she said coldly. *Ease up with the boot-face act, Florrie!* 'No need to apologise.' *That's better.* 'But you could've talked to me about how you were feeling. I would've understood, especially after what you'd told me about your family. Since you left, I've been worried sick about Dodgy Dick buying into the bookshop. There's no way I could've worked with a man like that; I'd have been forced to sell my share to him. Your grandad would've hated that and I would've felt so guilty at not respecting his wishes.'

'Yeah, I get that, and I'm really sorry.' He sighed, his eyes heavy with sadness. 'I don't suppose you'd be free for a chat any time today, would you?' he asked hopefully.

'Doubt it. I've got a lot on. I'm getting the old storeroom ready for Jack Playforth's reading; it's on Wednesday evening.' He wasn't going to get round her that easily. Her pride had been bruised and she was still smarting from it.

Ed's eyes lit up. 'Wow! That's fantastic. Please let me help with what's left of the painting, it's the least I can do.'

'The painting's done. The floor's been varnished too. My parents helped.'

'Oh, right.' He nodded, his smile faltering.

'Lark and Nate brought the chairs over last night after the bookshop closed. I'm going to arrange everything today, use some of the stuff that was stored in there as props, get the room set out exactly how I want it in plenty of time for Wednesday.' She was struggling to keep her voice flat, and regretted saying how *she* wanted it the minute it had left her mouth. 'It's where I'm heading now.' As if to prove it, she started walking. Ed followed her lead, silent for a moment.

'I know I'm too late as far as the painting's concerned, but I'd really like to help with the other stuff, Florrie.' He glanced down at her, but she refused to meet those deep-blue eyes, knowing they had the power to weaken her resolve. 'And, maybe I could explain the last few days to you?'

Her gaze fell to her feet and she chewed on the inside of her cheek, her mind swirling as they walked along, the sound of seabirds and lapping waves punctuating her thoughts. After his recent display of flakiness, the last thing she wanted was to put her trust in him again, only to be disappointed a couple of days later when he sloped off silently out of town without warning.

But the bookshop was his too, she reasoned and, from the sound of it, he didn't have much else to anchor himself to. She felt a twinge in her heart at that thought. And he had as much right to be there as she did. More, even; he was Mr H's flesh and blood. But what had sent her mind into a complete tailspin was the reappearance of her burgeoning feelings for him, the very ones she'd so forcefully packed away, vowing they'd never see the light of day again. Somehow, they'd annoyingly managed to escape. She'd felt them burst free the very moment he'd looked down at her not five minutes ago, turning her traitorous knees to jelly. And now the damned things were charging around her body with such shameless abandon, nudging her and urging her to fall head-over-heels in love with him all over again. Uh-oh, *you're in trouble, girl*, she thought as her head went into combat with her heart.

Florrie fought a valiant battle with her feelings as they made their way along the beach, managing to sustain her cool act, offering monosyllabic answers wherever possible, despite his guileless air making it difficult. They walked as far as the steps nearest The Jolly Sailors, Gerty stopping obediently as Florrie bent and fastened her lead to her collar. 'Come on, girl, time for this I'm afraid.'

They passed the familiar stack of lobster pots, the Labrador giving them a quick sniff as she went by. Florrie sensed Ed's eyes on her, but resisted meeting his gaze. This wasn't going to be as easy as she'd thought.

FORTY-EIGHT

Ed followed Florrie into the shop. She could feel the warmth of his presence behind her as she led the way to the storeroom, the occasional creak of the floorboards underfoot.

'Wow! It looks amazing.' He looked around him, smiling broadly.

Florrie felt a rush in her heart; she still wasn't used to seeing the room fresh and bright, or the rich patina of the old floorboards creating the perfect foil to the light-coloured paint on the walls. She'd earmarked some of the prints and framed vintage photographs they'd found when they'd been emptying the room; they'd just need a quick wipe over before she could hang them.

'I'm going to put some of the old books back on the shelves; I think they'll look good there and it's better than them being hidden away up in the flat. And some of the other old bits and bobs that were in here could be put to good use too.'

Ed nodded. 'I can bring them down for you; it'll take ages if you do it by yourself.'

Florrie didn't answer; she was too busy with the thoughts

rushing around her mind. She could feel his eyes on her but resisted meeting them.

Gerty trotted in, fresh from quenching her thirst. Florrie watched as she went straight over to Ed, plonking herself beside him. He bent, smoothing his hand over her head and she flopped down on the floor with a noisy harumph.

'Look, Florrie, I know I'm not your favourite person at the moment, and I get that; it's no more than I deserve. And I can totally understand that you'd rather not talk to me, but at the very least, please let me help you with this.'

She mulled over his words. He had a point, it would take her an age to bring all those books back down herself, but the thought of being stuck here with him for most of the day had triggered a mass of contradictory emotions. Her heart was saying, 'Yes! Yes! Yes!' while her head was wagging a warning finger at her, saying, 'The last thing you need is to spend time alone with Ed Harte. He'll worm his way under your skin then do a vanishing act again.' But the voice of reason, and the easiest one to listen to, told her he was an equal owner of the bookshop and had as much right to be there as she did. Florrie heaved a sigh. 'Okay, thanks.'

'Great!' He smiled. 'What would you like me to do first?'

* * *

'I don't know about you, but I'm ready for a cup of tea.' Ed brought down the last of the old books, setting them down on one of the chairs. He stood up, wiping beads of perspiration from his brow with the back of his hand. 'How about I put the kettle on?'

Florrie nodded, pleased with the inroads they'd made. Ed's help had taken hours off the time it would have taken if she'd done it on her own. 'Yep, okay. I'll get these put away while you're doing that.' She picked up one of the books he'd just brought down, reading the spine and avoiding making eye contact with him. Her tone may have softened towards him since they'd first arrived, but she still felt wary.

They hadn't stopped all morning, with Ed tirelessly running up and down the stairs to the flat, his arms loaded full of books, his biceps rippling. Florrie had found herself stealing a surreptitious glance on more than one occasion, quickly averting her eyes when he'd caught her looking.

Working so industriously meant it had been easy for her to keep conversation at a perfunctory level; she wasn't prepared to reinstate the closeness they'd shared before Ed's disappearing act. But it hadn't stopped the odd momentary lapse when she'd almost launched into a bit of banter with him, stopping herself just in time, the invisible barrier creaking its way back up. But sharing time over a cup of tea meant an opportunity for a more personal conversation and that made her feel uneasy. And it didn't help that, against her better judgement, she'd enjoyed being in his company again. It was all way too confusing.

She'd just slotted the last book into its new home when Ed came back into the room carrying a tray of tea, her wayward heart giving an involuntary flip. She quickly switched her eyes to Gerty who was following behind him, her tail wagging happily. *Hmm. No one's in any doubts as to where your loyalties lie, eh, Gerty?*

'I hope you don't mind but I've brought us a plate of biscuits, I figured we've earnt them after such a productive morning,' Ed said.

Florrie found herself returning his smile. 'You'll get no complaints from me as far as biscuits are concerned. Thanks.' She took the mug he proffered and helped herself to a ginger biscuit before parking herself on one of the seats while Gerty eyed the plate hopefully. 'And thanks for your help; there's no way I'd be anywhere near this far on if I'd tackled it on my own.'

Ed grabbed a chair and turned it to face her. 'No need for

thanks, it's only right I help.' They sat in silence for a moment, Ed dunking his biscuit in his tea. He left it submerged for a moment too long and the lower half dropped into his drink with a sploosh. 'Bugger!' he said, wiping the splashes from his jeans.

Florrie pressed her hand to her mouth, almost choking on her own biscuit as she struggled to stop herself from giggling. 'Nice one.'

He glanced at her through his fringe, his face breaking into a smile. 'I'll have to fish it out or I'll end up with a load of biscuit silt at the bottom,' he said, reaching for a teaspoon.

That done, he ate the remaining half of his biscuit, apparently lost in his thoughts while Florrie feigned interest in a leaflet about central heating.

Ed broke the silence, clearing his throat. 'How's Graham?'

'Graham?' She looked up, surprised by the directness of his question.

'Yeah, I just wondered what he thought of it in here? I'll bet he's impressed by the transformation you've made,' he said, looking around the room.

'I wouldn't know; either how he is, or what he thinks of it in here.' She sipped her tea, puzzled as to why he was asking about Graham, and why he thought he'd been in here. 'And I can't say I care either.'

'Oh, right.' He sounded genuinely surprised.

'He hasn't been in here; we're not together; I told you, we broke up just before... a few weeks ago and there's no chance of us getting back together.'

Ed straightened, a glimmer of hope in his eyes. 'Really? But I thought... I mean, I saw...'

Florrie listened, bemused. 'What did you think?'

'I saw you outside the shop... you looked pretty friendly from where I was standing.'

She spluttered, suddenly realising what he meant. 'Well, you seriously got the wrong end of the stick there.'

'But you were in his arms, kissing him. I saw it clear as day.'

'Not quite. Graham was the one doing the kissing. He grabbed me before I knew what was happening; I had a right struggle to push him off.' She briefly explained what had happened, Ed's eyes growing wide as he listened. 'I was stunned by it; he'd never been so impulsive when we were together. Not that it's made a difference to how I feel about him now. I still believe breaking up was the right thing to do.' She looked up, surprised to see Ed grinning from ear-to-ear.

'See, I was right; I told you he was still in love with you.'

Florrie felt the warmth of a blush tinge her cheeks. 'I'm not so sure about that. More like things haven't turned out how he'd hoped with Bethany. He hates being on his own so he thought he'd chance his arm with me; love doesn't feature.'

'You undervalue yourself, Florrie,' he said softly.

She snorted. *Ed Harte, you've got a bloody nerve!* 'Well, that's hardly surprising when my so-called business partner goes AWOL and I'm left with the impression that he's going to sell his share of the business to a notoriously dodgy crook without breathing a word of it to me, is it?' Florrie felt her anger resurrecting itself, burning in her gut. 'Don't try to deny it, you were seen deep in conversation with him before you left town.' He may have told her he had no intention of selling to Dodgy Dick, but Florrie still wasn't sure if she could believe him.

Ed ran his fingers through his hair, his face as red as hers. 'You're so efficient at running the bookshop, I didn't think for a second I'd be missed; you could run this place in your sleep. And you've got to believe me, I have no intention of selling to Dodgy Dick. I'm really sorry if it looked that way.'

Florrie's heart was pounding as she looked at him, searching for even the slightest of hints that he might not be telling the truth. Despite her anger, she found herself hoping with all her heart to find nothing.

Ed bowed his head. 'That last morning, you'd gone very

cool with me, you barely looked me in the eye and only spoke to me when necessary. I couldn't understand it, I thought we'd been growing close. I'd enjoyed us spending time together, thought you had too. Then I saw you with Graham and assumed your coolness was because you and he were an item again. I'd been seriously thinking about relocating here, but seeing you with him, well, that helped decide it for me.'

'Right.' Florrie got to her feet, massaging her crumpled brow with her fingertips; she could feel the mother of all headaches brewing. How she wished she could believe him.

Gerty observed her with silent interest.

'You were the only reason I'd hung back in Micklewick Bay,' Ed said quietly. 'If you didn't want me here, then there was no point me hanging around.'

Her eyes rested on him, her heart melting and her pulse surging as she added his comment to the melting pot of emotions swirling inside her. She didn't answer, words eluding her, but she could feel the pull between them growing stronger once more, drawing her to him, making her feel suddenly vulnerable. She stopped dead, clenching her jaw. She needed to stand firm.

He watched her expression change. 'I really am sorry for causing such confusion.'

Florrie's mind was in turmoil. 'But don't you see, running off as soon as things don't go your way isn't the answer? If we all did a disappearing act when things got tough, nothing would ever get resolved. And like I said before, you could at least have talked to me. You'd already explained how you felt about being around books, how you weren't certain you'd stay here permanently. I understood that. Don't you see it would've been so much easier if you'd spoken to me about Graham at the time, instead of shooting off? Doing that didn't give me a chance to explain.' She heaved a deep sigh. 'You left me panicking about Dodgy Dick.'

Ed flinched. 'I'm so sorry, truly I am. And I totally understand where you're coming from. I'm just not used to sharing how I feel, my parents kind of left me to sort things out on my own. I'm not used to discussing things with anyone; it's a hard habit to break.'

Her heart squeezed. His parents had a lot to answer for.

'And you've really got to get Dodgy Dick, his dodgy company– and anyone else for that matter – out of your mind,' he said vehemently. 'Though it wasn't through lack of trying on his part. He's a persistent sod and he was starting to become pretty intimidating but under the guise of a smile and over-familiarity, a hand-shake that was just that little bit too firm. It was starting to feel quite sinister to be honest.'

Stella's warnings about the man and the company he was involved with surfaced in Florrie's mind and she gave an involuntary shudder. 'But what made him think you'd be keen to sell?'

'He'd spoken to my parents at my grandfather's funeral, asking for first refusal. He gave them his business card, saying he'd give them a good price but he wanted to move quickly.'

'Tasteful.' Florrie's top lip curled in disgust.

'My parents were very keen, until the will scuppered their plans.'

Florrie flopped back down onto her seat; she could see how this would make things difficult for Ed.

'They were on at me,' he said, 'saying how it was only right that I should sell my half of the shop and invest in the house with them, which they said I'd inherit when they passed away. It's not the sort of conversation you want to have with your parents.'

'No, it isn't!'

He stole a tentative look at her. 'And they wanted me to encourage you to do the same. Seems they gave my phone number to Dodgy Dick and between them, they hounded me relentlessly about it.'

'All those phone calls you used to take, it was them?'

He exhaled sharply and nodded. 'Some were Luella too. And though I can understand my grandfather's reasons for not leaving the bookshop to my parents, it didn't stop me feeling guilty about it.'

Florrie understood where he was coming from; feelings of guilt regularly prodded at her conscience, telling her the share of the bookshop she'd been given should have gone to Ed.

'But this situation I've found myself in...' Ed threw his hands in the air, exasperated. 'I can't seem to win with anyone.'

Florrie suddenly felt sorry for him. Taking everything into account, maybe she could see why getting away from the building pressure was the most tempting option for Ed. But it still didn't excuse the way he'd left without offering an explanation. One of his postcards might have pacified his grandad, but they cut no ice with her.

FORTY-NINE

'I think I'll take Gerty for a quick walk,' said Florrie, getting to her feet and setting her mug on the tray. After the conversation with Ed an awkward atmosphere had settled between them and she felt the need to get some fresh air. Gerty leapt to her feet on hearing one of her favourite words. She looked up at Florrie eagerly.

'Oh, right. Mind if I join you?' Ed glanced at her as if testing her reaction.

'No, fine.' Florrie hadn't expected that; she assumed he'd take it as his cue to go back to the bed-and-breakfast, or wherever it was he was staying now. 'I'll just get her lead.'

Though they walked along in relative silence, Florrie's mind was banging and clattering with thoughts, occasionally being drawn out of them when her arm accidentally brushed against Ed's, sending a bolt of electricity fizzing through her. She did her best to ignore it, but from the way he flinched, she knew he'd felt it too.

From their vantage point on the top prom, they could see the beach was now teeming with visitors, a clutch of surfers bobbing about in the waves. The tide was even further back, the broad arc of sand glowing golden in the sun.

Florrie's eyes suddenly alighted on a familiar head of salt and pepper wavy hair, its owner sitting on a white painted bench facing the sea, apparently engrossed in a book. Florrie made her way towards her. 'Hi, Miss Davenport,' she said, smiling. 'Enjoying a read in the sunshine?' She was relieved to see no trace of sorrow in her friend's eyes.

'Florrie, how lovely to see you. Yes, I am, and I can't tell you how much I'm enjoying this Julie Spelton novel; I'm so pleased you suggested her to me.' The older woman carefully placed her bookmark on the page and closed her book, resting it on her lap. 'And, Ed, you're back.' She beamed up at him.

'Hello, Miss Davenport, yes, I landed back last night.' He smiled down at her, hands in pockets. 'How've you been keeping?'

'Very well, thank you. And how long are you here for?'

'I'm home for good... at least, I hope I am.' He caught Florrie's eye.

Home? For good? She fought hard to keep a poker face as her heart danced.

'Well, that is a bit of good news.' Miss Davenport's smile widened. 'And I expect Florrie's updated you about Jack's reading?'

'Now then, fancy meeting you lot here,' said a familiar voice before Ed could answer.

They turned to see Jack Playforth grinning at them, his usual overcoat swapped for a pale green shirt, the sleeves rolled up to his elbow.

'Jack! What a coincidence, we were just talking about you,' said Miss Davenport.

'Aye, I thought my lugs were burning,' he said, chuckling. He turned to Ed. 'And it's grand to see you back, lad, I was beginning to think you'd flitted.'

Ed smiled, the colour rising in his cheeks. 'I had to pop back to London for a brief visit but now I'm back and very much looking forward to your reading.'

'Aye, well, it's hard to imagine anyone being able to stay away from this place for long; captures your heart, it does.' Jack turned to Florrie, his dark eyes squinting in the sunshine. 'And how's the room coming on? Have you got the furniture set out yet, or do you need a hand?'

'We're pretty much finished, we just have some stuff to bring down from the flat, but it's looking good,' she said.

'Actually, I don't suppose you fancy giving me a hand with it, do you, Jack?' Ed asked. 'There's a couple of bulky items I could do with a hand shifting; if you've time, that is.'

Florrie looked daggers at Ed. 'I'm quite happy to help; I'm stronger than I look, you know.'

Jack chuckled and patted Ed on the back. 'Well, that's you told, lad. I thought you knew better than to mess with a York-shire lass. It's something I learnt the hard way years ago. And it's worth bearing in mind the little ones are the fiercest.' He winked at Florrie.

'Sound advice, Jack,' said Miss Davenport, turning to Florrie, a kind smile on her face. 'Though I think Ed was just being gentlemanly.'

Florrie cursed inwardly; since when had she become so bloomin' prickly? Her friend was right. 'I'm sorry, we'd be very grateful for your help, Jack; it'd be good to have your input with the room too.'

The melodic chimes of an ice-cream van spliced through the air, the tune growing louder as the vehicle approached and pulled into a parking space on the roadside. 'Now there's an evocative sound. Reminds me of the one that used to mosey round the streets where I lived as a kid,' said Jack, a wistful look in his eyes.

'Ah, yes, the sound always triggers great excitement amongst the children,' Miss Davenport said brightly.

'I'm not surprised, kids love ice cream. Come to think of it, so do grown-ups, especially this one.' Jack grinned. 'Right you lot, come on, ice creams are on me, we can eat them on the way to the bookshop.' He rubbed his hands together as though he meant business.

'Ooh, how lovely.' Miss Davenport popped her book into her bag, a beaming smile on her face. 'I can't remember the last time I had an ice cream.'

* * *

It didn't take the men long to bring the larger items of furniture downstairs. Miss Davenport had wiped the framed paintings and photographs ready for hanging by Florrie, who'd been busy working out how to arrange them before hammering picture hooks into the walls.

'I think we need a few more props if we want it to have the feel of an old-fashioned study.' Florrie stood back, appraising the room. 'I think a couple of books stacked here on the table next to the wingback chair would look good.' She waved towards the chair in question.

'And I'm sure I spotted a pair of old wire-framed glasses in one of the boxes we took up to the flat,' said Ed, his eyes suddenly brightening. 'We could add them too.'

'Ooh, what a lovely idea,' said Miss Davenport.

'Talking of lovely ideas, I quite fancy a crystal glass with a generous tot of whisky keeping them company,' said Jack. 'For display purposes only, of course.' His eyes twinkled mischievously.

'Tell you what, why don't I go and put the kettle on while you and Ed bring down the bits and bobs you mentioned?' said

Miss Davenport. 'I don't know about all of you, but I'd love a cup of tea.'

'You read my mind, Jean.' Jack smiled at her, making her face light up.

Florrie was busy positioning a folded woollen blanket in muted autumnal shades over an arm of the wingback chair when Miss Davenport bustled into the room with a tray of mugs. She set it down just as Ed returned, his hands full of vintage items. Jack followed behind, similarly laden, whistling happily.

'Excellent timing, Jean.' Jack dumped his finds on the desk he and Ed had brought downstairs earlier. Peering to see what had been chosen, Florrie's stomach clenched and she threw a concerned look at Ed. How on earth had Jack found that? She was sure it had been tucked well out of sight. Ed frowned, oblivious. She tried signalling to him with her eyes, but he just continued to look at her, nonplussed.

'You okay, Florrie, lovey?' asked Miss Davenport, looking between her and Ed as she handed him his cup of tea.

'Oh, erm, yes, I'm fine, thanks; just got a bit of dust in my eye.' She made a show of blinking rapidly and running a finger beneath her lower lid, aware of Ed watching her. She didn't dare risk any further signals for fear it alerted the suspicions of Miss Davenport and Jack. 'There, that's better.' *Think quickly, Florrie! Think quickly!*

'By, I'm ready for this.' Jack stepped towards the tray, his hand hovering above the mugs. 'Which one's mine, Jean?'

'The one with the blue and white stripes; I haven't added any sugar.'

'Champion. I don't bother with the stuff; I'm sweet enough,' he said, chuckling.

Florrie snatched another look at Ed who was looking back at her in puzzlement. He gave a subtle questioning lift of his shoulders. She darted her eyes to the wooden box on the desk.

His gaze followed, his mouth falling open. 'Oh shit,' he said, mouthing the word. He glanced back at her as Jack took his mug and stepped backwards, leaning against the desk.

'Hey, Ja—'

Florrie's words were silenced by a loud clatter as the wooden box hit the floor, the lid flying open, its contents spilling out. Unawares, Jack had rested his weight on a book which had nudged the box until it overbalanced and toppled over the edge of the desk.

'What the... ouch!' Jack jolted forwards, shaking scalding hot tea off his hand. He set his mug down and spun around, surveying the damage. 'I'm ever so sorry. I'm such a clumsy oaf.'

Florrie looked on helpless, her eyes wide, unable to speak as her heart leapt wildly in her chest.

FIFTY

Florrie heard Miss Davenport gasp beside her. She cast a quick sideways glance to see her friend clutching a hand to her chest, her face drained of colour.

Tension hung in the air, pulled taut, ready to give at any moment.

'Ey up, what's this then?' asked Jack, bending towards the scattered contents.

Florrie's eyes flashed over to Ed whose habitual smile had been wiped from his face.

'Er, why don't you let me do that, Jack?' Ed strode across to the poet who'd started gathering the papers together.

'You're all right, I've just about...' Jack straightened, looking intently at a black and white photograph in his hand.

Florrie's eyes slid from Jack to Miss Davenport to see an expression of horror on the older woman's face.

'Come on, folks, we're wasting good tea-supping time,' said Florrie, hoping the breezy tone she adopted sounded convincing. 'There's no need to trouble yourself with that, Jack, you can leave that for Ed and me to sort out. You might as well get your tea while it's hot.'

But Jack was peering more closely at the photo and didn't appear to hear her. 'By, if I didn't know better, I'd say the little lad in this photo was me; my parents had one just like it in a photo album. Almost identical it is,' he said, rubbing his hand across his chin.

Florrie's pulse started thrumming in her ears as he turned the photo over.

Jack frowned as he read aloud. 'Tommy. Fourth birthday. Fifth of August nineteen-sixty-nine.' He scratched his head and glanced around at the three shocked faces looking back at him. 'I was four on that very same day.'

Florrie could feel her mind trying to play catch-up with the events unfolding before her. She snatched another look at Ed who was rubbing his hand over his mouth; he looked as perplexed as she was. She looked across at Miss Davenport whose hand was still on her chest, frozen, statue-like, her breathing coming in shallow bursts.

Jack swallowed. 'And, how odd, there's another similarity; my birth mother gave me the name Tommy too.'

It suddenly felt as if the air had been sucked out of the room.

Florrie's mouth fell open, her mind running over Jack's words. *Birth mother?* She turned to see Miss Davenport trembling, tears pouring in rivulets down her cheeks. 'Oh, Miss Davenport, don't cry.' She rushed over to her friend, hugging her close, not fully understanding what was unfolding. Miss Davenport released a heart-wrenching wail, her legs buckling as she leaned heavily on Florrie. Quick as a flash, Ed was by her side.

'Come and sit down, Miss Davenport, you don't look at all well.' With Florrie's help, he guided her to the wingback chair. She slumped onto it heavily, sitting with her head bowed as sobs racked her body. Jack looked on, baffled, his usually ruddy complexion now pale.

'Here you go.' Florrie set a box of tissues in the older woman's lap. She knelt down beside her, taking her hand and squeezing it. Gerty ran over, looking between the two with concerned eyes. 'It's all right, Gerty,' Florrie said gently.

'Thank you,' Miss Davenport said, dabbing at her eyes. 'I've been... waiting so... many years for... this moment.'

'What moment, Jean?' asked Jack, looking utterly confused.

Miss Davenport's bottom lip quivered. 'The moment... the moment I'd... I'd be reunited with my son.' Her voice wavered as fresh tears fell.

'Your son?' Florrie choked back tears of her own. When Mr H had mentioned a baby being born several months after Johnny Jackson had unceremoniously left Miss Davenport, she'd assumed it was the other woman – Elsie – who'd had the child. Never in a million years did Florrie think it was Miss Davenport, until she and Ed had found the box of letters.

Jack fell back onto a chair, dragging his hand down his face. 'Bloody hell, I need a minute to take this in.'

'Sure you wouldn't like some sugar in that tea, Jack? It's supposed to be good for shock,' Ed said softly.

'Aye, I think I need it. You'd better chuck a load in there for me, lad. Actually, I don't suppose you've got any whisky, have you?' he asked, holding out his mug while Ed spooned sugar into it.

'Sugar's the best I can do, I'm afraid.' Ed gave a small smile.

Jack took a mouthful and sat staring into space. No one spoke, the only sound in the room was Miss Davenport's gentle sobs.

'So, let me get this straight, you're telling me you're... my... you're telling me you're my birth mother? Have I understood that right?' He looked over at Jean, his eyes brimming with emotion.

She lifted her head and nodded, her face puffy, her eyes

rimmed red. 'Yes, you've understood that right, Jack. I'm your moth... I'm your birth mother. I had no idea until just now.'

Jack nodded slowly. 'Bloody hell, I wasn't expecting any of this.'

Florrie felt suddenly conscious that she and Ed were intruding on this most private of moments. 'Would you like us to leave you to talk alone?' She looked between mother and son; it was difficult to tell which way this was going to go. A reminder of Jack's notoriously fiery temper flashed through her mind. Would he get angry with Miss Davenport for giving him up?

'No, I'd like you to stay... if that's okay with you, Jack?'

'Aye, I'd like you both to stay too.' His voice steady, he asked, 'So who's my birth father then? Is he still alive? Does he still live in Micklewick Bay?'

The air in the room was charged with emotion. Miss Davenport pulled at the tissue in her hands. Licking her lips nervously, she said, 'Your father's a man called Johnny Jackson, and I'm afraid I don't know if he's still alive. He left town at the same time I found out I was expecting you, and I haven't heard anything from him since.'

'Right.' Jack took a moment before he spoke again. 'So was I the reason he left?' he asked, his voice cracking.

Miss Davenport shook her head, fighting back tears. 'No, Jack, you weren't. He'd gone before I had chance to tell him. If he'd known about you, I know he would've stayed.'

Florrie stole a look at Ed to see tears shining in his eyes. He caught her watching him and cleared his throat, quickly brushing his fingers under his nose.

'Can you tell me what happened?' asked Jack.

Miss Davenport nodded, straightening herself. 'It's the least I can do.'

FIFTY-ONE

Eighteen-year-old Jean Davenport had been holding a torch for Johnny Jackson for as long as she could remember. Consequently, it came as a great surprise when he asked her if she'd "step out" with him in the spring of nineteen-sixty-three. At first, she'd thought it was a joke, or worse, a dare. After all, why would the local heartthrob be interested in a mousey little bookworm like her? Even Elsie Norwood, her best friend at the time, had been unable to hide her shock. 'What's he asked *you* out for? I mean, you're hardly his type.' Jean had ignored the sneer in her friend's voice.

With his slicked back hair, razor-sharp cheek bones and dazzling blue eyes, Johnny had turned her knees to jelly whenever she saw him. His black leather jacket and shiny motorbike had lent him a deliciously dangerous edge that made her heart race until she'd thought it would burst. At three years her senior, he'd seemed so glamorous and sophisticated and worldly-wise. But what she'd soon come to love the most was when he held her close at the dance in the local community hall every Saturday night, her head resting on his shoulder, feeling the strong beat of his heart as he whispered softly into her ear, 'You're the only girl for me.' Her heart had soared.

Jean had been surprised at how picky Elsie had been about her relationship with Johnny. From the moment Jean had told her he'd asked her out, Elsie had done nothing but pour poison into her ear, saying he wasn't right for her, that they were badly matched, that they wouldn't last. 'I'm not being funny, Jean, but you're hardly well-suited, are you? I mean, he's pretty much a man of the world; he's been to *London* and the furthest you've been is *Scarborough* to stay on your cousin's farm,' she'd said mockingly.

Jean had shrugged, too head-over-heels in love to let Elsie's words dampen her happiness. 'I don't think stuff like that matters when you're in love,' she'd said dreamily. 'And besides, I love Scarborough and so does Johnny. He's going to take me there on his motorbike.'

'I still can't get used to the thought of *you* on a motorbike,' Elsie had said with a snigger. 'And anyway, I'm only telling you all this 'cos I want the best for you. Honestly I do, Jean. I just don't want you to get hurt, that's all. But he'll cheat on you, just like I'm told he's done with all his other girlfriends. I know he will, you mark my words.'

'Well, I love being on the motorbike with him, it feels amazing.' Jean had been petrified when Johnny had first asked her to take a ride with him, but soon her fear had morphed into exhilaration as they flew along the roads, her arms hugging tightly around his waist, the wind rushing over her face.

And though she hadn't heard any rumours about him cheating, Elsie's words had sent a tiny niggle of doubt scurrying up her spine.

At least her friend, Dinah Harte, had been more supportive. 'Take no notice of her, Jean, Elsie's just jealous. I think it's so romantic. You look good together, and any fool can see he's smitten with you,' she'd said when Jean had shared Elsie's misgivings with her. As Dinah was five years older, Jean respected her opinion.

By the time Jean and Johnny had been together for a year the pair were more in love than ever. He'd even surprised her with a promise ring to mark the occasion which she wore proudly. Elsie had been proved wrong, much to her chagrin.

Not long after she'd seen the ring on Jean's finger, Elsie had broken her neck to tell her there was a rumour going around that Johnny had been seen in a compromising position with another girl. 'I have it from a very reliable source,' she'd said, not bothering to hide her satisfied smile, folding her arms across her chest. 'And from what I can gather, they've slept together.'

'I don't believe it! Whoever's telling you this, they're lying! Johnny wouldn't cheat on me! I know he wouldn't.' Jean had fought back tears as Elsie looked on, her eyes glinting maliciously. 'Why would he give me this ring if he was two-timing me?'

'Some men like to have their cake and eat it.' Elsie had shrugged.

Less than a week later Jean was to discover something equally devastating.

She was pregnant.

She'd been beside herself with worry, not daring to think what her father would have to say about it, or how Johnny would react. 'Oh, God, how can I tell either of them?' she'd said to herself, chewing her fingernails down to the quick.

Jean's father ruled the Davenport household with a rod of iron and woe betide anyone who stepped so much as an inch out of line. Life under his regime was joyless and run to a strict timetable, but it hadn't stopped Jean from sneaking out and meeting up with Johnny when the rest of the family had gone to bed. She'd tiptoe silently down the back garden path, her heart racing with a mix of excitement and fear as she'd slip through the gate and throw her arms around Johnny who'd be waiting on the other side. It was on such an evening of stolen pleasure their baby was conceived.

'What am I going to do?' she'd asked Elsie, sobbing into her hands as they'd sat on a bench looking out to sea

Elsie had listened, stony-faced. 'You scheming little idiot! You two were never a long-term thing! Did you think getting pregnant would make him marry you?'

Her harsh words had stopped Jean's tears in their tracks. 'No! How could you say that? I didn't do it on purpose! It was an accident.'

'Well, let me tell you this, boys like Johnny Jackson don't marry boring girls like you, Jean Davenport! Pregnant or not! And now nobody's going to want you! You're soiled goods!' She'd flounced off without a backwards glance.

Her so-called-friend's words had felt like a slap in the face. Is that what Johnny would think? That she'd done it to trap him? 'My life's over,' she'd said to herself.

The following night, as planned, Jean had sneaked out of the house to meet Johnny. Her heart had been racing like the clappers, though she still hadn't plucked up the courage to share her news or, rather, bombshell with him. And, after Elsie's reaction, she'd been even more afraid. As she'd closed the garden gate behind her she'd been surprised to find Johnny wasn't there, ready to scoop her up in his arms and rain kisses down on her. She'd waited for an hour, hiding in the shadows, the cold creeping into her bones, before heading back indoors, realisation dawning on her in a cloud of sadness. She'd been dumped. Elsie had obviously been right. Jean had never felt so afraid or alone.

A week later, Jean had been walking along the top prom, her face streaked with tears, when she'd bumped into Dinah Harte. 'Whatever's the matter, Jean?' she'd asked, guiding Jean to a bench and rubbing soothing swirls over her back. Dinah's kindness had been too much, and Jean had found herself blurting out the reason for her distress.

'Hey, nothing's ever as bad as it seems, trust me,' Dinah had said gently. 'Come on, let's go to my house, see what we can come up with.'

That conversation proved to be a pivotal moment in Jean's life.

FIFTY-TWO

'So what happened?' asked Ed. 'What did my grandparents suggest? Were they any help?'

Jean gave a juddery sigh. 'I definitely felt much better for talking to them.' She glanced across at him. 'They were lovely people, your grandparents, salt of the earth.' Ed nodded and smiled, swallowing hard. 'It was quite a scandal to get pregnant out of wedlock in those days, but they listened to me without being judgemental. Dinah had an idea brewing, she said, but needed to discuss it with Bernard first, so I went home with instructions to come back the following day. I still hadn't told my parents at this point. The thought was much too terrifying.'

Florrie stole a look at Jack who'd been listening silently throughout. He was breathing heavily, a shadow of sadness lingering on his face. She didn't know who she felt most sorry for, him, or Miss Davenport.

'So, I returned the next morning not knowing what on earth to expect.' She paused, taking a sip of lukewarm tea. 'They had friends over Harrogate way, a couple who'd been desperately trying for a baby for years but with no luck. Time, apparently, was running out. I knew as soon as I heard this where things were going. The plan was for me to leave town as soon as possible, before anyone found out I was pregnant – I'd have to tell my mother, of course, explain what I was doing. Then, once the baby was born, I'd hand it over to Bernard and Dinah who'd take it to their friends; my baby's new family. The woman would pretend she'd given birth without knowing she was pregnant, that way, they'd be able to register the baby's birth, instead of me.' A solitary tear rolled down her cheek and plopped into her tea.

With emotions welling inside her, Florrie fought back tears of her own. She couldn't begin to imagine what it must have been like to be faced with such a heart-breaking choice. She gave her friend's hand a reassuring squeeze.

'They told me not to make up my mind right away, but to think it over for a couple of weeks; that's what the family in Harrogate were doing. It was a huge, life-changing decision and, once made, there'd be no going back. Bernard had a relative I could stay with until I gave birth. It was on the moors, where no one would know me. My mind was all over the place. I was so young, unmarried and afraid of telling my father. But whatever decision I arrived at, there was one thing I was absolutely certain of: I loved this baby with all my heart.'

'So what made you reach the decision to give me away?' asked Jack, his voice thick.

Florrie felt Miss Davenport tense at the directness of his words. 'I asked Dinah and Bernard for more information about the family in Harrogate; I wanted to be sure if I handed my precious baby over to someone, he or she was going to a home where they would be loved and cherished.' She took a deep breath. 'It was my mother's reaction when I told her I was pregnant that made my mind up. I'd expected her to be shocked and angry at first, then calm down after a while, and be supportive. But she was apoplectic; I'd never seen her in such a rage. Told me I'd brought shame on the family, that my father would never forgive me. That she never would. That my actions were going to make life hell for her. She said I'd have to go away and have the baby, then give it up for adoption. There was no argument as far as she was concerned. When she'd finished screaming at me, she stormed out of the house, said she couldn't look at me. I rang Dinah who told me to pack a case and go to them; they'd heard from the family who were keen to go ahead with the plan. All I could think of at the time was at least this way I'd know my baby was going to a loving home.' She looked over at Jack, her eyes begging for forgiveness. 'Things moved pretty quickly from then on.'

'Where was I born?' he asked.

'At the little cottage on the moors, on the edge of a village called Lytell Stangdale.'

'Aye, I know it well,' said Jack.

The thought he'd mentioned doing a reading there for a television programme flittered across Florrie's mind. What a curious coincidence it was.

'It's such a beautiful place, and you were the bonniest baby, so content. I called you Thomas, after my grandfather, and I'd gaze at you for hours on end.' Miss Davenport dabbed her eyes with her tissue. 'I kept you for a couple of days before Dinah and Bernard came to collect you. Handing you over broke my heart, but I kept telling myself you were going to a family who would love you, and you'd want for nothing. They were to send me photos and updates of my little boy via your grandparents, Ed, but it was agreed it would be for the best if I wasn't told the identity of the family, nor they mine. Dinah and Bernard very kindly let me keep the letters with them since I'd gone back to live with my parents a couple of weeks after you were born and there was no way I could risk them finding anything. And, oddly, my time away and the reason for it was never mentioned by my family when I got back; it was as if it had never happened.' She shook her head. 'Anyway, Bernard even drew up some sort of formal agreement for me to sign, just to make it official – from my recollections, I think he must've had help from a solicitor, it looked very formal. Your new family stopped writing after your seventh birthday and I felt I'd lost you all over again.' Miss Davenport's voice crumbled as it gave way to sobs. 'I'm so sorry, Jack, please forgive me. Not a day's gone by when I haven't thought about you.'

Jack rushed over to his mother, crouching in front of her. He took her hands in his, rubbing his thumbs over her fingers, tears streaming down his cheeks. 'There's nothing to forgive. What you've just shared is heartbreakingly sad. I can't imagine how it must've felt to be forced into such a painful decision. I'm just sorry my adoptive family didn't tell me. I'd have come looking for you, but I only found out once my parents had died.'

'You didn't know you were adopted?' Miss Davenport looked up at Jack.

He shook his head. 'No, not until last year when I was sorting out their house. I found an old shoebox in the back of my mother's wardrobe containing a few baby items, a shawl, a little woollen hat. There was an agreement concerning the adoption of a baby and my parents, stating that they must never attempt to contact the child's birth mother, though she was unnamed on the document. There was a bunch of letters too, with a Micklewick Bay stamp on the envelopes. I was thrown at first as the baby was referred to as "Thomas" and "Tommy".'

Miss Davenport nodded. 'I signed something similar.'

Ed caught Florrie's eye, he didn't have to tell her he was thinking about the document bearing Miss Davenport's signature they'd found in the wooden box.

'And what about my father? Johnny? Did you ever hear from him again?'

'No, he never returned my calls, but a week after I'd shared my secret with Elsie, I heard he'd left town with her. Rumour had it they'd got married as soon as they could since she was pregnant with his child; he was two-timing me after all.'

'What?' Florrie felt anger push her sadness aside. 'After everything she'd said to you about Johnny? What kind of friend does that?'

'And what kind of boy cheats on his girlfriend with her best friend?' asked Ed before glancing down at Jack. 'Sorry.'

'No need to apologise, lad, I was thinking the same thing. They sound like a right pair; made for each other.'

'They sound horrible!' said Florrie. 'You were better off without either of them.'

Miss Davenport raised her hand. 'Oh, it hurt at the time all right, but at least they'd left town and I didn't have to face them and be reminded of them every day. And, if what I'd heard was true, it turned out Elsie wasn't pregnant after all; it was a false alarm.'

'Convenient,' said Jack.

'Hmm,' said Florrie. 'Doesn't sound like a "false alarm" to me.' She put finger-quotes around the words. 'More like manipulation.'

* * *

The next couple of hours flew by with Miss Davenport and Jack catching up on their missing years and looking through the letters and items in the box. 'I thought Bernard and Dinah had got rid of these years ago,' Miss Davenport said.

Florrie and Ed had offered to leave the pair alone once more, but both mother and son had urged them to stay. And though many tears were shed, they were punctuated by a generous smattering of laughter as Jack shared tales of the mischief he'd got up to as a young boy.

Eventually, the pair decided to call it a day and head home with their thoughts, both exhausted but happy. 'I'm chuffed to bits to have found you, but I just need to absorb everything in some peace and quiet; get my head around it all,' said Jack.

'I know exactly what you mean. I think I'll go and sit in the garden with a cup of tea and revisit all you've told me.' Miss Davenport smiled at him. 'And I can't tell you how happy I am to have found my boy after all these years.' She pressed her hand to his cheek, her eyes welling with fresh tears. 'And I'm so proud of you.'

'Thank you. And I'm just as happy to have found you,' Jack said, beaming at her. 'And it's only fitting it happened here.'

'Yes, you're right.'

'Don't forget these, Miss Davenport.' Florrie handed her the box that had been the catalyst to the day's revelations. 'I think it's okay for you to have them now.'

'Yes, lovey, I think it is.'

FIFTY-THREE

The room felt quiet and empty once Miss Davenport and Jack had gone, the awkwardness between Florrie and Ed springing back to life and filling the space around them.

'What a day. I wasn't expecting any of that.' Ed scratched his head, casting an uncertain look at Florrie. 'I should've kept a closer eye on Jack when we were up in the flat, made sure to keep him out of the way of the box. I'm sorry.'

'There's no need to apologise, it hadn't crossed my mind either. And it worked out well in the end; Miss Davenport and Jack were thrilled. Another one of those things that was meant to be.' Her shoulders sagged, her energy suddenly leaching away. She didn't feel strong enough to tackle the emotions that were bubbling under the surface, pushing to get out. Before she knew it, tears were falling unrelentingly down her cheeks. She covered her face with her hands and let them flow. In a moment, Ed strode across the room, wrapping his arms around her, holding her close, their awkwardness forgotten. He felt warm and safe, his arms as strong and sure as his heartbeat that was currently thumping in her ear.

Florrie didn't know how long he'd been holding her when

her tears finally subsided. She eased herself out of his embrace and stepped back, feeling suddenly embarrassed. 'Sorry about that,' she said, sniffing, unable to meet his eyes.

'Don't be. It's been one hell of an emotional day.'

She nodded, reaching for a tissue from the box on the table. 'Just a bit.' She headed over to a chair, slumping down onto it. Ed started pacing, dragging his fingers through his hair. Florrie watched as he strode back and forth, a torn expression on his face as he wrestled with his thoughts. Gerty glanced up; she'd obviously sensed it too. 'Everything okay?' Florrie asked.

'Don't suppose you fancy grabbing a bite to eat somewhere this evening, do you?'

His question took her by surprise, and much as she was tempted – being in his strong arms had felt indescribably reassuring – she wasn't prepared to simply pick up where they'd left off before he'd turned tail and rushed off to London; she couldn't just pretend everything in the garden was rosy. Just as Miss Davenport and Jack needed time to digest all they'd learnt today, Florrie did too; she needed to process all Ed had shared with her earlier in the day. 'Sounds good, but I think I'm going to call in on Maggie, then head home and have an early night.'

'Oh, okay.' Disappointment flittered across his face triggering a stab of guilt in her chest. He resumed his pacing, Florrie and Gerty watching with interest.

'Has something else happened?' Florrie braced herself for his answer. *Oh, jeez, I could really do without this.*

'If I don't say it now, I never will.' He came to a stop, grabbed a chair purposefully, set it directly in front of her and sat down.

Florrie's heart stilled; he seemed a little too close for comfort. And he looked uncharacteristically serious. Was he about to deliver the news she'd feared the most? she wondered. She couldn't keep up.

He dragged his hand over his face before looking into her

eyes. 'Florrie, what I'm about to say to you, I want you to believe every word of it, okay?'

Uh-oh, here we go. A feeling of disquiet fluttered in her chest. 'Okay,' she said, falteringly, her mouth suddenly dry.

'You're a decent person and you do everything properly, so I know you think me leaving the way I did was a bad thing. But for me, it actually turned out to be a positive thing – I hope that makes sense.'

Erm, not really. Florrie's brow crumpled. *Where on earth is he going with this?*

'Just hear me out,' he said. 'I'm rubbish at explaining my feelings, but here goes... See, the thing is, for the few days I was away, I managed to get rid of all the background noise and distractions that were filling my head, gave myself time to think, for my thoughts to get some clarity. And, for the first time as far back as I can remember, I was able to see everything crystal clearly; I knew what I wanted to do with my life; where I wanted to be; who I wanted to be with.'

'Oh?'

His frown lifted and his eyes shone. He took her hands in his, his fingers stroking hers. 'I want to be here... with you, Florrie... living in Micklewick Bay, working at the bookshop.'

'You do?' Her eyes widened as she absorbed his words, conscious of her hands, warm in his. Had she heard right? Was she hallucinating?

'It struck me like a thunderbolt. All I was able to think about while I was away, was you. My feelings for you...' He blew out his cheeks and shook his head as he couldn't quite believe them himself. 'I can't put them into words. All I can say is, I know we haven't know each other very long, but I've never felt this way about anyone.'

Dumbfounded, all Florrie could do was look at him, his confession charging around her mind. She was aware of his eyes searching hers; his words described her feelings for him perfectly.

Ed continued. 'It scared me at first. But when I realised it was actually what I wanted more than anything else in the world, it was as though a dense fog had lifted, allowing me to see everything clearly. I've never experienced anything like it before. I had to get the first train back; didn't want to waste a moment.'

Florrie blinked, aware that her mouth was hanging open. 'But how... I mean...' She swallowed, words failing her.

'I want to be with you, Florrie. I'd come back to fight for you; to get you away from Graham who I knew could never make you happy.'

Florrie blinked again. Had she got this right? 'But I thought... thought you didn't want to be here... you don't like being around books... you don't like the idea of getting close to someone after Luella... I mean...'

'That was before I met you,' he said softly.

She sat stunned, her heart thumping.

'I can see why my grandfather did what he did, putting us together, playing Cupid from up there.' He flicked his eyes heavenwards.

'You can?' Florrie's chest filled with emotion at the mention of Mr H.

'Yes, we're perfect for each other, Florrie.'

She sat back in her seat, releasing her hands from his. It would be the easiest thing in the world to agree with him but a flutter of apprehension made her hold back. She rubbed her fingers across her forehead, feeling almost dazed. 'This is a lot to take in.'

'I appreciate that.' Ed reached across and squeezed her shoulder. 'I suppose joining me for a meal's still out of the question?' he said, tentatively. 'Maybe chatting about it over food would help.'

Her mind was crammed with thoughts jostling for attention. 'I just need some time to think,' she said. She needed to process all he'd just told her before she talked any more to him. Before she made any decisions. Before she let herself trust him again.

'I can understand that.' He gave a disappointed smile, getting to his feet. 'In that case, it's probably best if I head back to the bed-and-breakfast, give you a bit of space. Am I okay to pop back tomorrow to finish what we need to do here?'

'Of course.'

* * *

'Come in, chick.' Maggie stood back, holding open the old oak door of Clifftop Cottage, the delicious aroma of home-baking wafting out onto the doorstep. Her smile dropped as soon as she noticed Florrie's puffy eyes. 'Bloody hell, you look like you've been through the wringer.' She closed the door, wiping her floury hands on her apron before wrapping her arms around her friend. 'Come on, there's fresh tea mashing in the pot and I've just baked some scones, we can have one when they've cooled.'

'Thanks,' said Florrie. She was sitting in a squishy chair, her feet curled underneath her, as Maggie handed her a mug of tea. Gerty briefly opened her eyes from her spot on the rug in front of the fire. The cosy warmth of the room, with its low beamed ceiling, cheerful furnishings and thick walls had a soothing effect and Florrie felt herself relax almost instantly.

Maggie flopped into the chair opposite. 'So, from the looks of things, I'm guessing you've had a bugger of a day and it's not just because you've been slogging your guts out getting the bookshop ready for Wednesday.' She peered at Florrie as she blew over the surface of her tea.

Florrie gave a heavy sigh. 'Yep, you guessed right.' She couldn't share all of what had happened; Miss Davenport and

Jack's news wasn't hers to tell and they hadn't discussed whether to go public with it just yet.

'Ed?' asked Maggie.

'He's back.'

'Really?' A wide smile lit up her friend's face. 'I knew he wouldn't be able to keep away from you.'

Florrie rolled her eyes before launching into the details of her conversation with him, Maggie's smile growing wider by the minute.

'But the burning question is, what are you going to do about it?' Maggie asked.

Florrie sighed again, resting her head on the back of her chair. 'In all honesty, I don't know. Despite everything he said, I'm still feeling wary; I'm not sure I'm ready to put my trust in him to stick around. I mean, ughh! I just don't know. And it doesn't help that there's been so many other things going on, it's hard to get my head straight. I honestly don't know what's happened to my life recently, it's been turned completely upside down.'

'Yeah, you've been through a lot in a small space of time, but things will settle down soon, I'm sure of it. And, for what it's worth, chick, I reckon you should follow your gut about Ed; you can't go far wrong with that.'

'I know, you're right.' Florrie could hear her gut loud and clear, but she was scared – actually, she was terrified. Once she made the decision, there'd be no going back. But it was one she wasn't going to make in a hurry, she was going to take her time. She wasn't prepared to expose herself to yet more pain; she wanted to be absolutely certain of Ed's commitment to the bookshop and Micklewick Bay before she did that. 'The thing is, Mags,' she said, holding her friend's gaze, 'he's the first man who's made me feel this way. When I'm around him, it's as if my heart sings with happiness. I know it sounds mega-corny, but it's true.' She smiled bashfully.

'I know, chick, it was patently obvious that night at the pub; me and the rest of the girls couldn't help but notice. You absolutely sparkled in his company, and he couldn't keep his eyes off you; it was lovely to see. And what you said isn't corny; I felt exactly that way when I first met Bear. Still do actually.' She chuckled softly.

Florrie gave a hefty sigh. 'Arghh! Why do things have to be so bloody complicated?'

'I think you'll find, sometimes, they're as complicated as you make them.' Maggie gave her an enigmatic smile as she popped a chunk of jam-smothered scone into her mouth.

FIFTY-FOUR

By the time Wednesday arrived, Florrie felt she could almost breathe a sigh of relief. The sign-writer had been the previous day and done a wonderful job. The rich gold cursive lettering declaring it to be "The Happy Hartes Bookshop" sat well with the ox-blood paintwork. Everything was now in place for the reading. The storeroom – or "reading room" as it had been renamed by Florrie and Ed – was set out, creating an intimate and cosy atmosphere. Unsurprisingly, all forty tickets had sold out almost immediately without the need for any advertising; simple word of mouth had been sufficient. And, better still, Jack had agreed to return for a book-signing session at a later date.

'It would be great to make author readings and book-signings a regular feature here,' Florrie had said to Ed, her enthusiasm returning.

'I think we should make it our mission.' He'd smiled down at her affectionately, making her dratted blushes return.

Since Ed's declaration the other day, Florrie had made a conscious effort to keep things on a professional level. She needed time to think over his words and, in truth, she was still feeling a little sore from his hasty departure, not to mention the little shadow of doubt that hovered in her mind. But there were too many other things going on for her to spend much time dwelling on it, for which she was thankful.

Since Sunday, Miss Davenport and Jack had popped into the shop together, all smiles having spent the last couple of days getting to know one another and making up for lost time. 'We're not going to broadcast our news just yet,' Miss Davenport had said to Florrie. 'Jack would like to get used to the situation first, it being a lot to take in and all.'

'That's understandable,' Florrie had said, though she had a feeling her friend would happily shout it from the rooftops.

* * *

The hum of chatter hushed as Jack walked into the room. He was looking smart in a sea-green shirt, dark grey moleskin trousers and a tweed jacket in complementary hues. His eyes swept the sea of heads as he took his seat. 'Evening all, thank you very much for coming,' he said. A burst of applause followed, making him smile. He retrieved a pair of reading glasses from the inside pocket of his jacket and slid them on. 'Right then,' he peered down his nose, a mischievous glint in his eyes, 'let's hope I don't bore you all rigid and make you wish you'd stayed home supping tea with your feet up in front of the telly.'

'Not a chance, we think you're fabulous!' a voice called from the audience.

'Nice haircut, Jack!' said another, the comment quickly followed by a wolf-whistle.

'Thank you and thank you,' he said, chuckling.

'It's the highlight of the year!'

'Bloomin' 'eck, no pressure then.' He rolled his eyes jokingly. 'And I'll refrain from saying you lot clearly don't get out much if that's what you think.'

Miss Davenport was smiling proudly from the opposite end of the room, standing alongside Florrie, Ed and Hayley; the young girl looked ready to bubble over with excitement. 'Omigod, I can't believe this! It's so awesome. My mum's wearing her best dress and her expensive perfume specially.'

Florrie caught Miss Davenport's eye and grinned.

Everyone listened, enthralled, as Jack read a selection of poems from his latest book, his rich broad accent the perfect instrument for the flat vowels of the North Yorkshire dialect. When he'd finished it was as if the atmosphere in the room was suspended, the audience holding a collective breath before breaking into rapturous applause, peppered with cries of, 'Encore! Encore! Encore!'

'That was amazing,' Ed said, leaning into Florrie.

'It was, and it's down to you he's here, Ed, having the guts to ask if he'd do it.' She beamed up at him.

'Sometimes it's worth taking the plunge,' he said, his eyes finding hers.

Something told her he wasn't only referring to Jack Playforth.

Jack's voice pulled her away from that thought. 'Thank you very much,' he said with a tip of his head, his eyes glowing. Florrie was surprised to see how bashful he looked. 'I'd be happy to answer any questions you may have, unless you're all keen to escape, which I wouldn't blame you for after listening to me bletherin' on forever more.' He removed his glasses and popped them back into his pocket.

Laughter followed and Jack launched into answering questions in his now familiar self-deprecating style.

'What made you come to Micklewick Bay, Jack?' asked a lady at the back.

'Ah, well, that's quite an interesting story,' he said, rubbing his hand over his chin, fixing his eyes on Miss Davenport. 'Hmm. I wonder if now's the right time to share it?' She nodded and smiled. 'Okay then, I've been given the green light so, here goes; I hope you lot have got plenty of tissues handy, 'cos it's a bit of a weepy one.'

He went on to share his story to a backdrop of silent tears, "ahhs" and much eye-dabbing. 'So you see,' he said, holding his arms out, 'this place couldn't be better named; it really is the bookshop of happy hearts.'

Florrie felt Ed's arm slip around her shoulder, the subsequent squeeze of the top of her arm as the room was once more filled with applause. She stole a glance up at him to see him gazing down at her. The look in his eyes made her heart melt.

'I think it's safe to say that was a roaring success. We'll have to celebrate on Friday.' Stella strode up to Florrie, dropping a kiss on her cheek. She was closely followed by Lark, Maggie and Jasmine, all trilling words of congratulations, each expressing their delight at meeting Jack.

'I'm so glad I could make it,' Jasmine said, beaming. 'But I'm afraid I'm going to have to dash now – babysitter issues again.'

'I'll catch up with you later, flower,' said Maggie.

'See you Friday, chick,' said Stella.

'Enjoy the rest of your evening.' Smiling, Lark made a point of sliding her eyes from Florrie to Ed, giving a barely discernible lift of her eyebrows. Florrie flushed, getting her meaning loud and clear.

'Thanks, girls, I really appreciate your support. See you all at the Jolly on Friday.' Florrie was distracted by a spike of alarm as she saw Stella lean into Ed, muttering something in his ear, an "I take no shit" expression on her face, which was usually reserved for the courtroom. Whatever she'd said had made him wince and raise his palms in a placatory gesture. Clearly satisfied she'd got her point across, with a flick of her hair, Stella made her way to the door, an air of fearless confidence around her. Florrie's stomach squeezed. *Oh, bugger.*

With the audience gone, the shop was strangely quiet. 'What a wonderful, wonderful evening.' Miss Davenport broke through it, her face wreathed in smiles, her eyes glowing. Florrie couldn't remember seeing her look so animated.

'And it's not over yet,' said Jack 'I took the liberty of booking us a table at Oscar's bistro to celebrate; I hope that suits everyone?'

'Oh, how lovely! I haven't been to a restaurant for more years than I care to remember,' said Miss Davenport.

'Cool,' said Hayley. 'I'll just text my mum, let her know I'll be late.'

Florrie caught up with Ed in the kitchen area where he was filling a glass with water. She felt herself hovering as she wondered how best to broach the subject of Stella.

'Everything okay?' he asked.

'I think so.' She looked up at him, relieved to see he still seemed happy. 'I spotted Stella having a quick word with you...' She didn't know what else to say without sounding like she was prying.

He threw his head back and laughed. 'Ahh, yes, that.' He looked down at her, his eyes dancing with mirth. 'She clearly thinks the world of you; in fact, they all do.' He laughed again. 'She basically told me that if I mess you around, I'll find myself separated from my testicles, and the "offending articles" – as she referred to them – would be deep fried and fed to the seagulls.'

Florrie groaned, clapping her hand to her forehead. 'She didn't?'

Smiling, Ed rested a reassuring hand on her shoulder, the warmth seeping through to her skin, sending a thrill rushing up her spine. 'Hey, it's okay. She's just being a loyal friend. And I tell you, if ever I need a barrister, I'll be sure to hire Stella. She clearly takes no prisoners.'

'You'd noticed?'

* * *

'Here's to new beginnings.' Jack raised his flute of champagne aloft, smiling as the others chinked their glasses against it.

'To new beginnings,' they chorused, grinning broadly at one another, oblivious to the interested stares and whispers of the other diners who'd cottoned-on to Jack's identity.

'And here's to my grandfather,' said Ed. 'If it wasn't for him leaving Florrie and me the bookshop, none of these new beginnings would've happened.'

'Aye, it's funny how things turn out isn't it?' said Jack. Everyone nodded.

'Mr H was a truly wonderful person,' said Florrie, emotion clogging her throat. 'As was Mrs H.'

'To Bernard and Dinah, two very dear friends,' said Miss Davenport, holding her glass up once more. 'I miss them both terribly.'

Florrie blinked quickly, sensing Jack watching her, but was unable to stop a couple of tears from escaping. She quickly swiped them away with her fingertips.

'Did I tell you I've booked a viewing to see a cottage in Old Micklewick?' he said, coming to the rescue and pulling the mood back up. All eyes turned to him. 'It's the little one on Smugglers Row, rather charmingly named "Contraband Cottage", so called because of an old smuggling connection, according to the details, that is. Needs a bit doing to it, but I'm up for the challenge.'

'I know the one,' Florrie said, nodding. It was a few doors up from Lark's and had stood empty for a couple of years.

'You mean, you're buying a holiday cottage here?' asked Miss Davenport, her eyes bright with anticipation.

'I mean I'm moving here permanently. I've never felt such

an attachment to a place; I feel like I belong, did from the very moment I set foot in the town. I'd been toying with the idea, but now I've got even more of a reason to put roots down here.' He smiled warmly at his mother. 'You're welcome to join me for a look around it, if you like? It's tomorrow afternoon, two-thirty.'

'Oh, I'd love to, Jack.' She touched his face with her hand. 'And you do, very much belong.'

'Aww! That's so cute!' said Hayley, grinning.

Florrie felt her gaze being drawn to Ed, their eyes locking as they shared a smile. She could feel the final vestiges of her misgivings about him ready to slip away, if only she'd let them. But tonight wasn't about them. Tonight was about Jack and Miss Davenport.

FIFTY-FIVE

'There, all done.' She looked up to see Ed walking towards her looking handsomely dishevelled. He'd been busy all morning, moving his stuff into the flat upstairs and unpacking, which was something they'd agreed on the previous evening. When he'd left London, he'd vacated his flat for good, handing in his notice to his landlord. Florrie had been surprised to see all his worldly possessions amounted to no more than two large suitcases. They wouldn't even have been enough to store her books, never mind her clothes, she'd thought when she saw them.

'How does it feel?' she asked.

'Surprisingly good.' He beamed at her. 'What are you up to?' He peered at her open laptop on the counter.

'Social media for the bookshop. I'm determined to increase our online visibility. Why don't I show you, while it's quiet? I'm working on a website too, and I think it'd be quite nice to have a blog attached to it, you know, just keeping people informed of what we've been up to, in a friendly, chatty kind of way.'

His face faltered momentarily. 'Oh, yeah, great idea.' She was disappointed to hear his voice lacked the conviction of his words.

Uh-oh, here we go. Don't tell me it's a case of Mr Flaky strikes again. Florrie drew in a quick breath. 'I'm sensing you're not keen,' she said, more sharply than she intended. 'But I think it's important for the bookshop to be on these forums; it's a wasted opportunity if we ignore them.'

He nodded, massaging his lips together, his eyes uncertain.

'I'm more than happy to deal with it all; I enjoy that kind of thing,' she said, watching his face closely.

His relief was palpable. 'Oh, right, well, I think it sounds brilliant. I know you've been itching to get this sort of thing established for the bookshop.' The shadow that had fleetingly troubled his face disappeared and his smile returned.

She felt a simultaneous rush of guilt and relief. His dyslexia! Florrie could've kicked herself for forgetting.

'Yep, I'm in my element doing stuff like this.' That wasn't strictly true, but he didn't need to know that. 'And it's what we need to keep us current and to keep our customers informed of our upcoming events and the like.'

'Yeah, it really is a great idea. I could take photos for uploading to all the social media sites, just don't expect me to do any writing or you could end up regretting it,' he said, laughing.

'I'll willingly hand over responsibility for all imagery. My photos never seem to turn out how I hope. Just look at this one, talk about cockeyed.' She showed him one she'd taken of a pile of books the other day. 'It was supposed to look artistic and stylish, and not something a three-year-old took by accident.'

'It's not that bad,' Ed said, chuckling as he peered at it.

'Then why are you laughing so much?' She couldn't help but giggle herself.

His eyes met hers and Florrie felt her heart leap as electricity crackled in the air around them. The expression in his eyes told her he could feel it too.

* * *

'Can I tempt you to an ice cream?' Ed asked, his eyes hopeful. The light breeze was ruffling his hair, the sun picking out golden highlights. Florrie couldn't help but think how achingly handsome he looked. Since his return, she'd been trying her hardest to ignore the yearning in her heart – despite his declaration – but it was proving difficult.

The pair had finished their work at the bookshop for the day and had walked down to the beach together with Gerty, making the most of the warm evening. The beach was still busy with day-trippers and the ice cream seller was doing a roaring trade.

'Mmm. You could actually,' Florrie said as she spotted a woman walking by, a whippy ice cream topped with lemon sauce in each hand.

Ice creams purchased, they headed down the few steps from the bottom prom to the beach, taking care as they negotiated the deep bank of pebbles. Florrie scraped her hair off her face, tucking it behind her ears before licking the drip of ice cream that was snaking its way down the cone. The sea air was filled with the delicious aroma of fish and chips from the nearby take-away, which was even busier than the ice cream bar. Seagulls wheeled up above, their shrill cries melding with the sound of the waves hitting the shore.

The pair walked along, eating in comfortable silence, the sea rushing up to them a couple of feet away, before scurrying back. Both were watching Gerty who was enjoying a wild dash around while keeping one eye on the ice creams. Since Ed had explained the reasons for his hasty exit from Micklewick Bay, Florrie had been glad to drop her hard act with him; she wasn't naturally disposed to being abrupt and cold, and it had been draining to keep up. And she couldn't deny it had been good to spend time with him again, see the familiar smile that lit up his face. Though, she was still reluctant to fully let her guard down; she'd told herself to be wary, to keeping her feelings for him in check. She had a funny feeling, given a free rein, they could very easily run away with themselves. And she didn't think she was ready for that just yet.

Ed stopped, focusing his gaze on the sea. 'I've really loved being back. Those few days I had at Dev's made me appreciate being here in a way I hadn't expected.' He heaved a lungful of salty air, a wistful expression on his face. 'Like Jack said, it gets right under your skin.'

Florrie smiled, not sure where this was going. 'Yeah, it is pretty special.'

Ed's eyes found hers. 'It's not the only thing.' His gentle smile made her pulse surge. 'You're pretty special too, Florrie.'

'Oh, um...' She could feel the warmth of a blush rising up her neck and looked away; she wasn't sure she was ready for this conversation.

'Argghhh!' Ed ducked as a herring gull swooped down with an ear-splitting shriek, flapping its huge wings noisily. Before they knew what was happening, it had snatched his ice cream out of his hands. 'What the hell?' He watched, his mouth hanging open, as it flew off with it clamped in its sharp, yellow beak.

'Oh, no! Are you all right?' Florrie asked, hooting with laughter. 'I meant to warn you about them, they've become a bit of a nuisance.'

'Cheeky bloody thing came from nowhere!' As Ed searched the sky for the ice cream thief, there was a resounding "splat". He looked at Florrie, who'd clamped her hand over her mouth, laughter spluttering between her fingers. He moved his eyes down to his shoulder to see a large white splash that travelled the full length of his sleeve. 'I've got a feeling that's not ice cream.' He pressed his lips together, shaking his head. 'As if stealing my cornet wasn't bad enough, the flaming thing had to add insult to injury.'

'That could've been so much worse,' said Florrie, giggling.

'You reckon?'

She nodded, still gripped by laughter. 'And don't forget, a seagull pooing on you is supposed to be lucky.'

'*Lucky?*'

'Mm-hm.'

'I suppose that's one way of looking at it.' Merriment dancing over his face, he threw his head back and roared with laughter, her giggles apparently infectious. Gerty, hearing him, bounded over, not wanting to miss out on the fun, clumps of wet sand flying behind her. She leapt up at Ed, her paws landing square on his chest. His eyes widened as he over-balanced. 'Waargghhh! Gerty! No!' His arms whirred like helicopter blades as struggled to save himself. But it was futile, and he fell backwards with a resounding splash, Gerty on top of him, just as a huge wave surged towards them.

Florrie yelped as the seawater ran over her shoes. Racing away from the encroaching edges of the tide, she turned around to see Ed heaving himself up onto his knees, seawater pouring from him as Gerty leapt around giddily, splashing water everywhere.

He spat out a jet of brine. 'What was that you were you saying about it being lucky?' he asked just as a wave reared up behind him, breaking over his shoulders. He scrunched his eyes tight shut. 'You've got to be kidding me!'

Florrie's cheeks were aching from laughing so hard as Ed walked over to her, pushing his drenched hair off his face with both hands. He stopped in front of her, hands on hips, an amused grin on his face, while Gerty tripped around him like a show pony.

'I'm so sorry, I can't stop laughing.' She made a concerted effort to stifle her giggles, though it was proving difficult.

'You don't look very sorry.' He gave an amused smile.

'I think we might need to cut our walk short.' Her voice was strangled by the laughter she was trying to contain.

'Hmm. Not your finest hour that, Gerty.' He lifted an eyebrow at Florrie.

They stood for a moment, neither of them speaking, her laughter subsiding as their eyes locked. A frisson of attraction set Florrie's pulse surging through her body. Before she knew what was happening, Ed had cupped her face in his hands and his mouth was on hers. She heard herself gasp as she closed her eyes, allowing herself to melt into him, his lips surprisingly soft and warm, tingling with a tang of salt. *Wow!* It was as if a thousand fireworks were going off inside her. She'd never been kissed like this before. Graham's wet-fish pecks paled by comparison. She reached up and wrapped her arms around Ed's neck, their kiss deepening, her emotions ablaze.

They pulled apart, breathless. Ed resting his forehead against hers. 'I've been wanting to do that since I first set eyes on you.'

'What took you so long?' she asked, a smile in her voice. Her guard fell to the ground with an almighty clatter as something inside her told her it was time to put her trust in him; to give him a chance.

EPILOGUE

ONE MONTH LATER

Ed pulled Florrie closer, dropping a kiss on top of her head. A contended sigh escaped her lips as she pushed her hand under his t-shirt, his skin warm to the touch. The pair were relaxing on the outdoor sofa, enjoying the last of the day's warmth in the back garden of Samphire Cottage. The evening light was imbued with an easy glow, the air suffused with bird song, the occasional waft from the barbecue drifting by. Gerty was stretched out beside them, her head on her paws, her ears twitching, hoping Ed might be inclined to throw another sausage or two on the still-glowing embers.

It had been the perfect lazy Sunday, just the two of them together with Gerty, no commitments vying for their attention. It was the first full day they'd had alone together; a welcome change after so many time-devouring days with the bookshop. Not that they'd minded any of it for a moment, but all the same...

Ed had stayed over at the cottage the previous evening, surprising Florrie with a pot of tea and croissants in bed that morning. A smile played on her lips as her mind revisited it.

'Morning.' Wearing his habitual grin, Ed had pushed open the door with his foot.

'Ooh, breakfast in bed; I could get used to this,' she'd said, pushing herself up on her elbows and smiling sleepily, her cheek imprinted with creases from the pillow. She'd picked up the rose he'd set out on the tray and inhaled its sweet, creamy fragrance. 'Mmm.' He'd leant forward and kissed her deeply, making her heart dissolve into a molten puddle.

'Would madam like her tea pouring?' he'd asked in a mock affected tone.

'I'm afraid you can't leave me dangling like that,' she'd said, grabbing hold of his t-shirt, pulling him to her and kissing him again.

'Ah, it's like that, is it?' With a lopsided smile, he'd removed the tray and slipped back into bed beside her.

The tea had grown cold by the time Florrie had returned to it.

'It's been a perfect day,' Ed said, curling her hair around his fingers, bringing her back to the present.

'It has.'

'I don't remember the last time I had a day where I felt as relaxed as this.'

'Mmm, same here.' She smiled absently as she watched butterflies dancing amongst the blooms in the jam-packed flowerbed.

They sat in silence, lost in their own thoughts for a few moments until Ed spoke. 'If anyone had told me a year ago that all this was going to happen, I would've said they were crazy. I mean, I'm devastated to have lost my grandfather, but so grateful to him for bringing me here to you. I know he intended us to be together.'

'There's no disputing that.' She'd had plenty of conversations with Mr H hinting at just that.

'Then there's Jack and Miss Davenport; we've all had our

lives transformed. If we hadn't been sorting out the storeroom and setting it up as a reading room, the box wouldn't have been knocked over and Jack would never have found his mum and be moving to the town to be closer to her,' he said.

'You're right. And it's so good to see Miss Davenport happy after being on her own for so long. I know they're taking it one day at a time, but everyone can see how happy she and Jack are to be making up for the years they've lost.'

'Yeah, and it was good to see her in her element at the first book club meeting; she sparkled,' Ed said.

Florrie smiled fondly. 'She did.'

The first Happy Hartes Book Club meeting, held in the newly named reading room, had been well supported, with Miss Davenport at the helm, and making everyone feel welcome.

'And as for us,' Ed cupped her cheek with his hand, brushing his thumb over it, looking deep into her eyes, 'I want you to know, I love you with all my heart, Florrie. Every last, tiny piece of it. I've never felt this way about anyone, and, hopefully, you believe me when I say I don't want to be anywhere but here with you. I'm in this for the long-haul.'

She put her hand over his, happiness swamping her chest. It was time to be honest with herself, and with him. 'I've never felt this way before either. I love you with all my heart too.' And it was true, but she'd been too scared to admit it to herself, fearful of opening her heart to rejection if he didn't feel the same way.

Gerty jumped up, pushing her head between them, her tail wagging happily.

'And, we love you too, Gerty-Girl.' Ed laughed, ruffling her ears.

'We most certainly do.' Florrie snuggled in closer to Ed, sending a silent thank you heavenwards to Mr H for setting her on this path.

A LETTER FROM THE AUTHOR

Huge thanks for choosing to pick up *The Little Bookshop by the Sea*. I hope you were hooked on Florrie and Ed's journey. If you'd like to join other readers in hearing all about my new releases and bonus content, you can sign up for my newsletter!

www.stormpublishing.co/eliza-j-scott

If you enjoyed this book and could spare a few moments to leave a review, that would be hugely appreciated. It doesn't have to be long, just a few words would do, but for us authors it can make all the difference in encouraging a reader to discover my books for the first time. Thank you so much. If you click on the link below it will take you right there.

I really enjoyed researching this book, not least because it involved lots of trips to some of the beautiful towns and villages that line the North Yorkshire Coast – my fictional town of Micklewick Bay is actually an amalgamation of these places. Starting with the Victorian seaside town of Saltburn-by-the-Sea, with its grand houses that boast panoramic views of the beach and the sea, not forgetting the magnificent Huntcliff. It's thanks to this lovely town that Micklewick Bay has its pier and funicular, and if any of you are familiar with Saltburn, you've probably guessed Huntcliff is the inspiration for my Thorncliffe. The quaint little fishing villages of Staithes, Runswick Bay and Robin Hood's Bay are the places I had in mind when writing about Old Micklewick, with their characterful houses that just ooze charm. I've spent many happy hours wandering their cobbled streets, ice cream in hand, keeping a watchful eye for those pesky seagulls! The bustling harbour town of Whitby must also get a mention, not least because of its delicious fish and chips.

It probably comes as no surprise when I tell you that many portions of the aforesaid fish and chips were consumed and ice creams devoured in the name of research for this book. It's a hard life but I battled on through! And I have to say, they were all delicious!

www.elizajscott.com

Bluesky: @elizajscott.bsky.social

f facebook.com/elizajscottauthor

X x.com/ElizaJScott1

O instagram.com/elizajscott

BB bookbub.com/authors/eliza-j-scott

ACKNOWLEDGEMENTS

So, now's the time for me to say thank you. I'm going to start by saying a great big thank you to my fabulous editor Kate Gilby-Smith for believing in me and my writing. Kate's positivity and enthusiasm is just wonderful, and I'm so looking forward to working on the rest of the Welcome to Micklewick Bay series with her!

Next up, a heartfelt thank you goes to the rest of Team Storm, in particular Alex Holmes for her keen eye and editorial skills as well as being so patient when I've wanted to add little extra bits. Thank you to the man at the top, Oliver Rhodes, for putting together such an awesome, experienced and super-friendly team. It's a joy and an honour to be part of the adventure. Big thanks to Melanie Crawley for her narration. As soon as I heard Melanie reading an extract of *The Little Bookshop by the Sea* in her wonderful warm tones, I knew she was perfect for the Welcome to Micklewick Bay series. I must also thank Rose Cooper for designing such a deliciously vibrant book cover! I think it captures Micklewick Bay perfectly.

I owe a huge thank you to the beautiful places I've named above for providing me with so much inspiration, not forgetting the residents for their friendly welcome.

I also have to say thank you to my two awesome author friends Jessica Redland and Sharon Booth (who is also a fellow Stormy!) for their kind words of support and encouragement – and for nudging me along. The cake's on me the next time we get together!

I must also say a heartfelt thank you to three inspiring women for their help in getting the first edition of *The Little Bookshop by the Sea* ready for publication: Alison Williams, Berni Stevens and Rachel Gilbey. Thank you!

My final thank you goes to you, the reader, for taking the trouble to pick up my book and read it. Thank you so much for being a part of this journey with me, I really am truly humbled and grateful. I hope you'll stay in touch and follow the adventures of Florrie's friends, next of which is Maggie and Bear's story.

Lots of love, Eliza xxx